On the back of the sea, who do we trust?
Our sisters.

When our ship falters, who do we trust?
Our sisters.

In a storm of Bullets, who do we trust?
Our sisters!

We fight together!
Or not at all!

Sisterhood Is Survival

PRAISE FOR

SEAFIRE

"A gutsy tale of sisterhood, courage, and unshakeable trust. You don't want to miss this book!"
Julie Murphy, #1 *New York Times* bestselling author of *Dumplin'*

"In these turbulent times, *Seafire* gives teens just what they need: A reminder that with unity and courage, they can rise up and ultimately change the world."
Dhonielle Clayton, author of *The Belles*

"A fast-paced, thrilling tale."
BuzzFeed

"One of the year's most anticipated new fantasies."
Entertainment Weekly

"As smart, ferocious, and uncompromising as its crew, *Seafire* is the adventure you're looking for. I have such a crush on this book!"
Kiersten White, *New York Times* bestselling author of *And I Darken*

Sisters fight with each other,
for each other,
and by each other's side.
I'm lucky to have one like you, Rosie.

First published in the UK in 2019 by Usborne Publishing Ltd., Usborne House, 83-85 Saffron Hill, London EC1N 8RT, England. www.usborne.com. Published by arrangement with Rights People, London.

The name Usborne and the devices ♀ ⊕ **USBORNE** are Trade Marks of Usborne Publishing Ltd.

Text © 2018 by Alloy Entertainment and Natalie C. Parker

alloy**entertainment**

Produced by Alloy Entertainment, LLC.

Cover design adapted from original artwork by Billelis.
Cover image wave background © Transia Design/Shutterstock

A CIP catalogue record for this book is available from the British Library.

ISBN 9781474966580 05363/1 JFMAM JASOND/19
Printed in the UK.

SEAFIRE

NATALIE C. PARKER

USBORNE

BEFORE

Caledonia stretched along the prow of the *Ghost* as the ship sliced through black water. At night, the ocean offered only a dark reflection of the sky above, and the promise of a cold grave below.

Her mother, Rhona, crouched near, a rifle balanced on her knees, eyes surveying the sea road ahead. "Our way forward is marred. Do you see?" she said.

Caledonia studied the eddies in the water, searching for the signs that meant there were rocks ahead, or a sunken ship, unusual swirls, or a sudden chop of waves. Rhona was always the first to spot them, but Caledonia was getting better.

"Rocks," Caledonia said, and without waiting for permission, she turned and called to her father where he stood on the bridge. "Three degrees port!"

The *Ghost* nosed south to avoid the sharp danger. On either side, familiar outlines of small islands rose around the ship. These were the waters of the Bone Mouth, a series of islands and rocky protrusions that offered flimsy sanctuary to anyone brave enough to sail them. They were treacherous in daylight, and nearly impassable at night, except by Caledonia's mother, Rhona Styx, captain of the *Ghost*. Under her command, they sailed as smoothly as if on open blue waters.

Years ago, Rhona liked to remind her daughter, they wouldn't have needed such stealth. When Rhona was a girl, she sailed from the colder northern currents, past the towering Rock Isles, all the way down to the Bone Mouth without any more danger than the occasional storm. Then, so gradually few noticed until it was too late, a man named Aric Athair had grown a fleet of ships armed and armoured for taking and killing. His fleet of Bullet ships stretched in a violent chain across the only way in or out of these expansive waters. Anyone on the wrong side of his notorious Net found themselves bent under the pressure of his thumb.

Now, after years of dodging Aric Athair and his Bullets, and facing dwindling resources, Rhona had decided the time had come for their small band to punch through the Net. For months, they'd searched for the best way. They'd studied the Bullet ships from a distance and determined the weakest point was at the tip of the Bone Mouth, where even Aric's ships were loath to sail. The *Ghost* could make it, but first they needed food – fruit, nuts and meat if they could get it – to supplement their stores for the unknown waters beyond.

Tonight, they resupplied. But tomorrow night, they ran for the very last time.

"You and your brother prep for the shore run." Rhona's red hair rolled behind her, battling with the wind.

A small thrill straightened Caledonia's spine. From the age of six, she'd campaigned for the responsibility of shore runs to be hers. Only in the last year had her mother finally conceded and assigned her the task. But as much as Caledonia cherished the trust her mother placed in her on those occasions, she knew her little brother hated those long dark rides to shore. He would spend the entire night terrified of being so far from the safety of their ship.

"Let me take Pisces." Caledonia climbed to her feet and followed her mother. "We're a good team. Besides, Donnally's too young for shore runs. He's only twelve turns, you know."

Rhona laughed her grizzly laugh. "You know this from all your experience?"

Caledonia pictured Donnally's eyes tight with fear, his mouth pressed into a stoic line as he struggled not to disappoint their mother. "I do," she answered.

"Cala, the only way your brother will learn is by your side," Rhona said with a sigh, but there was no fight in her words.

Mother and daughter skirted the bridge, then took turns sliding down the companionway ladder to the deck below. Even in the moonless dark, they knew their way easily around the *Ghost*. The ship had become a refuge for families looking to escape Aric's rule. As their numbers grew, every inch of the ship was transformed to meet a variety of needs

– masts supported sails and laundry lines, the galley was transformed daily from a mess hall to a bunk room, even the deck was host to stacked garden beds and two goat pens. While more than a dozen men and women were still topside at this hour, most of the crew was asleep in the small cabins below. There were lookouts posted forward and stern and up in the nest, but here in the Bone Mouth, the *Ghost* had never come across one of Aric's Bullet ships at night. Bullets were vicious and bold, but most lacked Rhona's seafaring skill.

Caledonia spied her brother crouched behind one of the four mast blocks studding the centreline of the ship, an overlarge jacket hulking around him like a grey cloud. He had their father's dark hair, their mother's fair complexion, and a nose that curled up at the tip, giving him a look of perpetual surprise.

The lines of a blunted arrowhead tattoo half-filled with black ink peeked out from beneath his curls. A matching one was drawn on her own temple. It was custom on the *Ghost* for parents to mark their children with unique sigils in case of capture. The mark would give those children the chance to find their family again someday.

"I'll take him next time." Guilt nudged at Caledonia. Her mother was right. The only way to prepare Donnally for the world was to take him into it, but sometimes she feared for her little brother. The gentle pinch in her mother's eyes said she did, too.

"Donnally!" Rhona called. "Hoist your eyes, son!"

Donnally started, rocketing awkwardly to his feet before he managed to spot his mother and sister. He trudged across the deck at a reluctant pace, dark hair flopping in his eyes. He schooled his features when he asked, "Shore run?" But the note of tension in his voice gave him away.

"Yes, but not for you. Cala's taking Pi, which means I want you and Ares on watch. Clear?" Rhona pointed towards the nest.

Donnally nodded eagerly. "Clear," he said, giving Caledonia a grateful smile.

Rhona pulled her daughter into her arms, planting a kiss on her head. "Get the job done."

"And get back to the ship," Caledonia finished.

By the time they dropped anchor near an island they called the Gem, Caledonia and Pisces were prepped and ready to go. They climbed into the bow boat harnessed against the hull of the *Ghost* and lowered it to the water as they'd done a dozen times before.

With quick strokes of the oars they covered the distance between their ship and the island. Recently, Pisces had grown several inches. She'd outgrown her little brother, Ares, and shot straight past Caledonia, and her height seemed to make her fearless. Pisces's shoulders were broad and strong, her skin a warm, pale brown, and she wore her hair in four long braids. As they rowed, her eyes were full of excitement, focused on the island and its bounty, while

Caledonia kept one eye on the black ocean.

"It's too quiet. I don't like it," Caledonia said.

Pisces pulled in a deep breath and tilted a ready smile towards her friend. "It's peaceful, like being so far underwater you can't see the surface."

"That's called drowning. Only you would find that peaceful."

Pisces laughed quietly to avoid unsettling Caledonia further.

Together they moored their boat in a sheltered cove, securing it in a thicket of tall grass. The girls split up to make their work faster, agreeing to meet back at the cove when their sacks were full.

The path down the shore was narrow, the ocean as dark as the night sky and nearly as flat. Caledonia moved along the rocky tree line, stuffing fallen coconuts and bananas and jackfruit into the canvas sacks draped across her shoulders. There was enough that she could afford to be picky, though the more she gathered, the longer they'd be able to sail. No one knew what to expect when they broke through the Net. They might need to sail for days or months, and they needed to be prepared for both. People once said that beyond the Net were wide-open seas and towns where children weren't forced into the service of a tyrant, but it was a world Caledonia could not quite imagine.

The tide was low and the waves sluggish, burbling and hissing as they surged and receded. In their wake, the sand glittered with the pearlescent shells of burrowing crabs and the slick backs of beached jellyfish. From the dense forest came the looping songs of insects and tree frogs. Perhaps she would return with meat after all.

Footsteps, hurried and heavy, sounded behind her.

Caledonia's heart tripped, her hands stuttered on the strap of her canvas bag, and she instinctively slipped through a fall of vines. There had been no other ships in sight for miles. These footsteps must belong to Pisces. They had to.

Still, the cadence of the steps refused to conjure the image of Pisces running, long black braids flying behind her.

Even away from the *Ghost*, the rules of the ship still applied. Number one: *Never be seen*. Caledonia stilled her breathing, adjusted her feet, and disentangled herself from the bag full of fruit. She would be ready to run. She would be ready to fight.

The steps grew louder and slower. A dark figure appeared: tall, muscled, male. Instead of racing past as Caledonia hoped he would, the boy stopped a few feet from her hiding place. His skin was suntanned and slick with sweat, his vest and trousers lined with guns and clips of ammo. His bicep was marked by a single scarred line that even in the dark was bright orange, saturated with the Silt in his blood. He was a Bullet, a soldier from Aric Athair's army.

Aric conscripted children, dismantling families in order to build his empire. Rogue families like Caledonia's had taken to the water rather than see their children stolen and transformed into soldiers. But because they'd run, if they were ever captured, none would be spared. Not even the children. People more readily offered their children up as payment when they knew the only alternative was death for all.

This Bullet couldn't be much older than Caledonia, seventeen at the most, but the mark on his bicep meant he'd already killed in service to Aric.

She smelled the salt of his sweat and the sharp pinch of gunpowder and something unrecognizable and sweet. Caledonia shivered.

The boy didn't look at her, didn't seem to be aware she crouched so near, her fingers inching her pistol from its holster. Instead, he began to do exactly what she'd been doing. He bent down and collected fruit.

She'd never seen a Bullet this close; her parents did their best to keep the *Ghost* as far from Aric's fleet as possible. Over the years they'd outrun dozens of Bullet ships and collected as many families from other ships and outlying settlements, all while staying out of sight.

Rule number two: *Shoot first.*

Her pistol was in her hand, finger curled around the trigger. When the boy turned his back and kneeled to inspect a coconut, Caledonia had the perfect advantage. She would only need one bullet.

She raised her pistol and stepped quietly out of her hiding place.

The boy froze, dropping the coconut as he raised his hands.

"Whoever you are, you have me," he said.

Caledonia didn't respond, her throat tight as she considered pulling the trigger.

"Would it make a difference if I asked you not to shoot?" the boy asked, face forward and eyes on the ocean. "If I begged for mercy?"

"Killing you would be a mercy," she told the Bullet.

"Maybe so," he said, voice at once piteous and resigned. "At least, if you're going to kill me, let me see your face?"

Caledonia's pulse quickened. There was no time for this. Where there was one Bullet, there were a dozen or more. She needed to find Pisces and get back to the boat, and she needed to do it now. *Shoot*, her mother's voice urged, but this was one rule Caledonia had never had to follow.

Sensing her hesitation, the boy shifted on his knees, spinning to face her. His hands remained steady in the air, but now he watched her.

Alarmed, Caledonia took an involuntary step back. "Move again and I'll shoot." She raised her aim to his head.

He nodded, star-pale eyes fixed on the barrel of her pistol. He had a long face with a jaw that looked sharp enough to be a weapon on its own. Blond hair, thick with sea wind and salt, framed his forehead like a crown. One ear stuck out a little further than the other, but the effect was endearing. She counted two guns strapped to each of his thighs, which likely meant there were at least two others she couldn't see. For the moment, she was the one in power, but she knew just how quickly that might change.

"At least if I'm to die, it'll be at the hands of someone lovely." His eyes charted a slow course across her face.

Warmth crept into Caledonia's cheeks. "Where's your crew? Your clip?"

"I – can I point?" When Caledonia nodded, he did, back in the direction he'd come from. "Ship's anchored off the northern tip of the island. Stopped for food."

"One ship?" Caledonia asked.

"One ship," he answered. "We were headed to the Net and moored here for the night. It's a bad moon for travelling."

He could be lying – he was probably lying – but this far from the Holster it could also be the truth. One ship on the opposite side of the island was survivable. As long as she and Pisces returned to the *Ghost* quickly.

But something had to be done about this Bullet.

"What's your name?" she asked.

The boy seemed to grow smaller under the weight of that question. "What does it matter if you're going to kill me?"

"It doesn't." Caledonia's finger found the trigger again, and again it stuck there.

A sad smile twisted his lips. "Lir. I'm called Lir. And I expect you'll be the last to know it."

He was so ready to die, and so young. Was he young enough to be saved? They said it didn't take long for the children Aric took to succumb to the dreamy pull of Silt. Addiction made Bullets both loyal and mean. But they also said an encounter with a Bullet always, always ended in one of two ways: either you died, or he did.

Shoot, my brave girl, she heard her mother's voice whisper.

"I'm…I'm sorry," she said, preparing to fire. Her fingers trembled.

Now his eyes grew wide, his hands stiff and splayed in the air.

"Please," he said, "please, show me the mercy the Father never does. Take me with you. Whatever life you have, it's got to be better than the one he forces on us. Please, help me."

This was precisely why the rule was *shoot first* and not *shoot as soon as possible* or *shoot when you feel ready*. But she'd broken the rule and now this wasn't a Bullet, it was Lir.

Lir, who desperately wanted a way out.

Lir, who hadn't hurt her.

Lir, who might be someone's brother.

If it were Donnally on some other beach with some other girl's gun to his head, wouldn't Caledonia want that girl to help him?

"Stand up," she said, lowering her aim to his chest.

Lir complied, and his expression softened when Caledonia moved in and pulled six guns and two knives from holsters on his thighs, calves and back. Up close, he smelled even more like the ammunition he carried, but with a pinch of something too sweet. He kept his hands up as she worked, eyes marking every place she touched him.

"Please," he repeated. "I'll never have a chance like this again. Please, help me."

The ocean rushed towards them and away, the waves quickening as the tide began to roll in. It was the same tide that would carry all the families aboard the *Ghost* far away from this terrible life that turned children into warriors, that made Lir plead for his life on an empty beach in the middle of a moonless night. She *could* help him. And she wanted to, but it went against everything her mother had taught her.

Shaking her head, she pressed the muzzle of her gun into Lir's chest.

Desperation surfaced in the tremulous bend of his mouth. "What's your name?"

It wasn't a secret, yet she frowned, refusing to give it up.

His smile turned mournful. "How about I call you Bale Blossom, then? It seems fitting." His eyes raised to trace the frame of her hair. The smile on her own lips surprised her. It wasn't the first time her hair had been likened to the deep orange of the baleflower, but it was the first time the comparison felt like a compliment.

"Call me whatever you like," she answered. "I still won't give you my name."

"You don't trust me. There's no reason you should, but I'm going to show you why you can."

Caledonia's finger tightened on the trigger as he slipped

one hand into his vest and produced a push dagger she'd missed. The handle was small enough to fit inside his grip completely while the black blade protruded between his first and middle fingers. He held it out hilt-first in the narrow space between them.

She snatched it, noting how his body had warmed the metal, and tucked it into her belt.

"How's that for trust, Bale Blossom?"

Caledonia wished desperately for her mother's wisdom. Rhona would know what to do in this situation. She would know how to do the right thing even if it was a dangerous thing.

But Caledonia had only herself.

"No one trusts a Bullet," she answered. "But maybe I can help."

"Are you going to take me to your crew?" Lir smiled sadly, seeming to know the answer before Caledonia had given it.

Rule number three: *Never reveal the ship.*

"No," she said, resolute. "But I'm not going to shoot you."

Lir nodded, the bravery on his face haunted by disappointment. Even in the dark of the night she could see his jaw was carved with dirt and old scars. His eyes glittered dimly, and his mouth settled into a hard line. The flash of hope Caledonia had seen a moment before had been swept away by resignation.

When he spoke next, his voice was hollow. "You should leave. Go back to your ship. Get out of here. I'll hide or I'll die, but I'll do it under my own sail."

She glanced in the direction of the *Ghost*, wishing it was as simple as taking Lir with her.

Lir followed her gaze, and before her eyes, he became as steady and as cool as the gun in her hand. He asked, "Do you know what we call this moon?"

"There is no moon tonight," Caledonia answered.

"It's the Nascent Moon," he said after a quiet moment, all trace of that sad resignation gone. "It's a time of potential and growth. A promise for things to come."

He touched her cheek, and Caledonia gasped, her arm lowering. She felt his hand slide into her hair, felt a spike of delicious heat follow his grazing fingers.

"It's the moon of beginnings and endings." His voice found a malicious edge.

Too late, she realized if she'd missed one dagger she might have missed another.

His fingers tightened in her hair. A slaked smile surfaced on his lips.

And the blade sank into her gut.

Lir gripped the back of her head. As hot blood spread across her stomach, he held her close. Her knees buckled and her gun hit the ground with a thud.

"Thank you for your mercy, Bale Blossom," he whispered, lowering her almost gently to the sand. Nauseating pain burned through her body. "And thank you for your ship."

Caledonia screamed, fighting to stay conscious. If they heard her, they might escape. She clutched at her wound and felt sand against her face, rough against her lips. She knew there was pain, but all she felt was panic. She had to get up, find Pisces, warn the ship. She screamed again.

Footsteps. This time, she knew them to be Lir's as he raced away, towards the Bullet clip that would soon find her family. She fumbled in the sand for her gun and fired three shots. It was still deadly dark, but she thought she saw him falter.

Even if those three bullets had missed their mark, everyone near the island would have heard the shots. Her family would have warning. They could escape, and as long as they followed the rules, they would.

Her nausea eased into a strange numbness. The blade, she realized, was still in her gut. A parting gift, and one that might just save her. Holding the knife in place to stanch the bleeding, she got slowly to her feet and began to stagger towards her cove and the bow boat, the only thought in her mind to see the *Ghost* safely on its way.

"Cala!" Pisces burst from the trees, her long braids swinging around her like ropes. "Oh, spirits, Cala!"

"Bullets." Caledonia barely managed the word before falling again to her knees. "We have to hurry."

Pisces nodded grimly and ripped a long strip of material from her shirt. The blade hurt even more coming out. Pisces worked quickly, binding the wound tightly before tucking her head beneath Caledonia's arm and lifting her friend to her feet.

Together, the girls stumbled through the woods, taking the shortest possible path to where their little boat waited. Caledonia tried to run. With each step her legs felt weaker, her lungs more shallow. Her gut burned as she moved. Thorny plants clawed at their legs and arms, leaving small trails of blood on their skin. Thick vines slowed their progress even more. Before the ocean was visible again through the trees, the sound of gunfire ripped through the air.

Neither girl spoke until they'd returned to the cove. The boat they'd used to come ashore was still there, bobbing as the tide came in. But now, out where their family's ship lay at anchor, a Bullet ship approached, flared with light.

It was an assault ship with a sharp nose and grooves along the hull where Bullets waited with magnetized bombs. The *Ghost* fought to weigh its anchor and gain speed, but the assault ship was already upon it. Bombs soared across the narrowing channel of water. A *boom* rent the air as the missiles exploded against the *Ghost*, ripping open the ship and knocking the breath from Caledonia's lungs.

Flames spilled from a hole in the side of the hull. It was everything the girls had been taught to fear, to avoid, everything their parents had spent a lifetime protecting them from. And Caledonia had brought it right to their feet.

Screams replaced the sound of gunfire. Caledonia lurched, pushing past the pain and into the shallow water. She surged forward once, determined to swim, but her body faltered and she cried out in defeat. Her feet sank into sand, salt burned in her gut, and Pisces gripped her shoulders to pull her back to shore. "Caledonia, no!" she cried.

The two girls could do nothing but witness. No one would be spared.

It lasted less than fifteen minutes.

The sun rose higher. Screams and gunfire waned.

Then the Bullets began their gruesome work of dragging the dead to their ship and hoisting the bodies of the slain on the metal pikes studding their rail.

One body, placed at the very front of the Bullet ship, wore an overly large coat that puffed in the air like a grey cloud. The feet dangled in the wind, and Caledonia choked on the memory of leaving Donnally behind just a few short hours ago.

Caledonia shivered in the warm dawn. Blood seeped down her body, but the pain in her gut was nothing compared to the pain in her chest.

"How?" Pisces whispered.

Caledonia slumped to her knees. She shook her head, unable to confess the truth to her friend. She'd failed her entire family; she couldn't fail Pisces, too. So she pushed the truth deep down, beneath her grief and her guilt and her anger.

"What do we do?" Pisces asked, her brown face bright with tears. "Cala, what do we do?"

Caledonia fixed her gaze on the Bullet ship, her ears on the final screams of her family. Fire reflected angrily across the black surface of the ocean. For all its darkness, it had failed to keep her family a secret. But so had she. Her heart hardened over the memory of Lir. He had taken her mercy and turned it red. Now she and Pisces were all that remained.

Taking her friend's cold hand in her bloody one, she gave the only answer she could find. "I don't know."

CHAPTER ONE

FOUR YEARS LATER

Just before dawn, Caledonia climbed into the aft rigging of her ship. The ropes were rough against her calloused palms as she scaled fifty feet of the mizzenmast, confident and sure, her hands and feet flying faster and faster, daring the sun to beat her to the top.

The sky filled with the hazy blue glow of dawn, and Caledonia pushed harder, relishing the first kiss of sweat against her skin. She'd scarcely reached her chosen perch when she yelled to the team of girls on deck below, "Haul!"

Eager voices repeated the command, and four sets of strong hands took hold of the lines and heaved. Along the mast, pulleys squealed and churned; Caledonia kept her eyes on the gaff beam moving towards her.

"Break!" she shouted as the gaff rose level with her chest. From it hung their treasured sun sail; hundreds of shiny black scales made to absorb solar energy and feed their engines.

The girls below began to secure the ropes while Caledonia moved to balance atop the beam. The morning wind that was so gentle on deck was bracing this far up, and a constant tension whirled in her stomach. Leaving one hand to grip the ropes, she stretched to retrieve the peak anchor and pull it down, snapping the cable in place.

The horizon was burning yellow now, and the approach of the sun brought a smile to Caledonia's lips. Below, she could see Amina perched on the starboard railing, tracking her with shrewd eyes. It wasn't necessary for the captain to secure the sail. Any one of Amina's Knots could do this just as easily as Caledonia, but this moment was unlike any other aboard the *Mors Navis*, and Caledonia craved the feeling of the world at her feet.

"Trim to port!" she called.

The sail angled towards sunrise just as the first gentle rays slid across the surface of the ocean. Light climbed the hull to paint the girls in their boldest strokes for just a second before it reached the black plates of the sun sail.

It was like fire.

Light leaped from a hundred scales at once in vibrant yellows, oranges and pinks; a cascade of momentary brilliance washed upwards as the sun climbed higher in the sky, and at the top of it all stood Caledonia. Wind tugged at her sleeves and her hair, light washed over her from boot to brow, and she felt as alive as the ship beneath her feet, charged and powerful.

It lasted for only a moment, then that dazzling morning fire was gone.

Sunlight glittered calmly in the sail, creating fuel to power all the systems of the ship once known as the *Ghost*. Repaired and renamed *Mors Navis*, the large vessel was sharp and elegant, all of it skinned with dark, grey steel except for a few patches of wood and tar. Everything on the ship was a mixture of old-world tech and whatever natural resources they could find. And they made it work. The *Mors Navis* now carried a crew of fifty-three girls, six cats and one goat. They'd made this ship both a weapon and a home.

Four years ago, this had been a fantasy. Trapped on a beach with nothing but a gut wound, her best friend, and this very ship in pieces, Caledonia could only dream of the day she had the means to stand up and fight. It had come sooner than she could have hoped, the morning Pisces looked at her square in the eyes and said she wanted revenge. It came as they bent their minds to the task of recovering their ship. It came one girl at a time. Caledonia and Pisces had stitched this ship and its crew together from odds and ends discarded by the world.

As Caledonia began her downward climb, she heard the bow boat drop from its hanging berth and hit the water. She saw it a moment later, pushing past the ship with five girls aboard and Redtooth at the helm, the red tips of her blonde braids visible against the bright blue morning. That team would scout a few miles ahead of the *Mors Navis*, looking for trouble or opportunity. Caledonia paused, watching as Redtooth raised her hand in salute to another dark shape in the water before speeding away.

Pisces. Some days it seemed the girl had been in the water since the attack on the *Ghost*. She'd risen before the sun that first, terrible day on the beach and walked straight into the ocean to drown her tears. When she came up for air, her sobs left jagged stitches in the hushed morning. Unable to move much on her own, Caledonia had no choice but to be still as her friend's grief washed over her. That grief was like a fever, one Caledonia could feel burning in her own blood. As Pisces sought solace in the ocean, Caledonia hoisted her eyes to the sky and let her own tears drain into the hard sand.

So much had changed in four years, but some things were very much the same. Pisces was in the water every morning as early as Caledonia was in the rigging. Just as Caledonia knew the surface of the ocean and her ship, Pisces knew what lay beneath.

Sunlight glinted off Pisces's smooth head and shoulders before she dived once again, vanishing from sight. Caledonia recalled the moment Pisces had come to her with a razor in her hand and tears in her eyes. "I want it gone," she'd said.

"You want what gone?" Caledonia asked as she cautiously reached for the razor, already afraid of whatever answer her friend was about to give.

"My hair," Pisces said, voice quiet. Tears slipped down her cheeks. "It drags in the water. And I need to be faster."

Caledonia began to cut, pausing every so often to blink away her own tears as she worked.

It had been the first of many sacrifices. But every one had made them stronger, brought them closer to the fight they ached for – to avenge their mothers and fathers and brothers and all the families aboard the *Ghost*. One day, they would take this fight all the way to Aric Athair himself.

"How's the view this morning, Captain?" a voice called as Caledonia reached the deck.

Lace was always among the first to greet her, no matter how early Caledonia rose.

"As bright as your hair." Caledonia faced the small girl, eyes appraising the pile of blonde curls that were as stubbornly cheerful as the girl who wore them. "What's the news?" Caledonia asked, turning her steps towards the bridge.

Though on the younger side of her command crew, Lace had stepped into Caledonia's trust almost as soon as she'd stepped aboard the ship. She was calm and competent, with a laugh as grizzly as Rhona's had been. Her skin was pale as seafoam and her curls, while not rusted red, were defiant. It was strange to associate someone so young with her mother, but Caledonia found something comforting in their similarity of spirit, and she'd loved Lace immediately for it.

Lace matched Caledonia's pace and began her morning brief of the day's activities. She covered changes to the duty roster, maintenance issues, health concerns. Lace had a knack for reporting dismal situations without sounding dismal, a talent that was exceedingly rare. Most of it didn't require Caledonia's direct attention, but the last item on Lace's list always landed heavy on the captain's mind.

"And finally," Lace began.

"And finally," Caledonia repeated with a sigh.

"Vitals. Far says we're down to beans and salt soup, and she can keep us running on that for five days at the outside."

"It's been five days for the past three, Lace. The soup is starting to look like water. Are you sure we can survive for five more days?"

Lace's smile was as sturdy as the deck beneath their feet. "We've survived worse than thin soup, Captain."

Five more days of meagre fare would make for a weaker crew. Caledonia felt the pinch in her own stomach amplified fifty-two times. Beside her, Lace had grown unusually quiet. "There's more?"

All around them, the deck buzzed with activity. Laundry lines were pulled taut and covered with clothes, the five Mary sisters were oiling the cable cutters and their clips beneath the railing, and Amina and the eleven girls who made up her sharpshooting team of Knots crawled through the rigging to polish the plates of the sun sail.

Lace's smile drooped when she answered, "We lost Metalmouth."

"Dammit." Caledonia stopped in her tracks, hands settling on her hips.

"Far thinks she got into some rot. Must've been bad to kill her."

That was an understatement. Goats were hardy in general, but Metalmouth had been named for the fact that she would have eaten the hull of their ship if she could. No goat meant no milk. Even less sustenance to go around. Finding a replacement wouldn't be easy.

"Bright bits?" Lace asked, her smile resurfacing. "We'll have meat for dinner."

"Youngest first," Caledonia spoke quietly. Her mind was already calculating the distance between them and the familiar waters of the Bone Mouth. If they changed course now, they could be there before they ran through their supply of beans. With any luck, they'd be able to forage on the islands and cast their lines for fish.

"Gather the command crew. We're changing course."

Before Lace had a chance to comply, a whistle pierced the air. It was followed by a shout from Amina high in the rigging. "Bow boat on approach!"

"That was quick," Lace mused, shielding her eyes to peer over the ocean.

The boat cut a straight line across the water, moving with strict urgency. It meant it was time to do one of two things: run or fight.

Immediately, the Mary sisters mobilized the deck crew, readying the hooks that would latch the boat and raise it into its hanging berth. The manoeuvre hadn't always been an easy one for such a young crew, but they hooked the boat on their first try and smoothly lifted the vessel from the water.

Redtooth was over the railing in an instant. Her blue eyes bulged like the muscles in her persistently burned arms as she made for Caledonia. "Captain," she said, clamping one hand on Caledonia's shoulder. "We found trouble."

Caledonia could see the future in Redtooth's eager expression. Trouble was code for a fight. Judging by the smile Redtooth couldn't hide, this wasn't just any fight. This was a chance to hurt Aric Athair, and that was impossible to walk away from.

"Can we eat it?" Caledonia asked.

Redtooth's lips spread in a devilish grin. "Sure," she answered. "We're the crew of the *Mors Navis*. We eat Bullets for breakfast."

CHAPTER TWO

The barge made a beautiful target. It floated on a glassy blue sea, covered in orange flowers turned towards the sun.

Under Redtooth's guidance, they'd come upon the baleflower carrier only moments before. The long, flat deck was a riot of mature flowers ready to be plucked and processed and eventually dehydrated and turned into Silt. This ship was on its way to rejoin Aric's AgriFleet along with other ships bearing harvested goods. He depended on these flowers, on the drug they produced, to force loyalty from his Bullets. They hungered for Silt almost as much as they craved Aric's approval.

He would definitely notice the barge's absence.

The day was clear, the air threaded with the distant, too-sweet scent of those poisonous flowers, the seas agreeable.

Caledonia lowered her binoculars and turned to face the five girls of her command crew: Pisces, Amina, Redtooth, Lace and Little Lovely Hime. Pisces was her second-in-command, while the other four commanded smaller crews of a dozen girls to oversee ship tech, training, navigation and medical respectively. In the time they'd been together, each of these faces had found harder edges. Little Lovely Hime no longer hid her hands in the pockets of her apron, Amina watched the horizon as much as she used to watch the sky, Lace smiled with more determination than joy, Redtooth's blonde braids were permanently tipped with red clay to signify she was ready for the fight, and Pisces spent so much time training in the water that her shoulders were always covered in fine sea salt. They were Caledonia's stones: some small, some large, each powerful in their own way.

From where they stood on the command deck, they had a clear view of both the barge ahead and the crew on the deck below.

Caledonia met Amina's steady gaze. In response, Amina raised her brown hand into the air like a sail, palm cupped. "There's a killing wind from the west, and the spirits are hungry," she said. "They will want blood. It does not matter from whom."

It certainly did matter from whom, but Caledonia wasn't in the mood to argue with Amina's spirits. Instead, she asked, "How charged are we?"

"Eighty per cent. Charging slower since our sun sail was gouged last week." Amina's voice carried fresh bitterness as she referenced their latest encounter. She turned thoughtfully towards the stern of the ship. "I'm working on a solution."

Like most salvaged ships, the *Mors Navis* ran on solar-powered jets. Unlike most ships, they had a system of retractable masts with patchwork cloth sails stowed belowdecks. At a moment's notice, the crew could erect the masts and convert the ship to wind power.

"Hime," Caledonia said, turning to the small girl. She had endlessly dark eyes and skin the cool beige of a seashell. Her mangled ear was hidden behind a long black braid, the end of which was tied in a simple blue ribbon. Her hands were folded quietly in front of her, a long apron blowing lightly over her trousers and boots. "You need to get below."

I want to fight, Hime said, her hands moving deftly.

Redtooth grunted her disapproval. "Not a smart move, little Princelet." She absently rubbed at a small scar on her palm.

Hime's cheeks flushed with anger or irritation – Caledonia didn't care which, only that Hime removed herself from the deck and the impending fight. Everyone on Aric's fleet was fed Silt. Even the Scythes, who were primarily responsible for tending the barges. And while Hime had been clean for nearly a year, the habit had long claws.

Amina laid a gentle hand on Hime's shoulder, communicating so much with a simple touch.

Hime raised her dark eyes to the baleflowers on the horizon, and then looked away with a nod.

One ship in the open blue, a hundred possible traps waiting where they could not see. Bale barges were never alone. There'd be at least two Bullet ships scouting wide for attack, ready to rush back and protect the precious cargo at the first signal from the barge.

This battle would cost the *Mors Navis*, but the only way to bring Aric's reign to an end was to weaken his hold over his Bullets. That required sacrifice – ammo, energy, blood. Caledonia was no stranger to sacrifice, but she preferred to make sure Aric's would be greater.

She spun, facing the crew below her on deck. Caledonia required every girl on board to know their strengths and pull their weight. Some, like Far, would do more harm than good in a fight, but even with a few tucked safely belowdecks, the fighting force was forty-nine girls strong. They stood with eyes trained on her. They'd seen the barge and had their guns and knives already in hand, their faces sharp and eager. They knew exactly what lay ahead of them. Raising her hand, Caledonia cried, "The only good Bullet…"

"Is a dead Bullet!" her girls shouted.

"Full speed!" The jets along the hull of the *Mors Navis* began to force water through their system. A plume of churned water rose behind them, and the ship surged forward.

Their speed was met by a flare from the barge, precisely as Caledonia had expected. It burst in the air like a great purple flower, then crackled and hissed as it faded to smoke. The countdown to Bullet ships began.

"You" – Caledonia pointed a finger at Lovely Hime – "belowdecks, don't come out."

Hime nodded and, with a final glance for Amina, slipped away.

Redtooth removed a small grey tin from a zippered pocket low on her leg and grinned as she dipped her fingers inside. She dragged red clay across her mouth, turning her lips into a bloody gash. Then, leaping from the bridge to the deck, she began organizing her raiding parties.

Amina was already halfway down the deck, shouting at her team of Knots to raise the masts and get into the rigging. No sooner were the masts locked in place than a team of girls began to climb, rifles strapped to their backs. They found positions among the bound sails and clipped into harnesses, ready to snipe incoming artillery.

The crew was in their rhythm. Tin, the eldest of the five Mary sisters, called out a list of orders to the deck crew until each of the twenty girls had a gun in hand.

"I have the bridge, Captain," Lace announced, tossing her sun-bleached curls as she turned to assume her position on the bridge. She was a bright spot among the crew, a sparkling citrine stone filled with warmth and light. Everything about her clung to cheer, from her ever-ready smile to the tattered lace she used to wrap her hands for combat. She was their Helm Girl, commanding the small bridge crew in Caledonia's absence. And she was the only person on board Caledonia trusted in that role.

"You have the bridge, Lace," Caledonia confirmed, leaving the shelter of her bridge and crossing the narrow

37

command deck to stand at the very tip of her vessel, in full view of the barge. She stood with hands on hips, eyes trained on her target, red hair blowing behind her like a deadly storm, as her mother had done whenever danger loomed. Let them see she was not afraid.

Pisces appeared at Caledonia's elbow.

"Cable mines," Pisces said as she pulled a charm back and forth on the chain around her neck.

Caledonia nodded. In all likelihood, there was a web of submerged mines attached to cables and suspended in a perimeter around that barge. They would need to be disabled or triggered before the *Mors Navis* sent its raiding parties in to destroy the crop. But first they would have to locate them.

They were closer to the barge now. Through binoculars she could see tiny figures rushing to secure the blossoms.

"Can you do it?" Caledonia turned to her friend, hopeful the answer was both yes and no.

"I can." Pisces dropped the charm. Seeming to sense Caledonia's momentary indecision, Pisces rested her fingertips against the arrowhead that marked Caledonia's temple.

In response, Caledonia raised her own fingers to the tattoo on Pi's temple. Black and starting to blur at the edges, it was a simple circle with two lines slashed vertically through one side. For Caledonia and Pisces, the marks had become living shrines to their murdered brothers, a symbol of the family they avenged with every battle.

38

The girls rested this way for just a breath before Pisces left like a gust of wind, flying down to where her submersible gear waited. As Pisces suited up, Caledonia imagined her own heart pinched flat as the ocean. Caring was what set them apart from the likes of Aric, but at times like this, it was only a distraction. Caledonia steered her mind to the fight ahead.

"Bullets!" The cry came from the top of the rigging.

Where moments before there had been water and dusty sunlight, now there were three black dots, which would soon grow into ships. They approached from the starboard side, coming to the aid of the barge.

"Get the tow in the water!" Caledonia shouted.

The tow, shaped like an oversized bullet, was a handheld propulsion device capable of pulling a person underwater. Combined with a blue lung that recycled air, that person could stay below for hours. That person was always Pisces.

Pisces would submerge and drive towards the skirt of mines, then trigger them from a safe distance using her pulse gun. It was the worst job on ship, but Pisces gave no evidence of anything except steeled nerves as she pulled on her mask, secured her flexible body armour, and checked her blue lung.

"Keep your distance, Pi. Come back to us."

Her tow ready in the water, Pisces leaped overboard. Then she was gone.

"Two miles to range!" Amina cried from her perch, eyes on the approaching Bullet ships. They were four miles out, but in two miles, they'd be close enough to open fire and hit the *Mors Navis*.

At this speed, that translated to minutes. And the crew needed each one.

On Caledonia's command, the *Mors Navis* slowed, coming to rest a quarter mile from the barge. Her crew was busy tightening armour over shoulders and thighs, checking their clips, and watching the enemy ships reveal themselves completely: an assault ship, a crusher and a mag ship. The assault ship was fast and would be heavily armed, the crusher designed for devastating impact, but the mag ship was the one that worried Caledonia. It would be armed with a system of magnetized harpoons. If they landed on the hull of the *Mors Navis*, they'd be able to hold her immobilized while the other ships attacked at will.

An explosion shot up from the water surrounding the barge. Pisces had found her first target and punched a small hole in the perimeter of cable mines. Now they waited for the second – to see how far the mines were spread apart, and to see if Pisces had survived the shockwave. On the deck of the barge, Scythes aimed rifles at the water and began to fire at Pisces.

These were torturous minutes. Caledonia inhaled slowly, scanning her crew. Amina hung in the rigging with the rest of her Knots, whispering a prayer to the sky. Redtooth crouched with her chosen raiding party in one of two bow boats swinging halfway down the starboard hull.

A second explosion spiked ten feet from where the first had been. Pisces was alive, and she'd just given them an entry point.

The barge would be theirs.

CHAPTER THREE

E verything moved at once.

Redtooth and her bow boats dropped to the water with a proud smack. Their engines roared to life, and the girls raised their plates of armour along the starboard side, locking them into a solid wall for cover from the approaching ships.

"Take them to the deep!" Caledonia lunged onto the cabin of the bridge, taking the shiny brass wheel from Lace and kicking the *Mors Navis* into high gear. She aimed her ship's nose directly at the Bullets, and her girls gave a vicious battle cry. Their focused rage reminded her that though she might be the force that kept them all together, they were here by choice.

The assault ship fired. Two precious missiles streaked across the sky. Amina's voice rang out, followed by gunfire. The Knots were sharp-eyed and shot each missile down midflight. They burst harmlessly in the air over the ocean.

Near the barge, another explosion erupted from the water. Redtooth now had plenty of room to manoeuvre right next to the bale barge and plant the mines that would sink it. Caledonia's job was to give them as much time as possible.

The approaching Bullet ships sped up. Wind sang through the ghost funnels mounted to their decks, creating a discordant, ethereal howl that sent an involuntary shiver down Caledonia's spine. Soon, the mag ship broke away, sailing over the remaining distance to the *Mors Navis*, trailed by the heavy-prowed crusher.

This was to be a halt and hit – the mag ship would move behind the *Mors Navis*, hook her with magnetic anchors, and hold her there while the crusher came in full tilt to hit her broadside. The *Mors Navis* was as tough as her crew, but she was shallow in the draught. A strong hit from a ship like that could topple her. Caledonia revved her jets again and turned her nose towards the mag ship, offering the smallest target possible.

"Cable cutters ready!" Tin's order travelled down the line as the girls prepared for the inevitable. She and her sisters commanded the deck with seamless efficiency. "Fire!"

Guns and rifles fired, the air turned grey with smoke, but the mag ship was undeterred.

With only feet to spare, the mag ship turned broadside and skated across the water to pace the *Mors Navis*. A small crew of Bullets greeted them with leering, hungry faces and a dozen gun barrels. The girls raised a wall of shields, and gunfire sparked against it. Before the girls could recover from the onslaught, the mag ship slipped into their wake and fired five magoons.

The hull of Caledonia's ship was a patchwork of metal and wood stitched together with heavy, waterproof seams of black tar. If even one of the mags hit wood, they stood a chance. But Caledonia heard the magnetized tethers attach one by one to patches of metal and knew they'd need grit over luck. She kept her ship's pace, but steered slightly towards the barge to buy a few seconds.

It didn't matter. As her crew traded fire with that of the mag ship, the five tethers connecting the two ships drew tight.

The *Mors Navis* began to slow.

Amina and the Knots turned their guns on the mag ship and opened fire, desperately trying to clear the way for their own crew to get over the rail of the *Mors Navis* and cut the magoon cables. The Bullets fired relentlessly. Shots sparked against their hull and soon found flesh and bone. Blood darkened the deck, the air thick with smoke and shouts and cries. Caledonia watched the scene unfurling with a sinking heart. Clearing the way for the cable cutters to dislodge the magoons would take time they did not have.

The assault ship drove forward now, heading not for the *Mors Navis*, but for the barge and Redtooth. That meant that the crusher – fitted with a deadly metal wedge on its nose – would turn on the *Mors Navis*. A direct hit from that ship would sink them for sure.

This was a perfect trap, but traps only worked when you thought your opponent couldn't surprise you.

"Amina!" she cried, and Amina slipped down the ropes to join Caledonia on deck. "Time to give your new web a try."

Shots hissed around them as the two girls hurried to collect Amina's latest design – three charges that could create a web of electricity. Anyone caught between them would get a deadly shock. But it required each charge to land within twenty feet of the others.

"Work fast," Amina instructed, calmly calibrating the charges and loading the three guns. "If they detach before we get all three in place, it won't work."

In the distance, the assault ship was closing in on the barge.

Time pushed at Caledonia's heart, but she breathed in once to slow it, then lifted the first gun to her shoulder and aimed for the deck of the mag ship. Amina did the same. "Three, two, one."

The kick of the guns was severe, but both shots hit their intended targets. Amina reached immediately for the third gun and fired. Caledonia didn't wait to confirm the shot landed before hitting the button on the remote trigger.

Blue-white light arced from charge to charge, spidering out to kiss the copious amounts of metal on each Bullet. Their bodies snapped in the air like sails in the wind, their eyes rolling skyward, mouths freezing with jaws clenched.

"Now!" Caledonia cried. The crusher was closing in, its nose lined up to ram the *Mors Navis* dead centre.

Five girls dived over the side of the ship, their feet caught by strong hands as they dangled and stretched to sever the cables of magoons holding the *Mors Navis* in place. One by one the cables snapped. Caledonia raced to the helm and drove the jets as high as they might go.

The *Mors Navis* jerked ahead, but she hadn't been fast enough. The crusher hit them with a glancing blow, ripping a patch of metal siding from the stern.

The ship heaved to one side, sending girls and guns sliding across the deck. Caledonia could do nothing but grip the helm and wait. From that position, she could see Redtooth and the bow boats racing home. Behind them, an explosion split the barge in two, filling the sky with vibrant orange petals that drifted slowly to the ocean.

Her girls roared in triumph. It was a vicious sound, and it filled Caledonia with so much delight she thought she could right this ship herself. Aric had lost a hearty crop today. And it was Caledonia and her crew who had taken it from him.

Not far from the sinking barge, she spotted something else bobbing in the water, a dark figure directly in the path of the approaching assault ship.

Pisces, she realized with horror. And the Bullet crew had her in their sights. Just as the *Mors Navis* began to right itself, a pick hook swung down from the enemy ship and buried itself in Pisces's shoulder.

As Caledonia watched, Pisces was dragged from the water straight into the hands of the enemy.

CHAPTER FOUR

C aledonia did not realize she was screaming until her girls answered her cry with a collective one of their own. Leaping up, she aimed her ship for Redtooth while the crusher, now several hundred feet beyond them, struggled to shift its momentum and return. The mag ship was dead in the water, and the assault ship, having slowed to collect Pisces, didn't have the momentum to catch up. The *Mors Navis* was faster than both remaining ships; they would get away easily now.

Except for Pisces. It took every drop of Caledonia's control to keep her course and not go after her friend, even though panic gnawed at the back of her throat.

The returning bow boats slid into the choppy waters near the base of the ship. It took three tries, but the crew successfully hooked and hoisted both boats back to their hanging berths. Her girls moved efficiently, unloading the bounty the raiding parties had collected before sinking the barge. Their joy in victory turned quiet.

That was it. Their goal completed. The bale barge

destroyed, her bounty claimed. Clear of combat, they were ready to run. They had to run. It was the mission she promised her girls: hit hard and hide fast, no unnecessary risks. But Caledonia's hands shook as she turned her eyes away from the assault ship.

"Caledonia." Lace stood beside her. Saying her name as though it were a command. How many times had she said it already?

"Yes, Lace."

"Your orders." She stepped in close. "Do we go for her? Say the word, Captain, and we'll go for her."

For one second, she considered a head-on fight with two Bullet ships. Her crew was brave and bold. If she asked them to, they'd churn like a storm to bring Pisces back. And she wanted to. She wanted so badly to raise her voice and ask them to prolong the fight. But the risk was too great. How could she justify the lives they might lose for the one she might save? Maybe if all she had to risk was her own life, she could. She would risk herself a thousand times over for Pisces, but asking her crew for the same was irresponsible.

"We make for the Bone Mouth," she said, voice hard.

"Captain," Lace began in protest.

"Now, Lace."

The engines churned. Caledonia's ears filled with a howling wind. Some part of her whispered that it wasn't real, and another part of her wailed that it was more real than the wheel beneath her palms.

She gritted her teeth and cast a final glance at the Bullet ships. The bale barge was only a smear of orange petals on the water, the mag ship bobbed without power, and the crusher had turned heel and was headed for the assault ship now two miles away. Two terrible miles that stretched between herself and the friend who had become her family. Her chest tightened, and something in her heart began to unravel.

Pisces was gone.

She'd never lost a girl in battle. Not one. And for Pisces to be the first? It was the one thing Caledonia didn't think she could bear.

Then, a cry from one of the Knots. "The tow!"

Caledonia's grip tightened on the wheel. Only when she heard it again – "Pisces's tow!" – did she pull the ship out of speed.

"Eyes on the Bullets!" Caledonia called up to the Knots, all too aware that the assault ship might view this pause as an opportunity to renew its attack.

The deck was alive with movement as Caledonia climbed down the companionway ladder. The railing was three girls deep, all of them peering over at the water below.

Pisces. The name repeated again and again, but Caledonia didn't believe it – couldn't believe it – until the sight of her friend, glistening and bleeding, appeared briefly above the heads of her crew as she was pulled over the ship's railing.

Caledonia raced across the deck, pushing through the

49

crowd with shaking hands, preparing for the worst. And suddenly, there she was. Blood coated one side of her face, dripping from a gash on her forehead. Her shirt was black against her wounded shoulder, and there was a deep puncture in the leather of her vest where the hook had found purchase. Alive. She was alive.

Caledonia closed the distance between them and pulled her friend into her arms, surrounded by a cheering crew.

Before Caledonia had a chance to say anything, another face appeared at the railing, hauled up with the tow. A boy. A Bullet.

All sound ceased.

The crew instinctively formed a circle with Caledonia at its centre. She turned, releasing her friend and facing the boy.

He was perhaps a few years older than her, with wide brown eyes and a strong nose. Slashing the deep brown skin of his bicep were the horizontal scars of his bandolier. He had three. Each was thick, ropey and saturated with the same dense orange as a baleflower. Caledonia had seen only one other bandolier scar this close before. They were a symbol of loyalty to Aric. Each represented some deadly degree of service to the tyrant, and for this Bullet to have three suggested his hands were thoroughly blood-soaked. He wasn't just dangerous, he was deadly.

"Throw him over," she commanded.

Pisces raised a hand. "Wait."

Caledonia could see the hope trembling in the corners of Pisces's mouth.

"He saved my life," Pisces said. "Please."

Pisces knew the rules as well as any girl on board, but she didn't know how the *Ghost* was discovered so many years ago. They'd lost their families because Caledonia had let her guard down with Lir. This Bullet would be no different, and she would not let her friend make the same mistake.

In the distance, the Bullet ships were shifting on the water, perhaps deciding to pursue the stalled prize in front of them.

"Good." Caledonia unsheathed her pistol and pulled the hammer back, pointing the barrel at one of the boy's wide brown eyes. "Now throw him over and save his."

"He risked everything to help me," Pisces protested. "He killed his own to get me off the assault ship, Cala. They won't take him back."

Caledonia trusted what her friend said, but she also trusted her gut. She of all people knew how deceptive a Bullet could be. Sacrificing one of their own to get a saboteur on board the *Mors Navis* would be an easy decision for their Silt-drenched minds. They would do anything to please Aric Athair.

Caledonia shouted, "First rule!"

And all around her came the chorus, "No Bullets!"

It had been the first rule from the beginning. When Caledonia's gut had healed and she and Pisces had repaired the damage to their ship, they'd agreed to form a crew.

Lir's betrayal was Caledonia's constant secret companion, and when she demanded an all-girl crew, Pisces had no reason to object.

Now Pisces stepped in front of the boy, placing her own head at the end of Caledonia's barrel. "He saved my life," she repeated, each word careful and precise.

Blood streamed steadily from the gash in her forehead. Maybe the boy had saved her life, but it was Caledonia who would make sure she *stayed* alive.

Redtooth appeared over Pisces's shoulder, her grin streaked now with sweat and ash. With one easy move, she had the boy's arms locked behind his back and his knees bent to the deck. He made no sound, no struggle.

"You have a few precious moments to save his, Pi." Caledonia lowered her gun and with her other hand gave Lace the signal to accelerate. "We get too far and he'll drown for sure."

"We send him back and he's dead anyway." Pisces kept her voice low. "He wants out. We abandon him and we're no better than them."

There was a dagger tucked into Caledonia's belt. It was small, with a wooden handle curved to fit completely inside her grip, and a short black blade meant to sit between the first and second fingers. The last time it tasted blood, it had been her own at the hands of a Bullet who said he, too, wanted out. There was no room on her ship for another who said the same.

The deck rumbled beneath their feet as the masts shuttered down into their holsters, no longer required by Amina's Knots. Half of the crew was in motion, clearing the deck for speed, their eyes on the boy, Pisces and Caledonia. The air between them smelled of brine and copper. Pisces kept one hand pressed over her wound, blood travelling down her arm in shallow rivers. She needed to be belowdecks with the rest of the injured where Little Lovely Hime could see to her wounds, not up here fighting for the worthless life of a Bullet.

The rules of their ship were simple: no Bullets, act together or not at all, and the captain's word is law. If there was flexibility on any of the three, it was the last – Caledonia's girls weren't afraid to make their opinions known. As long as they did it while they scrubbed the deck or peeled a potato or tended their wounds, she didn't mind. She liked that her girls had guts. But this was the kind of challenge that could slip beneath the skin of the whole ship if she didn't lock it down.

Caledonia stepped closer to Pisces, torn between wanting to knock her out and make her see reason. "We don't trust Bullets."

"We trust Hime," Pisces shot back, too quiet for any but Caledonia to hear. "How is this any different?"

"You *know* how."

"No, I don't." Pisces flinched, adjusting the hand over her wound. "We take the girls when they want out. Why not him? Why not the one who spared my life?"

Wind whipped between them. Its sharp sea spray did

nothing to cool the tension. It was true Hime had been one of Aric's and it was true that they'd taken her in. Even that had been a gamble.

"This is not a negotiation." Caledonia could feel the eyes of her crew clinging to this conversation. She raised her gun, again pointing it at the boy. "No Bullets. Not now. Not ever."

The boy didn't move. He barely seemed to notice the gun levelled at his head, but his lips parted and he watched Caledonia with a fearless kind of surprise.

Then he spoke. A single word that found no purchase in Caledonia's sympathy. "Mercy."

Caledonia's grin was as hard as her heart. "Not on this ship," she said. He was not the pale-eyed boy from so long ago, not the one she dreamed of killing, but Caledonia thought shooting him might feel nearly as satisfying. "You've done a good thing, so I'll spare my shot and your life. If you jump now, maybe your crew will do a good thing, too."

In the set of Pisces's mouth, Caledonia saw the determination she so admired in her friend. Nothing would convince Pisces to throw him over, just as nothing would convince Caledonia to keep him on board.

"I can help." The boy's gentle voice was jarring in the silence. Caledonia laughed and opened her mouth to share exactly what she thought of that, but he pressed on. "Please, I know how they think. I can—"

Redtooth abbreviated his plea with a blow to the back of the head. "It's rude to interrupt," she growled.

Laughter shuffled through the crew as the boy fell forward.

Redtooth wasn't one to pull her punches.

"Twelve miles out, Captain! Clear seas! No tails!" The call from Lace meant they'd put the remains of the Bullet fleet twelve miles in their wake with no signs of pursuit. Good news for them. Bad news for the boy.

"Throw him over," Caledonia said again.

Redtooth hauled him to his feet. This time he fought against her grip. "Wait! Please! I can help! You want to sink their barges? I know how to find them!"

Anything that came out of his mouth was nothing but noise, and every girl on that deck knew it. They would never trust a Bullet to tell her where to find Aric or his drugs. This time it was Pisces who stepped forward, and with a pained wince, she slammed her fist against the side of his head. It landed with a dull smack, and the boy's entire body drooped in response.

Out cold, he sagged in Redtooth's grasp, his head lolling to one side, knees splayed out at awkward angles. Pisces also drooped. Her broad shoulders hung like stones on her tall frame, hands loose at her sides. She looked ready to crash, but she wasn't finished.

"No Bullets," Pisces said loudly enough for all to hear. "We drop him in the shallows first chance we get."

This was a slippery slope, Caledonia knew. It didn't break the rule, but it came close. Her crew was loyal, and that loyalty was stitched together with rules and hard years of evasion and battle. To threaten a rule was to threaten the weave of their fabric.

Caledonia moved close enough to speak in her friend's ear. "You're alive, and I could not be more relieved, more grateful, but keeping him on board for any length of time is a risk."

The look Pisces returned was both gentle and strong. "We can resist them as long as we don't become them."

"Dammit." Caledonia couldn't argue with those words. She'd said them herself dozens of times over the years, but they weren't hers any more than they were Pisces's. "Rhona would be proud of you."

"And you, too." Pisces gripped Caledonia's hand, sticky with blood.

"Gag him. Bind him. Put him in the hole," Caledonia snapped. "First chance we get, we dump him in the shallows."

The crew rippled with whispers, hisses, grumbles. Caledonia stood tall and brought her gaze to bear on all who were near. "Now," she ordered, calm but firm.

Redtooth dropped the boy to his knees so the others could gag and bind him. Before they were done, he was conscious again, blinking meekly in the late afternoon light. If he was surprised to find himself still alive, he didn't show it. He remained compliant even when Redtooth stooped to make sure the ropes were tied so tightly that they cut into his skin.

"Captain," Amina called, approaching from the quarterdeck. She'd come to them from the Hands of the River, the folk who lived on the Braids and spoke with a breathy, musical accent. Sweat shone against her reddish-brown skin, and she moved like an ocean current, with rolling grace in every motion. Though she was shorter than Caledonia, she was just as imposing, with the sides of her head shaved smooth and a crest of thick braids coiled and twisted on her crown. The crew moved seamlessly out of her way, creating a path.

Caledonia braced, noting the way Amina's eyes strayed from her to the boy and back again.

Amina closed the space between them like a small storm. "We have a problem," she said.

Caledonia felt her pulse quicken. "Can it wait?"

"No," she said. "Our sun sail was hit. Again. It's not drawing power, so all we have is our reserves."

After the fight they'd just had, their reserves would be low. And they'd have burned through plenty making their escape. They'd need more to make it back to the waters of the Bone Mouth. And they needed to do it quick if they hoped to eat.

"What do we have left?" she asked, afraid she already knew the answer.

The ship bucked beneath their feet, slowing.

Amina held her captain's gaze, unflinching. "In another day, we'll be dead in the water."

CHAPTER FIVE

The sun sail hung from its mast in disjointed sections, dripping like rain where the weaving had come undone. Black scales littered the deck, some cracked or broken, others glittering in the late afternoon sun, turning the quarterdeck into a field of jewels. It was almost beautiful.

"Can you repair it?" Caledonia asked, eyes drifting over its ragged edges.

Amina collected a handful of fallen scales, turning them over like coins. She'd been with Caledonia and Pisces for a full three years. The girls had just finished patching the ship and were in pursuit of parts to repair this very sun sail when they rescued Amina from a small band of Bullets. They'd been too late to rescue her companions, and Amina had joined them with fury in her heart. Nearly half of the ship's systems were running due to her creative attentions. More than anyone, she knew the difference between broken for good and broken for now. If there was a way to fix it, Amina would find it.

One by one, she let the scales drop from her hand.

They hit the deck with hollow clatters. "No," she said. "It's done."

The word sounded deceptively simple when their reality was anything but. Done meant they were reduced to the power of whatever winds Amina's spirits chose to send their way. Done meant they'd never have a chance of outrunning another Bullet ship. They would still have power. The deck was littered with sun pips – small dishes set into the flooring that fed power and light belowdecks – and the entire bow was coated in sun paint which fed directly into the bridge systems. But without the sun sail to charge the engines, they wouldn't be able to outrun anything on these waters.

"Talk to me about options. Can we redirect power from the sun pips and bow? If we keep the cabins dark, can we—"

Amina's hand closed over Caledonia's forearm. Here, away from the crew, Amina let the depths of her frustration show. She had kept this sail alive for three hard years, had repaired it time and time again to keep the *Mors Navis* moving. And now it was scattered at her feet like spent rifle shells.

She shook her head. "I'm sorry, Captain. I could do as you say, divert what those cells draw, but it would provide less propulsion than the wind." Her eyes turned skyward as they so often did, searching for signs or hope. Finding neither, she released a slow sigh before adding, "It is not a solution, and I'm afraid I have none to offer."

The sun was harsh on Caledonia's face, reflecting from

the surface of the sea and toughening her skin. It was powerful. It was power. And it was just out of reach.

"We'll find a way." She'd been much closer to defeat than this moment, but even as she spoke, she knew their situation was precarious.

Caledonia turned her gaze to her crew. Every single girl on deck knew something was wrong. The *Mors Navis* always struck hard and hid fast. That was how they survived – by never sticking around to see what followed the first wave. The ship should have been moving at top speed, not cruising gently. Still, there was work to be done, and the girls were tending to it.

The wounded were belowdecks with Lovely Hime. The deck crew, under the guidance of Tin Mary and her four sisters, was making quick work of collecting bullet shells to be reused and debris to be discarded, reloading weapons, and scrubbing out bloodstains. A few girls hung over the railing, using rubber wedges to detach what remained of the magoons. They'd be reappropriated, crafted into whatever weapon Amina thought of next. Soon, all signs of their battle would be smoothed into their routine.

The boy was gone. Taken by Redtooth to the hole where he'd remain until Caledonia was ready to deal with him again. At the moment, she was happy to let him sit in the dark anguishing over whether his death would arrive in a few minutes or hours.

The day was won. They'd taken all the bounty they could

reach, sunk a baleflower crop, and survived an attack. The floor beneath the mainmast block was clear. All her girls had survived, and not a single shrouded body marred this day. It was a blessing and not one Caledonia took lightly.

"It was not our blood the killing wind wanted," Amina said, following her gaze.

"May it always be so," Caledonia replied, though Amina knew full well that Caledonia didn't believe in spirits.

Caledonia left Amina to collect the scales and returned to the bridge, where Lace greeted her with a determined smile and a report. Other than Pisces's shoulder, the injuries were minimal, the raid on the barge had supplemented their food and ammunition stores but not by much, and they'd set a course for the Bone Mouth.

"We'll reach it in three days at current speed." The last was offered with a raised eyebrow and an inquisitive tone. "Of course, if we push to top speed we'll be there faster."

"Maintain course and speed," Caledonia answered, leaving the bridge to stand at the bow.

So much had changed in the span of a single day. Caledonia needed time to cast her thoughts over the ocean, let them fall into a new sense of order. In light of the broken sun sail, everything else was secondary – Pisces's injury, the Bullet, their temporarily boosted food stores. Nothing else would matter if they didn't find a way to generate power. That was her job. Keeping this ship and its crew in food, ammo and power.

Caledonia knew the names of all fifty-two girls aboard her ship. Some were runaways – fled from the towns that traded children for safety – some, like the Mary sisters, were rescued from the fortresses of Aric's small tyrants, and others were like Caledonia and Pisces, the remnants of rogue families. They'd all been scarred by Aric's growing empire and wanted to destroy it piece by piece. No matter where they'd come from, every girl on this ship was here to fight.

They'd hidden in the rocky shoals of the Bone Mouth, they'd grown strong, they'd grown brave, and they'd downed seven bale barges all told. And now Caledonia would have to tell them that it was over. They were nothing more than a wind ship. And wind ships weren't fighting ships.

The sun was low in the sky when Caledonia finally called for Amina.

"Captain?" she asked, joining Caledonia where she still stood on the command deck. The *Mors Navis* boasted a low profile with only two short levels rising from the main deck. The command deck stretched forward from the bridge, just far enough for the two girls to speak without being heard by the bridge crew.

"What if I get you a new sail?"

Amina narrowed her eyes. "How?"

"The usual way. If we steal you a sun sail, can you make it work?"

"Of course," Amina said, clearly offended at the question.

"Good," she said, turning to the bridge. "All stop!"

The engines quieted, and the plume of seawater that rose behind the *Mors Navis* fell flat. The ship slid atop the water, letting the lapping waves coax it to a stop. For the first time, that gentle tugging felt ominous. It wouldn't be long before gathering even the smallest of speeds would be difficult.

"Captain?" Lace appeared before them, her blonde curls vibrant with sunset.

Caledonia turned her steps towards the main deck. Her body was beginning to ache from bruises she hadn't realized she'd gained during the fight. It was a good feeling, one she relished as she gave Lace the order to gather the crew.

Word raced through the ship, drawing Lovely Hime and her dozen wounded girls from below, the bridge crew from above, and even Far, the oldest woman on the ship at forty-two turns, from her preferred solitude in the galley. Caledonia stood by the mainmast block as they pooled around her like sharks. Pisces found her way to Caledonia's side, brushing a hand down the back of Caledonia's arm to let her know she was near. No one made a sound.

The sun was bleeding along the horizon now, setting fire to the ocean and turning the sky a brilliant, fish-scale blue. Soon the deck would be ringed in the dim blue glow of electric sun pips, just enough to remind the girls where the railing ended and the ocean began, but not enough to call the attention of a Bullet ship.

"We have a boy on board," she said when all were present. An uncomfortable whisper surrounded her, as she knew it would. "He won't stay. But he saved Pisces's life and in return we'll drop him in the shallows of the Bone Mouth." She allowed just a breath of a second to pass before she pressed on. "That is not our problem. Our problem is that our sun sail is dead."

Here she paused again, allowing the unease to settle in. No good would come from hiding this truth. Her girls needed to feel the reality of the situation before she offered her plan.

A rush of voices passed around the circle.

"Dead?" asked Pippa, unwilling to hear it. "We're good as sunk."

Tin called out in her deep voice, "Can't Amina fix it?"

"If I could fix it, that's what I'd be doing." Amina's answer was sharpened by irritation.

Caledonia felt every bit of their anger and fear, but she kept her expression calm. She lifted her hand, and the voices quieted.

"We will soon be a ship under wind and wind only. You all know what that means. We stay this way and we die or disband, and that's not something I'm willing to do."

She turned slowly, surveying the faces of her girls. Each was steely and bright. There was no hint of surrender here.

"We have options," she began. "Without power our best bet might just be to hide."

Redtooth made a sound that landed somewhere between a grunt and a laugh.

At one point in time, many of her girls might have preferred to hide. But that was before they'd found their rhythm as a crew and learned just how good at this they could be. Hiding now would be an insult to the small amount of pride they'd gained. Caledonia was counting on that pride as she pressed on.

"Hiding made us strong. It gave us time to make this ship strong. But there's something we do even better than hide," Caledonia said.

"Spend bullets," Tin replied darkly. "Sink ships."

Tin stood several inches taller than Caledonia, her spiked brown hair streaked with grime and sweat, her pale blue eyes full of the setting sun. She and her sisters had been the last to join the crew, eight months ago. They'd been a boon to the ship, smart and hardworking. But Tin made no bones about wanting to punch the Net and escape Aric's domain for good, and Caledonia knew there were more than a few girls on board who were tempted by the idea.

"Exactly," Caledonia confirmed. "We fight! And if we're going to keep fighting, we need a new sun sail."

"Are we going to port?" Redtooth asked, excited by the prospect of taking her raiding crew to shore. In all the Bullet Seas there wasn't a single port that could be called friendly, but there was at least one that didn't fall under Aric's rule.

"Not to port." Caledonia pointed towards the horizon they'd just left, now inky with night-time shadows. "We're going to power down and stay here until a Bullet ship spots us."

"And how are we going to run without power and no wind?"

Tin gestured to the sky where the air barely stirred.

"We're not going to run," Caledonia said, standing firm in the face of Tin's concern. Every piece of this had played to her favour, right down to Tin's final outburst. Her girls were ready to fight, and they'd do whatever it took to make that happen. She knew she had them even before she said it. "We're going to load every weapon we've got. And we're going to let them bring their sail to us."

CHAPTER SIX

Clear nights always reminded Caledonia of when this ship was her mother's, when they sailed under the moon and hid during the day.

Rhona Styx kept the *Ghost* out to sea for so much of Caledonia's life that her little brother had been born there. When she was old enough, Caledonia's father taught her how to climb the riggings, to tie knots and to judge distances, all under the dim light of the shimmering stars and moon. From her mother she learned how to steer the ship between the narrow straits of the Bone Mouth, how to rely on old charts and the eyes of their crew.

And sometimes, when it was calm and quiet for miles and miles around, she and her little brother would climb atop the bridge and he would sing. Donnally started with songs passed down from their parents and the others on board, a strange mishmash of tempos and long-forgotten languages, but soon he was creating his own music. He sang about Caledonia's red hair and about their mother's missing tooth and about riding on the backs of great whales.

There were too many songs to remember now. But when the night was calm like this one, she'd catch the refrain of one floating through her memory and suddenly his voice was there, a crooning, tremulous soprano singing about a crab who reached too high and was caught up by the stars.

Such memories were always accompanied by the threat of tears. She felt them squeezing the back of her throat like a bitter lime. She bit them back. There was room on her ship for tears, but not from her. She'd practised smoothing over that familiar bite of sadness with anger. It only took a single word: Lir. She conjured his face in her mind, those cold blue eyes, and let anger burn her sadness away, imagining how good it would feel to slide her dagger between his ribs.

One day, it would be more than a pleasant imagining.

Caledonia sat on the bridge, one knee pulled tight to her chest, eyes on the flat plane of ocean ahead, her mind tossing between Donnally's song and her own dark longing. In the old world, the little room would have been secured on all sides, wrapped in thick walls of protective metal. The crew didn't need to see with their eyes because they navigated the seas and even battles with soundtech. That kind of tech was all but extinct now, and the bridge of the *Mors Navis* was wrapped in panes of self-healing glass. Caledonia closed her eyes and willed her mind to be as clear as that glass.

"Cala," Pisces called quietly in the dark.

Each of the bridge stations were empty, her crew gone to their cabins to rest until the fight came to them. On deck, a skeleton crew of four girls watched for signs of Bullet ships.

"You shouldn't be up here." Caledonia turned to her friend. Pisces's white bandage glowed in the moonlight. "I need you rested. As well as can be."

Hime had stitched the cut on her head and smoothed it with a regenerating poultice. The wound on her shoulder wasn't as bad as they'd feared. Her leather body armour had taken the brunt of that vicious hook, but no wound was a good wound out here. As Hime had often reminded them, it wouldn't be so bad if they could get their hands on some Bullet skintech, patches and nanogels that could mend even the worst wounds. But they were incredibly hard to come by. Pisces's shoulder had been stitched with thread and bandaged, and she was under firm orders from Hime to keep it still until movement was absolutely necessary. She'd be back in the water as soon as another ship appeared. Wounded or not.

"I know, but I wanted to thank you. For letting him stay."

Caledonia hadn't thought about the boy in hours. He was still in the hold, rotting with his own thoughts. "Don't thank me until he's off my ship."

"I'm thanking you now." Pisces had been around Caledonia long enough to be undeterred by her hard exterior. "I put you in a tight spot with the crew, and I think you did a good thing."

In truth, Caledonia didn't want to be thanked at all. She didn't think she'd done a good thing. Keeping a Bullet on board was the most foolish thing she could think of, but if Caledonia had one weakness, it was Pisces. The girl lived in the softest part of Caledonia's heart, and she would do nearly anything for her. If not for Pisces, the boy would be treading water or back in the hands of his clip. Now he'd probably just end up dead.

Maybe they'd all end up dead.

"They had me, had my tow. They'd have filled my blood with Silt and let me dream my way to death. But he stood up for me. Spirits know why, but he turned his gun on his own clip and saved my life." Frowning, Pisces smoothed a hand gingerly over her bandaged shoulder. "He can't go back. You know how they feel about traitors, what they do to them. He deserves our help."

This was a place Caledonia wasn't willing to go. Pisces's ability to temper revenge with compassion felt like a dangerous vulnerability. Over the years, Caledonia's resistance to such compassion had become a line between them.

"No," she said, decisive. "He doesn't. He might have done a good thing for us, but there's a mountain of bad things behind him. Don't forget that."

"Cala," Pisces said, her voice sweeping down Caledonia's back like a mother's gentle hand. Calming and reprimanding all at once. "Just because there are bad things behind someone doesn't mean they only have bad things inside them."

Except when that person was a soldier of Aric Athair.

70

She let the line between herself and her friend grow a little thicker, imagined it curling around her own heart like a wall. Pisces needed her heart. Between the two of them, she was the one who knew when the crew needed room to breathe or scream or fight. It was good that one of them was aware of such things.

Eight bells chimed sweetly in the distance. A four-hour shift had passed, and it was time for a fresh watch to take over. The girls on deck moved quietly, passing each other like shadows.

One figure appeared in the doorway and stood just behind Pisces. Blonde curls gathered moonlight. "Captain." Lace's voice was quiet and soothing and as familiar as a warm blanket. "Nothing to report. Next shift's up."

Caledonia nodded, feeling cheered by Lace's presence as always. No matter how terrible things were, Lace could always find a reason for hope. Her mother had lived under Aric's rule and died smuggling Lace out of the Holster. When Lace told the tale, she ended it with a smile, saying, "There are good people in there, too. And they're fighting in all the ways they know how." True or not, believing it gave her a taste of Lace's optimism.

"Thank you, Lace. Get some sleep. You, too, Pi."

Lace left just as quickly as she'd come, but Pisces hesitated. "Pi."

"I'll keep watch with you." Pisces would stay with Caledonia even if she were bleeding from her ears.

"If I can't have you whole, I need you rested. Go to bed, or I'll get Red to take you away." She tried to make her voice light, but it was evident in Pisces's expression that she hadn't been entirely successful.

"What if he really is what he says?" Pisces pressed.

"He's not," Caledonia answered quickly.

"But what if it's true and he does want out? He could help us. He was a Bullet, he could know so much about how they—"

"He *is* a Bullet," Caledonia snapped. "And I'm not having this argument. He goes. As soon as we're near the shallows."

Pisces paced towards the door and back again, frustration evident in her brusque gait. "He's not the enemy, Cala. He's a tool of the enemy, and we shouldn't take his turning lightly. Promise me you won't."

This, at least, she could do. "I promise you, I won't take anything he does lightly."

If Pisces sensed the danger in Caledonia's words, she didn't let on. "Goodnight, Cala," she said, dropping a kiss on her friend's cheek.

Every hour that passed weighed heavily on Caledonia's mind. Bullets didn't like to travel at night, but the longer it took for ships to pursue the *Mors Navis*, the more ships there were likely to be. One ship would make this hard enough. Any more than two made it essentially impossible.

There were so many ways this could go wrong.

She'd almost been tempted to ask Amina what her spirits

would take in trade for a friendly wind. Instead, she'd asked her to install dozens of new hidden holsters around the deck and fit each one with a loaded weapon.

They were as ready as they could be. All they needed was a Bullet ship to spot them and take the bait.

No longer content to sit and stare into the dark, Caledonia left the bridge. With a quick wave to her deck crew, she slid down the companionway stairs leading into the berth. Her boots hit the cabin deck with a dull slap. A thick darkness surrounded her, and she took a moment to let her eyes adjust to the dim glow of sun pips in the ceiling above. As promised, Amina had redirected most of that power to the ship's propulsion system, leaving only a few pips with juice. After a moment, the light settled into a dusty arch along the hallway.

Even though she could walk the belly of this ship blindfolded, Caledonia let her hand drift along the wall as she moved. Years ago, the cabins of this hall had housed the families that made up the crew of the *Ghost*. Each family had its own room no matter how many bodies it contained. Now the cabins slept four girls in bunks with extra weaponry stored in chests beneath the floor.

While most were asleep, Caledonia could hear the gentle rise and fall of hushed voices behind closed doors. There was not always so much time before a fight, and nerves would only pull tighter as the night went on.

She continued through the dark galley, which smelled of coffee and tea even in these quiet hours. Dinner had been heartier than usual, thanks to the demise of poor Metalmouth and additional spoils from the barge. As usual, Far had brought her a plate knowing she wouldn't make time to sit for a proper meal in the galley. By now, though, Far was probably asleep on her pallet in the pantry, ready to feed the girls on dead watch if they came asking for food. On a different night, Caledonia might have looked in on the woman, but tonight she kept moving, sliding down the stairs to the storage bay.

She didn't know where she was going until she'd descended to level three, in the very bottom of the ship's belly, and reached a solid, metal hatch tucked into a corner at the forward end of the bay. Paint flecked the surface, peeling away little by little. In full light, it would be a patchwork of dark blue and yellow. Under the hazy glow of sun pips, it was cast in shades of grey. In the centre stood a heavy wheel, spun and bolted in the lock position.

It wasn't their custom to take prisoners, so the hold wasn't always used as such, but right now, a Bullet sat on the other side.

Caledonia shoved the bolt back and turned the wheel, unlocking the hatch.

The door opened to reveal the boy coiled in a spill of silvery light from the porthole. His hands were cupped before him, bound together with cords of pale rope. He wasn't asleep, as she'd expected, but neither did he look up. He kept his eyes focused on a spot across the room. A bruise had formed on the side of his face, and along the bare skin of his arms were several more. The gag pulled tight between his lips was damp with spit and blood. He looked smaller than Caledonia remembered.

"Sit up."

Letting the door hang open behind her, she stepped over the frame and into the room. The walls were lined with boxes, each packed with canvas and clothing and bandages. Nothing too easily weaponized. The remaining space was long and narrow, barely wide enough for a body to repose for sleep. This was no place for a long-term stay. There was only room here to breathe and wait.

The other time this room had been used for such a purpose was two years ago when they found Hime. And her needs had been dramatically different. For a moment, Caledonia could almost see the small girl curled on the floor like a fern, could almost hear the dull smack of her hands and feet as she pounded against the floor in anguish. It was clear that she could not speak, and they'd assumed the scar on her ear meant she was deaf as well. It had been Amina who realized they were wrong, who bent low to whisper words of comfort while the girl writhed helplessly.

Caledonia had almost forgotten how terrible it was to witness Silt withdrawal.

Shaking away her ghosts, Caledonia studied the boy. He was strong, well-fed as all Bullets were. His shoulders were rolled forward, his knees bent slightly towards his chest as

75

though his instinct was to roll into a ball for comfort, yet his body was tense, every muscle locked tight. The three scars banding his left bicep were spaced less than an inch apart. Two were gnarled and old while the other bore the puffed look of a fresh wound. Even in this silver light, the violent orange pigment left by Silt was visible. Bullets took so much of the drug that it settled in their blood, in their skin, blooming in their scars like the flowers from which it came.

Lost in a momentary surge of disgust, Caledonia was startled to find the boy had lifted his chin just enough to watch her. It was hard to discern his expression with the gag in place, but there was no malice in his dark eyes. Instead, he seemed thoughtful, curious even.

"I have questions. Give me lies and I'll split your tongue," Caledonia warned.

In response, the boy bowed his head, lowering his eyes briefly before meeting hers once again. He accepted her words without anger.

Caledonia stepped further into the room until she stood over him, one foot on either side of his legs. She crouched and roughly ripped away his gag. Blood darkened the corners of his mouth. He smelled like salt and metal.

The boy wet his lips, eased his jaw back and forth, the whole time keeping his eyes on her. "Thank you," he said after a long moment.

Caledonia frowned and tossed the gag in his lap. "Thank me again and it goes back on."

The boy wisely said nothing further. He didn't move other than to blink. He kept his shoulders rolled in, his chin slightly lowered, and his expression perfectly neutral. It was an obvious attempt to appear small and non-threatening, but whether it was genuine or deceitful, Caledonia wasn't sure.

Though he was in every way the opposite of the boy from the beach – brown skin instead of white, deep eyes instead of shallow, square jaw instead of sharp – looking at him stirred that hollow anger in her heart.

"Do you know a Bullet called Lir?" she asked, finally understanding why she'd come here in the first place.

The boy sat up straight, suddenly alert. He didn't speak, but he didn't need to. The answer was there in his reaction: Lir was alive, and this boy knew him.

Still crouched over him, Caledonia leaned in until her nose was only an inch from his. "Name his ship."

Caledonia didn't think she imagined the tremor in this boy's lip. He feared her. Or Lir.

"Let me stay with you," he said. "Don't drop me in the shallows."

"Don't mistake this for a negotiation." Caledonia leaned back so he might appreciate the full cast of her derision. "Name his ship or it's not the shallows for you. It's the deep."

He swallowed, gaze drifting from her eyes to her temple and snapping back again. "I can help you."

Her fist cracked out before he finished the words, crashing into his already bruised cheek. The boy slumped sideways, catching himself awkwardly with bound hands against a wooden box.

Bending close enough to grip his chin, Caledonia spoke in a deadly whisper. "I know that lie all too well. Speak it again and I *will* slit your tongue in two. Do you understand?"

He did, nodding only as much as Caledonia's grip allowed.

"Lir sails the *Bale Blossom*."

The name caught Caledonia by surprise. She heard Lir's voice in her ear, calling her *Bale Blossom*, calling it *fitting*, and a fresh fury began to burn in her heart.

The boy continued. "He's one of Aric's Fivesons. If it's him you're after, you're in for a hell fight."

In truth, Caledonia had been after him from the very first day she and her crew took their guns to the sea. She just never dared to hope it was possible to find a single Bullet in all the wide seas.

"There's more," the boy said, soft, daring.

"What makes you think I'll trust a thing you say?" He'd given good information, but the more he said, the less she trusted.

Shouts echoed through the hull, entering the hold like a resilient song. A ship had been spotted.

Dropping the boy's face, she stood to leave.

"Caledonia," he called in that daring and gentle voice.

She turned, immediately regretting her decision not to replace his gag.

His eye was swelling now, purpling from her blow, but still he met her gaze and said, "I won't lie to you."

"You just did," she answered. And then she left.

CHAPTER SEVEN

Not until dawn skated across the morning seas did the Bullet ship make its approach.

For three hours, Caledonia and the crew of the *Mors Navis* watched the dark shape against the horizon. Unwilling to get too close before first light, the Bullet ship hovered threateningly, waiting. When the sun pulled away the cover of night, Caledonia recognized the sleek bow of an assault ship marked with two vertical bands of red paint dripping down the nose. And on its quarterdeck, the black scales of a sun sail grabbed at the early light.

It was comparable in size to the *Mors Navis*, and like the *Mors Navis*, it could put on incredible speeds quickly, though it wasn't nearly as manoeuvrable and as a result worked best in concert with other ships. At the moment, however, it was alone on the horizon, observing its prey from afar.

With their wind sails bound and the sun sail in shreds, Caledonia hoped that their distress was convincing enough to entice the Bullet ship. To sweeten the pot, it was time to give the appearance of fear.

"Maximum propulsion," Caledonia called. "Ready the masts!"

The ship rumbled, pulling water in from the front and shooting it out the back in an attempt to gain speed. A tail rose behind them for mere seconds, sending them forward a few useless feet before the system cut out and the ship drifted once again. A second later, mast ports snapped open, and the posts climbed to only half their usual impressive height before stopping.

Let them think the *Mors Navis* was trying to run, and let them think she'd been caught off guard by the failure of her systems.

Caledonia kept her eyes on the assault ship. For a moment, it stayed put, hovering a few miles out. It would be just her luck to have attracted a Ballistic more concerned with caution than glory. Caution would sink them for sure.

Then a tail of water rose behind it, and the distance between them began to shrink.

"Pi!" Caledonia called, but Pisces was already diving over the port rail to her tow, packed with fresh charges. She wore the slim pouch of the blue lung on her back and the full mask of its regulator over her face. Testing once that air flowed from the tube connecting the two, she vanished beneath the chop. The action would do nothing good for her wound, but keeping her out of the water at a time like this would be worse for everyone.

"Stay low, girls." Redtooth's voice carried gently down the line. "Look beat."

If the assault ship decided to blast them from a distance, they'd be sunk. Her girls needed to stay low, needed to look like they were more ready to surrender than fight. But playing the victim went against fifty-three sets of instincts. They were a wall of clenched teeth and clasped fists, of blood hot with fire and fight, of voices barely cinched in throats. It wouldn't hold for long.

The approaching ship wasn't moving at full throttle but tacked left, then right, surely trying to ascertain whether or not the *Mors Navis* was as incapacitated as it seemed.

The crew held their breath. Most crouched beneath the cover of the starboard railing and a wall of plate-metal shields, while Amina's Knots were secured in their half-raised masts. Beads of sweat fell from their brows and prayers from their lips as they waited.

Caledonia stood. She lifted her chin, let her stormy red braid fall forward over her shoulder, and when she was sure she had the eyes of the assault ship on her, she lifted her pistol and fired a single shot directly into the ocean: *surrender*.

For a moment, the only sound was the shuddering of their tattered sun sail, then the air filled with a roar as the assault ship tacked towards the *Mors Navis* and sped up.

"Stay steely, girls!" Caledonia felt her own pulse spike. The urge to brandish her weapon was nearly overwhelming, but right now, being passive was the only thing keeping them alive. "Don't break!"

The assault ship gathered speed until the ghost funnel mounted to the bow crooned in unearthly tones. It was like the hollow cries of children lost beneath the waves. No matter how many times Caledonia heard that sound, it never failed to send a quiet shiver down her spine.

In moments, the ship was upon them. Its deck teemed with Bullets, faces alight with the impending conquest, arms bare to reveal bright orange scars. The ship veered around the *Mors Navis*, circling once to survey the situation. A spray of gunfire knocked into the hull, daring the girls to break formation and take up their weapons.

"Steely!" Redtooth called over the noise.

Not a single girl reached for her gun.

The *Mors Navis* rocked as the assault ship made a tighter circle, pulling in close.

An older man on the deck stepped up to the railing. His hair was close cropped and the bridge of his nose pointed in three different directions on its way down his face. On his right arm he bore five horizontal scars, each brilliant orange, and beneath them, the *A* inside a circle marking him as one of Aric's Ballistics.

The man's darkly placid expression shifted as he searched the deck of the *Mors Navis*, surprised to find it full of girls. Finally, his eyes settled on Caledonia.

"Weapons over!" he commanded. "Come peaceful and

83

I may give you a home in my clip!"

The reaction among his Bullets instilled no confidence that his words contained truth. Laughter, cheering, the cocking of guns. It did little to suggest that his home would be a friendly one. But the assault ship was still too far away for this to work. They needed to draw them close enough to board.

Caledonia spoke only for the ears of her crew. "Guns over, girls. Like we planned."

She raised her own pistol in the air and threw it into the ocean. It landed with a splash and was quickly followed by several more as the rest of her crew disarmed themselves. It was a loss. And not a small one, but they stood to gain so much more.

Satisfied, the Ballistic gave the signal. The assault ship moved forward, lapping the *Mors Navis* once more before sliding along her side. The grip hooks came down like curved teeth, latching on to the *Mors Navis* and allowing the Bullets to lower a gangplank connecting the two ships.

"Captain first." The Ballistic looked on shrewdly.

Caledonia stepped forward. Alone, she crossed the gangplank to the deck of the assault ship. She could smell the too-sweet perfume of Silt, see the glassy look in the eyes of every Bullet. She counted more than forty of them scattered across the deck. Their sun sail was hoisted at the rear on a single mast bolted in place, all but unguarded.

With great effort, she turned to face her crew, still safe aboard the *Mors Navis*, and for a moment, she was arrested with guilt. She had never asked them to take such a risk as they took now. But they looked on, their eyes alert and fiery, their mouths set and determined. They trusted her.

Turning back to the Ballistic, she spoke: "I am Captain Caledonia Styx of the *Mors Navis*, and I surrender."

"Caledonia Styx. Nothing but a girl." The Ballistic's grin was mirth and conceit. Then, with a movement so fast Caledonia barely saw it coming, he struck her across the face with the back of his hand. She crashed to her knees before him. Her vision split, but not so much that she missed the smug expression on his face when he said, "Surrender happens on your knees."

Blood slipped down Caledonia's chin. The taste of it was bright on her tongue. She felt sharp and bold, but she did not smile when she responded, "Yes, sir."

The Ballistic let one of his boys check her for weapons. Rough hands slid down her arms and back, searching for guns and large blades and finding none. It was a cursory search. Surely they planned something more thorough for later. Given the chance, they'd divest her of more than her weapons. Her senses would go next, riddled with Silt until she became one more piece of Aric's army.

Satisfied, the Ballistic returned his attention to the girls still aboard the *Mors Navis*. "Now the rest of you!" he called, resting a shotgun on his shoulder.

Amina was next. She led a small band of five girls across the plank, making a good show of looking defeated and defiant all at once. Lace led a small party over on Amina's heels, and reluctantly two more groups followed until they had twenty-six girls aboard the Bullet ship.

The Bullets moved around her girls, reaching for cuffs and ropes to bind them. While the attention was on her surrendering crew, Caledonia pulled a small remote from her belt. She hoped she'd given Pisces enough time, but there was none left to spare.

"This rain will only soak you. Last chance, girls." He said *girls* like it tickled his throat, with a purr and a smile. It coaxed a sneer from Caledonia's own lip, but she held her tongue and found the switch with her thumb. When none of the girls moved, the Ballistic raised his hand. Dozens of Bullets raised their guns and levelled their hungry eyes on the girls still aboard the *Mors Navis*.

"Fire!" the Ballistic shouted just as Caledonia flipped the switch.

An explosion on the starboard side rocked the assault ship, knocking everyone to the deck.

For just a moment, everything was still. The Bullets' sun sail glittered like jewels. Water hissed as it rained back into the ocean, and Caledonia's crew made their next move.

Amina and her five chosen girls recovered faster than the Bullet clip. They pulled weapons from boots and hidden harnesses and raced towards the sail. Lace and the others now moved with Caledonia, blocking the path Amina had just taken.

The assault ship listed heavily to starboard. While five Bullets raced into the belly of the ship to stanch the wound, the rest turned to Caledonia and her girls.

They were outnumbered. Caledonia counted at least thirty Bullets still on deck. As they raised swords and guns alike, she heard Redtooth shout, "NOW."

Those still aboard the *Mors Navis* opened fire, pulling guns from hidden clips.

The attack caught the Bullets off guard, clearing the way for Amina and giving Caledonia and her girls a fighting chance.

"Masts up! Knots high!" Caledonia called across the gap between ships. Redtooth repeated the order, and the masts climbed to their full height.

Half of the Bullets leaped to the railing, using whatever means possible to cross to the *Mors Navis*. Some raced across the gangplank, some jumped, still others used their own rigging and swung over on ropes. Those who remained closed in on Caledonia and her small band.

Lace was at Caledonia's side, pressing a pistol and sword in her hands, and then she was in the fray. Caledonia searched for the Ballistic and found him in pursuit of Amina, aiming his rifle at one of the girls high in his sun sail rigging.

Another of Pisces's bombs exploded, sending the ship heaving towards the *Mors Navis*, momentarily disrupting the fight. The gangplank cracked but did not fall, and the ship tilted towards the bow, heavy with water.

The Ballistic raised his gun again, this time aiming directly at Amina.

Caledonia lunged across the deck, aware that as she did, she removed herself from the protection of her crew, leaving Bullets at her back instead of sisters. But she had no time for safety. With all the speed she could muster, Caledonia aimed a kick at the Ballistic's wrist. She made contact just in time, the shot biting into the deck of the ship instead of Amina's head.

The Ballistic turned instantly, striking out with the full barrel of his gun. It whipped across Caledonia's cheek, stunning her.

A hand gripped her neck as the Ballistic bent close to taunt her. "If you'd come quietly, you might have saved a few of their lives. Now I'll let you watch as they die."

His confidence was as odious as his breath. He saw victory unfolding before him. Her crew was divided, spread out across two ships, while his was concentrated and brutal. He saw Caledonia's tactics as fractured instead of calculated.

His mistake.

A vicious scream split the air as a dozen girls spilled over the unmanned side of the assault ship, guns high. With all their attention on deck, the Bullets had missed the moment her girls slipped overboard into the bow boat and skirted both ships. Now it wasn't her crew that was hemmed in on all sides – it was the Bullets.

Using the distraction to her advantage, Caledonia slid one leg behind the Ballistic's and in two swift moves, the man was stumbling backward. He scrambled for his gun, but she was faster. She raised her pistol and fired.

It was a solid hit. Blood spilled from a blossom high on his shoulder, knocking the fight from him. His knees buckled, and he landed on the deck.

Her girls swarmed from all sides now. The fight swelled. Guns were traded for blades and fists. Caledonia caught her crew in flashes: Tin and Folly fighting back to back, Redtooth's braids swirling around her as she drove her blade forward. There was Lace, blood bright on her cheek, struggling against a boy twice her size.

In minutes, the battle was over. Amina's group had the sun sail halfway to the deck, and her crew was flush with triumph. Relief started to unfurl in Caledonia's chest.

Then, as her girls corralled the remaining Bullets around the mainmast, Caledonia saw a splash of blonde curls against the grey deck. A body lay there, unmoving and dappled in red.

"Lace." Caledonia rushed forward, dropping to her knees. "Lace," she repeated, voice choked. The girl's cheeks were still pink from exertion, and blood puddled beneath her small body. In one hand, she clutched a gun, a twist of lace around the handle. Next to her, Pippa crouched with tears in her eyes, desperately trying to cover the wound in Lace's chest with her own hands. But it was too late. The moment Caledonia caught the flash of Lace's face in battle had been her last.

Caledonia wanted to rage. She wanted to give her crew

the order to fire on the remaining Bullets, to remove their black hearts from this world. To give their bodies to the deep and send their ship after them.

But she took a steadying breath. Blood. Gunpowder. Salt. This fight had cost her crew dearly already, and there was no point in wasting more bullets.

"Surrender peacefully and you might live," Caledonia commanded, rising to her feet.

She hoped at least a few of these Bullets would give her the excuse for one more moment of violence. Caledonia felt their rage clutch around her like a noose, but one by one, the Bullets dropped their guns and knives.

Pippa and Folly quickly collected the abandoned weaponry. It would more than replace what they'd thrown over in their feigned surrender. Behind the crowd, Amina appeared with two others, the stolen sun sail bundled between them.

Caledonia stooped to gather Lace's body into her arms, her heart keening like a ghost funnel.

"You really think you can run from him? You're a dead ship." From where he knelt on the deck, the Ballistic spoke, his words as thick as the blood that now dripped down his arm.

Caledonia swept her cold gaze across the clip. She'd spent so long dogging Aric's ships from afar that she'd never considered what it might feel like to stop running. To turn and fight as they'd just done. It didn't feel like victory.

"You're right. Aric Athair killed us long ago." The smile

she offered them held no warmth. "We simply seek to return the favour."

While her crew held the Bullets at gunpoint, Caledonia hugged Lace close and walked calmly towards the gangplank, her crew following carefully behind. Her mother had once told her that there was more strength in calculation than in violence. Right now, she needed everyone – this clip and her crew alike – to know that she had won and she was not afraid to turn her back on a boat full of Bullets.

"Retract masts!" she commanded, feet once again on the familiar plane of her deck. "Release the plank!"

Tin appeared and gently lifted Lace's body into her own arms. "I have her, Captain."

The words were so familiar, so threaded with Lace's sweet voice assuring her, *I have the bridge, Captain*, that for a moment, Caledonia's breath caught and she clenched her teeth against a cry. She met Tin's sombre eyes and responded, "You have her, Tin."

In moments, the engines of the *Mors Navis* were humming with the last of their reserves. As they pulled slowly away, a final explosion rocked the assault ship: Pisces's parting gift punching the hull one last time and ensuring the ship would slowly submerge.

They were scarcely a mile away when flares glittered in the morning sky. Purple and yellow and red. The remaining Bullets calling for aid.

Caledonia hoped it never came.

CHAPTER EIGHT

Fifty-two.

Their number had increased over the years. Sometimes in ones and twos, sometimes in groups of five or more. Each time it jumped, Caledonia felt a strange twist of panic in her chest. As encouraging as it was to grow a full crew, it was also terrifying. She was responsible for each girl, for making sure they had food and drink and health, and she'd fought every day to keep them whole.

To keep them *fifty-three*.

And she'd failed.

It had been a night and a day since they left the assault ship. They'd driven hard to make the waters of the Bone Mouth, everyone determined and bent to their work. Amina got the new sun sail in place just as they ran through their reserves. It hung from the mizzenmast as though nothing had changed.

Redtooth sat constant vigil with Lace in the belly of the ship, growling whenever one of the cats got too curious. She was as steady and stoic as a marble statue, with streams of tears carved against her cheeks. Hime was the only one who could get close enough to bring Red her meals. Their friendship had found its footing on the perilous terrain of Hime's withdrawal, with Hime lashing out and Redtooth refusing to back down. Hime knew when Red's marble exterior was just that, a shield standing guard over a tender heart.

Pisces hid herself away with the engines, pouring her attention into something she could fix. And Caledonia took her position at the helm, the one she'd so frequently shared with Lace, and steered her ship with a firm hand.

When the islands of the Bone Mouth appeared on the horizon, Caledonia gave the order to stop and finally retreated to her quarters. They needed deep water for Lace, and Caledonia needed a moment away from the eyes of her crew.

Exhaustion tugged her towards her bunk, but she stripped out of her clothes and into something fresh, a simple pair of trousers and knit top in shades of brown. The fabric was a relic of the old world, neatly wicking away her sweat when it was hot, reflecting her own body heat when it wasn't, easy to clean and hard to tear. In spite of years of use, the top was as sturdy as the ship beneath her feet. Next, she wrestled her hair into a braided pile atop her head, sticking it in place with wooden combs. Tears cut warm paths down her cheeks and she did nothing to stop them.

Fifty-two. They were fifty-two when they should be fifty-three.

Fifty-one more opportunities to fail.

And this wasn't just anyone. This was Lace. Apart from Pisces, there wasn't a girl on board she trusted more. Lace had slipped into the fabric of the ship as though she'd always been there. She'd worked seamlessly at Caledonia's side, and whenever she laughed, Caledonia was warmed by a memory of her mother doing the same.

She'd gotten them both killed.

At a knock on her cabin door, Caledonia stamped out her thoughts. She smoothed her tears over her skin and stood to retrieve her gun belt. "It's open," she called.

The door swung and Pisces stepped into the room, her own eyes shiny and red. "We're ready."

Caledonia nodded. She didn't trust her voice to come out steady. Her throat, her lungs, her gut felt punctured by sorrow, as though the air were constantly wheezing from her through tiny holes.

"Cala, no one blames you." Pisces tried to catch Caledonia's eyes.

"They should," Caledonia answered, voice thin.

"It's not your fault. And any one of us would've taken her place."

A tremble began in Caledonia's hands as she cinched her gun belt and latched the buckle. *Any one of them would have taken her place.* It wasn't a threat, but it felt just as heavy. "Pi…" she started, and when she couldn't find the words she needed, she reached for her friend's hand instead.

Pisces squeezed tightly. "We all loved her, and we all love you."

There was a moment, years ago, when Caledonia and Pisces had decided which of them would lead their budding crew. After a year with only themselves to consider, they'd fallen into a kind of wordless rhythm. The pain of losing everyone they'd ever loved had left them with a powerful intimacy. Instead of hardening against each other, they grew together, their hearts and minds weaving around one another like the roots of an old tree. But as their numbers grew, so did their need for clear lines of command.

"One of us needs to lead," Pisces had said. "You need to lead us."

"Why not you?" Caledonia asked, though she knew Pisces was right. They were barely fifteen turns at the time, and she felt too small to take on the mantle of her mother.

"Because," Pisces began, "one of us also needs to follow."

She'd only dimly understood what that meant at the time. But with every day that passed, she understood it a little bit more. Today, it meant that she had to stand up under the great weight of this loss. And it meant Pisces would make sure she didn't do it alone.

Clenching her jaw against fresh tears, Caledonia let Pisces pull her down the dim hallway and up onto the deck. Before them, the entire crew stood quietly under moonlight. Behind them in the near distance rose the uneven outline of the Bone Mouth islands, and at their feet lay Lace.

She'd been washed and dressed in a simple white shift that fell to just above her feet. The Mary sisters had made it, singing softly as they stitched. Her hands had been wrapped in fresh lace, crisp and bright in the moonlight. On her arms, the crew had painted their names in black ink. Fifty-one names curled down her skin, and in her hands she gripped a gun against her breast.

For a moment, sadness threatened to overwhelm Caledonia like a great wave. Then she raised her eyes again to the faces before her and reached for the strength of her mother.

She didn't remember many deaths aboard the *Ghost*, but at each one Rhona Styx had stood tall and strong as she spoke the same words Caledonia now needed. Never once had Rhona faltered. As a child, Caledonia thought it was because her mother was too strong to feel sadness. But standing here now, she understood that Rhona had turned her sadness into another kind of strength. It was her responsibility to be strong for her crew even in the face of loss.

"Tonight, we say farewell to one of our sisters," she began. "The sea carries us in life. It feeds us and rocks us and challenges us. And in death, it gives us peace."

As she spoke, Amina, Hime and the Mary sisters began to secure stones to Lace's body. They were plain and grey, unremarkable sea stones, but Caledonia imagined each one a brilliant citrine, bright enough to light her way. One at the feet, one at the thighs, one over her chest. When they finished, they lifted her between them and carried her to the railing, blonde curls bouncing one last time. Pisces stood near with the paintbrush in her hand. Caledonia took it, bending to add her name on the back of Lace's hand.

"We loved you well, Lace," Caledonia said. "But you loved us better. Take our names and our hearts with you, and keep us from below."

Carefully, the girls lowered Lace's body over the railing, then let it slide into the dark waters. She vanished with a small splash, and the rest of the crew raised their hands into the air, cupping their palms like sails in final parting.

Long after most of the crew had dispersed and gone belowdecks for the night, Caledonia stood in the same spot with her eyes on the water below. She breathed deeply, forcing her mind to fold the death of her friend into the past. She needed clear eyes if she was going to keep this crew going.

But Lace was dead. Someone she loved was dead. And it was her fault. Again.

Redtooth leaned next to Caledonia, one hip braced against the rail. She looked as fresh as Red ever looked. Her blonde braids were smooth and the red clay at their tips renewed, her freckles were distinct and clean, and she'd taken the time to mend a few rips in her favourite grey jacket. But her eyes were puffed with sadness, and now Caledonia recalled the sound of her cries, echoing through the ship as they travelled to this resting place.

More than any of them, Redtooth was made for battle. She found joy in the danger and fought fearlessly beside her sisters, but all that battle fury came from a surprising softness. She loved as fiercely as she fought. And she mourned as deeply as she loved.

"Captain," she said, an apology for the interruption in her tone.

"I'm sorry," Caledonia found herself saying.

Redtooth's frown was severe, almost affronted. "She wouldn't want you to apologize."

"No?"

"No." Redtooth shook her head, assured of her answer even as she struggled to find her next words. "She'd want you to keep going. Keep fighting. And I think...I think she'd want you to have this."

She held in her hands a loop of dingy lace. It was long enough to wrap around a hand a dozen times or more, its creamy colour stained from years of use and fight. The scalloped edges had long since lost their shape, and the weave was soft to the touch. Lace's hand wraps.

When Lace's mother smuggled her out of the Holster, she sent her with a small spool of this very lace. It was the only thing of value in their possession, and she couldn't bear the thought of sending her girl away on her own without anything to trade. Even something as useless as lace.

It had been her opening gambit when she met Caledonia's crew – a spool of lace for a spot on their crew. That was how she acquired her name. And when the other girls told her lace was less useful than their goat, Lace decided to show them all. She wrapped her hands in that lace before every battle and hit Bullets harder for it.

Caledonia held out her hands and let Redtooth drape the lace between them. In her mind, she saw the flash of Lace's curls as she fought bravely against a Bullet twice her size.

Anger rose in her heart like the tide. Her hands closed around the lace in her hands. Her voice was deadly when she said, "Bring me the boy."

CHAPTER NINE

In moments, Redtooth had the boy on deck. He nearly dangled from her grip on the back of his shirt. His hands were a painful red from the bindings and his face paler than it had been when he came aboard. He blinked in the dim moonlight, eyes quickly coming to rest on Caledonia.

Redtooth paused, awaiting orders. The boy seemed to think this could go well for him, his lips parted once again in that strangely hopeful expression. It made Caledonia's skin itch.

"Unbind his hands," Caledonia commanded.

Redtooth complied, and as blood flowed freely to his hands, the boy hissed at the pain.

"Do they work?" Caledonia asked, prompting the boy to flex his stiff fingers and prove they still functioned. "Good. You're going to need them."

Redtooth grinned, and his face fell.

"Throw him over."

The boy struggled violently for the first time. He aimed a kick at Redtooth's knee, neatly knocking her to the ground.

The only crew left topside were the few on watch. They knew better than to abandon their duties, but when Redtooth went down all five of them turned.

Caledonia had her pistol out, ready to shoot him and be done with it. She pulled the trigger just as her hand was forced up at an angle. The shot barely missed the boy, and her gun was snatched from her grip.

The face that appeared before her was Pisces's, lips tight and eyes wide. She threw the gun down, once again putting her body between Caledonia and the boy.

Caledonia didn't give her time to settle. She stepped in and knocked her to the ground with a punch to her gut. Pisces was strong, she was tall, and she was fierce, but when it came to combat, Caledonia bested her every time because Pisces couldn't bear to hurt the ones she loved.

No matter how many years they spent sparring together, Caledonia could never quite explain to Pisces what it felt like to let your heart turn to stone and fight as if your life depended on it even when it didn't.

Pisces kneeled now, one hand clutching the new pain in her belly. It had been a kind hit – nothing was broken – but kind could still hurt.

"I'll go with him," Pisces warned. "I owe him a debt."

"You owe him nothing." Caledonia fought to keep the anger from her voice. "The only people you owe anything to are your crew. Your *family*." Her eyes flicked up to the boy, standing behind Pisces. "He is the reason our blood died.

He's the reason Lace died. All you owe him is a bullet."

"He saved my life. That *has* to mean something." She looked at the boy, once again kneeling on the deck beneath Redtooth's watchful eye. "We spent years wishing someone had stood up for our family, for our mothers or fathers or brothers. Well, he did! The thing we've always hoped a Bullet would do, and I won't let you kill him for it."

Drawn by the sound of gunfire, the crew was slowly emerging from belowdecks as Caledonia stood poised over Pisces. The boy was braced on his knees, his hands held out before him in a show of submission. He kept his eyes pinned to Caledonia, but he was sharp. She was sure he'd paced his distance to either railing and marked every new girl that joined the growing crowd.

Caught between the desire to ease her gentle friend through this and the urge to toss the boy, Caledonia took a few precious seconds for herself. It was impossible to ignore the similarity of this moment and the one four years ago on the beach. Only now it was Pisces treading in the deep-water eyes of a Bullet and their new crew at risk. She wanted Pisces to come to her senses and see this for the trap it was, she wanted the challenges to stop, she wanted this crew to rally around a single point of focus as they'd done for so long. They were nearly all here now, her crew, forming a dense ring around their captain.

"On the back of the sea, who do we trust?" she called.

Her crew answered together, "Our sisters."

Caledonia raised her voice a little more. "When our ship falters, who do we trust?"

"Our sisters."

She saw Amina and Hime and Tin move to the front of the gathering crowd. She shouted, "In a storm of Bullets, who do we trust?"

The voice of the crew rose to its highest peak. "Our sisters!"

And now Caledonia lowered her voice, speaking only to Pisces, who was still kneeling on the ground. "In the face of a known enemy, who do you owe?"

Slowly, Pisces lifted her head. Tears lay across her brown eyes, but she had too much practice to let them fall. She looked from the boy to the ring of her crew and answered, "My sisters."

Caledonia pulled Pisces to her feet and pressed a quiet kiss against her mouth. "He must go."

Finally, Pisces nodded.

It was all the invitation Caledonia needed. She moved around Pisces, collected her gun from the deck, and strode forward. The boy scrambled to his feet, but instead of fighting, he stopped and faced Caledonia. "I know where they are."

"I don't think you understand how little I care to hear you speak."

He studied her intently, eyes locking on the tattoo at her temple. "Your brothers. You both have brothers. I know where they are."

It was the last thing she'd expected him to say, and she drove the muzzle of her pistol into the soft underside of his chin. Redtooth stepped up behind him, becoming a wall holding the boy in place. He didn't try to escape.

"The marks on your temples?" he asked. "I've seen them before."

Caledonia gnashed her teeth. Pisces came to stand just behind her elbow, brushing fingertips along Caledonia's back. Even with violence between them, they were bound together by cords of trust. Caledonia nodded to the boy, trying not to reveal the depth of her own anxiety. "Go on."

He spoke softly, urgently. "Two boys captured years ago and brought into the family."

Caledonia barely stopped her hand from rising to her tattoo. Barely stopped the sudden press of tears. Pisces gasped so near that Caledonia thought the sound came from her own mouth. The fingers that had brushed her back now fisted in her shirt.

"Lies will only make your death more painful." Caledonia felt the words move through her lips, but her mind was cool and distant, as if muted by an icy rain. She couldn't let herself entertain the idea that the boy told the truth. Their brothers had died along with the rest of their family. She'd seen Donnally's grey coat at the end of a metal spit. They were dead.

He shook his head. "I told you, I won't lie. Two boys. One white, one brown, both perhaps twelve turns when they arrived, sixteen now."

In the year after the attack, Caledonia and Pisces had frequently found themselves hoping that they hadn't been the only ones to survive. They'd imagined someone – mother, father, friend – took a tow and a blue lung and submerged for so long, travelled so far that by the time they surfaced again they were long lost. They imagined their parents knocked unconscious and set adrift on some scrap of ship, scooped up by Amina's people, the Hands of the River, in the Braids far to the north. They imagined their brothers stowed away on the attacking ship and made a clever escape later.

But these were middle of the night ramblings, words neither of them meant to say aloud until it was too late, ideas they soon realized were weapons carving again and again into their hearts until one night, they agreed to never speak of the dead again.

"They may live in our hearts but not cloud our minds," Caledonia had said, doing her best to be brave and strong.

And tears had rolled down Pisces's cheeks as she agreed in a voice so much smaller than her friend's, "Our first family shall not be our last."

At these words from this hell of a boy, Caledonia felt her mind flood with thoughts of Donnally. His unruly black curls, his unfathomable stories, his insistence on splitting his portion of bread with her. Had he been alive all these years? Had she abandoned him twice? The thought was sharp as a dagger in her gut.

"Lies," she said again, but she found it difficult to force an edge into the word.

The boy before her licked his lips, pushing his chin down against Caledonia's pistol to meet her eyes. "The one with your mark liked to sing. At least…at first."

Donnally.

"The one with yours is strong as the tides." His eyes moved briefly to Pisces and back.

"Cala." Pisces's voice was little more than breath and pain.

"I – I know where they sail. I can help you find them." This time, the boy's voice took on an edge of distress. "I can help you find them, but…you have bigger problems."

"Be explicit," she demanded.

"Aric's placed a bounty on you, on this ship. That barge you sank? It was a trap. They were drawing you out, had a dozen ships within a day's sail of that mark. They're all on their way by now."

The crew was a silent wall, watching and listening to every word. Wondering if he told the truth. If he did, then every ship in all the Bullet Seas would soon be hunting them.

She had to acknowledge that he'd been terribly smart. If he'd fought harder than he had, against her or Redtooth, he'd be dead. And now here he was offering crucial information. Calculating, she decided. She must never forget that Bullets could be calculating.

"You're just a Bullet," Caledonia said, letting her words drip with derision. "How can you help us?"

Wind tugged the boy's hair across his eyes and pressed his shirt tight to his body. He shivered. "I've been on the inside since I was seven," he said without hesitation. "Your brothers are on the Northwater conscription routes, and I know where they're most vulnerable."

In four years, Caledonia had never considered sparing the life of a Bullet. But she wanted this hope he offered, and that desire stayed her anger long enough that he shifted from a devious Bullet to just a boy. He breathed in and out through his nose, trying not to look like he was trembling, but Caledonia saw the slight shudder in his shoulders. Shiver, she corrected herself. He'd need Silt before long, and when he hit that threshold, he might prefer the deep to her hold.

"They're together?" Pisces pressed. "You know the ship?"

The hope in Pisces's voice was what did it. Caledonia's heart squeezed. She held up her hand. "It doesn't matter."

Pisces choked as though Caledonia's fist had once again landed in her belly. "What do you mean? Of course it matters. They're alive and they're our brothers. We *have* to go for them."

For a moment, there was only the sound of the wind in their ears. Caledonia let the scenario play out in her mind – the *Mors Navis* heading directly into the Bullet Seas, and dozens of ships folding around them like a fist. Fifty-one more deaths she could have prevented.

No. If what he said was true and their brothers were alive, Caledonia would go after them alone if she had to.

"Red, give me some room," she said quietly.

Redtooth frowned at the order, but stepped away from the boy and turned her irritation on the crew. "Back it up!" she cried, herding the group out of earshot.

Caledonia holstered her weapon and stepped even closer to the boy, until all that might fit between them was wind. His breath was hot and unsteady, his jaw tight. Caledonia made her voice a hard-edged whisper. "I hate what you are more than anything in this world."

The boy flinched at that and answered, "I promise you, I hate it more."

Her first instinct was to dismiss the comment. She didn't care what he did or didn't hate, but there was a note of sincerity in his voice that she couldn't ignore. "What do they know about this ship?"

"Not much. A general description. They suspect you shelter in the Bone Mouth. But I guarantee they don't know you're girls. Or they didn't when I left."

"And if they did?"

A frown flashed across his face. "They'd send more after you than a dozen ships. Aric would never let it be said that any of his fleet might be bested by a clip of girls."

"Crew," Caledonia bit back.

The boy almost smiled. "Crew," he repeated.

It was true. With a few legendary exceptions, the Bullet fleet was predominantly male, all except for the Scythes, who were mostly female. Aric preferred that women spend

108

their time adding children to his fighting forces rather than fighting in them directly.

Caledonia studied the boy for a moment longer. She couldn't trust a word that left his mouth, but neither could she discount what he'd said.

"If you're lying about our brothers to save your skin, I will make sure you spend a very long time suffering for it."

He nodded, locking his eyes with hers as he answered, "I believe you, Caledonia Styx."

Again, she fought the urge to throw him over. Looking at him was bad enough, but when he was agreeable, it was somehow worse. She stepped back, turning to face her crew. "If there's a bounty on this ship, we need to lie low for a while."

"Lie low?" Pisces asked, horrified. "What about our brothers? We can save them, Cala. We can get them back!"

"We've just lost one of our number, and that was taking on a single ship. Sailing directly into the Bullet Seas? Even for our brothers, it's too great of a risk."

"But he knows where they are." Pisces's voice carried easily across the deck. Dozens of eyes looked between the girls, anxious, curious, and hearing every word.

Caledonia didn't want to have this discussion here in the open. She needed time to think, to consider all possible options. She couldn't leave her ship and her crew when they were being hunted, and she couldn't ask them to follow her into even more danger. But she also couldn't ignore that their brothers were possibly alive.

"It's not so simple," she said.

"Seems pretty simple to me." Redtooth locked her hands on her hips, towering above everyone. "Your brothers are alive. We go for them. We get them. We bring them home."

A murmur moved through the crew. There was a whistle of approval, a scatter of applause, all signs that Redtooth's opinion had traction. For a brief second, Caledonia wanted to take advantage of it and rally her girls to sail straight into danger and save Donnally and Ares. But it was foolish. And it was selfish.

"Home," Caledonia repeated. "There's nothing I'd like more than to have our brothers here, safe aboard this ship. But I can't – I *won't* ask any of you to risk your lives on something so dangerous. Especially with a bounty on our heads." She turned her gaze to Pisces. "If we go for them, we'll go for them alone."

"Apologies, Captain, but I don't think so." Redtooth shrugged, eyes falling on the lace now balled in her captain's hand. "The thing about family is sometimes you don't have to ask us to do stupid things, and sometimes you don't get to tell us we can't. Going after your brothers? Worth the risk, if you ask me."

Rhona's voice was brisk in her ear. *Loss is inevitable. Some losses will be harder than others. So remember this: never risk more than you're willing to lose.*

"We'd be risking all our lives for only two." Caledonia imagined her heart a stone, heavy enough to sink through the

110

tumultuous waves of the ocean. But then Tin stood out from the ring, her four sisters at her back. "Red's right. We're all here because that bastard took something from us. If we can't fight to get any of it back, then what are we fighting for?"

Heads nodded, not a single note of dissention among them.

"It isn't the mission," Caledonia protested. "We sink barges and get out fast. There's an entire ocean between us and the Northwater. There's no getting out fast up there."

She sought Amina for support and found that though her expression was conflicted, even she didn't look convinced. With a scowl, Amina raised her voice. "Sisters, how many of us had siblings taken by Aric Athair?" Hands rose across the deck, and Amina continued. "I saw my own brother murdered before my eyes. If he'd lived, nothing could stop me from going after him. Just as nothing should stop you, Captain. Let us use this Bullet to save them."

Hime stood forward next, hands moving smoothly. *We are your sisters, you've said so many times. If we are your sisters, then they are our brothers. Let us do this. Let us save them.*

Caledonia didn't know what to do with the tremor in her blood. She felt Pisces's hand slip inside her own and squeeze.

She turned again to the boy. It helped her to focus somewhere she could direct her fury. His shoulders twitched and he blinked hard. He needed a drug they would not supply. "You're about to go through a hell fight as the Silt leaves your blood. Survive it, and you might survive me."

111

He didn't smile. Caledonia thought she might have hit him if he did. But he breathed in relief. Nodding without speaking.

"Cala?" Pisces asked, daring to sound hopeful. "Your orders?"

"We need supplies and repair," she said, tasting salt on her lips and disbelief on her tongue. She drew a deep breath and began wrapping the long band of lace around her left hand. The Bone Mouth was within sight, but they needed more than they would find scattered across those islands. They needed a port. "We sail for Cloudbreak."

The crew held still until Caledonia finished threading the lace between each of her fingers and around her wrist. She made a fist as she tied it off. It was the smallest piece of Lace she could carry, but it was the part that was always ready for a fight. There was no doubt in Caledonia's mind that Lace would have agreed with her brave-hearted crew. And she'd have done it with a smile.

Caledonia lifted her eyes again to her girls. They waited, hopeful and ready.

"There's a storm on our tail, ladies. Not a small one. But we're fire on water." She paused, turning to meet Pisces's eyes. "Let's go save our brothers."

CHAPTER TEN

Caledonia spent the rest of the night wrestling with the ghost of her mother.

She couldn't shake the feeling that Rhona sat on the trunk across from her bed, back pressed against the wall, one knee folded beneath her, with a critical expression on her face that seemed to say, *What do you think you're doing, Caledonia?*

The answer felt selfish. She wanted to believe she was doing the right thing. More than that, she wanted to believe Rhona would have done the same thing. But Caledonia knew what her mother would have done. She'd have stood resolute in the face of her crew and set them on a course that increased their chances of survival. She never would have endangered the rest of the crew if there was a chance to escape. She'd say, *It's a captain's job to hold the line and make decisions that will keep her crew safe, even when their hearts cry out for something else.* And here Caledonia was doing the exact opposite.

For Donnally. Was he truly alive? Living amongst Aric's fleet? The Bullet's description was too specific to dismiss. She was helpless against the hope that now spun in her chest, kicking up old memories.

On nights when Caledonia lay stretched on her belly along the bow of the ship, studying the water below as her mother had taught her, Donnally would lie next to her on his back, eyes trained on the stars above.

"Nia," he said one night when the wind had turned cold and they were bundled in layers of precious wool. He was the only one who called her Nia. Everyone else chose Cala or Callie or even just Cal. But Donnally had needed something different, something all his own. "Nia, I learned a new story from Ares's papa. Want to hear?"

"No," Caledonia had said immediately, already annoyed with her brother's incessant storytelling.

"There's a sea monster in the sky, and if you'd turn over and hoist your eyes I could show it to you." "Hoist your eyes" was something their parents said when they thought their children were too focused on one thing. In Caledonia's case, that almost always meant the surface of the ocean. Coming out of Donnally's mouth it was just condescending. She ignored him and he continued. "It ruled the ocean, terrifying the king and queen, and in order to appease it, they had to sacrifice their own daughter. They called it Cetus."

In his excitement, Donnally had gripped Caledonia's shoulder in his small hands. She shoved him away with her elbow.

"That's a terrible story," she said. "I'm glad our parents aren't like that."

"Don't worry," Donnally had said, inching backward with mischief in his eyes. "A boy came to rescue her."

He was gone before Caledonia could demonstrate who among them required rescuing. His laughter rang throughout the ship like bells. Annoying, sun-bright bells.

Thinking of him lost somewhere in Aric's fleet made her blood race. She imagined his dark curls still falling into his eyes, she wondered if he'd grown into his nose, she fretted that he'd forgotten his stories.

He deserved a sister who would come for him.

Rhona's ghost sighed and clucked her tongue. At every sound, Caledonia prised open her eyes to look for her mother. But it was never a real ghost. It was a breeze through her open porthole, the pitchy slap of shallow waves against the hull. It was her own guilt over risking the lives of her crew based on the word of a Bullet.

Morning was still young when a tapping sounded at her door. Caledonia recognized the pattern and called, "Come in, Pi," without bothering to get out of bed. Pisces's tall frame was a shadow in the greying air. She slid through the door, pulling it shut behind her, then climbed into bed next to Caledonia.

When she was settled, she whispered. "I think it's real. It has to be real, right?"

Her dark eyes were wide and weary. She hadn't slept either, but not because of fear or guilt.

"He has every reason to lie." Caledonia's caution ran as deep as the ocean. "But—"

"But the details!" Pisces forgot to whisper. "No one could have guessed that about Donnally if they hadn't heard him sing. That's real. Isn't it? It has to be."

"I think…" Caution bent under the weight of her own hope. "I don't know, Pi."

A shimmer of tears caught the barely-there light of dawn in Pisces's eyes. She smiled softly and pressed her fingers over Caledonia's tattoo.

"You're hot." Pisces ran hot, but this was more than usual. "Do you have a fever?"

Careful of her wounded shoulder, Pisces snuggled into Caledonia's pillow. "It's just the healing process. Lovely Hime says a little heat is natural."

As much as Pisces worried over Caledonia, she'd turn herself inside out to keep Caledonia from doing the same for her. Most of the time, it worked. But the old world had left behind a few indestructible things: ship tech and fabrics and weapons, and a virus that burned through bodies like fire. Fevers were always cause for concern.

"It barely hurts any more," Pisces continued. "And honestly, I feel like I could swim for miles right now."

"Good. That's good." Caledonia's eyes drifted back to the trunk in the corner. "Rhona wouldn't like this plan."

"You can't know that." Pisces rolled onto her back, one hand coming to rest on the charm she'd worn around her neck for four years. It was a small glass circle, inside of which was pressed a single green plant. It had belonged to Ares, and she'd rescued it from the burned husk of the *Ghost*.

"I think I can. She never would have risked it. The entire crew for two people? It's bad maths."

"Only if you're thinking about people as numbers."

Caledonia sighed slowly. "A captain has to think about people as numbers. It's the only way. When a small number of your crew is unreachable, putting the larger number at risk is foolish. No matter who they are, if two people are cut off from the rest of the crew, you leave them behind and keep the rest alive."

In truth, Rhona wouldn't have agreed with the approach Caledonia had taken for years. It was too risky, too antagonistic. And it had landed her ship and her crew in the sticky centre of a bounty.

Pisces sat up suddenly. "Do you think she was leaving us on the beach that day?"

"Of course."

"Cala!"

"She had to." Caledonia frowned at her friend. "It was their only chance."

"Cala, think about it. There was a lot of time between your gunshots and the fight. They had time to weigh anchor and flee. But when we got to the beach, they were exactly where we'd left them. Because they were waiting for us."

"What?" Caledonia asked, feeling numb, trying to find

117

some shred of evidence in her memory that suggested her friend was wrong.

"They died because they loved us too much to leave," Pisces continued, hand fisting around the charm. "Your mother might have been all rules all the time, but that moment changed her. She would *want* us to go for our brothers. More than that, she'd want us to get the ones responsible for their deaths. I believe it and so should you."

A mix of dread and fear washed over Caledonia. It was rare for Pisces to display so much raw anger, but every so often, it was there, peeking above the surface like a shark's fin.

"This is our chance to do exactly that." Pisces's cheeks were flushed with fever and determination. Her voice found its steepest notes when she added, "We can avenge them."

Caledonia believed every word. She believed that if Pisces ever discovered who was truly responsible for the destruction of the *Ghost*, she wouldn't hesitate to bury a knife deep in their heart. Her heart.

That day would come. But first, Caledonia would get her own revenge.

"He's just a Bullet," she said, thoughts turning to the boy in their hold. "He's probably leading us straight to Aric."

Pisces laughed, pushing Caledonia's lips back into a smile. "Stop thinking it's a trap for one minute. Just…just enjoy this feeling. Donnally and Ares. Are. Alive."

It was such a dangerous dream. Let her heart linger there too long, and Caledonia was sure it would suffer. But here with Pisces, under the worn sheet of her bed, she let herself believe it for just a moment. If Donnally and Ares had survived, then maybe she could save them and redeem the smallest piece of her past.

"I could hear him sing again," she whispered, leaning her forehead against Pisces's.

"I could race him again." Pisces rolled her head back and forth. "He's probably bigger than I am now."

Even two turns younger than his sister, Ares could cut a path through the ocean as well as she, and he was just as fearless. Where Donnally was gentle, Ares was bold, but somehow the two had been as inseparable as their older siblings.

"I can't imagine Donnally being taller than you. He was always so spindly and awkward."

The image landed harder than Caledonia expected, causing her heart to thump painfully in her chest. "Up," Caledonia said, climbing over her friend and out of the bed. "That's enough. We have work to do."

"You held out longer than I thought you might," Pisces teased. "Were those real emotions or—"

Caledonia threw her dirty shirt into her friend's face. "You're lucky you're wounded."

CHAPTER ELEVEN

The sun was sliding pink rays over the lip of the porthole, and the scent of fresh teaco wafted through the halls. The girls were up, dressed and fed in moments. Tin was at the captain's side the instant she left the galley, giving a full report of the night's activities with a steady voice, though her hands seemed uneasy gripping the notebook Lace had used every day.

"What's the temperature of the crew?" Caledonia asked.

"Temperature?" Tin looked momentarily alarmed, afraid she'd missed something in her accounting.

"The mood," Caledonia clarified. "How's everyone handling it? Lace."

Tin narrowed her blue eyes and looked down at her list. It was an itemized record of their stores and duty rotations, nothing that would help her answer this question, but she studied it for a long moment before coming to a decision. "We miss her, but the chatter is about the brothers."

"What about them?" Caledonia asked, and when Tin hesitated, she covered the girl's hand with her own and added, "I need you honest, Tin. I need to hear more than the bright bits."

Tin nodded twice and plunged ahead. "Everyone's with you. We know it's risky and we won't all come back from it, but we're with you, Captain. They belong to us as much as they do to you."

Maybe her morning with Pisces had left her too close to her own heart, but the news stunted her breath, and it took every bit of her control not to let it show on her face. For a second, she felt fifty-one sets of hands braced against her back, holding her up, pushing her forward. She could not let them down.

"We're ready, Captain," Pisces called from a few feet away.

Grateful for the distraction, Caledonia nodded her thanks to Tin, then turned sharply on her heel and followed Pisces across the deck.

The map room was a windowless cube beneath the bridge. One wall was lined with shelves that contained the small number of maps they'd gathered over the years, each carefully labelled and organized according to region.

This space had been Lace's domain. Any time they found a new map, she spent hours in here studying it, trying to piece the old world together so that they might better understand the new one. The oldest maps contained large, unfamiliar landmasses surrounded by many oceans. None of those landmasses matched what they saw around them today. But Lace was determined to find some key that would unlock the past enough to explain their present.

Maps of the Bullet Seas were few and frequently unreliable, but she had used them to piece together her own map. As they travelled, she filled in each new region with observations from the bridge. The northern region was the least detailed. The Rock Isles were mapped only along the eastern borders, to the west was a span of ocean known as the Perpetual Storm, and the Northwater current was loosely tracked towards the Braids and beyond, though those rivers were just a suggestion of ink on paper. The southern quadrant was flush by comparison. There was the eastern peninsula where the Holster was clearly marked with an *X*, the Bone Mouth where each island was drawn to represent the true shape of the archipelago; trails of arrows indicated the directions of the currents. The Net was marked with a series of hash marks, and beyond it Lace had written simply *The Outside*. A world in progress, she'd said.

In addition to storing maps, this was also where the command crew gathered when they needed privacy. A second, larger table in the centre of the room was circled by chairs. In the chair furthest from the door sat the Bullet.

He was hunched over his hands, and though soaked through in sweat he shivered in waves. Each breath he took seemed more painful than the last, and his skin was both flushed and blanched in places. There was no danger in him at this moment, yet Redtooth stood behind him ready to quell any foolish action he might take.

They'd all seen this before. Bullets his age needed Silt every day to stay functional. And it had been three days since his last dose. The fever would intensify, and he would sweat until he ran out of salt; the shivering would turn to shudders, and before long the hallucinations would begin.

They could give him a dose. Keep him in his mind for another day or two. But offering him a dose meant revealing to Hime what she didn't need to know: they'd taken refined Silt from the last barge and meant to trade it when they reached Cloudbreak.

Hime stood far from the Bullet with her back pressed into a corner. She tried to look unaffected by his tremors, but her discomfort showed in the constant twist of her hands. When she'd been at her worst, she fought anyone who came near. And the first time they'd put a sword in her hand and took her into battle, she'd fallen into a blind panic, lashing out indiscriminately. If it hadn't been for Redtooth's intervention, she might have killed one of their own crew. As it was, Redtooth walked away with a single slash on her right palm.

Caledonia stood between Pisces and Amina facing the Bullet. They needed all the information they could get from him while he was still coherent enough to give it.

"Can you speak?" Caledonia stepped around the table, closing the distance between them.

The Bullet looked up, meeting her stern gaze and holding it. "Yes."

Caledonia's fingers curled into a fist, but she didn't strike. "Name their ship."

He swallowed, bracing against a violent shiver. "*Electra*."

Caledonia ignored the distant part of her that regretted his pain and pressed on. "What sort of ship is she?"

His shoulders jerked involuntarily before he could answer. "A hauler. Deeper in the draught, slower than you. Heavier."

"So we ram them," Redtooth said, already excited by the prospect. "Knock 'em off balance and scatter the rats in the cold water."

"You can't." The Bullet spoke without invitation, eyes on Caledonia.

"Why not?" Caledonia looked on him with unbridled irritation.

"Their hull is electrified. Hit them before you take it out—"

Redtooth loosed a string of her most colourful expressions.

"How does it work?" Pisces asked. She'd taken a seat on the Bullet's other side and was ready with a pencil and paper.

The Bullet struggled to keep his tone even as he spoke. "*Electra* bears a double hull, but it's not reinforced. The two hulls are separated. Only the external is insulated and charged with lethal voltage. It's meant to look weak enough to puncture, but the second your hull touches theirs..." He raised his hands and pressed his fingertips together. "That charge transfers to your ship, and everyone on board turns into a conductor."

It was all too easy to imagine – the crush of metal against metal, the shrieks of her crew as their bodies filled with deadly electricity. It wasn't all that dissimilar from Amina's electric web, only this was always live.

"How the hell do we board a ship like that?" Pisces asked, her expression imploring as she looked at the Bullet.

"We disrupt the charge," Amina said. "But to disrupt that kind of charge...we'll need a lot of power. More than we have."

"Can you find what you need in Cloudbreak?" Caledonia asked.

Amina's shoulders lifted in a shrug. "We can find anything in Cloudbreak. Getting it is always the challenge."

"If you can build something to kill that charge, I'll get you whatever you need," Caledonia said. "Can you do it?"

Amina gave a determined nod. "Of course, Captain."

She returned her attention to the Bullet. "Now, tell us where we can intercept them."

Clearing his throat, the Bullet pulled his arms tight to his body and began to speak again. "*Electra* sails the Northwater conscription route every ten-month to collect conscripts from the colonies. She'll be there in three weeks. Her most vulnerable point will be when she's furthest west." The Bullet took a steadying breath. Pisces looked concerned, but he pushed on. "It's an out-and-back run. They start at the furthest village and work their way back to avoid having too many conscripts on board at once."

They all knew "conscripts" was code for "kids". Aric swept the Northwater at least once a year taking a percentage of the children who were between seven and nine turns. How the colonies determined that percentage was up to them. There was nothing quite as terrible as turning a people in on themselves, making them police their own in service to a distant tyrant. Saving their brothers would be even sweeter if they could take down that ship in the process.

The Bullet shuddered harder, and this time Hime strode forward, hands raised. *No more. He needs rest.*

"He'll get his rest when the captain's good and done with him," Redtooth snapped.

And if he doesn't get rest, he'll be no good to us at all. Hime glared up at Redtooth, unaware that behind her, Amina had moved a step closer.

"Save your pity for someone who deserves it, Princelet," Redtooth said, but she was backing down.

Caledonia studied the Bullet for a long minute. "We have what we need for now. Get him up." Redtooth hauled the boy to his feet and moved him around the table to the hatch. Before they were through, Caledonia caught Redtooth's arm. "I have him."

The girl fought against her frown this time, but it was there, tugging her face into a picture of concern. "Yes, Captain."

Caledonia gave the boy a shove. "Move," she ordered.

The boy stumbled forward. His steps were uneven and sloppy, but Caledonia noticed that he required no direction to return to the hold. In spite of having only made the trip twice, he remembered every turn.

He stepped into the hold and immediately slumped onto a short stack of canvas, breathing hard.

Caledonia smothered the unwelcome sympathy she felt at the sight. Redtooth was right, he wasn't worth their pity, even if he looked pitiful.

"A ship with an electrified hull." She paused in the doorway.

"That's what I said." He barely moved, but his words carried an edge of aggression.

"Seems like an incredible kind of weapon. Why haven't I heard of it before now?"

"Maybe your previous prisoners died too quick."

He was angry. Good. Angry was honest. "Bullets never die quickly enough."

He laughed. It was a rough, pained sound, like sandpaper on metal. "I thought you enjoyed watching me suffer."

"I do."

She met his eyes again. And for the first time, they bore the hard edge of defiance. It didn't matter what he said.

A Bullet was a Bullet. One day, he'd prove that he was not worthy of any more trust than they'd already given. She was sure of it. And when he did, she'd be ready with a blade in hand.

CHAPTER TWELVE

The peaks of the Rock Isles appeared, gilded in the cool, fiery blue of dusk and rinsed in deep shadow. The mountain range was disconnected, separated by a circuitous, mostly impassable network of canals. Though the highest tips were frequently dusted in snow, the slopes bore some of the most arable lands around the Bullet Seas. Rich in resources and hard to reach, the mountains were home to Cloudbreak: a two-tiered market port that, by tradition and by circumstance, existed outside Aric's rule.

Surrounding it all was an archipelago of jagged metal islands meant to break a ship's speed. Between those fabricated islands, the waters were littered with the decaying hulls of ships whose captains had tried force and failed. In a very real sense, it was a graveyard, and it made this a dangerous stop for anyone on the run. As hard as it was to get in, it was just as difficult to get out.

They waited until morning to approach. When the market was sure to be open and a fine mist closed around the mountains, the *Mors Navis* moved at a crawl. Caledonia stood on the command deck, her sharp eyes steady on the dark water ahead, and selected a path through the jagged islands wide enough to accommodate them. Her ship was at the upper limit of what would be allowed to dock. Much bigger and she'd be forced to weigh anchor and take the bow boat in.

"What if word of the bounty has spread?" Amina stood next to the captain, mist gathering in small drops along the thick crest of her braids. "It will be more than Bullet ships after us."

The thought had crossed Caledonia's mind. A bounty offered by Aric Athair would appeal to more than just his loyal fleet. While Cloudbreak was not Bullet territory, it was sure to be far from friendly. Control of the market had changed hands a dozen times in as many years. The current ruler, Hesperus Shreeves, was known as the Sly King, a moniker earned by the way he managed to get the better end of any deal, no matter the odds. Even when confronted with Aric, the Sly King always seemed to come out unscathed.

"That's why we waited for morning." Caledonia forced a confidence she didn't fully feel. She raised her hand into the swirling mist. "If we can move faster than it takes for this fog to rise, we'll be gone before the Sly King spots our ship in his harbour."

Amina's mouth flattened. "The weather is a fickle ally."

"Yes, but it's all we have. Besides, there may be no bounty." Even as she said it, something whispered that the notion was false. No one sunk seven, now eight, of Aric's bale barges without consequence.

"I feel certain we'll know one way or another before long," Amina said, echoing Caledonia's own thoughts.

Where Pisces was the emotional balance to Caledonia's hard-edged approach, Amina offered grim insights with a selfless kind of ease that always felt like trust. Amina didn't expect the worst to happen, but she was never surprised by it. And she always trusted Caledonia to carry them through it.

The ship slid past a long row of sharp, metal teeth, and then suddenly the docks appeared scattered around the base of the mountain with no obvious method of organization. This was Lower Cloudbreak. As it was both a wharf and a market, they might find anything here from quick ship fixes to protein bricks if they were lucky. Caledonia saw clusters of smaller trade ships and two other vessels as broad as hers, but no Bullet ships among them. The Sly King of Cloudbreak had an understanding with Aric. Bullet ships stayed out of the docks, and Hesperus…well, Caledonia wasn't sure what Hesperus offered in exchange, but it was guaranteed to be a mark against him.

Usually, this was as far as Caledonia liked to go. But for anything of greater value, like the charges Amina needed to build an electro-mag and the ammo they'd need for the fight that followed, they'd have to travel to Upper Cloudbreak. That was a trip that involved riding the rope lifts up the towering cliffs, separating Caledonia from her ship for hours.

One of the larger vessels had taken the dock at the furthest edge, which had the greatest vantage over all comings and goings. The other had taken a spot near to the Cloudbreak lifts, giving their crew fast access to their ship should they need it. The smaller vessels filled in around them were probably exactly the trade ships they appeared to be while a few likely carried rogue crews like her own. If any had wind of the bounty, this wouldn't go smoothly. But while Bullet ships were equipped with radios for quick communication, almost everyone else avoided them to evade detection.

Joining them on the bow, Redtooth sucked her teeth. "No good option," she said darkly.

Caledonia nodded in agreement. "I suspect it's merely the first set of no good options of the day. Tin!" she called, raising a hand and gesturing to a berth nestled between two of the smaller ships. Of the two larger vessels, she'd rather be near the one that hadn't picked the most advantageous spot, and this put them closer to the lifts.

Tin nosed the *Mors Navis* in the right direction and slid the ship into the available space. The bow thrusters churned, slowing them down and nudging them right up to the dock. It was well done even if Lace or Caledonia would have done it differently.

No sooner had the ship rubbed against the thick bumpers than a dozen merchants appeared, holding up their wares.

They offered everything from fresh fruits, salted meat and wine to advertisements for tar or oakum or repair services. Caledonia's crew began the work of securing the ship and lowering the rear gangway. Others took up strategic posts, lounging here and there as if casually observing their new surroundings. Casually, but with guns close at hand.

"Time to go!" Caledonia called, and when she saw only Redtooth and Amina, she asked, "Where's Pi?"

As if on cue, a deep, groaning cry echoed through the hull of the ship. It was not the first they'd heard of the Bullet's withdrawal, but without wind and water to dull the sounds, this one raked across the deck like the slow twist of metal. A few seconds later, Hime emerged from the companionway with a frowning Pisces not far behind.

Pisces wore her bulky green jacket to hide her bandage from view. But the sweat on her brow was visible to everyone. The fever Caledonia feared had arrived in force.

Wound's infected. She needs a doctor. Hime's usually gentle expression showed signs of irritation. Her eyes landed on Caledonia, and she lifted her hands. *I need to come and see the doctor with her.*

"I don't need a doctor, I need rest," Pisces protested, eyes travelling up the cliffs towards Cloudbreak. She was not fond of heights, preferring the suffocating press of water to nearly anything else. "Just rest, and I'll be fine."

At the next howl from the dregs of the ship, Pisces's expression pinched just enough to tell Caledonia that this reluctance to leave had nothing to do with the rope lifts. An alarm rang in Caledonia's head, loud and clear. Pisces's sympathy for that boy was already a distraction, already having an impact on how she made decisions.

"Hime says you're not fine, and I trust her judgement on the subject more than yours. You're going," Caledonia stated, shouldering one of the four large sacks of solar scales they'd use for trade. To Hime, she stated, "You're staying."

With a heavy sigh, Pisces reached for one of the sacks. Before she could swing it onto her back, Hime caught the strap in her own hand, neatly pulling it away and shouldering the load. *She can't carry it*, she said. *I can.*

"Hime," Caledonia began, voice suddenly soft. "It's too dangerous, and I need you here."

I'm not afraid of danger, she insisted, the motions of her hands growing increasingly agitated. *I'm stronger than you think. I would show you if you would only give me the chance.*

This was delicate ground. After injuring Redtooth in battle, Hime had proven herself invaluable as a healing hand. She'd taken command of every health concern the ship had ever encountered, and they trusted her thoroughly in that regard. But whenever Silt entered the picture, Caledonia found herself trudging the line between protecting Hime's heart and protecting the rest of her crew.

"You are strong," Caledonia agreed. "And we need to keep you that way. Can you honestly tell me you're ready to be around a market where Silt is openly peddled?"

Hime clasped her hands against her apron, frustration blazing in her eyes. She looked from Pisces to Caledonia to the sack hanging from Red's grip. Finally, Amina moved to her side, lifting Hime's tight hands in her own and smoothing her thumbs across her knuckles. Hime so rarely let anyone touch her hands, but Amina was an exception. When they looked into each other's eyes, anyone near them disappeared.

"Princelet," Amina soothed, sure not to grip Hime's hands too tightly. "That boy will draw attention if he keeps this up. You're the only one who understands what he's going through. We need you to help him so he can help all of us."

This mollified Hime somewhat, but disappointment sat heavy in the bend of her mouth. She nodded, hands lingering in Amina's before dropping her bag and taking a small step back. *Don't let Pisces carry anything. She'll fall. And find a doctor with antibios. Expensive, but it's what she needs.*

Caledonia nodded. "Got it."

Amina shouldered her sack. Redtooth shouldered the remaining two. Pisces pulled her jacket closed, and as the four of them headed to the gangway, Caledonia instructed Tin to give the harbour master a bribe decent enough to find the best deals on the necessary repairs and a little extra for a heads-up on any trouble.

"Prioritize fresh foods according to Far's list. If there's a goat, see what you can do about making it ours. Keep the girls working on that patch in the stern. It needs fortifying.

And if you spy trouble, get out of here in a hurry. Remember the rendezvous?"

Tin nodded. "I remember."

"Good. Stay steely."

They made their way down the wharf and up the rocky shore towards the lifts. There were fishing crews sorting their early morning catch, traders packing their pallets to be hauled up to Cloudbreak, and the occasional man or woman left behind by their crew to guard the boat. They noticed Caledonia as much as she noticed them. But if any of them knew about the bounty, they gave no sign.

The system of lifts was impressive. Thick cords of rope, slick with oil to keep the moisture out, supported wood or metal pallets of all sizes. There were pallets barely large enough for a single person and others that might support half of Caledonia's crew at once. The ropes spiralled hundreds of feet up the cliff walls, disappearing into the mist. Midway up was a row of yellow flags. They fluttered limply in the gentle breeze, signalling that the winds were likely to be nearly as calm at the top of the cliff. Considering they were about to trust their lives to someone they couldn't see, it was far from comforting.

Redtooth tested several pallets, bouncing in the centre to ensure the material was sturdy, before selecting one big enough for the four of them and their goods.

"This one," she said at last, standing atop a wooden pallet with slats spaced several inches apart. "The planks are hearty, and the spacing should help if the wind is stronger up there. And since all we can see is mist and more mist, I like this better than the possibility of slick metal. Best of no good options, round two. Right, Captain?"

"Right. Let's load up."

Pisces groaned. Caledonia's own stomach cinched around her breakfast. Amina, however, stepped lightly onto the pallet, testing the ropes as if she might climb all the way to Upper Cloudbreak.

They secured their sacks in the centre of the flat, each taking a corner to keep the pallet balanced. Then, with a hard shake of a rope next to the painted image of a bell, the pallet lifted from the ground and they were drawn upwards.

It was faster than any of them expected. Pisces sucked in a sharp breath, and Redtooth laughed while Caledonia fixed her gaze on the diminishing shape of her ship. Cold wind pushed down on them from above, dragging Caledonia's hair into her eyes. The mist thickened like a blanket, and it wasn't long before the *Mors Navis* was only a blurry outline against a grey background. Then it was gone.

For several minutes, they travelled upwards at a dizzying pace. It was safe to assume they'd climbed more than half a mile before the pallet began to slow.

One moment all they could hear was the creaking of the ropes, and the next the air filled with the soft whistle of a dozen pulleys moving overhead. The sounds grew louder, the pallet slowed even more, and soon they stopped under the dim outline of several cranes curling over the cliff above. Ropes spiralled downward from each crane, disappearing into the mist.

All but Pisces climbed carefully to their feet, hands gripping the ropes for support. The pallet swayed in the breeze. For the first time, Caledonia was thankful that the mist obscured how far they'd travelled.

Directly across from their pallet, there was a small opening carved into the wall. But it was several feet away and barely wide enough for a single body to squeeze through.

"Do we jump?" Redtooth asked, not nearly horrified enough by her own question.

"You first," Amina said.

"Someone's coming," added Pisces in a choked voice.

They heard him before they saw him, the heels of his boots striking the stone at a neat clip. Caledonia imagined someone tall and broad, which turned out to be exactly not what this man was; he was no taller than Caledonia, with sloping narrow shoulders that seemed designed for the slender cut of the cave through which he walked. He was pale-skinned and tidy, with a yellow scarf bundled around his shoulders. When he saw them, his steps faltered and a crease of confusion appeared on his wide forehead.

"You're all girls!" he cried, peering down as though he expected to find a man somewhere on their pallet. "And so young!"

"Only in years." Amina was the closest to him, angling

her body to partially shield Caledonia behind her. Her tone carried a warning.

"Well, it's no matter." He shook his head as if to convince himself before continuing. "Welcome to Cloudbreak. I'm the Town Bell, but you can just call me Clag. How was your trip?"

His interested tone set Caledonia's nerves on edge.

"Very smooth," she answered.

"Good, good. No one got sick, did they? It can be unsettling on the stomach for some. Takes a while to get your sky belly about you." Though the cheer in his voice was relentless, his eyes moved from Caledonia and the girls to their sacks piled in the centre of the pallet, appraising.

"Our stomachs are fine. But if you don't mind, we'd like firm ground under our feet again." In her peripheral vision she saw Redtooth's hand stray near the gun at her hip.

Clag, however, was unmoved. "Of course, of course. Let's get on with it. Just a few questions and I'll have you on your way, whichever way that ends up being." He added that last with a private laugh. "Business in Cloudbreak?"

Caledonia motioned to the four sacks. "Trade."

"Will you be applying for a stall permit?"

"No, trade only." Caledonia breathed through the part of her that wanted to demand speed.

"All in good health?" He peered specifically at Pisces. "Your friend's looking a little peaked, a little shiny across the forehead."

"She's injured," Caledonia said in a firm voice, eager to

dispel his suspicions. "We'll be engaging the services of a doctor while we're here."

Clag's jaw worked back and forth for a minute as he considered. "We don't admit anyone who might have the Pale Fire. Or any other fevers for that matter."

"I don't have the fire." With a grimace, Pisces pulled herself to her feet and slowly shrugged out of her jacket, exposing the bandage on her shoulder. "Do you need to see the wound?" she asked, challenging.

Clag waved a dismissive hand in the air. "No, no. Ah, my dear, that looks painful. I do hope someone here can help, and I'm glad, very glad, that it's not a disease. For your sakes, of course. And how long do you expect to remain in Cloudbreak?"

"Only the day." Even as she answered, Caledonia felt the strain of time. The *Mors Navis* was not an inconspicuous ship. The longer they remained in port, the more likely it was that news of the bounty would reach Cloudbreak.

"That's not much of a stay, is it? Trouble in your wake?"

"No," Caledonia answered quickly. Too quickly.

One of Clag's pale, bushy eyebrows rose. "The Sly King doesn't take kindly to those who bring trouble to his port. Not kindly at all."

The Sly King did everything possible to stay on the right side of Aric Athair. If he knew Caledonia and her crew were docked in his port, she was sure he'd do everything in his power to keep them there until he could hand them over.

Caledonia forced herself to take a full breath before she answered again. "No trouble, we just have somewhere else to be." And she intended to be long gone before any of Aric's fleet sought her here.

"Very good. That's all my questions. Thank you for your candid answers," he said, clasping his hands before him expectantly.

"So," Caledonia began, "how do we get in?"

"Oh! You don't just yet. There's still the matter of payment for your journey. Trade or coin. Both are acceptable. But notes of service are no longer legal tender in Cloudbreak by order of the Sly King."

"We can pay. How much?" Caledonia asked, trying to strike a balance between nonchalance and irritation.

Clag studied her, a devious gleam in his pale blue eyes. "Well, that all depends. Are you pleased with the service?"

"Yes," Caledonia answered with caution.

"Good. Then, whatever you think is fair."

Fair? The last time they'd made this journey, the price had been set. And her cargo less precious. As the pallet swayed in mid-air, Caledonia reached inside her coat and withdrew the very small amount of Silt they'd stripped from the barge. Small, but valuable.

She held out a single casing, its bright orange colour leaving no doubt as to what it was. Or where it came from. Clag's eyebrows rose with interest.

"How many?" he asked.

"Six doses. Pure. Straight from the Bullet fleet."

"Six, hmm. Throw it over."

Caledonia hesitated for just a breath. The pallet swayed again, ropes protesting with a tinny shriek. He could take the doses and drop them or take the doses and demand more. She had no leverage here. And no choice. She tied the leather cord tight around the small bag, then tossed it into Clag's waiting hand.

Now Clag pulled a small notebook from his back pocket. He flipped through for a few moments, pointer finger running quickly down each page. Finally, he tapped a page three times, then snapped the book shut. "So nice meeting you," he said. He waggled his fingers in front of that endlessly cheerful smile. Without another word, he pulled a cord hidden just inside the tunnel and turned to leave.

Before Caledonia could speak again, the pallet gave way beneath them.

And they fell.

CHAPTER THIRTEEN

They hit something hard but continued to fall. Their bodies slid and scraped over stone, and all around them echoed Pisces's cries. When they landed one long minute later, their legs were too soft to support them. All except for Amina, who landed lightly on her feet, braids spooling around her body.

Caledonia pushed herself to standing, eyes searching out every entrance to the small chamber in which they now found themselves. The room was a roughly hewn cave with a small tunnel to their right, another to their left, and a larger one directly ahead. Above them was the hole through which they'd fallen, and as Caledonia craned her neck to see the top, the thin stream of light that had followed them down dried up. Doubtless, there'd been a trapdoor waiting just beneath their pallet to catch them as they fell.

A warning would have been nice, Caledonia thought grimly.

Amina pulled Pisces carefully to her feet, brushing gentle hands over the feverish girl's cheeks while Redtooth shouldered two of the sacks and Caledonia investigated each of the tunnels.

"There's a murmur in this one," she said, pointing down the largest of the three. "Sounds like town."

"Oh, good, on your feet already." Clag's cheerful voice came from behind, surprising them all. He emerged from one of the smaller tunnels, looking pleased but unsurprised to find they'd all made the drop. "My apologies for the delay. Takes a bit of time to get down all those stairs."

"Apologies for the *delay*?" Amina took a step towards the man, and while his smile stayed firmly in place, his right leg gave an involuntary flinch.

"Been a while since you've come to port, has it? Yes, the drop can be startling, but I'm sure you understand it's a necessary security precaution. Can't just have people pushing their way off the lifts without a proper interview any more. It's the cost of keeping our little town safe for business."

"You could have killed us," Caledonia protested.

But Clag only chuckled, shaking his head. "Nonsense. It's not even gusty today, and physics is a good friend if you know what you're doing. Now, I've come to give you your tokens," he said, producing four blue chips marked with a sequence of five numbers. He moved around the room, dropping them one at a time into each of their hands. "Trips down are complimentary, but only with the token."

"If they're complimentary, why do we need a token?" asked Amina.

Clag smiled a knowing smile. "We just like to know who's come and gone, that's all. It has no value for trade, but keep it on you."

Somewhere in the tunnels, a bell rang. Clag perked up, stepping across the room towards the tunnel opposite the one he'd come through. He moved silently, Caledonia noticed now, completely at home in what must be a network of tunnels and stairways and trapdoors for each lift they'd seen on the beach below.

When he reached the threshold, he paused. Sighed. Turned back to Caledonia. He was still cheerful, but something of his demeanour had changed. "I'm not supposed to do this sort of thing, but…" He looked over Caledonia's shoulder where Pisces stood. "The doc you want is named Tricius. She's in the Body Quarter. She'll get you right. And she won't take a pound of flesh to get you there."

"Thank you, Clag," said Caledonia. But Clag only shook his head and turned swiftly into the tunnel, muttering something about soft hearts and hard worlds.

Pisces was slumped against the cave wall when Caledonia turned to look. And suddenly she knew exactly what had spurred Clag to generosity. Pisces's skin was a pale grey-brown, devoid of its usual sunny tones, and the sweat on her brow now covered her entire face.

Swiftly, Caledonia swung her sack over one shoulder, propping her friend up with the other. Amina and Redtooth flanked them, and together they moved as quickly as

Pisces's leaching strength would allow.

"Almost there," Caledonia spoke softly to her friend, hoping it wasn't a lie. "Just hold on to me. We'll find this Doc Tricius in no time."

"I'm fine, Cala," Pisces said in a breathy voice. But her arm curled across Caledonia's shoulders and she leaned close, steps increasingly clumsy.

The tunnel was blessedly short, and soon the four girls found themselves at the mouth of a teeming market situated in a ravine with mountain peaks rising on all sides. Perched above it all, a stronghold of overlapping concentric circles sat high on the southern wall. Before them, stalls of every size sprawled in a chaotic press. They were wedged together in whatever space was available, flying flags or streamers or painted metal shields to attract attention. The cold air was spiked with the scents of roasting nuts and spiced meats and filled with the cries of vendors hawking their wares. In every direction, they were met with a flood of people navigating the haphazard paths between stalls. The whole thing seemed to operate on some internal logic that was completely foreign to the girls.

Red cursed. Pisces drooped. And Amina vanished.

Caledonia held tightly to Pisces. She studied the flow of traffic before her, certain that if she could just find something that looked like a main artery, they would manage. The longer she watched, the less certain she became. This place was designed to disorient, to put newcomers off their balance and keep them there.

Amina was back in moments, a small girl trailing in her wake. She was young, only thirteen at most, with beautiful scrolling scars over the tan skin of her left cheek and forehead. Her hair was a glossy black, tied up in multicoloured rags that fluttered lightly as she walked. Right away Caledonia marked how her eyes darted over the three of them and the easy way she strolled in this unsettling din with hands in pockets. She was wiser than her years might suggest, of that Caledonia was certain.

"Ladies," Amina said. Standing beside her, the girl smiled. "This is Nettle. I've engaged her to be our guide."

"You won't find better." Nettle's voice was still young, clinging to the higher notes like cresting waves. Her vowels bent over the ends of her words, softening and stunting them in a way that reminded Caledonia of Amina's own accent. "I know every inch of this place."

"You're just a child." Shifting her attention from the girl to Amina, Redtooth repeated. "She's just a child."

"You're hardly more than that." Nettle shrugged. "I understand you're looking for Doc Tricius. This way."

Without waiting for approval, Nettle stepped into the flow of the crowd.

"How do we know she'll take us to the right place?" Redtooth asked when Nettle was out of earshot.

"Never underestimate the girls of this world," Amina chided, stepping out in front.

Nettle was easy enough to track. Though she was short,

her multicoloured hair ties shone brightly in the crowd. She led them on a seemingly random path through the shopfronts, occasionally cutting down an alley so narrow none of the girls would have considered it a path. The smell of spicy meats, sweet stewed plums and fresh bread made Caledonia's mouth water. She was tempted to stop and spend some of their precious coin on a quick meal for all of them, but the looks she caught from the crowd encouraged her to keep moving. Most watched Pisces with a wary eye, sure she carried the fire or some other disease. But others looked on the four young girls with a hunger that set Caledonia's teeth on edge.

Nettle moved at a quick clip but always seemed aware of where they were, pausing to let them catch up if she got too far out in front. The crowd spoke and shouted in a handful of different languages, some Caledonia recognized, others she didn't. The people were grizzled and cautious, but none bore the orange bands of a Bullet's bandolier. At least not where it would be seen. The only identifying marks were the men and women in short, black capes, the shoulders studded with the cerulean blue bands of the Sly King. When they passed, people made room, held up their stall permits, or ducked between shops to avoid them. The presence of the Sly King was strong and not entirely welcoming.

On either side, vendors sold everything a person could possibly desire. There were furs in a variety of colours from the brightest fuchsia to inky black, salted meats perfectly prepared for long hauls at sea, solar tech, gunpowder, ropes and netting, and origin seeds guaranteed to sprout. At first, Caledonia tried to mark the vendors they might return to later, but the further they went the less possible that became. Even as they passed, the streets were changing. One vendor would just as quickly close down their makeshift stall as another would set up without a care for the flow of traffic. Caledonia would simply have to trust that if Nettle knew enough to get them to Doc Tricius, she also knew where to find the other goods they needed.

It had been nearly an hour by the time they stopped. Pisces's pace decreased rapidly, and even with Amina shouldering Caledonia's pack, it was slow going through the crowd. Finally, Nettle stopped in front of a medium-sized tent.

The Body Quarter was less overwhelming than the main market, with fewer open stalls and more closed tents. Here, the tent flaps were marked with simple paintings of the services available inside. Their path took them down a row of ornamental workers offering tattoos and scars and piercings, to one of pleasure workers, and finally to the healers. Most advertised the part of the anatomy they specialized in treating with a rough drawing of a foot or head or belly posted somewhere on the tent. But the flap of this tent was closed and painted only with the shape of a serpent wrapped around a staff. Above it, blocky red letters spelled out the name TRICIUS.

"I'm a girl of my word," Nettle said proudly, holding a hand towards the tent.

There was no bell, no means of announcing one's presence, so Caledonia pushed through the tent flap with a wilting Pisces leaning heavily into her body.

"Hello? Doctor Tricius?" she called, but the question was unnecessary.

The space was as small as it seemed from the outside and smelled strongly of dry, minty herbs. On one side of the room was a raised bed, on the other a narrow bench and work table near a chest containing dozens of tiny drawers. It was the first thing Caledonia had seen in the whole market that looked somewhat permanent.

As they entered, a woman stood up from the bench. Her skin was a cool, shadowed ochre with a wide scatter of freckles across her face. Her brown hair, twisted and piled neatly atop her head, was threaded with silver cords. She met them with an easy smile but didn't rush forward to greet them.

"Do all of you need attention?" she asked, voice kind.

It was only then that Caledonia realized Redtooth had followed them inside the tent and stood hovering behind Pisces's other shoulder, one protective hand supporting her elbow.

"Just her," Caledonia said. "Pisces."

"Can you pay?" was her next question. "I don't do trade. Coin only."

"We can pay." Coin carried the least amount of value amongst her crew. Their opportunities for trade were limited, and most places that used coin were in Aric's pocket. But they kept a little for occasions such as this.

"Are you coherent?" Doc Tricius asked Pisces.

"I am. Just wounded."

Doc Tricius nodded at Caledonia. "Help her to the bed, and then you and your friend can wait outside." She was already returning to her work table, uncapping a bottle of alcohol and smoothing the acrid liquid over her hands.

"She needs antibios. Do you have them? We can pay extra," Caledonia said.

"I'll decide what she needs," Doc Tricius all but snapped. "Now, you and your friend wait outside."

Caledonia did as instructed, pushing a reluctant Redtooth through the tent flap ahead of her. They found Amina outside, keeping watch over the slow shuffle of traffic, one hand ready on her gun. Nettle stood at her elbow, close but not touching, her eyes wide.

"*You're* the captain of your own ship?" the girl said eagerly to Caledonia.

"I am." Caledonia peered at the clouded sky, but it was impossible to gauge the progress of the sun. It had to be nearing midday by now. Splitting up wasn't ideal, but it had become necessary. "Doc will tend to Pisces, but we need to keep moving. Red, you stay here. Wait for Pi, and when she's done, you get back to the lifts and wait for us there. Clear?"

151

"Clear," Red answered.

"Amina, you're with me," Caledonia continued. "Nettle, we need to work fast. We need seaworthy food, gun tech, and – Amina?"

"Batteries, magnesium or air-breathers would do. Solid-state lithiums if you know where to find them."

"Solid-states aren't easy to come by." Nettle's smile morphed into a grin. "But I might know a guy."

"*Might?*" Redtooth stooped and pushed her nose against Nettle's. "You want me to help you be sure? I'm certain my friend already paid you to be sure."

Nettle took a purposeful step back. "You paid me to be your guide. You want privileged introductions, that's a separate fee."

Before Redtooth could advance on the girl again, Caledonia put a staying hand on her friend's shoulder. Though she was just as irritated, she had to admire the girl's gumption. It couldn't be easy to face three armed girls and demand more than she'd been offered. And if there was one thing Caledonia always admired, it was a girl with guts.

"Name your price," Caledonia said.

"I'll make the introductions...and in exchange you give me a spot on your ship with your crew."

"Off the table," Caledonia said immediately. "I'm not taking on more crew at the moment. Especially not crew too small to swing a blade."

Outrage blazed in Nettle's eyes at the insult, but she

didn't rise to the bait. Forcing a casual smile, she folded her arms across her chest and stood her ground. "I know some people who'll give you good trades for air-breather batteries. I can take you there right now if you like."

This was a familiar game. Some other time, Caledonia might enjoy playing it, but now wasn't that time. She pulled another small pouch from inside her jacket and gave it a good shake so Nettle was sure to hear how much coin it contained.

"I'm not taking on more girls right now, but I like you. We need solid-states. Lead us true and next time I dock in Cloudbreak, we'll talk."

Nettle's gaze never strayed to the pouch. She kept her focus on Caledonia, considering and unflinching. It was impressive.

"We'll talk about a spot on your crew," Nettle confirmed, and when Caledonia nodded, Nettle swiped the pouch of coin from Caledonia's grip. "Deal."

Shouldering their packs once more, Caledonia and Amina left Redtooth to wait for Pisces and followed Nettle back into the crowd. It was slower going with two of the large packs balanced on their shoulders, and more than once Caledonia envied Redtooth her immense strength, especially when she was jostled from one side of the row to the other.

In spite of the damp cold, sweat soon dripped from Caledonia's temples and down her back. The ground became steeper as Nettle directed them due south, where the paths turned into something more like roads and the structures on either side gradually transformed from temporary stalls to buildings of wood and stone. Here, the people around them seemed less hectic, and more wore the glassy blue of the Sly King's banner. High on the hill above them sat the stronghold of Hesperus himself. Caledonia bristled at being so close to the seat of power, but if this was where the deal was to be made, she'd make it fast.

"This is it!" Nettle jogged ahead, climbing a set of stairs and disappearing inside a stone building jutting out of the mountainside with four hewn columns caging it in. The door in the centre gaped wide, the room beyond lit from within by flickering candles.

They moved cautiously up the steps and through the door. The room was cavernous, lined with candles tucked into alcoves carved along the walls. Light danced over a large wooden desk squatting before towers of crates and piles of canvas sacks, each tagged with pale yellow strips denoting their contents. Next to them a stairway opened beside a lift not unlike the one they'd used earlier this morning. The cold air smelled faintly of animal fat and smoke. There was no sign of Nettle.

Before the girls could set their sacks down, a boy rushed into the room. At first glance, Caledonia thought she spotted a bandolier on his arms, but as he came closer, she realized they weren't lines but scrolling designs like the one Nettle

154

wore on her cheek and forehead, the scars the same soft ruddy brown as his skin. Silt didn't poison his blood.

Darkly, Caledonia wondered what kind of bargain kept a boy like this out of Aric's clutches. Whatever it was, it was surely the work of Sly King Hesperus and it was surely nothing good. Yet another sign that this was no place for a girl like her to linger. They needed to make their trade and get out before anyone realized they were here.

The boy stopped halfway to the desk and bobbed his head in greeting, breathing hard.

"Apologies for the wait," he said, though they'd barely stepped into the room when he arrived. "Nettle says you've brought goods for trade. We'll take the stairs. You can put your goods on the lift if you like."

"We'll hold on to them," Caledonia said, even as her muscles cried for reprieve. The scales were all they had for leverage, and she preferred to keep them close.

The boy nodded as though that were a common response and gestured for them to follow as he trotted up the stairs. Amina stepped in front, shielding her captain from whatever might be lurking around the corner.

The boy kept a steady pace as they climbed flight after flight of the curling stairs. They passed fourteen platforms between flights, and with each one the air grew cooler and thinner. Caledonia kept her pace behind Amina, but both girls breathed heavily. By the time the boy stopped, they were more than ready to let their sacks hit the floor.

"Captain Caledonia Styx," a voice boomed around them, and Caledonia's head snapped up to see a tall, broad-shouldered man with skin as black as the midnight ocean crossing the room towards them. His long greatcoat was tied at the waist and billowed around his legs like storm clouds, and he was trailed by six or seven others. Just behind him, Nettle followed, expression contrite but also pleased.

A girl of her word, Caledonia thought with a splash of humour. She was certainly that.

Caledonia forced her breathing to calm as she straightened her back and squared her shoulders with this man. "And you are?"

"My apologies, I thought you'd been informed," the man said with a quick glance over his shoulder for Nettle. "I am Hesperus Shreeves, and this," he added with a sweep of his hand, "is my court."

CHAPTER FOURTEEN

Caledonia made herself a rock. Before her stood the most dangerous person in all of Cloudbreak, the one man she needed to avoid. This was a man who went to great lengths to appease Aric Athair in order to continue operating with authority, who would certainly turn over Caledonia and her crew if it meant securing his own interests. And now she stood in his court with only Amina at her side.

The room was nearly a mirror of the one they'd entered on the ground floor. To one side was the lift, protected by a metal gate, and all along the walls were small, candlelit alcoves. Hesperus and his party had entered from a door opposite the stairway. He strode confidently across the stones to stand in the centre of the room. The rest fanned out behind him; four women and two men were now followed by four guards dressed in the short cerulean-banded black cape so prevalent throughout the market. While the guards placed themselves strategically around the room, the others stayed in Hesperus's wake.

"Nettle says you're the only one in this place capable of

making the trade we need," Caledonia said, determined to proceed through her growing sense of dread. The bounty was on her ship, she reminded herself, not on her, and her ship was safe in the wharf beneath a layer of fog.

"She knows her business." The smile Hesperus offered was as broad as his shoulders. "Just as I know mine. What have you brought me?"

"Solar scales, all in good working order. Ready to be repurposed into whatever device you need." As she spoke, Amina pulled open a single sack. The scales glittered darkly in the candlelight.

A man hurried forward to inspect the scales. Amina stayed put, her eyes pinned to him. He worked quickly, selecting a few scales from the pile and turning them over. When he nodded, Hesperus continued.

"And what are you looking for in exchange for such a treasure?" he asked, voice smooth.

Caledonia ran down her list of goods: protein, ammo, solid-state lithiums. Hesperus kept his expression neutral as she spoke, listening as casually as though she were discussing the currents and winds.

"A hearty trade," he said finally, when she'd finished speaking. "Shall we take refreshment while I have your scales tested?"

"They work," Amina protested, offence resonating in her tone.

"Of course they do, my dear." Hesperus shifted his gaze

momentarily to Amina, who bristled at the epithet. "But I don't trade until I know what I'm getting. So, take my refreshment or take your leave."

In spite of herself, Caledonia smiled. He was dangerous and not to be trusted, but he wasn't foolish and he wasn't a brute. She could work with that.

"We only drink red wine," Caledonia said.

Hesperus laughed loudly, his head tipping back to reveal all his teeth. "Kae! Red wine for my guests. Ladies, I'm afraid I'm going to ask you to climb a few more stairs, but I promise it will be well worth the effort. Please, follow me."

They travelled the curling stairs up two more flights to a circular room wrapped in cerulean-blue curtains which were pulled aside to reveal sky on all sides. This was the very top of the stronghold. In the centre of the room a fire blazed, and around the perimeter four telescopes on adjustable tripods pointed in the cardinal directions. The clouds that had been so dense this morning were thinning, and from this vantage they could see everything from the cliffs in the east to the beginning of sharper snow-capped mountains in the west. With a jolt, Caledonia realized the wharf below was clearly visible.

She caught Amina's eye. Saw her own alarm reflected but not amplified. If this was a trap, then they were squarely inside it. Their only way through was forward.

Two women preceded them into the room, both with skin as dark as Hesperus's and armed with blades and guns.

One took a seat along the lip of the wall, her back to the cloudy expanse outside, her eyes on Caledonia and Amina. Her head was shorn as smooth as Pisces's, her eyes wide and elegantly shaped like Hime's. Though she slouched against a column, she couldn't hide the power of her lithe body.

The other woman, Kae, went to a low table and filled three stone goblets with a ruby-red wine. Where the first woman was cool, Kae's presence was calming, surely meant to settle tensions before the work of trade began or encourage Hesperus's guests to drink a little too much. *Always assume the actions of those around you are intentional*, her mother had said. That was especially true of a man like Hesperus. He didn't rise to power by accident, and he certainly didn't keep it by being careless in his actions.

Hesperus took a hearty swig from his goblet, proving the wine was safe. Caledonia helped herself to a sip. It was sweeter than she was prepared for, with a tang that left her blinking in surprise.

"Cherry wine," Hesperus said, sounding satisfied. "The cherries grow in the mountains outside the city but are far too fragile for a life of trade. One of the many benefits of living in Cloudbreak. But you're not often in my port, Caledonia Styx of the *Mors Navis*, or you'd know such things."

Her ship. So he had seen it. He knew its name. Her pulse spiked, but she forced herself to take another sip of the wine before she answered.

"I'm not often in any port." She spoke as casually as her

tight throat would allow. "And I don't plan to be in this one very long."

"That remains to be seen," he said, dropping all pretence of humour. "You don't fly under the Father's banner. Tell me, Captain, how you stay outside his grip."

"I'm not here to discuss my tactics with you, Lord Hesperus. No disrespect," she added lightly, though her pulse was pounding in her ears. "I'm here to trade, and then I'll be on my way."

Behind Hesperus, the guard seated in the window shifted, her hand resting very near her blade.

"Trade is tactics, Captain. And before I engage, I like to know who I'm dealing with. It's not every day a young girl comes into my court seeking solid-states."

Trade is tactics. The words hung in Caledonia's mind as she considered her response and Hesperus's motives. It was possible he was exercising caution. Solid-state lithiums were rare. If she were caught with those in her possession, Aric would know where she'd found them. But surely the Sly King of Cloudbreak wasn't concerned with what people did with their goods. He was stalling. Searching for information that might be just as valuable as her solar scales. She needed to give him something.

"You know who I am. And I think you know more than you're saying."

"You are keen." His smile returned, predatory and pleased. "There is a bounty on you and your ship."

Caledonia's fingers became a vice on her wine goblet. The world was suddenly very small and very cold.

"Do you intend to claim that bounty?" she asked, hoping her voice didn't break.

The guard's hand settled firmly on the hilt of her blade.

Hesperus leaned forward in his seat, resting his elbows on his knees and clasping his hands before him with thumbs crossed on top. A small tattoo nestled in the thin flesh between his thumb and forefinger, a simple design in faded black ink. "I'm in the business of keeping my port, my market and my family safe. I do that by keeping the Father happy whenever the opportunity lands at my feet. So, yes, I intend to claim the bounty."

Caledonia's guts flattened. "Would you consider another exchange? My solar scales for our freedom? Surely their worth comes close to the bounty."

"If it were only numbers, that might be true, but they're not as valuable as the Father's goodwill." He shook his head. "I do like you, Caledonia Styx, and if not for the bounty, this might have gone another way, but I'm afraid I'll be keeping your solar scales in addition to claiming the bounty. Unless you have something else to offer?"

"Villain!" Amina cried. Her voice was followed by the snap of the guard's pistol leaving its holster, the bite of its hammer pulling back as a bullet moved into the chamber. Both Amina and the guard stopped.

For the smallest second, Caledonia considered the Bullet

in her hold. It was possible Hesperus would consider the value of returning a deserter of Aric's army a worthy replacement for the bounty. But an uncomfortable twist in her stomach kept her from putting it on the table.

She had nothing else of value to offer, and he knew it.

"Think what you will. I have more to consider than your small woes." Hesperus stood with the wine goblet held loosely in his grip. He crossed the room to stand with his back to them, eyes cast forward.

The guard kept her gun pointed at Amina's eye while Kae rose gracefully to her feet and spoke. "Keep your peace. We have no wish to spill your blood."

"The wind is in the north. Are you so sure it would be ours that spilled?" Amina gripped the pistol strapped to her thigh, shoulders angled to cover her captain.

"If not yours here, then that of your crew down there." Though the words were very clearly a threat, Kae spoke with calm command. "Keep your peace."

Through it all, Caledonia kept her gaze on Hesperus. "I have forty-eight girls down there on that ship. If you claim the bounty, you're killing every last one of us."

He spun. "And if the Father finds out I let you go, he'll make me watch my family die before he takes my life. I have no choice but to turn you over."

"Of course you have a choice! You can fight! You have endless resources here. Surely if anyone can resist him, it's you." She let the force of her words carry her forward.

But Hesperus stopped her with a laugh. "My girl, how would you propose I take on a fleet like his?"

"One ship at a time."

Now the Sly King's laugh turned soft, pitying. "That is no kind of strategy. Better to choose the path that costs us the least."

"Even if it costs the person next to you their lives?" Caledonia countered, feeling a surge of disgust for the man before her.

"I should throw rocks at the mountain, is that it?" Hesperus countered, unmoved.

"Better than hiding in one." Insulting him was reckless, but in that moment, Caledonia didn't care.

"Mino," he called to the guard, "bind our guests and take them to a cell while we welcome their crew to the Cloudbreak prisons. Forty-eight will be a squeeze, but I doubt they'll be staying very long."

"Brother." Mino's voice was tense and soft. She lifted her hand, pointing beyond the window.

The clouds that had crouched so steadily over the Rock Isles all morning had lifted away completely. The seas were long before them, the breaker islands gleaming dully in the sunlight. And just beyond, perhaps ten miles or so away, half a dozen Bullet ships sailed directly for them.

Their ghost funnels should have struck a note of panic, but for the first time in her entire life, Caledonia was glad to see them.

CHAPTER FIFTEEN

"Captain." Hesperus's voice was as hard as the mountains surrounding them. "It seems your wait will be even shorter than I thought."

"Brother." Mino's voice again, soft as a falling rain. She lifted her eye from the eastern telescope. "It's a Fiveson."

Hesperus cursed, spinning to press his eye to the scope. Caledonia waited anxiously, her eyes pinned to the approaching ships, her heart thready in her chest.

"The *Bale Blossom*." Hesperus lifted his head to glare over the water.

Without invitation, Caledonia moved between Hesperus and the scope to peer through the glass. Six ships of varying shapes and sizes cut towards the protected bay of Lower Cloudbreak. Five of the ships bore a single orange blossom on their hull. The nose of the sixth was covered in them. The blood drained from Caledonia's fingertips as she realized she was looking at the very ship that carried Lir.

Time fell away like the petals of a dying flower. A cold

kind of focus washed over Caledonia's mind as she surveyed the ships. Only four of them were small enough to make it through the breakers. The *Bale Blossom* and one other would be forced to stay behind. If the smaller four couldn't pin the *Mors Navis* down in port, they'd try to flush her out, crush her in the open. Before Hesperus could apprehend them, her crew would be locked in battle.

The sharp edge of a blade slid along her neck, and a firm hand landed on her shoulder. "I would appreciate it if you came without a fight," Hesperus said in her ear.

"I might." The thrill of finding the upper hand added heft to Caledonia's voice. "But my crew certainly won't."

"That isn't really my concern," he continued.

"It should be." Caledonia kept her eyes on the Bullet ships, on the shrinking distance between them and the port. "My crew will tear your harbour apart trying to fight their way out. And you think those Bullets care where their missiles land? There won't be a berth left intact in a few minutes. And when word gets around that Bullets are bringing the fight to your shores… Seems like bad business to me."

With a jerk, Hesperus spun her around. Frustration was apparent in the furrow of his brow, irritation in the clench of his jaw. He held her gaze for several long seconds before saying, "Speak plainly, Captain."

"I'm offering you a deal." Caledonia lifted her chin above his knife. "A chance to save your port."

Behind Hesperus, Amina had been contained by Mino,

hands held behind her back. Kae watched all four of them, expression flinty.

To Caledonia's surprise, Hesperus didn't look angry. He looked alert, impatient, as though the shift in circumstances delighted him in a very distant way. Sheathing his knife, he asked, "What are your terms?"

Caledonia pressed her eye to the scope, finding the ships much closer than she'd anticipated. Her blood sang loudly in her ears. She was mere miles from the man responsible for the death of her family. Her skin flushed and she felt light as air, filled with the desire to fight. But even as her body vibrated with the urge to charge directly for the *Bale Blossom*, she could see the field was stacked against her. Engaging them here would mean the death of most, if not all, of her crew. Even if they made it past the breaker isles, she'd never get close to Lir.

She preferred a fight she could win. Or one that got her close enough to see his face. If she took her crew into this battle, she was betraying them on every level.

"Lord Hesperus, are the Rock Isle canals passable?" Caledonia turned again to face him.

"Passable, yes, but it takes a nimble ship, a narrow one, and yours, as I understand it, isn't."

"I'll worry about my ship. Do you have charts?" When he nodded, she continued, "Then here is the deal: you get me and my crew back to my ship with charts in hand, and we'll take the fight out of your port."

Now Hesperus hesitated. It would be difficult to deny he'd done more than fail to hold them if he handed over charts of the Rock Isle canals. But a battle inside the breaker islands would be decidedly worse. It had taken decades for Cloudbreak to build its reputation as a safe port, but it would take only minutes to destroy it.

Kae pressed her hand to Hesperus's arm and revealed a small tattoo nestled in the flesh between her thumb and forefinger. If Caledonia had to guess, she'd say it was a match for the one on Hesperus's own hand and that Mino had one as well. He wasn't lying when he said he was in the business of protecting his family.

Hesperus bared his teeth at his sister. "Yes, dammit, I'll give them to you, but you must go. Fast."

"I have crew in town. I won't leave them." Caledonia knew she was pushing the limits of Hesperus's goodwill. But she sensed that they could be pushed just a bit further. He might not be an enemy of Aric, but he wasn't a friend either.

"Mino." Kae turned to her sister.

"Where?" Mino asked, releasing Amina.

"At the lifts," Amina said. "Two girls."

"That's it?" Mino asked, and when both Amina and Caledonia nodded, she vanished down the stairs.

"She'll find them and get them on the lifts. But you must follow me," Kae said, hurrying them down a single flight of stairs. Instead of continuing down the endless stairs they'd climbed to reach the observatory, she took an immediate turn, leading them through a corridor they'd passed on their way up. Hesperus followed at first but soon broke away, hollering to Kae to hold them until he returned.

The hallway was broad enough to walk two abreast until Kae turned sharply and they passed through a wooden doorway into a narrow tunnel. The air was even colder here and smelled more richly of earth and rock. Instead of descending the side of the mountain, they were cutting through it.

Panic pressed against the focus of Caledonia's mind, eating away at her thoughts until for a moment all she could think of was Pisces, her sister, the person who kept her heart from turning to stone. She would not leave her behind again.

Kae came to a stop before a latticed metal door and pushed it aside to reveal another lift. This one was crafted of metal, with railings wrapped around each side. It looked decidedly sturdier than the horror they'd ridden this morning.

"Get in. It will take you directly to the docks." Kae opened a panel in the wall and began flipping levers. Lights flared muddy green and burned orange. Distantly, Caledonia wondered if Clag operated controls like these.

"I can't go without Pisces and Red." Caledonia knew she wasn't thinking clearly, that she was prioritizing her heart over her crew. Amina knew it, too. She stepped in front of her captain, pinning her with an uncompromising expression.

"On the lift, Captain." Her hands came down on Caledonia's shoulders, and she applied firm pressure but did not shove. "Or I'll put you there myself." Moving in closer, she lowered her voice. "Staying here only puts your crew at more risk. You need to trust Pisces and Red to move quickly and get to the ship. And *you* need to have everything ready when they get there. That's what we trust you to do."

She was right. Of course she was right, but Caledonia's feet felt leaden as she boarded the lift.

The sound of footsteps rang through the tunnel. For the briefest second, Caledonia hoped it might be her girls returning with Mino, but it was only one set of footsteps. Not three.

Hesperus. He returned with a metal cylinder clutched in his hand. Sweat gleamed on his brow. He didn't offer the cylinder immediately but held it across his body like a weapon.

"No map of the canals is completely true." All his earlier resistance was gone. This was a different Hesperus, earnest and concerned. It was a Hesperus Caledonia instinctively trusted. "Each contains a purposeful flaw – a mistake meant to mislead those unfamiliar with the channels. It's one of the things that keeps them impassable. On this one, it's the northern corridors; their depth, width, length, everything is off. Sometimes by a few feet, sometimes by a lot more. Don't trust them. Find another way and you'll be fine."

"You said the flaw is one of the things that keeps them

impassable." Amina was far sharper than Caledonia in this moment. "What are the others?"

Hesperus's smile was grim as he handed over the metal cylinder. "Most of the Rock Isles are unstable. They fracture and cave daily. No map can help you with that."

"There's no more time," Kae urged. She slid the cage shut between them. "You must go now."

The lift gave a small hiccup and began to move down.

"Thank you, Lord Hesperus," Caledonia said, tipping her head to maintain eye contact. "I won't forget this."

"Don't hurt my port, Captain Styx," Hesperus called, just before they moved out of earshot. "I hope you survive."

The lift slid downward, picking up speed as it descended the shaft of rock. A damp wind rushed upward, bringing the familiar scents of brine and chalky sands. Though Hesperus's stronghold was higher than the market level of Cloudbreak, the trip down seemed to take half as long as the trip up.

The lift slowed before it came to a stop, and the girls pushed the lattice door. Caledonia wasted no time. They were across the small antechamber and through the blessedly unlocked door in seconds, only to find themselves standing on the beach, mere paces from the wharf they'd left this morning.

In moments, the two girls were climbing aboard the *Mors Navis*. From this vantage, the Bullet ships were not yet visible and the crew had no reason to suspect anything was wrong until Caledonia sent up the cry, "Make ready! Bullets on approach!" Her crew sprang into action, readying the ship. Caledonia's eyes strayed to the cliffs. Three lifts moved downward. If her friends were not on one of them, then it was already too late.

"Masts up!" she shouted. "Amina!"

"Knots to the rigging!" Amina's voice all but lifted her team up the four masts, now shooting from the deck to pierce the sky.

Tin appeared at her side. "Orders, Captain?"

Caledonia hurriedly uncapped the cylinder from Hesperus and poured its contents into her hand. A map, just as he'd promised, showing the canals in meticulous detail.

"The canals? Captain, no one sails the canals. Not in ships like this. We'll never make it," Tin protested.

"We'll make it. We just need the right path." Her eyes skated over the maze-like passages. If they picked the wrong way, they'd find themselves trapped. "Lace would have found a course," she said with a strange and uncomfortable mix of irritation and loss.

If Tin had further protests on the subject, she bit them back and studied the map over Caledonia's shoulder. "Here, these canals look wide and deep enough." Tin's fingers charted a path through the northern canals.

If only it were true. "Those dimensions are likely false, according to Hesperus. Look south of these canals." Caledonia selected the first channel she felt sure couldn't be

172

considered northern. "Anything south of that line should be reliable."

Passing the map into Tin's hands so she could ready the bridge crew, Caledonia returned her attention to the lifts. One had paused midway down, one was already on the ground, and the third was somewhere between the two.

"Amina!" she cried.

As if reading her mind, Amina's answer came from high on the mainmast. "It's not them. I can't see if they're on either of the other two."

"Two ships threading the breakers!" The call came from the stern, where one of the Knots was perched atop the sun sail with eyes trained on the approaching threat. "I see two more just beyond!"

Frustration clawed up Caledonia's throat. "Engines! Get ready to shove off!"

Hime was there in a flash, standing before her with panic pulling her mouth into a shape of distress. Her hands flew. *Redtooth? Pisces? Where are they?!*

"They're coming," Caledonia promised. "They'll be here."

The ship rumbled beneath her feet, echoing the growing fury in her heart. They needed to move. She needed to give the order to move.

"Captain!" Amina's voice. "They're on the beach!"

Caledonia spun, spotting them right away. Redtooth's blonde braids flew behind her as she ran, one hand fixed on Pisces's arm. Even at this distance it was obvious Pisces

173

struggled to keep her pace. Her long legs moved with a sluggish rhythm, and her head was tucked low with the effort.

"Halfway through!" Amina's Knots called.

The crew stood at the ready, bodies tense. They could have been under way minutes ago, gaining a healthy lead on the Bullet ships. Instead, they were still in port, floating there like easy pickings. But every girl on board looked towards the racing forms of Redtooth and Pisces. If the two girls could have been drawn forward by the combined will of their crew, they'd have been on the ship fifty times over.

"Shove off!" Caledonia cried at last.

Her crew began the work of untethering the large ropes keeping them steady in port, as up on the bridge, the girls ignited the thrusters.

Pisces stumbled, and the ship seemed to hold its breath as she recovered her feet. They heard Redtooth shouting, saw Pisces dig fists into the sand, and then they were up again, racing towards the departing ship.

"Be ready, Tin!" Caledonia called.

Slowly at first and then picking up small bits of speed, the ship moved out of berth towards open water and the two hundred yards that stood between them and the canal entry point. Redtooth and Pisces hurtled down the wharf, Redtooth pushing Pisces ahead of her. With one final burst of speed, the girls raced down the dock, leaping onto the deck just before it moved out of reach.

Pisces landed on her hands and knees before collapsing against her good shoulder while Redtooth rolled the landing, coming to rest on her back.

Caledonia waited just long enough to see them safe aboard before she shouted once more to Tin and the ship sped towards the narrow opening of the Rock Isle canals.

Chapter Sixteen

Tin pushed the *Mors Navis* as fast as the shallow waters would allow. Their wake rolled behind them, adding chop to the already dangerous waters between the breakers. It would slow the Bullet ships down but not stop them.

"Amina!" Caledonia called as they raced along the wall of cliffs towards the narrow mouth of the Rock Isle canals. "Masts down! High speeds!"

Amina released a piercing whistle, and all her Knots quickly disentangled themselves from the rigging. Caledonia spared a glance for Pisces, now seated with her back pressed to the mizzenmast block and under Hime's stern attentions, before darting up the companionway ladder towards the bridge.

"Guns up, girls! Shield's high!" Redtooth shouted as two ships emerged from the breaker islands and the first shots exploded behind them.

Tin stood at the helm, her grip as steely as her gaze. Behind her the bridge crew monitored the rest of the ship's systems. Caledonia spotted the map, spread out on a table near the helm, each corner tucked beneath metal clips to keep it in place.

They were fast approaching what appeared to be a solid cliff wall. Though the entry to the canals was clear on the map, it was impossible to see from this distance. On the map, it was narrow, barely wide enough to accommodate the full girth of the *Mors Navis*. If they'd been moving at a reasonable pace, they'd have plenty of time to plan the tight turn. As it was, they'd have to rely on Caledonia's sharp eyes and quick instincts.

Taking the wheel from Tin, she felt more connected to her ship, its power vibrating up through her palms. It was reassuring and familiar. Still, Lace should have been at her side, counting down the distance in her steady way. Instead, it was Tin, who was untested in the role. Caledonia couldn't yet trust her ability to gauge the distance.

Water splashed along the rock wall as the *Mors Navis* sped past. Two hundred yards ahead, the splashing ceased and the water flowed smooth. "Ready on thrusters. Hard turn to starboard on my go."

Tin sent out the call: "Hard turn! Hard turn ahead! Strap in!"

Caledonia gave Tin the wheel long enough to wind a strap around her own waist and snap it into place.

"Do you see it?" Caledonia asked.

"I think so." Tin's voice was tentative.

"Counting down!" Caledonia called for the entire bridge

crew. "Three!" The opening still wasn't entirely visible. "Two!" Wind whipped through the bridge. "One!" She pulled the wheel sharply to starboard. "Port bow thrusters on full! Starboard stern thrusters on full!"

The ship rotated, biting in and slewing across the top of the water at a steep angle. Caledonia gripped the wheel. The rock wall slid past, and just as the ship righted itself and regained forward momentum, the mouth of the canals revealed itself.

"Ahead full! Thrusters out!" Her commands were executed immediately, and the ship charged straight into the narrow opening with only feet to spare on either side.

On deck, Redtooth called the girls to battle stations, focusing her gunners aft. Knowing they would be attacked from behind was a small advantage, but one they could use. From what Caledonia had seen of the Bullet ships, they were smaller craft, which also meant they'd be faster than the *Mors Navis* in these twisting canals.

Tin's voice was strained as she called directions to the bridge crew, adapting to Caledonia's pace and the narrow canals. It was too fast and they all knew it. Metal sliced against rock more than once, but never enough to harm the hull.

The roar of engines billowed around them, the sounds growling off the tall walls as four Bullet ships entered the canals in their wake. Caledonia pushed harder, her hands steady on the spokes, her muscles tense, her stance wide.

She knew this ship better than anyone.

Shouts rose on deck. The first Bullet ship was near enough to engage, and they opened fire. Caledonia did her best to ignore the dull snap of shots hitting her hull. The canals curled tightly one direction, then the other. Each time they made a turn, they lost the Bullet ships for a span of a few short seconds, but they needed more.

"What's ahead, Tin?" she demanded.

"Three hundred yards to the first fork!" Tin called from her post by the map.

The ship dodged around another long bend, earning them a small moment of reprieve from the pursuing ships. But what lay ahead made Caledonia's lungs freeze. Before them, the canal walls tilted away from each other, bowing out like arms opening towards the sky. It left the waters within wide and welcoming. Perfect for several smaller ships to overtake a larger one.

They had room for speed now. And they would need it.

Caledonia ordered engines to full. The *Mors Navis* darted ahead, and for a brief second it was only them and the water, the steady hum of their engines the only sound in the broad canal.

Then it was over. Behind them, four Bullet ships thundered around the bend and poured into the canal, sun sails glittering fiercely on their tails. They fanned out across the space, ready to attack the *Mors Navis* from every angle. They were smaller, lighter, faster. Three hundred long yards ahead the canals narrowed and forked. They'd gone from a race to a fight.

Turning the helm over to Tin, Caledonia rushed to the deck. Redtooth was already shouting orders, dismantling the shield wall from the aft deck and reconfiguring her crew for a fight on all sides. Amina's Knots perched on top of the bridge, bodies low and guns trained on each of the approaching ships. It was exactly what they should all be doing. And as Caledonia studied the ships, now gaining on them, she knew it wouldn't be enough.

Caledonia whistled, and Amina, Redtooth, Hime and Pisces circled around her. "Options," she said.

"Deploy the cable mines we collected from the barge." Pisces was barely on her feet and her arm was in a sling now, keeping her bad shoulder immobilized. Hime hovered at her side, one hand steadying Pisces's hip.

"Risky," Redtooth said, fresh red clay painted in a wide swathe across her mouth. Her eyes shone in this pre-light of battle. "Those things are designed for floating, not dragging. Could backfire on us."

"Then we hold it as a last resort. Other options."

"Spin the ship." Amina spoke decisively. "We hit the thrusters hard and break their line before they have time to regroup. If we get behind them, we take the advantage."

Caledonia played it through in her mind. The ability to spin the ship in a tight circle at top speeds was the benefit of their powerful thrusters and shallow hull. The manoeuvre would scatter the Bullet ships and give the crew time to pick one or two of them off, but they'd still be left with two and the advantage would be spent.

"Possible. Other options," she pressed.

Lovely Hime raised her hands, hesitated. She squinted in the sun, her eyes straying to Amina before she resolved to speak. *We have quicklime in the hold.* Now she turned to survey the four ships in pursuit, and added, *And we have the wind.*

They'd taken the quicklime off a previous barge and stashed it in the cargo hold, far from the desalination tanks and other sources of water. The caustic powder was useful for scouring pipes clean and dangerous when it came into contact with wet surfaces. Like water or eyes or lungs. Caledonia had nearly forgotten it was in their inventory.

"Vicious," Redtooth said, lips bending into a smile. "I like it."

It *was* vicious, and it was clear by the way Hime braided her fingers together and looked away that she wasn't proud of having made the suggestion.

"Do it," Caledonia ordered.

Redtooth gladly complied, calling orders to the crew.

In moments, the quicklime was on the rear deck. Each of the girls handling the canvas sacks wore gloves and covered their mouths and noses with scarves or bandanas. Caledonia ordered everyone else upwind. Tin steered the ship into a slow fishtail, letting the stern of the ship sweep lazily from side to side. Thinking they'd gained some advantage, the Bullet ships moved in close. They didn't see the smile that sliced across Redtooth's mouth as she raised her blade.

The bags were cut, and the air filled with a powdery white cloud. It puffed and swirled in the tugging wind, travelling towards each of the four ships. If the Bullets knew what was coming, they had no time to react. The powder engulfed their ships like a deadly fog, filling their noses, mouths, eyes, and lungs with a burning they were powerless to combat.

As the roar of their engines fell away, the canyon filled with the screams of boys and men. Their ships faltered and slowed, and soon the screams stopped altogether; the quicklime had burned its way through layers of delicate skin, making it painful for those Bullets to draw a simple breath, much less issue a cry.

Hime wilted, her eyes filling with glossy tears she fought to contain.

I am like them, Hime said.

Caledonia considered her response. Hime had never felt like a Bullet to her. She'd felt like a girl who'd been forced to adapt to a violent way of life or die. She'd felt like a survivor. Now she wondered at all the ways surviving could change a person, all the ways it might have changed her brother. And then she stopped wondering.

"A little," she said carefully. "But that's one of the reasons we have to keep fighting. So maybe one day, no one will have to be even a little bit like them."

"Come on." Amina moved to take Hime's hand. She pulled the girl close, wrapping one arm around her shoulders. "You don't need to see this."

But Hime pulled away, keeping her eyes on the ships in their wake. *No, I do.*

Caledonia watched for any of the ships to recover and renew their chase, but they passed into the next narrow channel with no signs of immediate pursuit.

Her girls cried out in victory, their voices pounding along the canal walls. They were tired and hungry, but their eyes shone in the full light of the sun. Even knowing they'd left Cloudbreak without the supplies they needed, the crew was committed to this journey. It filled Caledonia with a twist of guilt and pride.

It was only as Caledonia made her way again towards the bridge that she realized something shocking: the bounty was real. The boy had told the truth.

CHAPTER SEVENTEEN

Dusk slipped down the canyon walls long before the sun had set. Caledonia's arms trembled with cold and effort. Every movement of the ship needed to be precise. Fast. When Amina finally climbed into the cabin to announce there'd been no sign of pursuit since releasing the quicklime, Caledonia pulled the ship out of gear. They might not have much of a lead, but they'd gain more by reducing their wake, travelling in silence, and letting these twisting, enigmatic canals cover their path.

"Go silent and dark. Thrusters for drift only," she said, giving the helm over to the bridge crew. "Tin, take a rest, too."

Everyone needed a rest, but more than that, they needed a safe course through these canals. Caledonia and Amina spent hours tucked away in the map room, their lights as low as they could keep them, their backs bent over Hesperus's flawed map. Usually, this was a task that would involve the whole command crew, but with Lace gone and Pisces injured, they needed Redtooth on deck and Hime with the wounded while the two of them studied.

An ideal course took them through the northern passages, depositing them west of the Rock Isles. From there it was a straight shot towards the Northwater conscription routes. But it was the northern canals they couldn't trust. More than once, Caledonia found herself tracing that course, wondering if they could risk the uncertainty.

Eventually, they found a path that would take them safely out of the canals. It would drop them due south, west of the southernmost thrust of the Rock Isles. Barely closer to their desired course than when they'd docked at Lower Cloudbreak. But it was an area that wasn't frequented by Aric's fleet, and that, at least, was a small victory.

By the time the two girls returned to the main deck, night was thick and several of the crew had taken up watch posts. The sky was a narrow slip of glittered black far above them. The sun pips remained dark, and the only sounds were the occasional whisper of pebbles tumbling into the water.

It was the first still moment they'd had since fleeing Hesperus's observatory.

"I lost everything." Caledonia kept her voice quiet. "Everything we had to trade, I lost."

Amina stood silently at her side, offering neither comfort nor censure. She watched the captain with her steady, dark eyes. Witnessing but not judging. For some indefinable reason, it was a relief to be heard and not challenged or calmed. It was a relief to let her failure feel like a failure.

"I shouldn't have taken all the scales with us. That was

reckless." Rhona never would have done something so irresponsible. She'd have taken half and held half back. Just in case.

"I agree." Amina's honesty was jolting. "But I didn't at the time. It was a good risk, just a bad outcome. I would have made the same decision."

"Are you sparing my feelings, Amina?"

Amusement narrowed Amina's eyes just as it widened her smile. "When have I ever spared you anything?"

Amina was the only one among them who had purposefully left her home and people to fight. The Hands of the River fought only as much as was necessary to keep Aric's influence out of the Braids, but at fifteen turns, Amina, with her small family, had joined a band determined to do more than keep Aric at bay. She'd lost her family in much the same way Caledonia had, at the hands of a merciless Bullet clip. She was like a hewn piece of granite, formed in fire and tougher for it. She would be the last to spare Caledonia any hard truth.

"Are you sure there's nothing on this ship we can use to neutralize *Electra*'s hull?"

"I'm sure." Amina stood quietly for a moment, head tilted into the breeze as though listening to another conversation. "Captain, we made mistakes. But our reasons were good. *Your* reasons were good."

It felt like an accusation. It didn't matter that her reasons had been good, the result was the same. She'd lost the only viable option they had of building the weapon they needed to save their brothers, and in the process failed to acquire the food they'd need for a long haul at sea. She opened her mouth to say as much when a dreadful howl erupted from the bowels of the ship. It echoed around them, blossoming in the narrow canyon like a bomb.

The Bullet.

Without another word between them, Caledonia and Amina raced belowdecks. The sound had called several curious crew members into the hallways, but the instant they heard the captain coming, they made room for her to pass.

The two made quick progress through the galley and down to cargo hold on level three. Here, the cries were so much louder, splintered with shrieks of real pain. Even though he was a Bullet, it was still difficult to bear witness to such agony.

She made for the door, but was arrested by a voice calling out. "Captain!" Pisces hurried into the cargo bay, face stricken with worry. "Captain, I'll take care of him."

"I need him quiet." Caledonia paused with her hand resting on the hatch.

"I'll take care of him," she repeated. Pisces looked more rested. Some of the colour had returned to her cheeks, but racing here had taken more energy than she had to give. At another cry from the hold, Pisces's lips pressed with concern.

"I need him to get quiet and stay quiet." Caledonia made sure there could be no confusion about what needed to happen.

Pisces straightened her shoulders, forcing her breathing to remain even. "I said I'll take care of it. He's my responsibility."

"No, he's mine," Caledonia corrected her.

Inside the hold, the boy raged against himself. He banged against the floor, and his cries plunged into dreadful moans. Pisces's fist wouldn't be any kinder than Caledonia's, but it didn't matter who knocked him out, just that someone did.

"Make it fast," Caledonia said.

Pisces needed no more invitation than those words. She spun the hatch and was through the door in an instant, pulling it shut behind her. The boy's cries dimmed immediately, and after another moment, the hold was silent.

Sending Amina to rest, Caledonia returned topside where she sat high on the bow, a worn blanket wrapped around her shoulders against the cold, listening for any sign of pursuit. Every so often, the bow thrusters churned softly beneath her, keeping them in the centre of the canals. A gentle wind curled around the ship, and now that she had time to look, Caledonia saw the channels were lined with small trees, clinging to the crags and narrow shelves of rock.

Along the deck, her girls moved quietly through the night. The bell stayed silent. When it was time for a new watch to take over, the girls met briefly in the dark to confirm the transition.

Redtooth watched over the deck crew from her nest atop the mainmast block, her gun cradled across her knees, a thin

188

blanket for warmth. She was as tough as her past had made her. She never said much about it, but they knew she'd been rescued from the ship of a hard man by Captain Annee, who sailed under a single law: harm no women. Annee took the girl among her crew, and after her death, Redtooth had come to them looking for a new crew to serve and love. When it came to her girls, she made sure they all had what they needed even if that meant she went without. That included the captain. If Caledonia spent a sleepless night topside, Redtooth did, too.

The boy in the hold didn't make another sound. It was difficult to think about him now without thinking of Donnally and Ares. The bounty was real, he hadn't lied about that, so what were the chances he was lying about their brothers? For the first time, hope spun through Caledonia's heart unchecked, surprising her with the hot press of tears. Hard on its heels was the dread of knowing she'd just lost their best chance of saving them. But she still had this Bullet. If there was another way, she would make him reveal it.

And then there was Lir. For that brief second, she'd had him in her sights. If she closed her eyes, she could see it again: the nose of his ship burning with baleflowers, the dark tower of it climbing four levels into the sky. She would never forget its profile, and now that she'd seen it, she wanted nothing more than to make it burn. But Hesperus had called him a Fiveson. He would always sail with a small fleet around him like armour, insulated and protected from every threat.

But he lived. Lir was alive. And that meant one thing: she could kill him.

Caledonia's fingers strayed to the dagger in her belt. The metal of the blade was always warm, as though flush with the memory of her blood. One day, she would give it another memory to keep it warm.

Just before dawn, Pisces settled in next to Caledonia, two steaming cups of weakened teaco in her hands. The drink was a mix of whatever they had – coffee beans, chicory root, tea leaves – all brewed together and rarely the same from day to day. Today, it was worse than usual. Though Tin had managed to supplement their stores in Lower Cloudbreak, Far was already working to stretch their pantry. Without her knowing how long she'd need to do so, their fare would once again get thin and salty.

"He's sleeping," Pisces said.

It took Caledonia a moment to realize she was talking about the boy. It didn't matter to Caledonia if he slept, only that he wasn't shouting, but she nodded as if the information pleased her.

"I think he may be coming through the worst of it, though his pain is far from over."

This did please Caledonia. "Good," she said.

A soft, disappointed sigh eased from Pisces. "I know you hate them. But if you want to believe our brothers will be okay, that they can come back to who they were before Aric, then the same has to be true for this one."

It was all Caledonia could do not to argue. She remembered their brothers. Donnally was too kind, too generous to submit entirely to Aric's cruelty. Ares, she wasn't so sure of. As a boy, he'd been just as self-possessed as Pisces, but he nursed an anger that surfaced occasionally. When there wasn't enough – meat, bread, time – he would explode out of his child's body. At the time, it was directed at Aric's fleet, but he was just a boy, and Caledonia feared that his anger might have found an encouraging home among the Bullets.

Without the solid-states Amina needed to build her electro-mag, they might never find out. Their mission had gone from rescue to survival. But she couldn't bring herself to crush whatever hope Pisces still had of saving their brothers. She was having a hard enough time maintaining her own.

Sunlight landed, light as a bird, on the tips of the tall channel walls. In moments, they would have enough light to drive the ship faster. Caledonia sipped at her teaco, and her stomach growled in response.

"Hime says Doc Tricius gave you skintech as well as antibios." It was a piece of luck to find antibios, and a little bit of a miracle to find any kind of skintech outside of the Bullet fleet. She'd have to thank Clag if they ever found themselves in Cloudbreak again. "She thinks you'll be back in the water in no time. How does your shoulder feel?"

Another sigh. "A little better today."

"Good. Keep resting. Do whatever Lovely Hime tells you to, and nothing Red tells you."

That earned a laugh from Pisces. The girls climbed to their feet as the sun glided down the walls towards the ship. It was time to move, and her crew was already making preparations. The dead-watch girls shuffled belowdecks for a few hours of sleep while others emerged bright-eyed and ready for the day ahead. Weariness settled along Caledonia's limbs. As soon as Tin appeared, she'd follow the dead-watch crew and sleep.

"Captain!"

Every head turned to the woman now emerging from belowdecks. Far's voice was infrequently heard, and never at such a volume. It was always strange to see her outside the galley. She was a tall, broad-hipped woman with black hair that curled densely around her face and shoulders and skin as pale as quicklime.

"Stowaway!"

In front of her, held in the woman's iron grip, was the form of a small girl, struggling to keep on her feet. She twisted to face Caledonia. Her left cheek was decorated in a single raised spiral, and her hair was filled with colourful ties: Nettle.

CHAPTER EIGHTEEN

"I found her scavenging in the pantry." Far gave the girl a shove but didn't release her. "Like a rat."

Nettle didn't struggle, but she had the decency to appear guilty as she met Caledonia's eyes. She clutched a bag to her chest that was half as tall as she was, and though she was armed, she hadn't gone for her weapons.

Every bone in Caledonia's body ached for rest, her groaning stomach reminding her she'd had nothing except weak teaco, and she hadn't slept since their arrival in Cloudbreak. A stowaway was the last thing she wanted to deal with.

"I thought you were smarter than this, Nettle." Redtooth pulled the girl from Far and pushed her to her knees facing the captain.

"I know you said to wait, Captain Styx, but you said yourself you don't come to port often. I couldn't not take this chance." Nettle's words came in a hopeful rush. She looked from Caledonia to Redtooth to Pisces to the whole gathering crew. "You're all girls! You're *all* girls. Please keep me. Please, please keep me."

Caledonia considered the girl. She'd dropped them right in the court of the Sly King without warning. Had she known about his plan to claim the bounty? "You've already disobeyed me once. Why would I keep someone I can't trust to follow orders?"

"I disobeyed you to serve you," Nettle said. "And I've come bearing gifts."

She laid her bag on the ground and started tugging at the ties. With a laugh, Redtooth pulled the bag out of her reach. "You talk, I'll open."

"Batteries. Two of the solid-state lithiums you were after, and a box of string conductors. Not as powerful, but lightweight, and they hold their charge for ever as I understand it. Very valuable." As she spoke, Redtooth pulled each item from Nettle's meagre belongings. "Hesperus always takes more than he gives. But I know all his hiding places."

"You *stole* them? From the Sly King of Cloudbreak?" Pisces nearly shouted.

"I did." This time, Nettle didn't look guilty. She looked proud.

"So you brought us batteries and a new enemy, is that what you're saying?" There was a trembling anger in Pisces's voice. Caledonia understood her point. They had more than enough adversaries as it was, but they'd left Hesperus with a small treasure and hadn't damaged his port on their way out. She was willing to consider this part of their bargain, even if the means of trade was indirect.

"Someone get Amina up here," Caledonia called. To Nettle she said, "If these are as good as you say, I won't put you over for stealing aboard my ship without consent. But if they're not, you should count yourself lucky that we're still inside the channels."

Amina arrived a moment later, blinking sleep from her eyes. After a quick inspection of Nettle's gifts, she confirmed they were exactly what the girl had promised.

"Solid-states, fully charged," Amina said with a knowing look for the captain. "They'll do."

The crew was very aware that adding hands to help with the work also meant adding a mouth to feed. And there wasn't a girl among them who hadn't noticed the thinning of the soup. Keeping Nettle on board might breed resentment, but Caledonia wasn't in the business of abandoning girls. Especially not smart girls. Though it irritated her endlessly to be held hostage by Nettle's selfish desires, having solid-states meant Amina could build her weapon. This was exactly what they needed to resume their pursuit of the *Electra* and their brothers.

"She's more trouble than she's worth," Pisces said into Caledonia's ear.

Caledonia spoke just as softly. "No more than a Bullet."

Nettle raised her chin, projecting confidence. Her hair ties fluttered in the wind, and her dark eyes shone like the black scales of their sun sail. Her bravery was defiant but also calm. In spite of herself, Caledonia liked her.

"Amina says these are good, and that's the only thing saving your life right now," she said. "You'll stay aboard, live by our rules, but until you prove otherwise, you're worth less to us than the barnacles on our hull. One wrong move and we trade you for a goat next time we find shore. Clear?"

Nettle's mouth struggled against a smile. "Clear."

Before Caledonia could assign someone to orient the girl to her new position on the ship, Amina stepped up. "I'll show her to her bunk and her work. Anyone have issue with her, you have issue with me."

"Red, take Nettle's gifts to Hime for inventory. And Amina, make sure she gets to work right away. The waste drain-line should be a good place to start."

For the first time, Nettle's smile wavered in place. She knew exactly what that was, which meant not only did she know her way around a ship, but she knew exactly how bad this particular job smelled. Fifty-two girls were a lot to clean up after.

"Consider it done, Captain," Nettle said with less enthusiasm than she'd shown just a moment before.

A few of the girls cheered, the ones who'd been on drain duty. If Nettle did well and finished the work on her own, she might gain a few easy allies.

"Amina will tell me when she thinks you've earned your place." Caledonia walked towards the young girl and stopped a foot away, testing her resolve. "I expect it will take a while."

Nettle stood with her back straight and her eyes up.

Undeterred by Caledonia's nearness. "You won't be disappointed, Captain Styx. I'm here to help."

Caledonia spared a pointed look for Amina before leaving the deck. They weren't fifty-two any more. Between the boy in their hold and this clever girl, they were fifty-four. She tried to fix the number in her mind as she descended one level and took a meandering path to her quarters.

There was still so much to do. They were travelling south instead of north, the repairs in their stern were patchy and needed more attention than they could give while under way, but she could feel her energy draining through the soles of her feet, puddling on the ground behind her as she walked. Food would be good, but by the time Caledonia finished a round of level two, she was all but dead on her feet. Her path ended at her chamber doors, and there was nothing, not even this piercing hunger, that could pull her away to the galley.

It didn't matter. Inside her cabin, she found a plate of food waiting for her – a thin slice of bread, a scoop of something green, and a small wedge of seed brick. Only a few bites in all, but they were bites she didn't have to work for. She would have to thank Far for her thoughtfulness later. For now, she needed rest.

She stripped, showered and forced herself to stand upright while she scrubbed her teeth before hitting her bed. She fell asleep with her mind casting a line in their wake.

Somewhere behind them, the *Bale Blossom* sat amid dark waters, awaiting the return of its ships. Caledonia's mind lingered there, trying to conjure an image of what Lir must look like now, but over and over again all that surfaced was the boy from four years ago: the boy with a sun-stained nose and one ear that stuck out a little too far, who had smiled softly as he drove his knife into her belly.

There was no doubt in her mind that running had been the right choice. They'd been outnumbered, pinned in port, and a fight would have cost them all very dearly, but here in the dark of her cabin she let her disappointment burn. It was a wound in her gut that would never heal.

CHAPTER NINETEEN

C aledonia felt as though she'd slept for days when she finally peeled herself out of bed. Sounds of the ship in full swing filtered through the hallways. The rumble beneath her feet told her the ship sailed sure and steady.

She opened her cabin door to find Nettle leaning against the opposite wall, a plate of food in her hands. She perked up immediately, sloshing hot teaco over her hands and cursing as she regained balance.

"Captain. Good morning. Well, afternoon. Sun's been going for a long while."

Caledonia reached for the mug first, giving herself a good long sip while Nettle clearly tried not to squirm. "Nettle. What are you doing here?"

Nettle held the plate out in response. "Lunch. Well, it's sort of dinner now. Amina told me to sit right here until you stirred and then make sure you put something in your belly. So, I sat right here and when I heard you moving, I ran down to the galley. Far says she'll only accept an empty plate in return."

Small as it was, the meal was still larger than it should have been for a single portion, but there wasn't a girl on the ship brave enough to send food *back* to Far. Caledonia wolfed it down and sent the empty off with Nettle.

By the time she made it topside, the sun was sliding west and the end of the canals was in sight. Ahead, the seas were wide, with no towering walls to squeeze their skies, no perilously shallow channels lurking beneath. Behind them, the waters were empty and silent; no Bullet ships trailed in their wake. In no time, the *Mors Navis* would be cutting through open waters, and Caledonia breathed deeply of the salt-fresh air. For the moment, they were free and clear.

Tin came forward with a ship's report. Her spiked brown hair had been scrubbed, and she looked well-rested and alert as she began to run down the list.

"And, finally, vitals," Tin said, coming to the end of her reporting. "If we keep to this rationing, we've got stock to hold us for five days. I recommend reducing speed and dropping nets for a while."

Five days. On seas that were entirely foreign to them, five days was far from comfortable. But Tin's recommendation was a good one. "Bring us to a stop before we leave the cliffs. We'll need the cover if we're going to have any luck with the nets. Dispatch the bow boats to scout for signs of trouble. We can spare an hour, maybe two, but then we need to move."

The ship slowed, and a team got to work unrolling the

fishing nets and readying them for the water. Caledonia found the rest of the Mary sisters stringing lines and hanging laundry beneath the sun sail with a song on their lips. Redtooth had a small group of girls spread across the bow, their guns in pieces, their fingers shiny with oil as they scrubbed the powder from their barrels.

She found Amina and Hime on one side of the rear deck, legs draped over the starboard rail, feet knocking together in the wind. They peered down every so often at Nettle, now harnessed and dangling to repair some of the heavier bullet damage. They leaned towards each other, cradling the conversation of their hands with their bodies.

With so much activity on deck, the levels below were thinly populated. The cargo bay was quiet, as it should have been this time of day. But when Caledonia arrived, she found the door to the hold slightly ajar. She rushed across the room, afraid she'd find the hold empty, the Bullet missing and at large on her ship. But what she found instead was infinitely worse.

The boy was still there. Hands bound. His body curled tightly in the centre of the room like a shell. His brown skin was pale and shiny with sweat, his clothes soaked with the same, and sitting with his head cradled in her lap was Pisces.

She looked up when Caledonia entered. Their eyes locked. Pisces tensed but didn't get up. Instead, she looked defiant, defensive, all over this dissolving boy on the floor. On the ground sat an empty cup and a small teapot. A gentle breeze floated through the open porthole, loosening the stale clutch of air.

Seeming to sense something had changed in the room, the boy's eyelids fluttered open. He spotted Caledonia and froze.

"Out," said Caledonia.

Pisces pressed a hand to the boy's arm, then carefully slid her legs out from beneath him, gathered the cup and teapot from the floor, and stood. She moved without haste, as if to defy Caledonia with every step she took. It was a small rebellion, but one Caledonia wouldn't forget.

The boy's gaze darted to Pisces as she crossed the threshold. Caledonia didn't give her the opportunity to look back before pulling the door shut on her heels. It wouldn't lock from this side, but she didn't need security. She needed privacy.

She gave herself two slow breaths to calm her blood. She focused on the state of the room. Someone had brought him more than teaco over the past days. There was a thin blanket, a dirty plate and a carafe of fresh water.

Drenched and still shaking through his withdrawal, the boy forced his long body to uncurl. He sat up now, straining through his pains, and met her gaze with one more present than before. His brown eyes were ringed like the inside of an ancient tree. Surely the most notable thing about him.

"You survived." She leaned against the stacked bolts of canvas near the door, considering him with arms crossed.

He looked weak, but she would never underestimate a Bullet. She kept her hand near her gun.

"Some of me." His voice carried the sand of too little sleep and long-distant screams. He smiled dimly. "Feels like there's still a little left."

"Bullets aren't made of much to begin with."

It was hard to tell if the sound he made was a groan or a laugh. "We're made of the same stuff as you. It just gets distorted."

"Distorted? You press children into service, slaughter families by the score, and you call that a distortion?" Caledonia felt her anger gaining quick ground over her sense. She'd come here for information, not a fight.

The boy shivered where he sat. "It's the only word I have for what happens to us."

Us. Them. The group that now included her brother. Suddenly, it was Pisces's voice in her head, telling her that if she wanted to believe their brothers had survived, she had to believe this boy might have, too. But this boy was nothing like her brother.

"You know, you might have survived if we'd dropped you in the shallows. You were beyond his reach. But you stayed on my ship. You knew there was a bounty on it and you stayed."

"I'm not made for just surviving."

It was almost laughable coming from the boy sweating his way through an illness second in intensity only to the Pale Fire. "What are you made for, then?"

Now he smiled, grim and stubborn. "Fighting back."

A glimmer of the boy he must have once been was tucked into the corner of that smile, and for a brief second, Caledonia pitied what he'd gone through to become a Bullet.

"How many ships accompany *Electra*?" she asked.

"None."

"I don't believe you."

He nodded as though he'd been expecting this. "*Electra* sails alone. Her hull is her greatest defence, and the Northwater is so sparsely populated they never have to worry about attack. But beyond that, she sails alone to demonstrate Aric's perfect control of the region. It's as much a mind game as it is conscription." When he finished, he closed his mouth and watched her. Shivers occasionally stirred his shoulders, but his eyes remained firm. Caledonia turned this new information over in her head.

"There's something else," he said after a minute. "Something you need to know."

Caledonia's eyes narrowed. "Every time you volunteer information, I trust you less."

His jaw clenched around what might have been a grimace or a smile. "I'll wait, then."

It was the first thing he'd said that teased a smile onto Caledonia's lips. At least he wasn't delusional.

The boy caught sight of her smile, and his whole body stilled. His eyes lingered on her mouth, his own lips curling so faintly she almost missed it. It occurred to her then that this boy wasn't dissolving, he was consolidating; as the Silt left his blood, he was rediscovering his edges. Soon, he would rediscover his strength. And looking at him now, Caledonia realized that strength would be considerable. His frame was dense with muscle, and his moves against Redtooth had been enough to show just how agile and competent he was in a fight. It was even possible he'd been holding back. Struggling just enough to buy time without hurting anyone.

"I will convince you to trust me," he said at last.

Caledonia laughed, harsh and only once. "The day I trust a Bullet to do more than die is the day the sea turns to stone."

This time he didn't speak. Caledonia had more questions. She needed to know when the optimal time to strike the *Electra* was, and she needed ship schematics and to know where their brothers were likely to be located. But she'd bent her trust as far as it was willing to go for one day.

CHAPTER TWENTY

It was early dinner hours, and the galley was a flood of noise. As Caledonia approached, she heard shouts and laughter and teasing. It was always hot in here by midday, with the stoves fired up and plenty of bodies to raise the temperature. At the moment, the heat was a perfect match for Caledonia's mood.

In the centre of the room, the rounded post of their mainmast took up a wide circumference of space. On either side were the kitchen and room for tables and chairs, which were stored and secured whenever they weren't in use. In rough seas, a loose chair was almost as dangerous as a gun.

She found Pisces seated at a table near the door. She wasn't eating. She was waiting. When she spotted Caledonia, she stood and moved to join her.

Caledonia strode past, knowing her friend would follow. This was not the place for the conversation Caledonia intended to have.

Neither girl said a word until they were safely inside Caledonia's quarters, the door shut firmly behind them.

"Cala—" Pisces began, but Caledonia cut her off.

"What do you think you're doing with him?"

Pisces crossed her arms. "Helping him. Helping us."

"You had his head in your lap." Anger trembled in Caledonia's voice. "That's not helping him."

"He's sick. We needed him quiet. You said to keep him quiet."

"Yes! By using your fist, not singing him a lullaby!"

"That's not what I was doing, Cala."

Caledonia waited, fists punched against her hips, lips pinched shut.

Pisces sighed with her whole body. "I got a tincture of nightcast from Doc Tricius. I've been giving him a few doses a day to ease his symptoms, help him sleep."

Nightcast was not difficult to come by, but they had none on the ship. While not as addictive as Silt, it put the recipient in a heavy sleep. It could knock out a person of any size, suffering all manner of pain. It wasn't only dangerous, it was expensive. And Pisces had taken it upon herself to purchase some for the comfort of a Bullet.

Caledonia's lips fell into a steep frown. It was Pisces's gentle heart she'd put at risk by allowing that boy to remain on board. No matter what he promised them, she should have trusted her first instinct. She should have thrown him over.

But she hadn't, and now they needed him.

"Bullets are poison. That Bullet is a poison."

"His name is Oran," Pisces said, biting at Caledonia's attempt to keep him a faceless captive. "And he's not poison, he's a boy. I know you want to convince yourself that they're all the same – drugged, violent, evil – but I'm not willing to believe it's true. Oran saved my life. He's human. With a mind and heart. Maybe he's done terrible things, but I don't believe he's a terrible person."

"Of course he's done terrible things! And will again. This is why I didn't want him on board in the first place. We have rules for a reason – they keep us safe from exactly this kind of insidious deception. No. Bullets."

"Until we find our brothers."

"What?"

"No Bullets, until we find our brothers."

The words knocked against Caledonia's lungs. "They – they're our brothers," she stammered.

"And they're Bullets." Pisces spoke firmly, her words brushed with pain. "Someone did this to them. Someone turned them into the thing we fight against. And if I could find the ones responsible, I'd let that little seed of anger they planted inside me four years ago turn me into something even more terrible than them. I'd make them pay." Her fingers closed into trembling fists, and she exhaled slowly. "But that's never going to happen. What is going to happen is we're going to get our brothers back. And that rule is going to change, so we might as well start now. With Oran."

Oran. She hated knowing his name. She hated the way

Pisces said his name. She hated that where she saw only danger, Pisces saw hope. Most of all, she hated that she was going to have to hurt her sister in order to keep her safe. "You are not to see him. Don't visit him again. Don't look at him again. Understand?"

"I understand." Pisces's voice was cool as the ocean water. "I understand that you're afraid. You've always been afraid. It's your deep dark secret, and you judge the people around you based on what *you're* afraid of. Well, this may be surprising, but we're just as smart as you, Caledonia. We're as brave as you, and you have to trust us to act like it."

The words were like a sharp wind that left Caledonia gasping. Pisces didn't know that Caledonia was responsible for the death of their families and their brother's capture, but she knew Caledonia.

"I do trust you. I just don't trust the world. That's why we have rules. The rules keep us safe." And if she'd believed her mother when she'd said the same thing, she'd have prevented the slaughter of all the families aboard the *Ghost*. Rhona had known better, and now she did, too.

Frustration showed on Pisces's face. "I don't think you do trust us. Not the way we trust you. If you did, you'd know I'm not letting myself be deceived by Oran."

Silence settled between them. It felt like the air had gone brittle and was ready to snap in half. Caledonia knew she should tell Pisces that she trusted her. She should go further than that and prove her trust by encouraging Pisces to visit the boy in their hold, but her mouth sealed itself around the knowledge that he was dangerous. Her skin burned at the memory of Lir's fingers brushing along her jaw and into her hair. That single moment of intimacy had destroyed so much, and Pisces had held this boy's head in her lap. He would lure Pisces into thinking he was better than he could possibly be. He would convince her to help him. And then he'd hurt her. Maybe the whole crew. All the girls they had fought so hard to keep alive. When that happened, that seed of anger Pisces spoke of would explode. It would destroy her.

"Well," Pisces said at last, sadness evident in the dip of her chin. "Someone should tend to him. The faster he gets through this, the more use he'll be to us."

The room felt much smaller than it already was, yet it seemed that Pisces was miles away. The two had fought often over the years, sometimes furiously, but they always came back together. This would be no different, Caledonia was sure. She *was* sure. But it was strange to realize that as much as she trusted their friendship would survive, she didn't trust Pisces as much as she meant to. If she did, she'd tell her about Lir and the *Bale Blossom*. She'd tell her about what really happened that night on the beach, about what she was responsible for.

But if Pisces knew the truth, she might leave Caledonia for ever. And that was a risk Caledonia couldn't take. At least, not yet.

A pounding on the door startled them both.

Caledonia had barely shouted for the girl to enter when Nettle appeared, breathing hard and sweating. In the next moment, the engines roared to life.

"Captain." Her tone carried the hard edge of battle. With her next word she confirmed it. "Gulls."

CHAPTER TWENTY-ONE

On deck, the scene was dramatically changed from just a few hours earlier. The bow was cleared of guns and girls, no lines of laundry hung below the sun sail, and a team of a dozen girls was quickly folding away the fishing nets and making the ship ready for high speeds. Anything that could fly loose from its riggings was tied down or strapped into place.

"There," Nettle said, pointing to figures running high on the cliffs, now racing by as the ship gained speed. "The bow boats spotted them."

The *Mors Navis* raced into open waters, leaving the shelter of the canals. Breaking away from the southern tips of the Rock Isles were more than a dozen surface craft, only large enough for a single person to ride. They shot off the lower cliffs, landing with so much force they dived beneath the surface and disappeared from sight for long moments. When they reappeared, they flew several feet into the air before hitting the water and zipping forward. Each rider wore a blue lung, enabling them to stay under for as long as they needed. It was this ability to dive and resurface that earned them their name: Gulls.

They were pirates in the oldest sense of the word. Scavenging and looting their way across the seas. Knowledge of a bounty on the *Mors Navis* would certainly have piqued their interest, but they'd take any ship that crossed their path, even a Bullet ship if they thought they could get away clean.

Until now, Caledonia had only encountered them in stories. It was the sort of tale you heard in port from men slush-mouthed and thick in their cups, the sort a few of her girls told in constricted, traumatized tones.

"Masts up! Knots high!" Caledonia called, racing towards the bridge where she could see fore and aft.

The mast blocks snapped open. Soon the posts were up, and Amina's team of Knots were climbing high with rifles slung over their shoulders. On deck, Redtooth scattered her crew on all sides, setting up two-girl teams to shield and shoot.

Pisces stuck with Caledonia, eyes tracking the approaching vessels.

Thirteen Gulls raced south. Their arms and torsos were wrapped in segmented armour, polished to reflect the sun into the eyes of their prey. Their faces were obscured by masks covering their eyes and nose and holding the respirator of the blue lung in place. They were eerily quiet, the only sound the chorus of their individual engines. They fanned out, leaving long tails in their wake.

"Captain." Amina came up behind her. "The two just there."

She pointed towards the centre of the flock. Caledonia followed her line, her eyes landing on two Gulls dragging small trailers behind them.

"Hull breakers." Pisces moved forward with small, stunned steps. "Big ones."

Amina clenched her jaw and raised her eyes to the sky, swearing beneath her breath.

"Put me in the water," Pisces said, rolling her shoulder and doing her best not to wince. "I can plant stasis mines in our wake and get out before they close in."

Stasis mines would float at a depth of ten feet and ignite when a Gull passed within their range. It would require many mines for no guaranteed return. And the more the Gulls spread out, the harder they would be to pick off.

"No, we need them to close in. Pi, stay out of the water. Amina, as soon as they're in range, you and your Knots target the bombers. We're going to reduce speed and let them come."

The girls' hands met briefly between them, squeezing tight, then all three moved at once. Amina ran towards the main deck. Pisces raised her voice, telling everyone to prepare to take fire. And Caledonia ducked onto the bridge to give the order to reduce propulsion.

The distance between the Gulls and the ship began to shrink; the space between each of the Gulls widened.

Caledonia kept her eyes on the hull breakers, densely packed shrapnel bombs with enough power to puncture the hull several times over. The devices were too heavy to launch through the air, and so the Gulls would get as close as possible before slingshotting them across the top of the water towards the *Mors Navis*. Caledonia would have to lure the hull breakers close enough that her Knots could do their best work and take out the Gulls dragging them.

For a few seconds, the only sound was the whip of water against the hull, the happy purr of her engines, the seabirds overhead. Then the air split around a scatter of gunfire. One Gull fell from his vessel into the ocean, dead by a single, perfectly placed bullet from a Knot high on the mainmast. Before another shot could be fired, a horn sounded, and one at a time the Gulls dipped below the water until none were left.

Caledonia's gut sank with them. She'd underestimated their tech. Allowed the gap between them to diminish. And now they were out of sight.

"Oh, hell. Eyes sharp, girls, eyes sharp!" Redtooth raced down the line, scanning the water for any sign of where they'd gone.

Behind them, the ocean frothed white with their own wake. It was impossible to determine which bit of chop might point to a Gull some distance beneath the surface.

"Engines to full!" Caledonia called.

At the helm, Tin worked with a steady hand, responding

to the captain's commands but not quite anticipating them, creating a gap in the rhythm.

Caledonia turned her eyes forward. The sea was a wide, unknowable plane. They could only drive south and hope they were faster than the Gulls below.

Every girl on board was tense, their eyes and guns trained on the invisible enemy. With each moment that passed, the tension grew, thickening in the air like dough.

Then, finally, a cry from a girl posted on the port side of the aft deck. It was followed by a quick rattle of gunfire. Caledonia spotted the pops of water several yards away. Some short distance beneath the surface, silver flashed in the sun as it travelled towards the ship.

Her girls concentrated their fire on that spot, and suddenly the water exploded, surging upward with the dangerous force of a destroyed hull breaker bomb. It was followed by the sound of metal snapping against metal. The girls hit the deck, pressing their bodies tight to the gritty surface as shrapnel flew overhead.

It was over in a second. Redtooth's voice carried them all to their feet. "No damage!" And Caledonia knew they'd gotten lucky in more ways than one. Not only had they hit one of the hull breakers, but it had been far enough beneath the surface that the shrapnel was all but useless.

She had no time to enjoy the victory. Gulls shot from the water on all sides of the *Mors Navis*. One bobbed to the surface, pierced by shrapnel that glittered terribly in the sunlight, dripping blood and oil into the clear blue sea. Oil. It snagged Caledonia's attention. They didn't use sun tech. Their range would be limited.

Three down. That left ten, one of which carried a second hull breaker. Caledonia counted the Gulls now pacing them on either side. Nine. And no hull breaker in sight. She would have to drive them up.

"Hard to starboard!" she called.

The girls latched their harnesses to whatever was nearest as the bridge crew complied. With no more warning than Caledonia's command, the ship pivoted sharply. The hull bit into the water, swivelling in a tight semicircle and driving a violent wave forward as they changed directions.

No matter how agile the Gull's vessels were, if any were lurking beneath the *Mors Navis* during that, they'd be tumbling like a shell.

Those on the surface, however, skirted the resulting wake and regrouped faster than Caledonia had hoped was possible. Her crew fired relentlessly. The Gulls stayed just shy of full range, which meant they were spending ammo for nothing more than a comfortable lead. Eventually they'd run out of both.

One of Amina's spider nets would be more than a little useful right now. Caledonia tried not to let her mind linger on the charges they'd failed to get from Hesperus. They'd need all of Nettle's stolen charges to take on the *Electra*. Not even one could be spared.

Caledonia turned and found herself face-to-face with Lovely Hime. The girl had divested herself of her apron and strapped a gun belt around her waist. Her long braid rippled down her back in the wind, leaving the lower part of her scarred ear and jaw uncharacteristically exposed.

Protest was instinct when it came to Hime. But something about the look in her eyes stayed Caledonia's objection.

Hime lifted her hands. *They're driving us. Herding us towards the tall grass flats.*

Caledonia recalled the area of Hesperus's map directly south of the Rock Isles covered in hash marks for no discernible reason. Tall grasses would gum up their system and pull them to a dead halt. If the Gulls wanted them stationary, that was an excellent way to ensure it happened.

Behind them, the Gulls rode in a V formation, and now Caledonia noted how they were holding their pace. Sunlight gleamed sharply off their metal plates, their masks menacing and cold, and they hung back just far enough to apply pressure, hemming her in on the port side and pushing gently west. They were doing exactly as Hime said, and Caledonia had missed it.

Caledonia let the scenarios unspool in her mind. If they kept this course, they risked finding themselves mired in the tall grass waters. If they pushed east, the Gulls would resume their attack, applying pressure until she ran out of ammo and relented. They could survive the onslaught, but the threat of the hull breaker was too much to ignore.

She needed to draw them into a fight.

"Get belowdecks and stay there. Amina! Knots low! Retract the masts!" Caledonia raced towards the bridge, taking the stairs two at a time. "Reduce propulsion. We're going to pull them in close, spin the ship, and swat them away. Ready on thrusters," Caledonia continued. "We need them synchronized. Ready, Tin?"

"Aye, Captain." Tin's hands fidgeted on the wheel, dancing away and back as though it were uncomfortable to hold.

"Good. Adjust heading four degrees port, then slow it down and wait for hard spin on my mark."

The ship began to slow, and shouts of "Hard spin! Hard spin, girls! Latch in!" were tossed down the line. Caledonia stood just outside the bridge where she could keep her eyes on the Gulls. As they realized the *Mors Navis* was pushing east, they adjusted course and, one by one, slipped beneath the surface.

When she was sure the Gulls had caught up to them, she gave the order for maximum acceleration. And as the *Mors Navis* drove through the waves, Gulls shot out of the water on all sides. Their guns were ready, and they fired mercilessly as they flew through the air.

Without the Knots to shoot from above, it was up to the girls on deck to return fire. They rotated shields and gave as good as they got.

Caledonia watched the scene. Her girls were vulnerable on the deck, taking fire from above and below. It was impossible to defend against. In their midst, she spotted Hime, guns raised, teeth gritted, the blue ribbon in her hair catching the sunlight for a split second. There was a voice in Caledonia's mind screaming to protect them, to change course and find another way. But she'd made this decision because there was no other way.

She waited. Watching for her opening. The Gulls wove around the stern of the ship, never crossing the midsection, never trying to get in front of her. Then, there was the moment Caledonia was waiting for: the Gulls clustered on their port side, the one dragging the hull breaker now visible beneath the chop. If they did this right, they could take out all ten with the body of the ship itself.

"Now!"

The ship began to nose into a wide arc. Not the hard spin she'd planned.

Caledonia could see the moment unravelling around her. On the bridge, Tin was at the helm, panic in her eyes as she tried and failed to bring the ship into a spin. Just as she feared the plan was done, Tin slipped from view. The thrusters roared, and the boat spun.

Caledonia could do nothing but hold on as the entire ship rotated like a top on the water's surface. Fast, much faster than she'd expected it to be. Her stomach lurched against her backbone and stayed there.

The moment felt longer than it must have been. By the time they stopped, the sea frothed in all directions, and

Caledonia heard the sounds of crew members coughing or vomiting over the sides.

But they'd done precisely what they'd meant to. The remaining Gulls had been helpless in the face of so much spinning metal. Their vessels were spread across a quarter mile of ocean in all directions, their riders flailing between them. It would take them time to recover, and by then, the *Mors Navis* would be too far to chase. Somehow, they'd done it. Someone had.

Caledonia unlatched herself, ready to commend whoever had saved the manoeuvre. But the bridge was silent, stunned. To one side, Tin slumped against the open windows, drawing in deep breaths of fresh air. Behind her, the bridge crew adjusted thrusters in anticipation of a new course. And at the wheel, with her hands planted firmly against the brass, was none other than Nettle.

CHAPTER TWENTY-TWO

When they'd put a comfortable amount of distance between the *Mors Navis* and the Gulls, the command crew retreated to the map room.

Nettle now sat in the seat Oran had occupied four days before. The girl kept her hands in her lap, her chin up and eyes wide. A strategy, perhaps, for a young girl who'd made an art of appearing more vulnerable than she was, of slipping through crowds and out of minds as quickly as she appeared in them.

To one side of the girl, Redtooth stood with her back to the wall, almost but not quite out of Nettle's peripheral vision. Hime sat at the table, hands resting lightly on top. Across the room, Pisces leaned a hip against the map table, her fingers tangled in the chain around her neck. Amina was the last inside, and she pulled the door shut behind her.

"Why were you on the bridge?" Caledonia stood across from Nettle, hands braced against the table.

Nettle's eyes skated nervously around the room before she answered. She knew she was trapped, and for the first time, fear slid across her eyes. "I'm better at the helm than I am with a gun, and I thought you might need the help."

"Did I ask for your help?" Caledonia asked, even though everyone in the room knew the answer. Her point was in the following question. "Did I give you an order?"

Nettle gulped. "Yes, Captain."

"And what was that order?"

"To do as Amina instructed."

"And did you follow that order?" The girl had done good work, but only by dismissing the rules of the ship. Caledonia could not let that go unexamined.

Nettle looked to Amina. Her shoulders straightened, and she sat up. "Captain, I did." Caledonia opened her mouth to call out the lie, but before she could speak, Nettle pressed her advantage. "Amina told me that every action I took should serve you and the crew. I saw the execution of your order failing, and I stepped in to make sure you succeeded." She paused, looking from Caledonia to Amina and back. "For the good of the crew. We act together or not at all, right? That's rule number two? Well, I acted with you."

Redtooth's brow furrowed sharply, and she shifted on her feet as she frequently did when working through a puzzle. Across the room, Pisces's expression remained unreadable, though Caledonia felt certain she knew her friend's opinion on the matter.

"For the good of the crew," Caledonia repeated. "And what made you think you could do what my bridge crew couldn't?"

Nettle's bravado faded a little. "I've done it before. I told you, I'm better at the helm than I am with a gun." Her sincerity was tinged with a sadness Caledonia recognized and didn't want to touch.

"You will stay off my bridge until I put you there, or I'll put you over."

Amina took a step forward. Not towards the girl, but towards Caledonia.

"I'll serve you well anywhere you put me, Captain," Nettle said, tentative yet daring. With a glance towards Amina, she added, "But I'll serve you best as a member of your bridge crew."

Caledonia let that sit in the room for a second before dismissing the girl. "Out."

Nettle didn't wait for a second invitation. She pushed her chair back with a heavy scrape and hurried across the room, where Amina held the door open for her.

"We need a new heading." Caledonia turned her attention to the map when the girl was gone and the door shut again. She would deal with Nettle after they had a new course.

"She did good, Captain," Amina said.

"She can't follow orders."

"We need a crew that can take initiative when the moment calls for it," Amina pressed.

"We also need a crew who can do as they're told. Even when, and especially when, they disagree with me."

"Don't forget, her obstinacy is the only reason I have

224

what I need to make an electro-mag strong enough to disrupt *Electra*'s hull." It was unusual for Amina to argue in favour of anyone outside her small team of Knots. A fact that escaped no one's notice. "Her skill is undeniable."

"I don't disagree on that count." Irritation stirred in Caledonia's chest. "Say what you mean, Amina."

"I only say what I mean, Captain."

"Then make your point!"

"We need you to do your job! You've left Tin at the helm for long enough, and she's done a good job, but we need someone who can do the best job." And suddenly Lace was in each of their minds. Startlingly present.

Caledonia bit down on that same strange blend of loss and irritation. Lace had hardly needed to hear an order before she was completing it, had been sound and capable at the helm, and Caledonia hadn't realized just how much losing her had shaken her until this moment.

"I know," she said simply. "We need a new heading."

For a moment, sadness wrapped them together in the familiar silence of loss. Replacing Lace at the helm wasn't the same as replacing her in their hearts, but it felt just as terrible. Still, it had to be done and the only person who could do it was Caledonia.

The girls drew in around the table. Pisces pulled Hesperus's map from its cylinder and spread it out, weighing down each of the four corners with smooth stones. None of their other maps contained much detail of the seas south or west of the Rock Isles. Further west and north than where they now sailed, Lace's map marked the Perpetual Storm, where the skies were known to be violent and dangerous, but they'd never come this far to know for sure.

Caledonia had a dim memory of sailing waters in search of a way out of the Bullet Seas. The waves rushed from all sides, the seas biting at the hull. The sky grew suddenly dark, as though the sun had set in the middle of the day. Pisces's mother had gathered the children and rushed them belowdecks, where they strapped in to keep from being heaved from one side of the room to the other. It had seemed to last for days, which couldn't be true. However long it was, Rhona had reversed course and taken them safely south again, to the Bone Mouth.

They had never returned. Any notes or maps Rhona might have kept about the event had been destroyed in the attack, and there had never been a need to travel further than the Rock Isles. Until now.

Hesperus's map centred on the canals, but the waters around it were charted for at least a hundred miles. Even if there was a chance it couldn't be trusted, it contained more information, in more detail, than anything else in their collection.

The girls studied it in silence. Amina marked where they were with a small black stone. The waters east of their location would be dense with Bullets, while directly west the tall grasses stretched towards the Perpetual Storm. Directly north were the Rock Isles they'd just left, and south was the wrong direction entirely. If it were possible to sail a straight line through the Rock Isles, they'd reach the Northwater in only a week's time. As it was, two options lay before them: they could cut due west, pushing through the grass flats and risking their propulsion system in the process, or they could return north, risking another encounter with the Gulls, and from there skirt the western edge of the Rock Isles.

"According to the Bullet—"

"According to Oran," Pisces cut in. "His name is Oran." She lifted her chin, daring Caledonia to argue.

"We have two weeks to reach the Northwater and intercept *Electra* to save our brothers. We know there's a small fleet after us in the east, which leaves west and north. So." Caledonia looked up, ready for suggestions.

"Gulls or grass. No good options," Redtooth remarked with irritation. "It'd be nice to have some good options for a change."

"I'm inclined to take the grass over Gulls," Caledonia admitted. "We've been running hard, and grass will slow us down, but we're unlikely to encounter any more Bullets that way, and we know how to manage grass."

Hime held her nose close to the map, her finger tracing a section of land that skirted the southern bend of the tall grasses, as if looking for a hint of deceit from the mapmaker.

Pisces leaned in. "I think we should return north. We can run slow and quiet and cut west as soon as possible."

Caledonia studied her friend, unable to determine if this was a real suggestion or another attempt to argue. "If we end up in another fight, we could deplete our ammunition," she countered. "And we don't have much to spare."

"Those Gulls will think twice before coming after us again." Pisces's tone was uncharacteristically cool. "And grass is risky."

"We've sailed through grass before."

Pisces nodded. "But we don't know how far the flats go. We've never sailed these waters, and the Gulls were herding us in that direction for a reason."

"The map shows that they thin here." Caledonia took a steadying breath and pressed a finger to a spot on the map where the hash marks were obviously further apart.

"You really want to trust Hesperus? The man who tried to turn us over for the bounty? How is that any better than trusting a Bullet who saved my life?" Pisces argued.

"I'll trust a crooked merchant over a dirty Bullet in a heartbeat," Caledonia fired back.

Pisces eyes widened; she was losing patience just as quickly as Caledonia. "Based on everything we know, the fastest, most reliable way to the northern currents is to move north and cut west as soon as possible."

"It might be fast, but it could be a minefield. We don't know how many crews like the Gulls hang close to the Rock Isles, and I don't want to find out. We've been fighting for days. The crew needs a break."

"What about food?" Pisces pressed. "Far says we have five days, but we all know what that means. It'll be five days until all we've got left is water. If we go north, towards the Rock Isles, we can at least send the bow boats to forage on the coast. There's no promise of food if we go west."

"There's never a promise of food, Pi!"

This wasn't the familiar terrain of their disagreements, the place where Pisces challenged Caledonia to ensure her plans were sound. Instead, there was fear and frustration between them. They both wanted the same thing: to save their brothers. They were about as far from that goal as they could possibly be. They had no notion of how they would board the *Electra* when they found her. And the wrong choice now might mean losing Donnally and Ares for ever.

Hime straightened and raised her hands decisively. She pointed, drawing all their attention to the same spot on the map she'd been inspecting. *These are the Drowning Lands. Dangerous sailing, but many settlements where we can trade for food.*

"Are you sure?" Amina asked. "The grasses are still an issue."

The captain is right, they're thinner here. Passable, if we do it right.

They'd all heard of the Drowning Lands, a long stretch of marshy lands tucked away in the south. They were rumoured to be inhabited, but the people were all but ghosts. Ships that entered the Drowning Lands were never seen again.

The location was only speculation, but Hime seemed certain.

"How do you know?" Caledonia asked.

Hime faltered, her hands fluttering momentarily. *I've been here before. Long ago.*

"Long ago?" Caledonia rounded on the gentle girl, frustration brimming over. "You knew exactly what those Gulls were up to, now you say you know the location of the Drowning Lands, and I'd like to know how."

Before Hime could answer, Amina's voice crashed down like a yardarm. "Captain," she warned. "She just told you she's been here before."

Caledonia held her ground. "She also told me she'd stay belowdecks, but that didn't stop her from taking up arms today."

I've told you. I can fight. I want to fight. Hime's cheeks flushed as she spoke, her hands moving decisively. *You protect me too much.*

"You have always needed our protection!" Caledonia nearly shouted.

But I never asked for it!

Amina turned fully to the captain, eyes dangerous. "If she says she's ready to fight, I believe her. You should, too."

"She broke the rules, and this entire crew saw her do it!"

"Caledonia!" Pisces shouted.

The breath caught in Caledonia's throat. Her small world was spinning too fast.

"You need to remember that we are not your enemy.

We are your crew. We're loyal and we will serve you until the end, but that doesn't mean we'll be blindly obedient." Pisces's hand clenched into a fist.

"I'm not asking you to be obedient. I'm only asking that you follow the rules. To follow me."

Hime and Amina glanced at each other. Redtooth took a step back.

"The rules don't keep us safe, Caledonia. We keep one another safe. If you'd trust us to do that, we wouldn't need rules at all."

Heat tightened around Caledonia's neck. Pisces had never challenged her so directly in front of the command crew. And never would have if not for that damn Bullet in their hold. Her small rebellion had turned into something so much more, encouraging Amina and even Hime to act against her orders. It was like sand shifting beneath her feet.

"We need to pick a route." She pressed her eyes shut for a moment, then resettled them on the map. Grass was trouble, but less trouble than another gunfight. And the possibility of trade for food was stronger than a chance to forage.

"We go west." Caledonia gave the order with as much conviction as she could muster.

Pisces gave her a hard look. The wall between them grew thicker in that instant. Then she turned and, without another word, left the room.

CHAPTER TWENTY-THREE

Caledonia stood alone on the wing of the bridge as the *Mors Navis* approached the tall grass flats.

They'd decided to wait until morning to navigate the grassy seas, and it had been a long night for the captain. She tossed in her bunk, hot even though a fresh breeze moved through the cabin. She played through her argument with Amina, but her mind stagnated on the memory of Pisces and her accusations. She couldn't shake them and couldn't pinpoint the place where she'd gone wrong. When she eventually slept, her dreams were haunted by a girl whose face flashed between Lace's wind-chapped cheeks and Nettle's curling scars. She dreamed of drowning in seas thickly corded with grass and kelp, surrounded by one of Donnally's sweet songs.

By the time the sun spilled over the horizon, she'd been covered in a thin film of sweat and her hair was a nest around her neck. She'd washed and wrestled her wet hair into a braid so tight it hurt.

The crew was quiet this morning. They moved through

their duties without the usual banter that accompanied the rising sun. They may not have been in the room yesterday, but they knew their command crew was uneasy, and it cast a pall over the entire ship.

The *Mors Navis* was anchored in place and floated without propulsion or thrusters, giving Caledonia time to study the way ahead. While the map gave her a good sense of where to go, finding the specific path was up to her. The longer she looked over the water, the more determined she was to prove she could take them through it. Rhona would have done it without a second thought.

There were no swirls or eddies to suggest large rocks, but there were variations in the surface that spoke to what lay beneath. Most of the water was covered in little ripples, sharp and small with no sense of depth. This was where the grasses were the thickest and most likely to gum up their systems. At a glance, it encompassed the water for miles around. But Caledonia had been watching, letting the water reveal itself, and she'd found a path where the water rose and fell in small waves. That was where the grass was thin, and that was where the *Mors Navis* would pass.

Something brushed lightly against her arm, and she turned to find Lovely Hime standing with her on the wing. Her braid was tied with one of her bright blue ribbons and pulled forward again, hiding the scars once more. The morning light splashed against the glossy, black strands and shone through her wide oval eyes. She was like a beautifully banded agate, thin layers pressed together in a crescendo of colour, but only ever knowable from one inadequate angle.

When they'd brought her aboard, before any of them had learned to speak her language and before she was capable of communicating at all, they'd been struck by the loveliness of her. Even sweating through her withdrawal, raging against demons no one could see except for her, she was lovely. And that was what they'd called her. Little Lovely.

It was only a few weeks before they learned her loveliness ran as deep as the ocean. By that time, the name was a part of the crew. The only difference was that they'd learned her real name, too.

"Good morning," Caledonia said with her voice and her hands.

Hime smiled, licked her lips and raised her hands. *I'm sorry.* Two words, and Caledonia was cast into the press of emotions she'd worked all night to lock away. A captain needed to care, but even more than that, she needed to keep her mind free of caring too much. Hime had a right to fight, and Caledonia had a right to stop her.

"I understand that you want to fight. But that didn't go well for Red the first time, and we need you safe, Hime." Caledonia's sign was slower than her words, but when it was just the two of them, she didn't mind. "You are the best healing hand we have. We need you when the fighting is over."

234

I am not as fragile as you think. Hime pressed her lips tight together. Her fingers clenched, and she took a moment to ready herself before she spoke again. *Do you ever think about going somewhere else?*

The sudden change of topic stunned Caledonia enough that she said the first thing that came to her mind: "You mean beyond the Net? No."

Every girl on this ship had thought about it from time to time. Caledonia would be lying if she said she never had, but the terrible truth was that nothing brought her peace like the thought of driving Aric's fleet beneath the waves. Like the thought of driving her dagger into Lir's heart.

And, now, like the thought of bringing her brother home to fight at her side.

Hime's expression tightened. Her eyes travelled over the water, and Caledonia had the very clear sense that she'd misunderstood the girl. Hime raised her hands. *Pisces is right. These grasses are trouble. It's very rare that anyone gets through them.*

There were many things from Hime's time among Aric's fleet that Caledonia had chosen not to ask about. No one on this ship needed any more information than Hime was willing to share. As a Scythe, she'd been kept on the barges, her task to tend the bale blossoms from seedling to harvest and transform them into Silt. It was also her job to test every batch. Her addiction was no small beast.

If Hime knew something of these waters from her time

as a Scythe, it was worth listening to, though she'd been so thoroughly drugged that it was hard to know if the information was entirely trustworthy.

"Did you sail these waters on your barge?"

Hime looked out over the rippling waters, her gaze travelling further than she could possibly see. She raised her hands. *Yes. Once. We – we didn't make it.*

Barges were much larger than the *Mors Navis*, their hulls just as shallow, but they used propellers rather than propulsion that relied on pulling water through the ship at high speeds. It was enough of a difference for Caledonia.

"We will," she said, eyes still cast ahead. "Is there anything else I need to know?"

Hime paused. Nodded. *You read the water like it's a book. If anyone can get through, it's you.*

Caledonia smiled and called to her deck crew, "Weigh anchor!"

Overhead, the air was peppered with seabirds scooping low over the grass-infested waters to catch fish trapped near the surface. To the north, the Rock Isles had been swallowed by the horizon. The air was warm, the sun climbing, and Caledonia listened to the rhythmic clink of the rising anchor with a sense of confidence in the task ahead. She would take them through these waters, and they'd be that much closer to finding their brothers.

When she returned to the bridge, Tin was at the helm, her bridge crew secure in their stations, and there was Pisces coming off the companionway ladder and heading towards her. Caledonia braced for another argument.

"Ready when you are, Captain." Pisces gave a nod. All traces of their previous argument were gone. Tucked away and stored while they stood in front of the eyes of the crew. "I have fifteen girls down in propulsion. We're with you."

A smile threatened, but Caledonia fought through it. "Engines on full. We're going to gain as much momentum as possible, then kill the engines and coast. Tin, nose two degrees starboard. We're aiming for the water with the most chop."

The *Mors Navis* climbed quickly to speed, driving faster and faster until they were nearly upon the tall grass flats. Caledonia moved out onto the command deck where her view of the water was clear, waiting as long as possible before giving the order to cut the engines. They powered down, and the ship slid neatly into the slim bend of water that looked like a path.

Suddenly, a hissing noise filled the air. On either side of the ship, long grasses brushed the hull, bending over to drape themselves along the length of the ship. There was no space between the blades; they obscured the water completely. It was as if the sea had transformed into a silky, green fabric that now embraced the ship.

The loss of inertia was so immediate that the force of it tugged at Caledonia's body. On open seas with the current at their back, the momentum they'd gathered would have kept them going for a mile. But here, the grasses kissed their speed away, dragging them down like the mermaids of legend.

Caledonia kept her eyes on the barely there slice of water before them and saw that it narrowed. "Engines to minimum," she said, and when they'd used up the available space, she gave the order to drift again.

They continued in this way for several hours. Moving in and out of speed whenever the grass thinned enough to warrant it. Pisces sent runners back and forth to the bridge with updates. Her team was working as fast as they could to clear the grass now threading their system. They climbed into the narrow outtake valves and hacked at the fibrous stalks, which they could only do safely when the engines were down. It took time, but they were finding their rhythm, moving forward little by little. It was slow, steady progress, and Caledonia was starting to breathe a little easier.

Until the path ahead disappeared entirely. Before them, the grasses braided together in thick cords, lying on top of the ocean as though there were nothing beneath it.

Caledonia searched for a way through the green. The path she'd chosen had taken them further south than she'd hoped to go. So far that she could see the beginnings of a swampy shore reaching towards them. They were surely the first ruffling skirts of the Drowning Lands. There was no path to shore, and the surface of the water was flat as glass as far ahead as the eye could see.

"Captain." A runner appeared in the doorway. "Pisces says we need to power down."

She shook her head. "We can't. Tell her to keep the girls out of the valves until I give the word."

The girl hesitated, then ran off to carry the message belowdecks.

The only chance they had was to power up and hope their momentum carried them across the slick grass. "Engines to full. We need all the speed we can get."

Her crew complied. The ship rumbled and with less agility than usual began to pick up speed. Grasses hissed against the metal hull, dragging and slapping in displeasure, when suddenly the ship bucked and the rumble of the engine vanished.

Caledonia cursed. The ship drifted, slowing until they stopped altogether. If they tried to spin the engines up again, they'd pull even more of the thick grass into the propulsion system. They could send up the masts, rig the sails. But the breeze that rippled over the water wasn't the sort that would budge the ship.

They were stuck. And until they could clear the engines or a firm wind drove in, they'd stay that way.

Caledonia cursed again. Even now the *Electra* was probably preparing for her journey along the Northwater conscription routes. Every single moment was precious.

She drew a deep breath. Blood. Gunpowder. Salt. They could work through this. She just needed to be patient.

Before she could convene her command crew, a cry: "Ships! Port bow!"

There, six vessels raced across the grass-infested waters in boats that seemed to barely touch the surface. The crafts were flat, with large fans whirring behind a steering console, and on each stood several figures. They poured out from between long reeds and scrub plants, clinging to the swampy shore. Behind them, five more vessels appeared, and behind those were another seven. Eighteen vessels in all.

Immediately, her crew reached for their weapons, training sights on the approaching vessels. Steely and ready to fight.

The air hummed as the small fleet approached the *Mors Navis*. Each vessel held at least four figures, some more, but none less. They outnumbered Caledonia's crew nearly two to one. They were armed, and not lightly.

One vessel pulled away from the group, aiming for the bow with guns up. A shower of gunfire scattered across the nose of the *Mors Navis*. None hit the ship, but the point was made. They had firepower, numbers and mobility. Without propulsion, Caledonia only had firepower.

"Hands up, girls," Caledonia called with bitterness in her voice.

"Captain." Redtooth came to her side, a fight bristling in her voice. "We still have the advantage of height. We can at least thin the herd."

"They're not Bullets. And those were warning shots.

240

We may be able to talk our way out of this."

As they watched, the swarm of boats multiplied yet again, even more sliding away from shore. They circled, guns pointed at the deck, but not a single shot fired. The soldiers, men and women, trained their guns expertly and wore plates of blackened metal not unlike the armour of the Gulls. It was the presence of the women that gave Caledonia hope. Women standing shoulder to shoulder with men. They might survive this yet.

"Surrender with peace and we will do no harm!" It was a woman's voice. Strong, firm, demanding.

"I am Caledonia Styx, and this is my crew! We will do no harm and surrender!"

In response, two hooks appeared over the rail, trailing a rope ladder. It pulled taut under the weight of someone beginning to climb.

Panic was ready to bloom in Caledonia's chest.

Redtooth was the first to greet the newcomer as she topped the rail. She stood too close, forcing the woman to carefully straddle the railing unless she wanted to collide with Redtooth's chest. The woman ducked her head, hiding a smile as she gripped the rail with strong hands and swung one leg over without hitting Redtooth.

She was the soft taupe of an oak tree, with arms corded like thick ropes. Her armour was plated across her chest and banded around her shoulders, each piece curved to meet her body. Her hair was pulled back from the temples in twists, clasped with metal beads in steely grey and black and the pearlescent colour of an oyster shell. The woman met Redtooth eye to eye, and now that she stood on the deck, she crossed into Redtooth's space and didn't back down.

"Push back, girl," the woman said, her voice dipping to show Redtooth exactly what she thought of her youth.

"Red," Caledonia warned, though she would have liked to see Redtooth knock the woman back a few paces. She stepped between Redtooth and the woman. "We can offer you coin in exchange for aid." She spoke as though negotiation were expected. As though these people didn't have the obvious advantage.

The woman's smile withered, all humour draining away. "You know that's not how this will go, Caledonia Styx. This is the Drowning Lands, and you and your crew will disembark peacefully."

"Or?"

"What has given you the impression that you have an alternative choice?"

"Captain." Amina's urgent whisper was in her ear. "Tugs. And welders."

On the water, the mud-runner boats were making room for the tugs. The crews tucked in close around the base of the hull, attaching lines fore and aft. And before another word was spoken between Caledonia and the woman, sparks flew as the welders got to work.

They were taking the *Mors Navis* apart.

CHAPTER TWENTY-FOUR

Caledonia had lost this ship once. Every single decision she'd made in the four years since had been designed to keep it running. She'd imagined if she ever lost it again, it would be the same day she lost her life. She'd imagined it would be bloody, the *Mors Navis* in flames and her crew lost. Nothing like the unsettling peace of this moment.

"This ship is worth far more than its metal." Caledonia could barely think past the hiss of fire against her hull.

But the woman was unmoved. "Not to a Scavenger. You can make your case to the queen."

A twist of dread and fury tangled in Caledonia's throat. She was helpless. The ship was braided into the ocean, immobile and useless. And the entire crew had lowered their weapons. The only option before them was surrender.

"We'll go peacefully." Caledonia's lips felt numb as she spoke.

The woman before her shouted an order, and dozens of grip hooks appeared over the railing in response. From each dangled a rope ladder like the one she'd used. "I'm Ceepa."

She gestured to her own ladder. "After you, Captain."

It was all Caledonia could do to put one foot in front of the other and descend the ladder. On deck, her crew was thoroughly subdued, their expressions just as stunned as she felt. As her hand left the cool metal of her hull, she tried not to think that it was for the last time. Distantly, she registered how quickly her crew was funnelled down the rope ladders and loaded onto mud-runners. She spotted Amina and Hime nestled together; Nettle's multicoloured ribbons caught her eye; Redtooth growled as she was directed to a boat apart from Caledonia. But she caught no sign of Pisces.

There was always a chance that Pisces had heard the commotion and hurried her team into the valves to avoid detection. Or perhaps she'd taken the blue lung and her tow and submerged. Whatever the reason, Caledonia hoped that her friend hadn't been harmed.

Ceepa climbed into the mud-runner with Caledonia, and with a nod of her head, the soldier at the tiller revved the engine. A humid wind embraced them as they rushed away from the ocean. It carried with it a smell of rotting wood and sunbaked mud. Water gave way to muddy terrain which gave way again to water so rapidly Caledonia couldn't track it. The boats travelled seamlessly from one to the other, startling long-legged birds and round frogs.

After several miles, the first real trees appeared. They were scraggly, with knobby spines protruding from the water around them. Puffs of evergreen needles dripped from thin branches, allowing room for the sun to spill between them. They were not the glossy-leaved trees that sheltered the islands of the Bone Mouth, and Caledonia doubted they carried any fruit on their pale branches.

She was peering between the jagged-looking trunks when she saw a building. It was a squat wooden shack elevated above the water on stilts with a canoe tethered beneath. Once she'd spotted it, she noticed several others like it. There were dozens of the little houses, each raised on stilts and squatting high over the water. In the doorway of one stood a small child wearing a green smock that hung heavy to her knees, watching them pass as though the sight before her were a common occurrence. She raised her hand to wave, oblivious of the distress that brought them here.

Soon they arrived at a building much larger than any of the others. It was round and capped by a sloping roof trimmed in solar lanterns and surrounded by a wide, wrapping porch. From the front, a staircase led directly down to the water and on one side a ramp arched like a bow. Caledonia's craft was the first to skid up the ramp, the vessel travelling less seamlessly over the rough tracks than it had over the swamplands.

At the top, they were met by four guards. While one relieved Caledonia of her gun, another bound her hands. She didn't struggle. If their captors wanted them dead, they could have killed them back at the ship. And if they were meant to be prisoners, they'd have taken her blades in addition to her gun. They'd brought Caledonia and her crew into their home, which meant they wanted something from them. She just wasn't sure what.

Caledonia was paraded down the porch to the front of the building, where she was visible to the rest of her approaching crew. The message was clear: should anyone struggle, their captain would be the first to pay the price.

One by one, her crew was unloaded and bound. Caledonia tried to count, but once her captors were satisfied that all her crew had seen her, they directed her through the front doors of the building and into a wide hall with vaulted ceilings. Though the walls were constructed of thick wooden planks, each contained a vein of polished metal snaking through the beams like little rivers. It made the room wink and glimmer like it was surrounded by stars.

At the far end stood a throne. Like the walls, its thin wooden reeds were braided through with bands of silver, with feet that curved away from the base like the roots of a great tree. Upon it sat a woman. Her hands rested on either arm, and her chin was raised just enough to be intimidating. Long robes of purple and grey pooled around her feet, and her wrists were banded in the same polished silver that decorated the room. She was surrounded by men and women on all sides, their attention turned towards the girls now being driven across the room.

When they were still some distance from the throne, Ceepa pulled Caledonia to a halt, stepping in front of her and kneeling. "My queen, we bring you a crew of fifty-four. They have sacrificed their ship in the grass flats and surrendered without a struggle. None were injured. We lost nothing in the taking."

The queen turned her head to survey her catch, solar lights reflecting off the elaborate earrings that dripped along the full length of her ears. Her curly black hair was braided away from her temples in a manner similar to Ceepa's, except the queen's hair was twisted around cords of metal. It gave the impression of a crown.

"The water provides," the queen said at last.

The room repeated the phrase, and Ceepa rose to her feet.

The queen stood. Her skin was a pale satin brown, her eyes a cool grey, and though she wasn't tall, her presence was towering. Everyone in the room arranged themselves so that they stood apart from her, as though her regality created a palpable perimeter around her.

"My queen," Ceepa said. "This is Caledonia Styx. She leads this crew."

The queen took a few steps forward, her gaze steady on Caledonia. It was a little like being approached by a towering wave, ready to submerge you.

"Caledonia Styx." It was more a statement than a greeting. The queen moved on, passing down the line of girls. "You are in the Drowning Lands. Your ship is no longer your own, but your lives remain yours to direct."

She continued to walk down the line as she spoke, casting her calm gaze from girl to girl. Some of them met her eyes, others looked away. She didn't seem to prefer one response over the other but, like a wave, moved on at a steady pace.

"You are not our prisoners. The water has brought you to us, and you will always have a place among the Scavengers. But you are also free to go."

"In what ship?" Caledonia's voice sounded harsh after the smooth tenor of the queen.

The queen didn't bother to turn around when she answered. "No ship. If you choose to leave, you leave by your own means."

"On foot. Through the Drowning Lands?" Caledonia tried to keep her fury contained. "That's a dying choice."

The queen turned this time, not to face Caledonia but to move to the centre of the room. "It is a challenging choice, just as this is a challenging world."

Now Caledonia understood how they had maintained secrecy for so long. Once a ship had been taken in by Scavengers, its crew became Scavengers, and the room was filled with evidence of their undertakings. The fabrics of their clothing were tightly woven and missing the rips, patches and odd seams that prevailed among her crew. Even the walls were ornamented with items that surely didn't come from these swampy lands – long tapestries and segmented maps and even paintings and photographs of the old worlds. These people weren't warriors or merchants. They were collectors.

"You've captured more than just my ship and my crew." Caledonia stepped forward, setting herself apart from her crew as the queen had done from her own people. "Aric Athair has put a bounty on our heads. There's an entire fleet of Bullet ships after us. If you hold us here, you're making yourselves a target."

At the mention of the Bullet fleet, a ripple passed through the men and women still standing to either side of the throne. The queen, however, gave no reaction.

"Then we are doing you a great favour," she said. For the first time, her lips broke the plane of her face and edged a smile towards her grey eyes. "There will soon be no ship left for them to track, and once you have chosen your place among my people, we will protect you. From any threat." She stepped back. "Now, we must have decisions from each of you. Who will say first: stay or go?"

Panic was a shock in Caledonia's lungs. She needed her ship. She needed her crew. Donnally's life depended on it. Ares's life depended on it. Staying here was not an option. But neither was wading through the Drowning Lands with no boat, no guns, nothing but the clothing on their backs. Why would her crew choose to follow her when all she had to offer them was a potentially fatal slog through the swamp?

Suddenly, Hime broke away from the crew, racing towards the throne. Amina was there in an instant. "Hime!" she called, but Hime didn't stop.

The room was in motion. Ceepa's grip came down hard

on Caledonia's shoulder. Four guards converged on the queen, while two more made for Hime, and Redtooth darted after Amina.

Hime was lifted from her feet and hauled back towards the centre of the room. She didn't struggle, but she raised her hands, signing a single word: *Mother.*

"Hime?" A woman in a soft brown blouse and black trousers stepped forward. She was short and slender in the way of willow reeds, with strength evident in the curve of her arms and legs. Her hair, tied in a long braid, was a glossy black, threaded with copious strands of grey. "Hime, is that really you?"

The guard holding Hime in his grasp placed her gently on the ground as the woman moved forward.

The closer she came, the more Caledonia saw it. The skin as pale as sparrow feathers, the eyes dark and ringed with grey and brown, the uncompromising beauty in the slope of her mouth.

In the next moment, the woman confirmed it. She took Hime's hands in her own and, speaking softly through the fall of her tears, said, "My daughter. You've come home."

CHAPTER TWENTY-FIVE

There was a tangible shift in the room. The air itself seemed to hush as the woman hurriedly unbound Hime's hands and pulled the girl into her arms. Hime collapsed into her.

Daughter. The woman had called Hime her daughter. It was the kind of story no one told. When children were separated from their parents, they never found them again. It wasn't a safe thing to hope for. Something Caledonia had never allowed herself to yearn for. Yet it had happened. Right in front of their eyes. Every person in the room understood that this was as close to a miracle as they would ever witness.

Finally, the queen stepped forward and placed a hand lightly on the woman's shoulder. In response, the woman released her hold on Hime, reluctantly prising herself away.

Gaining control of her tears, she lifted her hands and began to sign. She asked what had happened to Hime and where she'd been for so many years. Hime's answers were long, her hands unsteady and mostly blocked from Caledonia's view.

"My queen," the woman said when Hime's hands came to a rest. "This is Hime. My Hime. The water has returned my daughter to us."

"Your daughter was taken several years ago, before she entered her maturity." The queen studied Hime's face, assessing with that same unbreakable calm. "Sera, are you certain?"

"I could not be any more certain, my queen. She says it was as we feared, she was taken by Aric Athair's fleet along with her brother. Her father – my husband – was killed, his body given to the water."

Here, the room paused, and together they lifted their hands to the level of their hearts, palms down as though resting on the surface of the ocean, and slowly pushed them downward with a soft exhale.

A fresh wash of tears appeared in Sera's eyes as she repeated the gesture. "She was taken into service, forced to work among the Bullets until this woman and her crew discovered her. She says they saved her when they did not have to."

Hime turned to the queen, her face paler than usual, but with a determined gleam in her eye Caledonia was only just beginning to realize had always been there. She lifted her hands. *I would not be alive if not for these girls. They fight against Aric Athair's reign and search for their missing family.*

To Caledonia's surprise, no one interpreted Hime's words for the queen. The woman listened, clearly understanding every sign. It struck Caledonia that nearly everyone in this room seemed to be comprehending Hime. This was a language they knew. Perhaps a language they all shared.

Hime continued. *Their fight is a good one. Please, help them.*

Beside Caledonia, Amina was a spear of energy, firmly planted in place but packed with power. Every bit of her attention was focused on the shape of Hime.

"My queen." A man stood out from the crowd. Tall and broad across the chest, with a brow that had been ploughed years ago and was now stuck in an expression of concern or disapproval. The lower half of his face was covered in a rusty beard that was twisted into ropes and decorated with fine metal beads.

"Jon," the queen said, giving approval.

"Accepting what the water has brought us is one thing. We will have their ship off the sea before anyone else can spot it," he said. "But giving aid to a crew the Father has already marked makes us vulnerable. It is not our way. We accept what is given and release what is taken."

Several others nodded their heads in agreement. They weren't afraid to make their opinions known, which suggested that while the queen was commanding, she also listened.

Sera spoke next. "It may not be our way, but why shouldn't we release what is needed in this case? When they have returned something so dear."

"Unintentionally," Jon continued, looking sour. "They have not brought you your daughter because they meant to, Sera. It is a welcome coincidence and no reason to make ourselves vulnerable."

"Aren't we always vulnerable?" Sera asked. "Keeping a marked crew is just as dangerous as aiding them."

"You're right." Jon crossed his arms across his chest. "We shouldn't do either. We should let them go as they are. Let the Drowning Lands decide their fate."

The crowd rumbled again. Caledonia was reminded sharply of those terrible moments in Cloudbreak, when Hesperus held her fate in his hands. But whereas he'd been seduced by the promise of the bounty and Aric's favour, these people seemed committed to avoiding both. Like Hesperus, they would make their decisions out of fear, and Caledonia had nothing left to bargain with.

An old woman shuffled to the front of the crowd. She was hunched, with tired eyes and silvered hair piled atop her head, yet her body was strong and it was clear her mind was sound. "Queen," she began.

The queen acknowledged this woman with more deference than she had for either Jon or Sera, bending her head slightly as she spoke her name: "Jules."

Jules continued, "We keep our peace with the Father because we have to, not because we want to. Sending this crew into the Drowning Lands is doing him a favour, one that puts blood on *our* hands. Perhaps the water has brought us this crew so that we might support those who resist him. Sending them on their way might be better for our community than keeping them."

Here, Caledonia saw her opening. She took one small step forward. "Queen," she said, mirroring the grandmother's speech. "This crew was built on the back of the water. We are brave and we are determined, and the sea calls us to fight where others cannot. Please, let us continue. I won't ask for your aid, but I will ask for release. And for our ship."

When the queen spoke, the entire room turned towards her, flowers seeking the sun. Even Caledonia felt the tug of her magnetism. "The water has brought us an opportunity. We have lost many of our children to the Bullet fleet over the years. The peace we hold with the Father rests on our labour. Our scavenged metals and ore expand his power and protect our families. But only so long as we stay hidden." She turned her gaze on Caledonia, and for the first time, it felt as though she spoke directly to her. "This crew is not hiding. They are fighting a war none of us started, and so instead of keeping them here, we will help them to do what we cannot."

It felt like a time to say thank you and also like a time to stay quiet. Caledonia chose a middle ground and nodded once to the queen.

The queen's gaze remained on Caledonia for a full breath before she continued. "We will give you our aid for the good you've done our daughter. We will repair your ship, supply what stores we can for your journey, and feed and house you while you remain in the Drowning Lands." Caledonia realized with a start that this still wasn't a negotiation. That the queen in no way viewed Caledonia as an equal. Even more startling was the revelation that Caledonia didn't think of herself as an equal. The queen had yet to raise her voice, and this entire room was riveted by her every word. It was a kind of power Caledonia associated with her mother, and the kind of power she wasn't sure she'd ever truly have.

Now the queen spoke for her court. "The crew of Caledonia Styx will be our guests until their ship is seaworthy again. All except for the boy."

The boy? Caledonia spun. Her eyes met Oran's.

"Bring him forward."

As the queen returned to her throne, one of the guards pushed Oran to the front of the crew. He looked better. His skin wasn't slicked with the sweat of illness and had regained the warm brown tone he'd had when Pisces first brought him aboard. He winced as the guard tugged on the bindings around his wrists.

"A Bullet," the queen said, marking the orange scars on his bicep. "Your prisoner?"

"Yes," Caledonia confirmed quickly.

"Good." The queen's voice was dispassionate and cool. "Kill him."

The guard gripped Oran's neck with a firm, meaty hand

and began to drive him from the room. Oran planted his feet, his body hardening for a fight.

"No!" Pisces was there in a beat. Once again throwing herself between that Bullet and death. "Caledonia!"

Irritation reared in Caledonia. At Pisces's passionate plea, at the Bullet for putting this tentative alliance at risk, and at herself for what she was going to do next.

"My queen," Caledonia began, layering deference into her voice. "He is a Bullet, and for that alone he deserves to die. But he's also the only hope we have of finding our family."

The queen said nothing. She raised a single, graceful hand, and the guard stopped pushing Oran forward. She waited for Caledonia to continue.

"Pi," she said, extending a hand. With a glance for Oran, Pisces crossed the room to Caledonia, braiding their fingers together. "We lost our brothers to the Bullet fleet four years ago. This boy has seen them. He knows where they sail. It's unfortunate, but we need him. His death would mean nothing to you, but a great deal to us."

The queen didn't deign to return her gaze to Oran. She stared into Caledonia for a long, uncomfortable moment. The room became a drop of silence.

"Very well," she said at last. "But while he is here, he will stay by your side. If he is discovered anywhere except in your immediate presence, he will die."

Caledonia heard a sigh emerge from Oran. She'd rather

have her toenails split and soaked in the salty ocean than spend time with him, but that, unfortunately, wasn't an option. She dipped her head for the queen and said words she only barely meant. "Thank you, my queen."

CHAPTER TWENTY-SIX

C aledonia tried not to think about the boy sitting in the canoe behind her, or the rope that was now tied around her waist, tethering him to her. The queen's command was even worse than it sounded. Not only was Caledonia to keep Oran by her side at all times, but she was to do it some distance from the village.

"They're poison," Ceepa said with a dark look for Oran. "You don't bring poison into the heart of your village."

Again, irritation swelled in Caledonia's chest. But she couldn't argue. She didn't exactly want his poison on her ship either. While her crew was released and loaded into canoes headed for the centre of the village, Caledonia and Oran were tethered together and pointed away from it.

The Scavenger village was broad if not dense. Beyond the main hall was a network of stilted houses just like the ones they'd seen before, only these were arranged in clusters. Three or four houses sat around a broad deck and were connected to one another by footbridges of rope and wooden slats. Most appeared to be family homes, but each was oriented around a larger, central building. Children of all ages raced across the bouncing bridges, their shouts and laughter unchecked as they chased and ran from place to place. The adults moved more carefully, their steps easy on the precarious bridges and ladders. They kept a steady pace on the water, gliding between the clusters but never beneath them. In a distant way, it reminded her of life aboard the *Ghost*.

"What happens to the people you capture?" Caledonia asked, marvelling at the size of the village. "After you've taken everything they hold dear?"

Ceepa didn't acknowledge Caledonia's dig. "Everyone shares equally in what the village produces. As long as you work."

"Ships like ours can't come by that often. What do you do while you wait?"

"We pull ore from the iron bog, then we smelt it down and trade it." Ceepa pointed south, where a thin curtain of smoke was just visible above the trees. "It's as honest as it gets."

The sun set faster here than it did on the seas, and soon the village filled with the cool blue-white glow of solar lanterns strung from every available perch. It was beautiful, like a field of stars hovering just above the water. It reminded Caledonia so suddenly of Donnally that the back of her throat squeezed. He would have called them the souls of the ancestors, hanging low to light the way for their loved ones.

Or he'd have said they were the hearts of trees, visible only to the people who lived here. Whatever the story, it would have been both unfathomable and magical.

It was almost full dark by the time Ceepa nudged their canoe beneath a stilted house. This one stood alone several yards from the nearest housing cluster.

"Someone will come by with food. There's a canoe there for you to use." Following the aim of Ceepa's gesture, Caledonia made out the shape of the little boat against a post across from where they floated. "Whenever you do come to the village, make sure you tether your beast." Ceepa spared another dispassionate glance for Oran, who wisely kept his eyes on his lap.

Caledonia didn't bother assuring her that Oran would stay firmly bound at all times. She stood, balancing as the little boat rocked sharply, and pulled herself onto the ladder.

The ladder extended upward, leading to a closed hatch in the wrap-around deck above them. Caledonia heaved herself up and waited while Oran awkwardly did the same with bound hands.

When they were through, Caledonia let the hatch fall back into place and gestured for Oran to precede her into the little house. He might be bound, but that was no reason to turn her back. He complied, instinctively searching for the light panel as soon as he entered. Blue-white light dusted the room, not enough to eradicate the darkness but enough to lift the heaviest shadows.

The space was divided into two rooms, one large and open with a chest in one corner and rows of hooks along the ceiling, the other containing something like a bathroom.

They found hammocks in the chest and together hung two from the ceiling hooks. The windows were open and lined with curtains of a finely woven netting to keep out the bugs, but even so the corners were littered with insect carcasses and clumpy spiderwebs. It was warm. The air clung to her skin and seemed to intrude on the fabric of Caledonia's clothing, making it feel dense and damp.

It was going to be an uncomfortable night in a strange place. And she was tethered to a boy she'd tried to kill. Twice.

Perhaps she'd make it three. For a brief second, she entertained the thought of finally putting him over the rail and letting him drown. Without his hands to tread water, he might survive for a little while, but eventually his legs would give out and he'd slip beneath the surface.

The thought didn't give Caledonia as much pleasure as she'd expected. It left an uncomfortable crook in its wake, a sea snake disturbing the flow of water. Ceepa was right to call him poison. There was something truly insidious about him. So insidious, Caledonia had stopped wishing for his immediate demise.

Oran stood four feet away. Just far enough that the tether drooped between them. No matter how they arranged themselves, it would pull taut between the hammocks, and there was the possibility that Oran would wait until Caledonia fell asleep and strangle her with the slack. She would have to undo the tether and bind him to the hammock.

She had no weapons to consider. She'd given her blades to Pisces for safekeeping, and Ceepa hadn't offered to return any of their guns. Though it left Caledonia feeling unbalanced, she could admit it was the better move. Both for the Scavengers, who, in spite of Hime, had very little reason to trust the girls, and for her current situation. If she were armed right now, she'd be removing bullets and securing knives in case Oran got creative. There could be nothing worse than being stabbed with your own blade. That was a fate she saved for Lir.

She gestured to one of the two hammocks hanging in the middle of the room and, when Oran was settled, lifted his hands above his head and secured them to the chain of the hammock. The skin around his bindings was red and raw in places. Painfully so. Caledonia tied her knots with a careful hand, jostling the wounds only a little in the process.

Oran watched her work, dark eyes strangely unyielding, supine body relaxed despite her ministrations. She waited for him to beg for her to loosen his bonds, or to promise he meant her no harm. But he didn't speak. He simply watched her.

When the knots were set, she settled into her hammock and an awkward silence. Now that she no longer had to acknowledge him, Caledonia leaned into the scoop of fabric and closed her eyes. There was no better way to demonstrate she didn't consider him a threat than to pretend she barely knew he was there.

But she couldn't have been more aware of him.

Every little creak of his hammock reminded her that he swayed a few short feet to her left. She could hear his breath well enough to know he inhaled through his nose and exhaled softly through his mouth. She thought she could even smell his sweat, though if she was being very honest with herself, there was a good chance it was her own.

At least her crew was somewhere comfortable and safe. At least her ship wasn't being torn apart. At least they still had time to get to the Northwater and save their brothers.

"Thank you."

Her eyes snapped open. She turned to find Oran still watching her. Had he been watching her this whole time? She scowled.

"For saving my life today. I know you didn't have to, and I'm grateful."

"I'm not concerned with your thanks. Or your gratitude." She thought she detected the hint of a smile on his mouth, and she wanted to hit it. Hard.

"You don't have to be." He shifted, finally turning his eyes away from her. "But you have it regardless."

"It's worthless," she snapped. "The gratitude of a Bullet. I didn't save you from the Scavengers because you deserved it. I saved you because you have intel I need. As soon as this is done, I'll turn you over to the first person who asks nicely."

His hammock creaked, but he said no more. A small but welcome breeze slithered through the windows, whispering against the netting and sipping at the stifling humidity. Outside, the night birds were beginning to sing in long, looping voices. Bugs clacked and chittered, and every so often there was the very distant sound of laughter or a door slamming. Missing from it all was the sound of water. It was an odd sensation, to know that she was on the water and yet so removed from the rocking of its arms.

Something bumped beneath them, and Caledonia shot to her feet.

"Food," Oran said calmly. "Ceepa said someone would come to deliver some food."

He was right, of course, but the fact irritated Caledonia as she hurried out to the deck and opened the hatch in time for a silver-haired woman to deftly swing her bundle onto the floor. She stayed on the ladder, showing no signs of wanting to come all the way up. With some surprise, Caledonia realized it was the grandmother from the court. Jules, who'd argued in their favour.

The woman shook her head slowly, small silver trinkets clinking in her hair. "So young. Up close, you're even younger than I realized."

In her head, Caledonia heard Amina's response to Clag in Cloudbreak. *Only in years.* It had only been a matter of

265

days since that moment, but she felt every one as if they stacked up on her shoulders. Nothing had gone well since that strange man directed them to Doc Tricius.

"Maybe too young." Caledonia surprised herself with her honesty, but it felt good to show this small corner of her worries to someone she wasn't responsible for. Maybe it was seeing Hime reunited with her mother. Maybe it was all the ways the queen made her think of her own mother. Whatever it was, suddenly, Caledonia didn't want this grandmother to leave.

"Young, but not a child." With one hand, Jules reached out to caress Caledonia's cheek. Her calloused fingers were rough and gentle at the same time, hardened by work and softened by age. "There are no children any more. Just babes and the rest of us. Remember, when they call you *girl*, they're trying to tell you something. They're trying to tell you that they're more than you, that the body you're in makes you less. But you know, and I know, that you're exactly what you need to be."

Caledonia put her hand on the paper-soft skin of the woman's arm. "Thank you."

"There's enough for the boy," Jules said with a grim smile. "But make sure you take the whale's share, love."

And then she was gone, leaving words that resounded like bells in Caledonia's mind. She sat there on the floor of the deck for a long moment after Jules left, letting those words burrow into her mind and take root.

Whatever Jules had left for them smelled divine. Caledonia's stomach roared, reminding her just how long it had been since she'd eaten. She scooped up the basket and took it inside, unpacking it on the floor some distance from Oran. There were several wooden boxes, each containing a steaming delight – a dark meat in thick gravy, white turnips on a bed of leafy vegetables so dark they looked black under these lights, and in the last a small loaf of fresh, buttery bread. Two bottles contained clear, drinkable water, and in a very small tin she found coarse salt.

Oran didn't even try to hide his hunger. He sat up at the only awkward angle his bindings allowed, braced his legs on the floor, and watched as Caledonia revealed each dish, his mouth slightly agape.

Her first thought was to deny him. Make him watch as she took her fill and his portion grew steadily smaller. But there was something about hunger, something about the hopeful way his eyes studied the steam. As empty as her belly was, his was surely worse.

With an internal groan, Caledonia got to her feet and untied the rope tethering him to the hammock.

"C'mon," she muttered. "You can't help me if you starve to death."

They sat with legs crossed around the arrangement of dishes. There were no utensils, so they ate with their hands, using the bread to scoop up every bit of the gravy. It was good. There was no question about that, but they ate too quickly to know if the turnips were more tender than the meat or if the greens were bitter.

Oran waited for Caledonia to take her fill of each dish before diving in. The bindings on his wrists did little to slow him down. He lifted the gravy dish to his face, licking the corners clean and acquiring a dab of gravy on the tip of his nose. Caledonia almost laughed as he hurried to wipe it away, embarrassed by the mess on his face, but somehow not the method of making that mess.

"I think the only thing I'll miss about the Bullet fleet is the food," Oran said, licking the last of the gravy from his fingers. "Aric is a demon and a bastard, but he knew what he was doing when he built his AgriFleet."

The bale barges were only one slice of that fleet. The rest supported a wide range of fruits and vegetables, ensuring the Bullets were healthy and strong, even while their minds dulled under the constant pressure of that drug.

"What about Silt? It's only been a few days, but they say the first days are the worst. Don't you want it again?"

Oran's expression darkened. "I will not miss the Silt," he said, as though convincing himself.

"You sure?" she asked. "I've never seen anyone break the habit as cleanly as you."

His body tensed. "This isn't my first time."

"What does that mean?" she asked.

Oran stood and moved to the window. He took a long draught of his water before answering. "Sometimes Silt is withheld. For a day, maybe two. It's a punishment."

"Seems counterproductive." Caledonia climbed to her feet, studying the Bullet from behind. "Why weaken your fleet like that?"

"Because it reminds them how much they need it and him," Oran answered quickly.

Caledonia shivered. "But a day or two isn't enough to break the habit," she pressed.

He nodded, keeping his face turned away. "Sometimes the punishment is worse."

She wanted to know more. She wanted to know why he'd been punished and whether or not Donnally had suffered in the same way, and without thinking, she leaned close to skim one of the three bands on his bicep with her fingertips.

He spun, snatching her wrist in his hand as though the touch had burned. His breath was hot on her mouth, their bodies inches apart. He looked boldly into her eyes. Angry and somehow also afraid. For just a second, it undid her. Then, just as quickly, he dropped her hand again and leaned away.

Caledonia's heart pounded. The place where he'd gripped her was hot, but he hadn't hurt her. He'd stopped himself on the precarious edge of violence.

She didn't speak, and neither did he.

They cleaned up, setting the empty tins outside on the deck. Oran offered his hands to be rebound to the chain, and Caledonia sank into her hammock feeling unsettled.

For a moment, the only sounds were of the night bugs and the breeze through the window. Then Oran's voice rumbled, "I'm sorry, Caledonia."

Caledonia turned her back to him and shut her eyes.

CHAPTER TWENTY-SEVEN

When Caledonia next saw the *Mors Navis*, it was moving past her window at daybreak.

She was up in an instant, peeling back the window netting to see her ship propped in a floating dry dock and moving more deeply into the Drowning Lands. She took note of every gash and seam. They couldn't always make solid repairs at sea, but they'd done their best. The *Mors Navis* was a tough ship, and Caledonia was relieved to see her all in one piece. The repair shouldn't take too long.

Oran was still asleep in his hammock, arms bound firmly above his head. In the grey light of dawn, he was drawn in softer strokes. Though the air had cooled to a pleasant temperature overnight, his forehead was covered in a thin layer of sweat and his brows were delicately furrowed. He looked almost gentle. Vulnerable to whatever gnarled demons Aric had left inside him.

Caledonia rubbed her wrist. Reminding herself what happened when she forgot how vicious those demons were.

"Get up." Caledonia made her voice loud and hard.

Chasing away his sleep and her flash of sympathy in the same breath. "It's time to go."

To his credit, Oran didn't ask a single question. He was up as soon as his hands were free and was ready to go only minutes later.

They nearly tripped over breakfast on their way. Someone had cleared their empty dinner dishes and replaced them with a bundle containing rolls, soft cheese and fresh berries. They paused long enough to cram cheese-stuffed rolls into their mouths, but took the berries and bottles of water with them.

She briefly considered positioning Oran in the front of the boat where she could keep him in her sights. It would remove opportunities for him to surprise her, but she didn't want to spend more time than necessary staring at his head, and putting him at her back was a stronger message. It said, *I'm not afraid of you. You are no threat to me.*

Early daylight filtered through the scatter of trees in rays of warm orange and cool yellow, bugs stitched the surface of the water together with little nips and tucks, and beneath darted minnows and fish. Canoes slid between the trees and stilts, ruffling the water as people went about their morning tasks. The Drowning Lands were awake, above and below.

Bound as he was, Oran added his strong strokes to hers, and they soon found their rhythm in the unfamiliar boat. At first, Caledonia offered directions, but after a short time Oran responded to the subtle shifts in her oar, adjusting his

272

own before she could give a command. There was something very calming about the work, the slow, steady rhythm of the oars, the music of water dripping from them. The air was fresh and cool, and though they were surrounded by the waking sounds of the village, it felt serene.

They arrived at the crew's cluster of stilted houses to find Ceepa and Pisces seated at an outdoor table chatting over steaming cups.

"Tea, Captain?" Ceepa offered as Caledonia drew near. "I have none for the Bullet."

Pisces didn't bother hiding her disapproval at the snub.

"Thank you." Caledonia accepted a mug of the fragrant drink, taking a seat near Ceepa. Oran stood as far from the table as the tether allowed, but it was more awkward knowing he lurked than having him close. Caledonia gestured to the seat next to her, and Oran took it.

"We've had a chance to assess the damage to your ship," Ceepa said. She was already dressed in plates of grey armour. Caledonia had the impression the woman was never without it. "She's taken quite a beating. Needs work."

Four encounters in the past ten days. But that ship had taken more than the sum of these skirmishes combined.

"I don't need her perfect, I need her capable." Caledonia didn't like the casual tone in Ceepa's voice. "How long will it take?"

"With your crew assisting? Nine days," Ceepa stated. "Maybe ten."

"Ten days?!" Caledonia was on her feet. "We don't have that kind of time."

If Oran's timeline was accurate, they had fourteen days to reach the Northwater ahead of the *Electra*. It would take four days under ideal conditions to sail from the Drowning Lands to the Northwater. More if they encountered trouble. Ten days for repairs would leave them scrambling. Their brothers might be gone before they reached the Northwater at all.

"She was sailing just fine when we left her," Pisces said smoothly, her gaze urging Caledonia to stay calm. "Propulsion was gummed up, but we could have had it cleared in a day. What did you do to her?"

Ceepa merely shrugged, rising from her seat. "Taking ships apart is what we do, friends. And we do it fast. Putting them back together takes us a bit longer."

The crew was beginning to awaken, emerging from houses on all sides of the deck in search of breakfast. Caledonia bit down on her irritation. In the distance, her crew grew louder, seeming to echo the rumble in her own chest.

"No one knows the *Mors Navis* like my crew. We'll cut that time down. A week is all we have to spare."

Oran cleared his throat. "Our timeline's actually a little shorter than you think. *Electra* will start her run with the waxing crescent moon. That's our timeline."

"What?" A familiar anger tinged Caledonia's response. "Why?"

274

"We do everything in alignment with the moon. The waxing crescent is a time of growth and potential. Perfect for gathering recruits."

She'd heard it before – Bullets were deeply superstitious and looked to the moon for signs and portents of things to come – but this was the first time she'd heard it in such detail.

"The waxing crescent is in twelve days," Pisces said with renewed alarm.

Twelve days. Not fourteen. Twelve. They had to get out of here.

Before she could say another word, the noise from the crew spiked. The rumbling rose in a sharp crescendo, and the girls danced into an excited circle across the deck. That's when the cheers began. It was a sign of one thing only: fight. While she was usually in favour of the girls blowing off steam, this was not the time or place for it. Oran followed as Caledonia strode across the deck and released a piercing whistle. "Heads high, girls!"

Immediately, her girls quieted, raising their heads and releasing the circle. In the centre stood two figures: Redtooth, which didn't surprise Caledonia at all, and Amina, which couldn't have surprised her more. Redtooth would fight with anyone, but Amina? Amina wasn't the brawling sort.

The two girls stepped apart. Amina, with her hands braced against her hips, eyes hard and pinned to the captain; Redtooth, with blood tracking down her chin and a pained look for Amina.

"Whatever it was, is it settled?" Caledonia asked. "Or do you need me to settle it for you?"

Amina's eyes cut away. Redtooth grumbled under her breath.

"Louder, Red," Caledonia ordered.

"I only said—" She paused to put another foot of distance between herself and Amina. "I thought Lovely Hime was going to stay with her mom."

Understanding washed over Caledonia, taking her anger with it. In its place was a quiet and sudden squeeze of apprehension. It had been an unspoken possibility since they landed here. Everyone knew they might be losing Hime. And in this moment, Caledonia feared there was no other possible outcome.

She saw that same fear humming through the girls still standing near, a chord in search of a song. These girls were so accustomed to the fight that if they went too long without, they'd find one. Being still for too long was no good for girls with the current in their blood.

"Ceepa!" She called to the woman leaning against a doorframe with a full view of the show. "My crew's ready to get to work!"

CHAPTER TWENTY-EIGHT

It took twenty-one canoes to transport the crew to the *Mors Navis*. By the time they had everyone there, the sun was high overhead, the air thickening with humidity.

At first glance, the ship looked much as it had when they left it, but closer inspection revealed significant damage to the forward hull. Ceepa had not exaggerated her people's destructive expertise.

While the crew boarded, Caledonia and Pisces surveyed the exterior of the ship. The dry dock was a marvel all on its own, two walls and a floor of rusted metal capable of lifting a ship completely out of the water and moving it long distances. The girls were able to walk right up to the lowest point of the *Mors Navis*'s hull and run their hands over the distressed seams.

Oran followed along behind, careful to never let the tether pull tight between them. Every time he moved, Caledonia was reminded of how aware of her he was. No matter what she did, he was prepared to move in some corresponding fashion. It wasn't obedience, she realized, it was perception. She must always be in the corner of his eye and the front of his mind.

"I think we can do it in six days," Pisces said, breaking into her thoughts. "We know these tools. If we work through the nights, our girls can get it done."

"Good." Caledonia swept her mind clear of Oran. "Get Lace to draw up the work teams. If the cabins aren't damaged, we can have rotations here and in the cabins in town."

"Tin," Pisces corrected her in a soft voice. "You mean Tin."

Caledonia's stomach pitched, and for just a second it was like losing Lace all over again. If Lace were here, she'd have run this operation without a hitch. But Lace wasn't here. They'd lost her. *She'd* lost her. And her crew still hadn't found its footing again.

Or maybe it was just that she hadn't.

"Of course. Tin," she said, nodding too quickly and forcing her mind to hurry past its grief. "We'll get Tin on the duty roster. I want one of our crew here at all times. The queen may have ordered her people to help, but there are at least some who don't agree with her. I don't want to give them any opportunity to take what's ours."

"Done," Pisces confirmed, eyes casting back towards the village.

"Any sign of Hime?" Caledonia asked. Perhaps it was the fight between Amina and Redtooth that made her think of it. Or perhaps it was the nagging fear that she was about to lose a second crew member.

"She was here last night. Briefly. But she left with her mother." Pisces paused, glancing up towards the deck at the sounds of their crew settling into their work. The ship began to rumble gently as some of its systems were tested. "It goes without saying, but Amina's not taking it very well."

"You think she'll stay?" Caledonia asked, though she felt like she already knew the answer. All she could remember were the moments Hime had expressed frustration with Caledonia, with her own role on the ship. At every turn, they'd held Hime back, kept her from the fight she so desperately wanted to join. Why would she stay with them when all Caledonia had done was tell her no?

Pisces looked pained for a moment, as if she were pondering the same thing. "I don't know," she said softly.

"I think she'll stay with you." Oran's voice surprised them both. They turned to find him leaning against the weathered hull, brown eyes flashing in the sun.

"Why?" Pisces asked, voice gentle.

"She was a Scythe," he said simply, apologetically. "The fight is part of her now."

"What does that mean?" Caledonia asked.

Oran's mouth dipped into a brief frown. "Kids who end up in the family of the Father go one of two ways – they either fight or they don't. If she wasn't a fighter, she'd have left you long ago. One way or another. But she's with you. She needs to fight almost as much as she needs anything else." He gestured to the long clutch of silvery trees, the still-surfaced water surrounding the dry dock. "She won't get that here."

Caledonia understood that he knew this because he was talking about himself as much as Hime. She didn't know if the sensation in her chest was a resigned kind of sadness or an unsettling sense of comfort.

She met his eyes and was surprised when her first thought was that they looked honest.

"Captain!" Redtooth appeared, standing in the gash at the front of the hull. She leaped to the ground with a firm smack of her boots. A long bruise was darkening along her pale jaw. Amina had not pulled her punches. "The hold's in good shape. You can dump that Bullet while we're here. So you don't have to cart him around with you."

"Or I can help." Oran stepped closer to the small group. "My hands work, and I'm pretty good with ships. A ship tech, actually."

Redtooth pushed a finger into his face. "Damn dirty Bullets don't touch my ship. Try it and I'll put you down." Then, as an afterthought, she added, "Unless the captain says otherwise."

"Believe me," Oran said with a grim smile for Redtooth. "I've felt the hammer of your fist. I'm not touching anything until you tell me to."

"We should let him help," Pisces said. "There's a lot of work to get done, and he's capable. I'll watch him."

"No." Caledonia's voice was decisive. "The queen's orders are clear. He's to stay tethered to me at all times. I'm not going to give them any excuse to think I've disobeyed, so he'll stay with me. Basic tasks only."

Pisces wasn't fast enough to hide her frown, but Redtooth gave the boy a satisfied glare.

He smiled in return, saying, "I might not be quite the hammer Redtooth is, but I'll do my best."

Redtooth leaned in to answer, "Don't feel too bad about it. The way you take a beating, you make one helluva nail."

CHAPTER TWENTY-NINE

The next days vanished between long hours of work and short hours of sleep. Tin put the crew through its paces, implementing a punishing duty rotation. Caledonia and Pisces took turns, ensuring one of them was always present on the ship, and Nettle was given the task of sounding alarms when it was time for the next shift to wake and return to work. By the end of the sixth day, the *Mors Navis* was in better shape than she'd been in years. They would be ready to leave in the morning.

Caledonia's cabin was a lot smaller with her command crew crammed inside, but they made do, taking down the hammocks to make more space. Oran sat in one corner of the room beneath the shadow of Redtooth, who loomed over him like a mast pole. Caledonia had released the tether again, more for her comfort than his. After days of working side by side, they'd found a strange sort of harmony that consisted mostly of Oran anticipating Caledonia's movements.

They'd taken Lace's map of the Bullet Seas from the *Mors*

Navis and spread it out between them. A small chunk of metal representing the *Mors Navis* was mired in the Drowning Lands.

"Starting tomorrow, we have six days," Caledonia said. "And from here, we're headed straight up through the Perpetual Storm." She tried to sound confident, but none of them knew what to expect in those waters. "Oran, show us the best point of interception once we reach the Northwater."

Oran was on his feet before she finished speaking. Taking a gnarled pencil from Amina's hand, he lightly laid out the Northwater conscription routes. They were as expected; the only difference was that Oran worked with a confident hand, marking each specific stop along the northern colonies with precision.

"Here," he said, marking the westernmost edge of the routes. "If we get there early enough, we'll have time to hide in one of these coves and catch them off guard."

"And what about *Electra* herself?"

Oran flipped to the schematic he'd been drafting every evening after returning from the *Mors Navis*. He'd located the coils that generated the electric field around the exterior of the ship and indicated the most strategic point of impact that would compromise the ship without tipping it over.

"I can't guarantee it, but your brother used to be assigned to the engines. Here," he said to Pisces. "And yours is more likely to be in the command tower somewhere," he said without raising his eyes to Caledonia.

They studied the schematic in silence. Placing Amina's electro-mag was easy in theory. As long as they got close enough, they'd disable the hull before the *Electra* knew they were under attack. It was the second part of this plan that was challenging: how to storm the ship without accidentally killing the brothers.

Every single plan the crew had ever executed was designed without a care for the lives of their enemies. Saving Bullet lives ran against every natural instinct they possessed.

"Never thought I'd be trying to figure out how *not* to kill Bullets," Redtooth grumbled.

"There has to be a way." Pisces studied the schematic feverishly, as if in looking away she would miss the moment it revealed the answer.

"There is." Every head snapped up at the sound of Oran's voice. "Send me in. I can get aboard without much trouble. Once I'm there, I can find your brothers and get them off ship." No one spoke, and Oran continued. "There's a good chance they won't have heard that I turned traitor, so they'll have no reason to suspect me."

"Bullets have radios," Amina said.

"Yes, but short-range only. And *Electra*'s hull makes even that a challenge. Her own electrical field gets in the way of communication."

"That's true," Amina confirmed. "And their radios are shorter range in the north because there are fewer towers. The colonists destroy them whenever they find them."

Amina spoke with the confidence of someone from the region. Aric had tried to subdue the Hands of the River in the same way he had the northern colonies, but the Braids were too winding and expansive to control.

"Send me in." Oran spoke again. "It's a low-risk plan."

He was right. They could send him in, let him bear all the heavy lifting. If he was discovered they'd have lost nothing. Unless this had been his plan all along. Gain their trust, learn their ship, and lure them into an elaborate trap.

"Drug rot," Redtooth said, getting close to peer into Oran's eyes. "Got his brain."

"Seems like a good idea to me." Amina turned back to her own plans, unconcerned with whatever fate awaited Oran. "It's no loss to us if they catch him."

"No loss to us? It's a suicide mission!" Pisces rounded on Caledonia. "Cala, you can't consider this. You know what they'll do to him."

"I'm considering everything." Caledonia took Pisces's hand in hers, naturally weaving their fingers together, trying to ignore the twinge of concern she felt whenever Pisces leaped to the defence of this boy. Turning to Oran, she asked, "Why would you do something so risky?"

Here, Oran stumbled, but he covered it quickly with a wry smile. "You're going to hand me over eventually anyway, right? Might as well put the time I have to good use."

Pisces's fingers curled around Caledonia's. They all knew what would happen to a disloyal son of Aric's. And it was

285

no easy death. That didn't bother her. Or, it shouldn't. What bothered her was the thought of sending a Bullet to do their work. What bothered her was the thought of *trusting* a Bullet to do their work. Making him the linchpin of their plan put everything, and everyone, at risk.

"No," Caledonia said decisively. "We'll find another way."

In the end, the only plan that seemed to have any chance whatsoever was the first: disable the electrical field, ram the ship, and board with a low-kill order. It wasn't perfect, but it was what they had. If they didn't take this chance, it would be another ten months before the *Electra* travelled the Northwater routes again, and by then Oran's information would be old enough to be all but useless.

The command crew departed as Jules arrived with another stack of boxes containing dinner for Caledonia and Oran. This time, there was a young girl who scampered up the ladder ahead of her.

On her back was a small satchel, which she offered to Caledonia with a soft smile.

"Blankets," she said. "We could have a chill tonight. There's even one for...*him*." She was easily as old as Nettle, yet somehow younger. Her long brown hair was thin, like Jules's, and wrapped in a bun on the top of her head to match.

"Thank you, Tilly," Jules called. "That'll be enough. She wanted to meet the pirate queen and her boy."

"Pirate queen?" Caledonia laughed kindly. Tilly stood

286

before her with eyes alight. "Pirates were thieves and scoundrels. I'm not a scoundrel, but you know what I am?" Tilly shook her head, and Caledonia responded, "I'm a rebel."

"And him?" Tilly asked.

"Pirate," Caledonia conceded, winning a shy laugh from the girl.

"You've had your words, now let's get, Tilly." Jules tapped her hands on the floor of the deck, starting to descend.

Tilly's eyes strayed to Oran even as she backed towards the ladder and followed her grandmother to the canoe waiting below.

"Queen says to meet her after sunrise in the main hall," Jules called from halfway down the ladder. "Whatever fight's ahead of you, I hope you give them hell."

When Caledonia returned to the cabin, Oran had both hammocks hooked into the ceiling with a blanket on each and dinner laid out on the floor – chicken tossed with glossy brown grains in a bed of gravy, a dish of the same greens as every night before, and twists of a hearty bread.

It took them very little time to clear the containers of each and every crumb.

As promised, a chill pushed through the windows before long, and the blankets were not only welcome but necessary. There was still a smear of light in the sky when they settled into their hammocks, bellies full and eyelids heavy.

Oran raised his arms without complaint. The skin of his

287

wrists was getting worse, rubbing away in places. Caledonia hesitated.

"Sit on the floor."

She found what she needed in the small stash of supplies in their bathroom: a glass bottle of disinfectant, a flat tin of salve, and a packet of gauzy bandages. She returned to find him seated on the floor, holding his hands away from his body so they didn't bump or brush unnecessarily. He was hiding his pain, and she wondered just how long he'd been doing so. She crouched next to him, arranging the tin and bandages on the floor, then gently began to work at the knots of his bindings. They were tight, and in the end there was no other way to release them than to tug.

Oran tensed but didn't make a sound. Caledonia did her best to crush a sudden swell of sympathy. It was easy to ignore a thing you didn't care about. But this was not easy. The ropes finally came away, leaving ghostly bindings of blood and ravaged skin in their wake. Oran released a long breath, and Caledonia winced as she inspected the wounds for rot or infection.

"This is going to feel like hell," Caledonia said, soaking one of the smaller bandages in alcohol.

"Don't enjoy it too much," Oran responded, voice taut.

"Don't tell me what to do," she muttered.

He laughed until she pressed the bandage firmly to the top of his wrist, letting the alcohol penetrate the places where the skin was rough or rubbed completely open. Oran's muscles clenched from jaw to thigh, but he held still and didn't flinch when Caledonia lifted the bandage and repeated the process several times over until she'd covered both wrists. Next, she applied the salve, smoothing it across his skin in a thin, oily layer. Finally, she wrapped clean bandages around each wrist.

"These next?" Oran nudged the old rope bindings with his foot. They were stained with his sweat and blood, the fibres darker where they'd pressed against his skin for so many days. They should be burned, their ashes scattered in the ocean.

But she had no other options. The only other length of rope was the tether, and if she left him untethered when they left this cabin, she'd be breaking the queen's rule.

Surprising even herself, she frowned. "Yes."

Oran held perfectly still as she worked. She gathered the ropes and carefully wound them around his wrists, then tied the knots gently, giving them more slack than before.

"I know I risk my tongue by speaking," he said, climbing into his hammock when she was done. "But I would help you even if I weren't your prisoner." He looked up, not challenging except in his sincerity.

Caledonia rose to her feet. Dusk had finally faded into the horizon, tossing dusty shadows across the cabin. Oran's eyes gleamed with diffused light. The irritation she expected to feel remained distant and dulled. All she felt was a kind of curiosity. "Why?" she asked.

"He took my family, too."

"Aric is father to all," she reminded him. It was the lie Aric wanted them to believe, the one he told over and over again. If he was father to all, then no one needed a family elsewhere.

"I was born in the Holster, given to service by the time I was seven. Even our parents tell us Aric is the only father we have, the only father we need. Not all of us believe it."

"Did you?" Caledonia's voice was nearly a whisper.

"Mostly. At first. I had no reason not to." He paused, searching for something in her eyes. "But last year, Aric ordered me to prove my devotion and kill my birth father."

Again, Caledonia's voice was thin when she asked, "Did you?"

"No," Oran answered. "But I didn't save him."

A cool breeze shivered through the room, tightening around Caledonia's throat.

"Aric shot him in front of me." The edge of bitterness in his voice was blade-sharp and ready to cut. "Aric is not my father."

And suddenly, Caledonia heard it, the casual way he said Aric's name without the honorific – Aric Athair or even simply the Father. She thought of his knowledge – how he knew the shipping schedule. How he had drawn the *Electra*'s schematic from memory. How he knew where their brothers would be on the ship. It was not the knowledge of a lowly Bullet.

"Who were you to him?" she asked.

Hesitation. A flash of regret. A flash of defiance. Oran was steady as a star in the night sky when he answered, "A Fiveson."

And for the first time, Caledonia believed him without a doubt in her mind.

CHAPTER THIRTY

That night Caledonia dreamed of storms.

Winds that plucked her ship from the water like it was no more than a shell, flinging them high in the sky where Bullet ships waited, guns ready to riddle their hull with fresh holes. They fell again into a sea of glowing blue waters, shadowed and thick with monstrous whales whose bodies were made of twists of shiny metal and dark green sea grass. When they breached the surface with mouths agape, the sound they made was the cacophonous roar of a hundred ghost funnels.

When she opened her eyes, she found Oran turned on his side, pulled from sleep by whatever noise she'd made and watching her with a pinch of concern between his brows.

"Don't," she said.

"Don't what?"

"Think of me," she said, unable to find any other words in her early morning state.

She heard more than saw the smile in his voice when he answered. "I'm afraid our situation has made that impossible, Captain."

By the time they arrived at the main hall, the sun was just beginning to slip through the trees and stir the village to life. The queen's people led Oran away as soon as they docked, and a young woman with a babe rounding her belly informed Caledonia that the queen was ready for her.

Caledonia was instantly nervous. This was not a woman she wanted to keep waiting.

She was sent into a room adjacent to the main hall, where she found the queen seated at a low table. Today, she was draped in robes of sage green and black, and though she sat on a cushion on the floor, she might as well have been in a throne. Her back was tall and her chin effortlessly high, as though she possessed a vein of precious metal within her, running through her backbone. Before her, a mottled brown teapot woven with cords of silver released fragrant steam, and the doors and windows had been flung open to the morning light. At each entry two guards stood with ready weapons.

"Your ship has been repaired, Captain," the queen said, leaning forward to pour the tea as Caledonia took her seat across the low table.

Caledonia didn't know what to make of the moment. Shouldn't she be the one to serve the queen and not the other way around? But this wasn't her queen. Merely a woman she'd swiftly come to admire. "Yes, thank you."

The queen continued in her placid way. "Your galley is stocked with all we can spare, your batteries fully charged, and I understand we've even reinforced your bow. It will make you heavier than before. You'll feel the difference, I expect. Might slow you down, but not by much."

Pisces had overseen this particular improvement. The stays had shown signs of buckling, and the Scavenger engineers had recommended a full reinforcement of the nose. It had required a considerable amount of Scavenger resources.

"All of this for saving one of your people? I'm grateful, but this is more than I can promise to repay."

"You saved one of ours and we are grateful, but I suspect it was not your intention that day. Tell me, Captain, did you set out to save Hime from the Bullet fleet?"

Caledonia remembered each of the barges they'd destroyed, but none so clearly as the one on which they'd found Hime. It had been early in their campaign against the AgriFleet. They'd only taken down one other, and the barge had appeared before them like a gift. It floated, unguarded, far from any shore. They approached cautiously at first but soon realized that the barge was in distress. The flowers were wilted under the brutal summer sun, and no one stood on deck to tend them. When they boarded, they found four Scythes belowdecks. One was dead, her small body stiff in her cot, one was feverish and pale, shivering on the floor. The other two, deranged by a combination of fever and Silt, rushed at Redtooth's boarding party. They died quickly, and Redtooth returned to the *Mors Navis* with the only surviving girl in her arms. The one who'd been collapsed on the floor.

The terrible truth was that Hime only lived because she hadn't been well enough to fight them.

"No," Caledonia answered simply.

The queen paused, drawing her steaming cup into her hands and rolling it between her palms. "We have no choice but to feed Aric's demand for iron, silver and most of all steel. These are the things he knows we have. We cannot resist."

Caledonia felt herself mirroring the queen's movements, pulling her own cup into her hands and rolling it between her palms. The steam smelled of honeysuckle and moss.

"When he takes more than our metals, we have no recourse. If we resist, we will lose the very small amount of freedom we have here." The queen sipped her tea, then set her cup on the table. "But the danger of preserving small freedoms is complacency, complicity. I cannot do much for you, Captain, but I can do this. Take your ship, take your crew, and prove to that man that he has not quelled all of us. Prove that there is a fire on these seas he cannot contain."

The words wrapped Caledonia in a fierce embrace. Her skin felt hot, her heart both buoyant and heavy. She wasn't sure of her voice, but she was sure she needed to speak. She clenched her teeth and responded, "I promise."

The queen nodded, sipped her tea, then gathered her robes and rose to her feet. "I hope the water returns you to us one day, Captain. But if it does not, then I hope it carries you well."

Caledonia searched for something to say in return. "May the seas bring you all that you need."

A smile spread across the queen's face. A smile like the bending crest of a wave, brief and beautiful. Then she turned and left Caledonia alone in the room.

By midmorning, the crew was ready to depart. The *Mors Navis* had been taken out of the village and awaited them in deeper waters, where Ceepa also waited to lead them safely through the grasses. Caledonia stood on the deck of the main hall as her crew boarded mud-runners and was carried away. Redtooth stood at her side, carefully scrawling each girl's name on a small pad of paper.

Pisces had gone ahead with Oran in tow to make the ship ready and organize the crew as they arrived. Amina should have gone with her but refused. She stood on the deck with Caledonia and Redtooth, but while they watched after the departing crew, Amina kept her eyes on the village waterways. Waiting.

Hime had been absent since that first day in the Drowning Lands. But the entire village was aware they were leaving today.

When all but the three of them were accounted for, it was time to go. A single mud-runner waited on the ramp. The water below was littered with a few boats, curious villagers come to see the crew of girls leave. The deck, however, was clear; it was the three of them and no one else. Fifty names in all lay on Red's list. They made fifty-three. One less than it would have been seven days ago.

For the first time, Caledonia felt the hard truth of this

moment. Even though their ship was in new repair and their stores were replenished, they were leaving with so much less than they had when they arrived.

"This is our fault," Amina said, voice thick. "My fault."

"This isn't your fault," Caledonia insisted. "If you need to blame anyone, blame me. I'm the one who kept her belowdecks, and I'm the one who got us stuck here in the first place."

"Don't you think she'll at least come say goodbye?" Redtooth asked.

It was hard not to recall Oran's words. He'd been sure that Hime would come with them, and Caledonia found now that part of her had believed him. But it simply wasn't true, and Caledonia didn't want to linger in this moment. The longer it lasted, the harder it became. "C'mon."

"I don't think I can just leave." Amina's words sounded deflated. "How can I just leave her?"

"What do the spirits say?" From Caledonia, this question would have sounded antagonizing; from Redtooth, it was just a question.

Amina tipped her head towards the sky, eyes searching for the things Caledonia never seemed to see. Tears welled and spilled down her cheeks. "It's time to go."

The three girls boarded the mud-runner, Caledonia the last. She was angry now that Hime had not even come to say goodbye. Hadn't she loved them enough for that?

The journey to the ship was a quiet one. They whipped through the ghostly tunnelled trees and into the marshy lands beyond. The sun was brilliant overhead and so much hotter without a cover of trees to protect them. Redtooth sat close to Amina, occasionally reaching out to stroke the girl's cheek or drop a kiss on her shoulder. Caledonia turned her face upward and tried to think kindly of Hime. With them or not, she was still a girl of her crew. She owed them nothing beyond what she'd already given.

When the profile of the *Mors Navis* appeared ahead, sharp and sleek against the sparkling water, Caledonia felt a knot inside her release. Home. That ship was the only home she'd ever known, and once again it was whole and powerful and ready. Her feet tapped on the floor, anxious to settle into the variable rhythm of the waves, hungry for the grit of the main deck. They'd lost days to the Drowning Lands, and she was ready to make up for it.

As they drew near, they found the empty mud-runners now fanned around the nose of the ship, ready to move just ahead of them through the grass flats and clear anything that might cause problems for the *Mors Navis* and her newly recovered propulsion system. On deck, the crew was active, moving through their paces and prepping for sail. And snuggled up next to the rear of the ship, beneath the ladder they would use to board, bobbed a smaller boat with only two people seated inside it. Two women with long glossy black braids.

A new knot formed in Caledonia's throat. Maybe it would have been better to have no goodbye. As their mud-runner buzzed over the surface of the water towards the little boat, Caledonia felt the unsteady peace she'd reached over Hime listing to one side. In front of her, Amina sat rigid.

It was cooler in the lee of the ship. The hull was smooth in places where it had been patched or scarred for years. Even the metal they'd lost to the crusher had been newly smoothed over, the seams of the patch nearly invisible. The work was so satisfying to see that Caledonia almost asked the woman at the tiller to take them around so she could lay her eyes on all of it here in the glorious embrace of the ocean. But there were more pressing matters to attend to.

Amina was on her feet before they came to a stop alongside the ship, nose-to-nose with Hime's boat. Hime stood while her mother sat in the back of the canoe, holding the little boat steady with a skilled oar and strong arms.

No one seemed to know what to say. Amina and Hime stood locked in place, one with jaw clenched, the other with fingers curled. Redtooth chewed on her lip, looking from the pair to Caledonia, and Caledonia waited as long as she possibly could.

"Red, topside." She spoke as casually as she could manage. If Amina and Hime needed a moment to say goodbye, she could give them that much. "Amina, you have five minutes." She turned to follow Redtooth up the ladder. A sharp clap pulled her attention back to Hime.

Captain, she said. And stopped. *Captain,* she said again.

"Hime," Caledonia responded, waiting.

Permission to come aboard, Captain.

"Hime," she said again, sadly now. Was she going to have to be cruel? "There's no time. We must go. You'll have to say your goodbyes here."

Her frown was delicate as a flower, petals closing as the sun slipped away. *I'm not saying goodbye.*

"Hime, please." The sadness she'd worked so hard to hold at bay was here now, sitting heavy in her chest. It was hard enough to let Hime go, and harder still to deny her a last moment among her crew. But this would be easier. For everyone. "It's time to let go."

No! You're always making decisions for me. But this one is mine. My choice. My crew. Hime's words came furiously, toppling one over the other. *I'm going with you, and I'm asking for permission to come aboard.*

The words finally landed. Hime wanted to stay. With them.

Amina had become a statue. She faced Hime, but even without the benefit of her expression, Caledonia could feel the anxiety rolling off her in waves. Behind Hime, her mother watched. Caledonia couldn't imagine the conversation they must have had to get to this point. But her mother sat there, eyes steady and proud of the daughter she was once again losing to the water.

A strange laugh fell from Caledonia's lips. "Hime, of course you have my permission."

Conditions, Hime said immediately, keeping her eyes resolutely away from Amina's. *I am allowed to fight, and I am allowed to determine for myself when a situation will or won't be too "tempting". You took care of me when I needed you, now you have to stop. Let me be a part of this crew.*

They were fair demands, even if Caledonia didn't like them much. "Done," she said. "But I am still the captain, and when I decide we can't risk your healing hands in battle, you sit out. Deal?"

Hime nodded. *Deal.*

"Then welcome aboard, Hime."

CHAPTER THIRTY-ONE

There was nothing more glorious than standing on the deck of the *Mors Navis* with a friendly wind at her back.

True to their word, the Scavengers led them safely west on a path through the tall grasses. When it thinned enough that the *Mors Navis* could move on her own again, they peeled away one at a time, melting into the flat-surfaced waters that had caused so much trouble for her crew and her ship.

The girls were in high spirits. Not only were they finally under way, but Hime's return had brought everyone to their smiles. The minute she appeared over the railing, Redtooth had scooped her up, spinning her around with a cheer.

Tin fell into step at Caledonia's side with a report. Already, she'd taken stock of their new supplies and repairs. She was nearly giddy as she reviewed the list of vitals. "Grain, rice, dried meats, tea, some bag of something I don't even know what, but Far's excited about it."

Caledonia smiled. "How long will it last us?"

"Oh, 'A good long way', according to Far. That's a direct quote."

Since they might not make land again for a while yet, that suited Caledonia just fine. The queen had done more than was fair, and Caledonia intended to use these gifts well.

"Those sound like bright bits to me," she said. "Get the crew to their stations and take us to full speed."

The only thing the queen hadn't been able to give them was time. They had six days to cross the world and intercept the *Electra*. Getting through the tall grasses had taken a bite out of their first day, and Aric's bounty was surely driving ships in all directions searching for them. On their side was the tempestuous reputation of the waters ahead.

They sailed unhindered for the rest of that day and just as smoothly through the night. Caledonia had to prise herself away from the helm when it was her turn for rest, and returned as the sun rose to push her ship towards the northern horizon. Every moment brought them closer to their brothers, and she felt her pulse driving with the current.

But by midmorning, she'd smelled the distant promise of rain on the air, and not long after that the wind turned brisk. Ahead the skies flashed with an approaching storm.

The crew came alive at once, removing loose items and stashing them belowdecks. The scene in the belly of the ship would be the same. Any loose item in high seas could cause injury. The girls would make sure everything was secured before the storm hit.

Caledonia raced to the bridge, where Tin stood ready at the helm. "Are you steady?" Caledonia asked.

Tin braced her hands against the wheel, answering with forced confidence. "I'm steady, Captain."

"Fill the ballast," Caledonia ordered. "Drop the keel."

The *Mors Navis* wasn't built for rough seas. She was intended for the shallows, favouring manoeuvrability over heft. But she had a few tricks that might help her weather a storm like this one; a ballast chamber along the belly that would add weight when filled with seawater, and a keel that would add leverage below. With any luck, the combination of the two would keep them upright.

"All hands!" Caledonia cried. "All hands to stations! Get those masts down!"

Three of the four masts collapsed into their chambers. The mainmast remained perilously high.

The waves were picking up, slapping the ship broadside.

"Red?!"

"Captain!" Redtooth shouted, coming close. "It won't come down. Must be a gear stuck. We can work on a manual fix, but it's going to take time!"

There were always hitches after a repair. Caledonia knew this, and still frustration threatened to tip towards panic. Wind pushed across the deck, ripping their time with it. If that mast didn't come down, it might tip them or break.

Pisces appeared at her shoulder. "I'm going to get Oran out of the hold."

Caledonia caught her arm in a tight grip. "We don't need him."

"We do!" Pisces pointed at the mast. "He's a ship tech, remember? He can help."

A ship tech and a Fiveson, she thought grimly, but Pisces was right. If he could help them get that mast down, then they needed him. Caledonia swallowed her irritation.

"You help Red. I'll get him," she growled.

The hallways were full of action, but no one looked twice at the captain as she continued down to level three. The cargo bay echoed with the sounds of footsteps and the rush of water filling the ballast. She crossed to the hold and opened the door to find Oran dismantling the piles of supplies, making them smaller and lower to the ground. Through his little window, he'd glimpsed the storm and knew better than to wait for someone to come secure the room for him.

"Looks like it might get rough out there." He paused in his work, hands held carefully away from his body. It occurred to her then that he might be explaining himself. He wasn't afraid of her exactly, but he regarded her with caution.

"I need you topside." Caledonia looked to the porthole. Through the little pane of self-healing glass the clouds were a gunmetal grey and rolled like waves. "We have a problem with the mainmast gear. Think you can help?"

"Yes," he answered quickly, giving his bound hands over to her so she could untie him. "If you trust me to do it?"

The ship pitched more sharply than usual, and Caledonia gripped his hands. Warm and rough and responsive. In the distance, the ship's bell began to ring. The storm was here.

"I trust you not to die," she said, dropping his hands abruptly.

"It's a start." Oran fell into step at her heels, following as she raced topside. He was easily as tall as Pisces and had to duck frequently to avoid the low piping, but he was quick on his feet.

When they arrived on deck, rain was pelting from a nearly black sky. The mast still reached upward, and now there were half a dozen girls lashing themselves to it with tools in hand.

Oran eyed the mast block with a practised gaze. "Do you know where the gear is catching?" he asked.

"It won't come down," Caledonia answered without humour.

Another wave knocked against the side of the ship, tipping them roughly. She was needed on the bridge. Tin had never navigated a storm and needed to change course, drive into the waves, or they'd capsize in mere moments.

"Red will know more. Go, and make sure you strap in," she said, sending him off to join Redtooth.

She moved towards the bridge, then stopped, suddenly nervous. She'd sent a Bullet in with her crew. She turned to find him, to ensure he was there, that he was strapping in, that he was doing exactly as he'd said he would. And he was. Standing at Redtooth's side, taking instruction while he strapped in and began moving expertly up the mast.

Fiveson.

The memory of his confession flashed like lightning. Oran had been a Fiveson, and she'd trusted him with the safety of her crew. She stared after him. It was just a moment, but in that moment, another wave seized the ship, sweeping across the deck with driving force.

Caledonia was knocked from her feet. She hit the deck hard, her head cracking painfully against the gritty metal.

The sky was an electric blue. Her body was slipping towards white water. And the last thing she saw was Redtooth, sliding down the deck towards her like a bird of prey, blonde braids flying and a look of panic in her blue eyes. Caledonia blinked.

And nothing followed.

CHAPTER THIRTY-TWO

Pisces was frowning. Scowling, really. Half of her face was drenched in light, the other cast in shadow as though the sun perched on her shoulder. She opened her mouth to speak. Her lips moved, but the words came out muffled at first, soggy as though worming their way through water.

"Pi?" Caledonia muttered, her own voice thick and muddy.

Pisces bent close, and Caledonia felt a cool cloth press against her forehead. "Easy, Cala. Then we'll get some food in you."

The edges of the room came into focus. Her room. She was in her bed, and the sun was rising on Pisces's face.

"I'm not hungry." She sat up and regretted it instantly. The movement sent her belly and her head to spinning, and she vomited at Pisces's feet.

Pisces threw a towel on the mess. "Of course you're not, but you should be, so you'll sit there and you'll eat."

She didn't have the strength to resist, so she nodded – carefully – and shifted so she could lean against the wall and inspect the knot on the back of her head. It was a sizeable nugget, tender to the touch and crusted with blood.

Pisces sent for a plate and then opened the porthole to freshen the room with brisk sea air. "Do you remember what happened?"

The sun was fully risen now. The storm had hit around evening, which meant Caledonia had been out for the whole night. She squeezed her eyes shut and tried to remember. But all she saw was Redtooth, skidding across the deck as her own body slipped towards the edge. She hadn't been strapped in. The water should have swept her out to sea.

She opened her eyes to find Pisces seated across from her. Arms crossed. Frowning with her entire figure.

"I remember hitting the deck. And Red..." But what had happened? She couldn't find it in her memory. It was obvious that Pisces knew exactly what had happened, and it was equally obvious that she wanted to say so. "You tell me."

"You *hesitated*." Her arms unfolded, hands landing on her thighs as she leaned in. "I saw it. I was just in time, in fact, to see how you stopped in the middle of a storm to second-guess yourself and your crew."

"That's not what I was doing." Was it? She remembered the moment. The bridge crew needed her, but so did the deck crew, struggling with the mainmast, a Bullet in their midst. A Fiveson.

Pisces narrowed her eyes. "I *know* you. Maybe better than you know yourself sometimes. I saw it. You don't trust your crew, and I'm beginning to think it means you don't trust yourself."

"That's not what happened, Pi! It was Oran! I sent Oran off to work with Red, and then he was there and I couldn't bring myself to move away. Because I don't trust that *Bullet*."

"What more do you want?" Pisces threw her hands out in exasperation. "He's done everything you asked, and he performed beautifully during that storm. If he hadn't helped get that mast down, this ship would be on the bottom of the ocean by now, and your crew would be dead."

"I want—" Caledonia's head throbbed. "I want you to understand that no matter what he does to gain your trust, you can't give it to him."

"I think he's done more than enough to gain our trust already."

"He's tricking you!"

"Tricking me? How?!" Pisces was on her feet, pacing in front of Caledonia's bed. "Tell me how I'm being tricked."

"You're enamoured with him!"

Pisces couldn't have looked any more affronted. "I'm not enamoured, Cala. I like him. I'm grateful for him. And I treat him like he's human because that's what he is. I can do that without falling for him. Can't you?"

They were interrupted by a single knock at the door. It was the plate of food, piled high and still steaming. And even though a moment before she'd have sworn she wasn't hungry, her stomach growled. She took the plate.

"What happened to Red?"

"She nearly cut herself in half going after you like that, but she's fine. Sore. Maybe a little grumpier than usual." Pisces filled the gaps in Caledonia's memory. The ship was pitching hard to starboard, and Caledonia was washing away with the water. But Redtooth used the roll of the ship to her advantage, sliding down the deck just in time to catch Caledonia around the chest. Caledonia hit her head again, but Redtooth's tether held, and when the ship rolled back to centre, they hurried the captain belowdecks.

It could have killed both of them. *She* could have killed both of them. Pisces was right, she'd hesitated and those seconds had nearly cost everything she had to give. It wasn't like that moment on the beach, but it felt close. She'd flinched. And when she flinched, she lost, but those around her lost even more.

Her mother wouldn't have flinched. Rhona would have stood firm in her decisions, raced to the helm and steered the ship boldly into the storm. Of course, Rhona's ship never would have been crosswise of a storm to begin with. Even when they'd sailed these seas long ago, she kept the *Ghost* on the right side of the storm. That was the kind of ship she ran. But Caledonia wasn't Rhona. It didn't matter who had been at the helm; their course was determined by the captain. *She* had let the crew down.

Pisces reached over and gave her thigh a friendly slap. "Don't mope. Eat. When you're done with that, we're going topside so you can see that we did just fine without you. Because of you." She stood to gather a fresh shirt from the old trunk she'd been sitting on, tossing it on the bed next to Caledonia. "You've got maybe three days to get your head straight. Going up against *Electra* is a new game. And we need you steely. This is the finest crew on all the seas, Cala. Believe it."

She nodded, careful of her head this time. "I do and I'm sorry. I messed up." She felt herself shrinking. Felt the tears warming her eyes. If she couldn't keep her feet during a storm, what made her think she could take on a ship like the *Electra*?

"I said 'don't mope'." Pisces nudged her again. "Or if you're committed, then talk to me."

"What is there to say? I lost us everything in Cloudbreak, I got us stuck in the Drowning Lands, and now this. How am I supposed to go up there and face everyone again?"

Pisces was wearing a different kind of frown now. Angrier. "How about my shoulder? Was that your fault, too?"

"Yes! Don't you understand, it's all my fault. Every mistake, every injury, every bad move. They're all my fault because I am the captain of this ship."

"Just because things didn't go the way you wanted them to doesn't mean you're at fault. Cloudbreak was rough, but I needed a doctor. And you convinced Hesperus – the Sly King of Cloudbreak, need I remind you – to not only release

312

us but give us the map that saved our lives. The grass flats was a situation of no good options, and we'd have made it there, too, if not for the Scavengers."

"And you argued against me! Even you think I made a bad call there."

"I'm not saying that. North might have been just as bad. Maybe worse. Fighting the Gulls a second time could have been disastrous."

"Then why did you fight me?"

"Because that's my job!" Pisces threw her hands down in exasperation. "I am your sister, your friend and your second-in-command. I stand by your side and I argue with you because someone has to be brave enough to do it. You made a good choice in a bad situation, and we ended up with full stores and a stronger hull because of it."

"Because of Hime," Caledonia corrected. "That only happened because we had Hime with us."

"And we had Hime with us because you're the kind of captain that saves lost girls. Spirits, Cala, you've always been so frustratingly myopic. If we didn't win, we lost; if you're not good, you're bad; if it's not day, it's night."

It hurt her head to do it, but Caledonia scowled. "I fail to see your point."

A laugh like a fish leaped from Pisces's mouth. "Of course you don't. Listen. We are being chased by the Bullet fleet. They know our ship. They know your name. We have no good options available. Everyone on this ship knows it.

313

We rely on you to make the best possible choice in whatever situation we find ourselves, and then we follow you. Highs and lows. We follow you."

"And what happens when I make too many bad choices? When we have too many lows?"

"What do you think? That we're all going to wake up some morning and leave you because things got hard?"

Caledonia looked away. It was exactly what she thought. And what she deserved. If Pisces knew the truth about that night on the beach, she'd be the first to leave.

Pisces wilted. "Cala," she murmured, moving to sit next to her on the bed. "We only have bad choices. We trust you because you always find a way through them. The only mistake you made last night was not trusting your decisions as much as we all do."

Caledonia released a long breath. A few tears found their way down her cheeks, and she clenched her jaw in case they had friends. Pisces draped a careful arm around Caledonia's shoulders and let her lean in. The wall Caledonia had worked so hard to maintain, the one she held between her heart and Pisces, didn't feel as solid as it once had. She imagined Pisces sitting on the other side with a chisel and hammer, picking away at a single spot. One day she would get through. She would learn her single, tremendous secret. And it would be the last day she looked on Caledonia with love in her eyes.

But for now, for this moment, it was just the two of them,

she wasn't responsible for fifty-three other lives, and she wasn't hiding a terrible secret. She leaned into her sister's neck and let the tears fall.

CHAPTER THIRTY-THREE

Strapping in during a storm was basic. It was different from strapping in before a hard turn in the midst of battle. Those frequently occurred with only a moment's notice. But a storm had to approach. You had time to strap in. Caledonia had certainly had time. And she'd wasted it on doubt, endangering everyone.

She felt like a novice. She didn't have time to act like one.

Her head throbbed and her steps were unbalanced, but the more she moved, the easier it got. Caledonia had let Pisces pick the worst of the bloody knots from her hair and pull the snarls into a loose braid down her back. Later she would stand under a stream of hot water and work the tangles loose with oil and a comb. For now, she needed to push through this sluggish melancholy and get in front of her crew. They needed to see that their captain was still on her feet, and that she could own her mistakes.

By the time they climbed to the deck, she was almost at full speed. The eyes of the crew fell on her immediately. Curious, concerned, relieved. She did her best to bear it as casually as possible. She nodded, made eye contact, smiled tightly and kept moving.

The ship was cruising freely across restless waters. Blue chop expanded in all directions; it was a sea recently stirred and full of energy. Behind them and some distance west, the skies hung dark, but here, the sun was powerful behind puffy white clouds.

"We broke free of it sometime after midnight," Pisces said, following her gaze. "We don't think it's travelling this way, but Nettle's moving us as though it is."

"Nettle?" Caledonia turned her attention towards the bridge. "You put her at the helm?"

"She put herself there. Again, and just in time, too." Pisces braced her hands on her hips as she gave Caledonia the rest of the story. How Tin had done her best to keep the ship steady, and how Nettle planted herself at Tin's side and shouted commands like Caledonia herself. Soon, Tin stepped aside and Nettle was the one navigating the steep waves and lashing winds. "She did good. I doubt Lace could have done better."

The name still stung. Pisces didn't use it lightly but to show the depth of her approval.

"More trouble than she's worth?" Caledonia asked.

Pisces ran a hand over her head. Her hair was nearly an inch long and falling softly against her forehead. "Aren't we all?"

"I'll have a talk with her. And with Tin. It's overdue."

Caledonia felt the mantle of captain settling more firmly around her shoulders. It hadn't fitted well since Lace died. She'd let her discomfort become a distraction, and when she was distracted the whole ship was off balance. It was time to provide her crew with the firm ground of her decisions again.

Continuing their route around the deck, they found Redtooth standing on the mainmast block, her head tipped back to look up. Several feet above her, Oran was balanced along the lower yardarm near the mast, using the footrope but no harness. Around his waist he wore a belt of tools. His arms were slicked with sweat and full of the late morning sun.

"Could you move any slower? I thought you said Bullets were fast!" Redtooth cupped her hands to be sure he heard her. "Fast and hard," she added, barely containing a laugh at her own joke.

"I said" – Oran paused to give whatever he was working on a sharp crank – "we hit our targets!" Another crank. "And yes, we hit them hard."

"Not in my experience," Redtooth teased.

Oran's shoulders moved in laughter. He didn't volley back immediately but bent over his work. On the rear deck, a small cluster of girls sat with a sail spread out between them. They were repairing it, but they sat in full sun to do it. And in full view of the unusual sight of a Bullet in the rigging.

"Captain!" Redtooth leaped from her post beneath the

boy, consuming the distance between them in three long steps and wrapping her massive arms around Caledonia before she could protest. "You're here. You're good. Are you good?"

"I'm good." Caledonia allowed the hug, then gently but firmly pushed Redtooth back a step. "Thanks to you."

Redtooth shrugged and looked away. "Anyone would have done it. I'm just glad you're okay."

Sometimes, Caledonia was briskly reminded that Redtooth was a girl just like the rest of them. She was hard and bold and forthright, and she felt so rough that it was easy to think her heart was also those things. In reality, that couldn't be further from the truth.

"I don't want you risking your life for me again, clear? I'm grateful, but that was a one-time thing."

Redtooth regarded Caledonia with amused disbelief. "Ah, sorry to disagree, Captain, but that's not something I can promise. If I see you're in trouble, I'm going to do something about it. That's just the way it is."

"Red—" Caledonia started, but was cut off when Redtooth gently grabbed her face in her rough hands. Ducking her head to look straight into Caledonia's eyes, she repeated, "That's just the way it is." Before Caledonia could respond, Redtooth pulled her close and pressed a quick kiss against her mouth.

This time Caledonia's smile won out, and she pressed her palms to her sister's sunburned cheeks.

"Got it!" Oran shouted from above. "Sail's back in its gear and ready to come down." He'd moved from the footrope along the yardarm to the tines along the mast. "Like me."

"Why isn't he in a harness?" Pisces asked, scrutinizing Oran's situation, twelve feet up and loaded down with tools. "We have plenty."

Redtooth grinned, conspiratorial. "Yeah. And they're all made for *girls*."

"You're not saying he believed that?" Pisces sounded like she couldn't decide if she was amused or horrified.

The grin on Redtooth's face grew. She squinted up at Oran as though considering the question. "I like him," she answered resolutely.

"Red," Caledonia warned. "Get him down."

"Yes, Captain."

He didn't need much help. Redtooth stood beneath to offer guidance, but mostly ended up teasing him about his grip. Oran laughed easily with her, letting the jabs land and throwing a few of his own. Whatever had transpired between them in the hours since Caledonia's injury had been significant enough to win the smallest amount of Redtooth's trust.

He hopped to the ground at Redtooth's feet. "You wanted the gear snapped in, right? No chance for movement."

Alarm showed on Redtooth's face. "Snapped in? No, I didn't want it snapped in! I—" Her teeth crashed together. "You're joking. You're a damn dirty Bullet and you're joking."

"I am," Oran confirmed, satisfaction bright in his eyes. He was sundrenched and in the full blush of health for once. The tone of his brown skin was even instead of blotchy or fever-pale; he'd bathed and washed his clothes, and even his wrists were free of their bandages and less violently red.

Pisces hadn't moved, but her attention landed on the Bullet like a ray of light. "You know any of those harnesses would have fitted you just fine, right?"

"I know." Oran's smile was easy, his tone light. "But you always trust your clip."

Redtooth's smile returned at that, clearly pleased that he'd taken her challenge and run with it.

"Crew," Caledonia corrected. "There's no clip here."

"Right, crew," he said. "My mistake. I'm glad to see you on your feet."

"Don't get sentimental," she fired back.

He laughed. "That's what you call sentiment?" He shook his head in disbelief, then he heaved a sigh and raised his hands. "I assume my time in the sun has come to an end?"

The answer was yes. She should be standing here to bind him and return him to the hold like the unwelcome guest he was. Except, he wasn't as unwelcome as he'd been only two weeks ago. He'd given good information, he'd survived his withdrawal, and when she hadn't been looking, her crew had folded him into their patterns. She could remove him from it. Lock him away until she needed him again, or she could lock him into the routine.

321

The fight ahead of them was filled with unknowns. He was their single biggest asset, their single greatest advantage. If she didn't demonstrate even the barest amount of trust in him, how could she expect her crew to do the same? If they were going to risk their lives taking on the *Electra*, they needed to know they were doing so with good cause and good information.

Caledonia regarded the boy before her. Once a Bullet. Once a Fiveson. What would he be next? Friend or traitor? As she stood there on the deck of her ship with a brisk wind at her back, she realized there was only one way to find out.

She placed a hand on his wrists and pushed them firmly down. "Don't make me regret this," she said.

"Caledonia Styx," Oran said, his smile as vibrant as the noon sun. "I suspect your regrets are few and legendary."

He didn't know how right he was.

CHAPTER THIRTY-FOUR

On the wall of the bathroom that wasn't reserved for Caledonia but was treated that way regardless, hung a mirror. The seamless, silvered surface was made of the same self-repairing polymer that made up every glass pane and window on the ship. It could break, but within moments, the splinter would knit itself back together. More than once, Caledonia had studied the unmarred surface with a sense of wonder. The old world had been so skilled at making unbreakable things, and yet they'd failed to keep themselves whole. They'd left behind tools and weapons and half stories and a desperate legacy.

Rhona had once said that the history of their predecessors was a living creature they'd be running from their whole lives; history was a disease they weren't equipped to fight. She thought if they could escape its reach, they could make their own history. One that wouldn't harm or chase or infect anyone else.

Caledonia felt like she'd been running from her own history for four long years. But two weeks ago, she'd turned around. She was in pursuit, and with every minute they drew closer to the ship that carried their brothers. Every mile that swept along their hull was one less mile she'd have to run. Maybe it was running from the beast of history that gave it power. Maybe, just maybe, if she could win their brothers back, she'd feel like she could stop running from her past. And maybe when that was done she'd find the courage to tell her friend the truth.

Caledonia studied Pisces's face in the mirror before her. She sat on a low stool with her chin tipped up, all the angles of her jaw, nose and cheeks looking harsh in the blue wash of cabin lighting. On her chest, the green seedling inside Ares's glass charm seemed more alive than usual. Pisces waited, one eyebrow lifting when Caledonia paused for just a moment too long. Shaking away her thoughts, Caledonia wet the razor in her hand and pressed her fingers to Pisces's throat, tipping her head back even more. Then she pulled the razor steadily across Pisces's scalp. As the feathers of black hair scattered around them on the floor, Caledonia was struck by how similar this moment was to the first time she'd cut her friend's hair. Those tresses had been much longer and Pisces's expression less bold, but it marked their loss in a way neither of them had expected. Just as this moment marked something else.

"Will you grow it again? When we have them back?" Caledonia asked when she'd finished moving around the delicate skin of Pisces's ear.

Pisces pressed a few pieces of shorn hair between her fingers. Their eyes met briefly in the mirror. "I don't think so."

"Why not?" Moving on to the other side, Caledonia pulled the razor from the crown of Pisces's head to the centre, wiping the blade on the towel over her shoulder to clean it before repeating the gesture. "You loved it long."

"I did. But..." Pisces dropped the hair and looked up. "Cala, have you thought about how different they're going to be?"

"Of course." Caledonia tried to sound matter-of-fact and unconcerned. "What does this have to do with your hair?"

"Nothing really." Pisces was quiet for a moment as she reconsidered her approach. "They won't be the same. I don't think there's any way they can be."

"I know." Caledonia's response was short. But Pisces was determined to continue.

"It's just, we're not the same either. I don't think I'll ever be the same girl I was that night on the Gem. Maybe it sounds strange, but my hair was sort of wrapped up in that girl, and I don't think I can go back to that, even though I loved it." She waited for Caledonia to swipe the last of her hair from her head, then turned in her seat. "And we won't be able to make them who they were either."

The metal in her hand felt hot. In spite of the frost blooming on the round porthole, the room was suddenly too warm. She forced herself to answer calmly. "I know they'll be different. But they'll come back to us. I know they will. You said yourself, if Oran can change, so can they."

"I know." Pisces stood and took the razor from Caledonia's hand. "We just have to be ready to let them discover who they want to be when given the chance."

Perhaps Pisces's caution was prescient. Caledonia hated to think what four long years had done to Donnally's gentle nature. And what if Ares didn't want to come back to them at all? It was too terrible a thought to voice. She didn't want to burden Pisces with the same grim thoughts that haunted her, so instead she smiled and said, "After we force them off that ship and through detox, of course."

"Of course," Pisces answered, cheered. "Force first. Choice later."

It was an uneasy thought, but there was no other way. When they found their brothers, they'd be indoctrinated and drugged. While it was tempting to imagine winning them back would be easy, recovering their minds could prove to be even more challenging than saving them in the first place. Caledonia tried to brace herself for both options, but in her heart she knew it was more likely to be the latter.

If it had been her, if she'd been the one stolen from the ship and forced into a violent way of life, she wasn't sure she'd have survived. But she'd never tasted Silt. And there was no way to know how that one thing might have changed her.

"It's just," Pisces said, catching Caledonia before they

parted ways in the hall. "It's just that I'm worried. And you don't seem worried."

"I am," Caledonia admitted. She imagined herself like the mirror on the wall, a single crack splitting her face in two before melting together once more. "But not about them."

For two days, the *Mors Navis* travelled steadily north, pausing only in the thick of night to reserve power and let the engines rest. The storm had stolen nearly a full day and night from them, and now they raced to reach the Northwater ahead of the *Electra*.

The air gathered a constant chill, and the waters were full of bite. None of them was used to this kind of cold, and soon they'd raided their stores for every sweater, wool coat and set of gloves they could find. They had enough for nearly everyone. And the remainder set to work in the galley stitching warmth together from various pieces of clothing and unused blankets.

Pisces, stubborn, anxious and probably dying a little from being so long above the surface, used their midnight stops to get herself back in the water. Redtooth stood watch with her new friend Oran by her side. Caledonia could never tell which of them was more ready to leap in after Pisces at the first sign of distress. Even covered in the thickest wetsuit they had on ship, Pisces emerged with a purple tinge to her lips and clattering teeth beneath a strangely refreshed smile.

When a blue-grey coast appeared in the north, it was midday on their second full day since the storm. The land tumbled towards the ocean like pebbles tossed down a hill. Uneven ridges climbed sweeping valleys lined with the smallest racing rivers. The shoreline was jagged and temperamental, sometimes curving smoothly along and sometimes diving sharply in or outward. It created coves and peninsulas of all sizes, perfect hiding places for a ship to lie in wait.

The colonies were a scattering of towns and villages across the area. Given how frequently the land shifted, they were known to move. Once, they'd done so aggressively, always seeking to outsmart Aric's men. Now when they abandoned one site and chose another, they were required to report the location or risk egregious consequences. Like everyone else in and around the Bullet Seas, they were a subdued people, and once a year they were stripped of many of their children.

At the helm, Nettle kept a good distance from the shore and drove forward at an even pace. Caledonia's conversation with the girl had been easy enough. She'd already proven herself capable and had asked for the responsibility, and Caledonia was ready to give it to her. Nettle was no longer on probation but their Helm Girl.

Her conversation with Tin, however, landed hard. It was Caledonia's fault. Instead of moving forward and assigning Lace's work to other girls, she'd let Tin try to fill her myriad roles for far too long. And while she was well suited to one, letting her try to do both was rough on her and the crew. Tin had blinked hard when Caledonia made her Operations. "Just Operations?" she'd asked, her blue eyes narrowing. "And you're making the *stowaway* Helm?"

"Yes," Caledonia had responded without flinching. "Nettle is Helm. You are Operations. I need you in your best element, clear?"

To Tin, this was a stripping of her power, and it showed in the clench of her jaw. "Clear," she answered darkly. Then she balled her fists and rallied. It was the kind of gesture Caledonia had come to associate with her whole crew. They were grit and determination, a kind of raw battle cry born of the extraordinary tangle of despair and desire they were built from. And when they finally found the *Electra*, it was that cry that would win their brothers.

But knowing where the colonies were likely to be wasn't enough. They needed a location and it needed to be specific. It took several hours for Oran to get his bearings. He sat on the command deck with Caledonia, wrapped in a coat of burnished red wool, shoulders hunched against the wind. Beside him was a cup of cold teaco and an empty plate, and he alternated between peering through binoculars and making notations on a small piece of paper. Finally satisfied, he relinquished the binoculars to Caledonia.

"There's a cove just around that bend. That's the furthest colony. Where *Electra* will start gathering."

Caledonia lifted the binoculars to her eyes and focused on the protrusion of land. "You're sure?"

"As sure as I can be." The wind pushed through his hair, whipping it across his eyes and ears. "But I haven't been a Fiveson in months. And they don't tell Bullets much at all. Things might have changed. I doubt it, but it's possible."

It had been nearly three weeks since Oran told her about this run, since they'd brought him aboard. If he'd said something like this back then, she'd have dismissed it offhand, suspected him of leading her off course. Today, none of that doubt coloured her thoughts. If he was right, they had only a day before the *Electra* came into view. Alternatively, it might already be anchored around the next bend, raiding the colony for children.

"Understood. Nettle! Get us into this cove," Caledonia called, climbing to her feet and gesturing to the one next to Oran's mark. The ship rumbled immediately, and Caledonia turned her steps towards the main deck. "Red! Get ready!"

Redtooth whistled to her team in response, and the crew sprang to action.

Leaving the deck, Caledonia raced down the companionway ladder, ducking to avoid the pipes. She hurried through the corridors to level three, where Amina and Hime were locked away in the room they'd claimed as their lab. It was directly beneath the bridge and forward from the cargo bay, a room the size of several bunkrooms combined, with lockers and secured cubbies along the walls that were perfect for cataloguing and storing tech, most of which was now spread across the floor. There were wires and panels and charges of every shape and size. The walls were covered in drawings, each held in place with magnets, some of which were as large as the paper they held.

It looked like chaos to Caledonia, but the two girls fitted neatly into the metal tapestry around them. They found what they needed instantly, parts and pieces passing between their hands as naturally as if they shared a meal. If Caledonia watched them instead of focusing on the mess around them, the pattern of chaos suddenly looked like a logical dance. It was beautiful. It was exciting.

"Amina. Tell me we're ready."

She didn't answer right away. She stood, crossing to the opposite side of her work with long, careful steps. Her braids had been collected into a single larger braid down her back and tied off with a familiar blue ribbon, and her brown cheek was smudged with black grease.

Hime crouched off to the side, her apron puddling on the floor at her feet, hands resting atop her knees. Each of her fingers bore some sign of the work they'd been doing, pricked or sliced or peeling.

After a moment, Amina looked up. "We're ready."

Ready. They were ready. They were in the right place. They had the right weapon. Now all they needed was a target.

CHAPTER THIRTY-FIVE

Caledonia crouched in the front of the bow boat, her eyes pinned to the rocky outline between them and the cove. She felt certain that just behind that bend, the *Electra* spliced through water. She felt it like a vibration in the ocean, and her blood reached for the fight.

In order to run silently, the bow boat had to run slowly, and in order to scout unseen, they'd have to moor the boat and hike over the hill on foot for the best vantage point. Redtooth sat at the tiller, guiding them smoothly towards the shore, and Oran sat in the middle, feet braced against the gentle bounce of the boat. A small team, but the work ahead didn't require anything more.

Under normal circumstances, Redtooth would have taken her usual team to scout for the *Electra*. As it was, Caledonia wanted Oran's eyes on the ship before they moved in to attack, and where Oran went, she also went.

The shore was braided with driftwood in all directions creating a barrier between them and the hill beyond. Redtooth nudged them as close as they could get, but there was no getting to shore without also getting wet. One after another, they leaped over the side of the boat, the bracing water reaching above their knees.

Redtooth released a strangled curse. "Now I know Pi is part fish. How the hell does she do this? No, I take that back. I want to know *why* she does this."

"Peace of mind," Caledonia answered, grateful for the distraction from her freezing flesh.

"That girl has a strange notion of peace," Oran added, joining Caledonia at the back of the boat where they could push while Redtooth pulled from the prow.

They manoeuvred the boat over the bleached stacks of wood to the beach, and soon it was secure enough to leave behind.

The three of them squeezed frigid water from their clothes, pulled their jackets tighter, and began to pick their way up the steep hillside. The ground was peppered with rocks covered in a slick moss, making the climb a challenging one. They slipped and scrabbled over the uneven surface, winning fresh bruises on their knees and shins. By the time they reached the top, they'd all broken a sweat and were breathing hard.

They moved quickly, settling behind a crop of boulders, which offered mild protection from the cold wind and a good view of the water.

The cove on the other side of the hill was much like the one they'd come from, only this one was empty. Caledonia felt dread sink through her stomach. What if Oran was wrong? What if this was the wrong cove? But then Oran pointed.

"There!" he said.

Smoke rose in hazy streams from the trees a half-mile inland. The colonists were near, anticipating the same ship they now waited for.

"Maybe they won't lose their children today," Caledonia said.

"It won't stop them." Oran turned on his back, shoulders braced against the cold stone. "They'll lose their children one way or another."

This was the way of the world. It had been the way of it for Caledonia's entire life, but hearing it now dug a trench of sadness she hadn't expected. She turned her eyes to the trails of smoke and imagined families gathered around each one, holding their boys and girls close for the very last time.

"What would it take to stop him?" Redtooth surprised Caledonia with her question. "You were a Bullet. Not good for much, if you ask me, but you must have some idea."

Oran almost smiled. "Destroying the AgriFleet is a good tactic, honestly, but you'll never do it on your own."

"How many ships do we need? Five? Ten?" Redtooth pressed, her mind fully engaged.

"A fleet," Oran answered, sombre. "You need a fleet."

Redtooth slumped, scowling at Caledonia for a long minute.

"Red," Caledonia said when that minute went too long. "Speak or avert your frown."

"You need a fleet," Redtooth said matter-of-factly. "If anyone can command a fleet, it's you."

"You're dreaming." Caledonia turned her eyes back to the mouth of the cove. "I'm not saying you shouldn't dream, but maybe set your sights somewhere more reasonable."

"You mean somewhere like taking down a ship with an electrified hull?" Redtooth nodded. "Good advice."

Caledonia scowled.

"She's right," Oran said from beside her. "If anyone could lead a fleet, it's you."

In spite of the cold, Caledonia felt a small warmth bloom in her chest.

Redtooth groaned. "Things have gone very wrong when a Bullet agrees with you. Quick, say something terrible. Shouldn't be hard. Just open your mouth."

"Red, you're faithful and strong, and if I die tomorrow, I hope you remember I considered you a friend," Oran said brightly.

"If you don't die tomorrow, just find me the next day," Redtooth responded, but she didn't even try to smother her smile this time. "I'll take care of you."

Oran offered some response, but Caledonia didn't hear the words.

Her gaze moved as though drawn to a point on the ocean. The wind that stung her cheeks suddenly filled with an electric hum. She felt it in her skin, tasted it on her tongue. And in the next moment, *she* appeared.

The *Electra* sailed around the peninsula like a harpoon. Blue-white lightning crackled along her hull where the ship met the ocean. It sizzled and snapped, flashing unnaturally bright in defiance of the daylight. There was no ghost funnel mounted on her bow. Instead, an old holo projected orange numbers into the dimming sky. A countdown to the moment they would come ashore and take the colonists' children.

The ship was a nightmare coming to call. And it was the cage that held Donnally and Ares prisoner.

"She's here," Caledonia said, raising the telescope with numb fingers. "And she's alone."

The sun was falling behind them as the *Electra* turned towards the colonist fires on the beach. She was just as Oran had described – a hefty belly and short command tower, broad and slow. They watched her move slowly into the centre of the cove and weigh anchor there. It was too late for them to begin their work of retrieving their conscripts. For that, they would wait until first light. So Caledonia would move even sooner.

"See how they take care with the anchor?" Oran spoke into Caledonia's ear, sure to keep his voice low.

Caledonia found the anchor with her scope, noting how the Bullets on the chain avoided touching the hull at all costs. It was the only evidence of the danger. Not even the water below seemed affected. As Oran promised, the electrical field was designed to stop just above the waterline so as not to charge the water for yards in all directions.

"Red, how many Bullets do you count?" she asked.

"Twenty-five topside," Redtooth answered promptly. "Not sure about belowdecks."

"They cap these crews around fifty or sixty." Oran spoke with confidence. "They save as much room as possible for the conscripts."

They held their position for another hour, studying the movements of the crew and trying to get a more accurate count. It was safe to assume they outnumbered Caledonia's crew, but if Oran was right, perhaps not by much.

It was strange to think that she could be looking at Donnally or Ares right now and she'd never know it. More than once she caught herself letting her sights rest on a single Bullet with dark hair, searching for the feature that would confirm it was her little brother. She was so close to him. So close to having him back in her life. Part of her wanted to go now, to return to the ship and mount the attack immediately.

But that was foolish. And she was not a foolish person.

"We have what we need," she said when the sky was full dark and the Bullet ship portholes filled with a cool blue light, while above the orange countdown ticked steadily. "Let's go."

Chapter Thirty-Six

Night felt darker this far north. Maybe it was the cold. The way it slithered through the fibres of coats and trousers or curled around ears and throats. It wasn't the constant pressure of a hot night spent around the Bone Mouth, but a seeping discomfort that made everything feel endless.

But maybe it was simply that the morning was a time of promise and possibility, a time Caledonia had convinced herself would never come. A time when Donnally and Ares existed in more than just her dreams. Maybe that was why the darkness felt so complete. Because the promise of what lay just beyond it was so incredibly bright.

The news of the *Electra* stirred the blood of the ship. Everywhere she looked she was met with bright eyes, hands ready to fight. She gave the order to rest, but with the fight so near, there would be little of that.

Far pushed her kitchen crew to their limits, whipping up as much of a feast as they ever enjoyed. Girls gathered in the galley to eat and later in the cargo bay to double and triple check their guns, to refill a few more spent cartridges with powder even if their own clips were full. Some bathed, some slept, some shut their doors and spent their energy on one another. Everyone had their own way of preparing for battle.

In the hours just before the sun glazed the cold ocean, Caledonia and Pisces collected cups of black and blue paint and moved through the ship drawing their individual sigils on the hands and cheeks of every girl, anywhere that would be easy for the brothers to see. Pisces's mark went on easily, but the brushes weren't fine enough to fill only half of Caledonia's blunt-tipped arrow. Every time she tried, she produced a shapeless smear, so she gave up and just drew the outline.

There was no way to anticipate how the brothers would react. Caledonia's imagination insisted on presenting her with a tearful, easy reunion. She wanted it. But she was certain nothing about this would be easy, including, and maybe especially, winning their brothers' minds back. They drew these sigils in the hope that it would distract the brothers from the fight long enough to be subdued without injury. Since they couldn't guarantee it would be one of the two of them to find the boys, every girl needed to bear one of the marks. Surely, they would see and remember. Donnally would. She knew that with unbridled certainty.

Caledonia came to Oran last. Days ago, he'd been moved from the hold to a cabin near her own, and she found his door ajar, the room inside dark. Keeping her eyes firmly on the hatch and not beyond it, Caledonia raised a hand and knocked.

She heard movement right away, the slow unwinding of limbs from a bed, and then the light was on and Oran stood before her, layering on a second shirt.

"Time already?" he asked, his hair stiff with sleep, his eyes pinched with the same.

"Nearly."

He noticed the cup of paint in her hands and raised a curious eyebrow.

"It's for my sigil. To mark you as one of my crew, and as someone they can trust."

His eyes travelled to the mark at her temple and back to the paint. Then he stepped aside to let her into the room.

They'd given him a room alone, and though the space was just as large as Caledonia's, the number of beds it contained made it feel smaller. Two sets of bunk beds climbed in uneven steps along two walls, their ends overlapping in the corner. The third wall contained a set of four lockers and little else. There was no window in this room, which many of the girls preferred for easy sleeping. Judging by the swipe of the blankets, Oran had chosen the second-lowest bunk.

He stopped in the middle of the room, as though suddenly unsure of what to do. Caledonia chose a perch at the end of his bed, motioning for him to sit on the lower bunk on the adjoining wall. He followed her lead, resting hands on knees.

Over the past days, Oran had been at her side more often

than not, but there was something decidedly different about being alone with him now. She stirred the black paint, though it was smooth already, and eased the unexpected tension with a question. "How are your wrists?"

"Nearly back to normal." Oran lifted his hands to show the colour of his wrists had improved. "How's your head?"

She frowned at the memory of her blunder during the storm. "Still not as hard as the deck."

Caledonia wasn't sure if he laughed first or if she did, but in the space between her words and their laughter, some final braid of tension unravelled. The boy who'd landed on their ship in the colours of the Bullet fleet was now just Oran.

"Lean in." Caledonia lifted the brush from its cup, the hairs thick with black paint.

Oran did as directed, leaning in and tilting his head towards her. Lightly, she pressed her fingertips beneath his chin and jaw, turning his face so she could work. She started one inch beneath the corner of his eye and drew a long line vertically towards his jaw before hooking it towards his ear. Another one followed, this time hooking towards his lips, then she drew the smiling curve that connected them.

"They'll know you're a friend now."

"Is that what I am?"

His breath ghosted warmly over her palm and wrist; his eyes remained trained on her. Those layers of brown and grey were even more textured up close, the inner rings bursting outward like the arms of a starfish. She tried not to look, but they pulled her back again and again until finally she didn't look away.

"Yes," she answered, knowing it was too much of the truth, and also knowing that part of trust was giving people the truth when they asked for it.

They were suddenly closer. His chin resting in her palm. Her lips so near to his.

There was an unfamiliar warmth growing in her chest, an unexamined desire singing in her ears. Every thought in her mind was suddenly centred around his brown eyes, his long nose, his lips, his lips, his lips.

He leaned up. Lips brushing hers like the warmest southern wind. He paused there, waiting, the touch of his lips so light against hers it could barely be called touch. She wanted more. And in that moment, she snapped back.

The brush lay on the floor in a smear of black paint, and it was only by some small grace that the cup was still upright. Caledonia sat up straight to repress the unwelcome tremor in her body.

"Did I overstep?" Oran asked, eyes intent and otherwise unshaken.

Retrieving the brush, she drew in a deep breath and gripped his chin, a little tighter this time. "When I want a kiss, I will be the one to take it."

Ignoring the smile that slipped across Oran's mouth, she set to work. She drew the next sigil with quicker strokes, a circle intercepted by two vertical lines just off centre.

"For the record," Oran said when she was done with her work, expression deadly serious, "that kiss is there for the taking."

Caledonia laughed again. There was a new kind of tension between them now. One that drew them closer instead of pushing them apart. It wasn't entirely uncomfortable.

"I'll add it to Tin's inventory," she teased.

Caledonia knew the time had come to ask the questions she'd held in reserve. The ones that had nothing to do with how they bested the *Electra* and found their brothers. The ones that had everything to do with what happened after.

"You said my brother liked to sing at first." Now that she'd started, she found it was difficult to continue. But she pushed on. "Can you tell me what he's like now? Is he like you? Does he want out?"

"Caledonia." Oran leaned back, lips tightening in reluctance. "I told you, I don't want to lie to you."

"Then don't," she said quickly, suddenly panicked. "What do you know?"

"I know that it goes hardest for the kids like Donnally. He's not the same boy you knew from the *Ghost*. He's been out here a long time, and for Bullets survival is violence."

Caledonia's mind reeled. What did Oran know? What had he seen of her brother? What had he become in the four years since she'd seen him? And then, another question. This one brought her to her feet. "No one knows that name except me and Pi."

Surprise widened Oran's eyes, his mouth opened in silence.

"You didn't hear it from us, so tell me the truth: *how* do you know its *name*?" Caledonia demanded.

The small space suddenly felt smaller. Oran rose to his feet, moving towards Caledonia as if to take her hands. She snapped them away.

"Oran," she warned.

"I – everyone knows the *Ghost*."

"Why?" she demanded. "Be explicit."

"Because," Oran started. "Everyone knows Ballistic Donnally."

Caledonia stepped back.

"You said—" She took a breath. Blood. Gunpowder. Salt. "You said…he was a member of *Electra*'s command."

"He is." Deep regret painted Oran's features. "He's the first in line. Donnally commands *Electra*."

The world she'd known a moment ago had been wholly changed with those three words: *Donnally commands* Electra. She had no bearings. And she wouldn't find them in this increasingly small cabin with the boy who – what had he done? Had he lied? *No.* It was too confusing to unpack, so she clamped it down.

"Find Red," she said, pulling the hatch open behind her and stepping unsteadily through. "She'll make sure you're armed."

And then she left.

CHAPTER THIRTY-SEVEN

Caledonia stood in a circle with her four most trusted girls, her stones. Pisces looked more herself than she had in weeks, with her hair freshly shorn and her arm in good repair. Amina had her head turned up, listening to everything the winds had to share. Hime had removed her apron and bore holsters on her hips, and her silky hair was woven in a tight braid down her back. Redtooth had a fresh smear of red clay across her mouth and looked hungry for the fight. In the centre of the circle, Caledonia dropped a bit of the bedraggled lace she'd worn since Lace's funeral.

The night was thick around them, the wind cutting, but they stood strong on the nose of the command deck as they reviewed their strategy. Amina's electro-mag would provide a pulse capable of interrupting the electrified hull, but no one knew for how long. They had one shot. If the *Electra* got its hull charged again before they made contact, the game was up. It was this need for swiftness that brought them to it: they would storm the *Electra*, and when they were close to impact, they would fire the electro-mag, disabling her hull before they rammed her.

"Hime," Caledonia began, speaking with her hands and her voice, "there's still time to go below. I won't deny you this fight, but we will certainly need you after."

I understand, Hime said, shaking her head as she spoke. *But my place is with you.*

Caledonia swallowed her protests. Much as she would prefer to have the girl below, she knew this was an important moment for both of them. She turned to Amina. "How are the winds today?"

"Conflicted," she answered with her eyes on the dimming stars above. "But in our favour."

"That sounds better than usual. Red, how are your boarding parties?"

"Steely," Redtooth answered quickly. "Ready to jump as soon as we hit her."

"Pi?" Caledonia asked.

And Pisces reached for her hand, squeezing tightly when she said, "Let's go get our brothers."

Caledonia ignored the flash of fear in her chest. Pressed it down, down, down and covered it with the memory of Donnally's clever smile, the slippery feel of his dark curls, the sound of his voice saying, *Hoist your eyes!*

And now that same sweet boy was not simply aboard the *Electra* but in command of it. She couldn't bring herself to say it aloud to Pisces. A Donnally in charge of a Bullet ship

346

was not a Donnally she could conjure in her mind, but if she saw her own horror reflected in Pisces's face that would change. And maybe it didn't matter. He would still be among the command crew, and if he was in fact the Ballistic of that ship, she'd know exactly where to find him. She would get to him first.

They walked together to stand on the small deck behind the bridge where they could be seen by the entire crew gathered on the main deck below. They were armed and ready. Among them, Caledonia found Nettle, her young face braced for the fight ahead, her bright ribbons ornamenting her dark hair. There was Tin, standing in the firm clutch of her sisters, each one more steely than the last. And there was Oran. He'd abandoned his burnished red coat in favour of the closer fit of his long-sleeved shirt. Over it, he wore double holsters lined with guns and a short sword.

The crowd was dense, their eyes turned towards Caledonia and the four girls behind her. All around them, the sun pips glowed blue in the darkness, ringing them in starry light. It was time for her to speak, to rally and inspire. She stood silently for a moment, studying the shape they made on the deck. Knowing that there were forty-nine souls before her and in a few hours there would very likely be less. Knowing that those losses would follow her for ever.

Rhona would have taken this moment and turned them around. Rhona would have kept her ship and her crew whole and hidden. She believed small losses were unavoidable, but the same was not true of big losses. Rhona wouldn't have taken this risk. But Caledonia was not her mother.

Somewhere along the way, she'd come to the hard realization that there was nothing she could do to keep them all safe. But she could help them to fight. It wasn't her job to save them; it was her job, as Pisces had known from the very beginning, to lead them.

"Sisters!" Caledonia called. "I thought that you came across the world to the Northwater because of me, and for days I've struggled to understand why you would take such a risk to rescue two boys you've never known. But I've learned something over the course of this journey. You're not here because of me. *I'm* here because of *you*. If not for you, I might have tried to do this on my own. If not for you, I'd have failed early in this journey.

"I cannot promise you safety. I thought I could, but we don't live in a safe world. We live in a world of no good options, but it's because of you that we can make the best of them." She paused. She could feel their energy rising, could almost hear the collective pounding of their blood. On their cheeks, the sigils of her family and of Pisces's family shone in the blue glow of sun pips. They were marked, all of them, as her family. It was beautiful and terrifying.

"On the back of the sea, who do we trust?" she called.

Her crew answered together, "Our sisters."

Caledonia raised her voice a little more. "When our ship falters, who do we trust?"

"Our sisters."

She shouted, "In a storm of Bullets, who do we trust?"

Their voices spiralled together, rising up like the early morning sun. "Our sisters!"

With a grin, she finished the call. "We fight together!"

And they responded, "Or not at all!"

"Here we go, girls!" Redtooth shouted.

The *Mors Navis* roared to life. They'd moved slowly closer to the bay over the course of the night, but they needed room to build up their momentum. Now they pushed to speed with Nettle at the helm.

Amina and Hime took their position high on the nose by the gun that would fire the electro-mag. Nearby, Pisces held the binoculars to her eyes, marking the pace and watching for unexpected troubles. Redtooth stood with Caledonia halfway between the nose and the bridge where they could carry commands to the crew waiting on the deck below. And the crew was divided into raiding parties that would attack together.

An icy wind stole tears from Caledonia's eyes and tugged furiously at her hair. In spite of the cold, her body was coated in sweat, and she shed the grey coat she'd worn all morning.

Redtooth leaned in close, raising her voice to be heard over the wind. "No good options," she said with a grin. "Seems like our speciality."

Caledonia was reminded of the moment weeks ago when she'd stood on this very deck with Amina discussing the possibility of intentionally engaging a Bullet ship and stealing its sun sail. It had been the first in a long series of no good options.

"I'll take that," Caledonia answered with a matching grin.

The sky was just beginning to show signs of dawn when they rounded the peninsula and entered the bay. Before them, the *Electra* was nestled in the centre of the cove, her nose pointed towards them. The orange numbers of its countdown floated in the air, ticking ever closer to zero. That blue-white fire shattered repeatedly along the waterline, making the ship appear to hover just above the ocean.

"Swing starboard!" Caledonia called to Nettle, who only barely needed the command.

The ship swung in a sharp arc to starboard, bringing the *Electra*'s port side into full view. According to Oran, the best place to strike would be the forequarter where they were most likely to take out the engines. But since Ares was also more likely to be down in the engine room, he'd suggested a hit dead centre.

Nettle lined them up, and the ship accelerated.

Pisces raised a hand.

Amina and Hime adjusted their grip.

A wall of Bullets appeared above the *Electra*'s railing. They raised guns and shields and opened fire. The crew of the *Mors Navis* held their fire even as their own hull echoed with rain. Any stray shot from them might be the one that took Donnally or Ares. So they pressed low to the deck, heads ducked behind battered shields, and they waited.

After what felt like an eternity, Pisces's hand came down and Amina's gun exploded. The electro-mag was heavier than a bullet and so it was slower and easier to track. It flew through the air, directly towards its intended target, landing with a loud pop.

And nothing happened.

The distance between the *Mors Navis* and the *Electra* was fading fast. In another second, the impact would leave every member of her crew electrocuted.

"Amina!" she shouted, knowing there was nothing to be done.

Just as she was about to give the order to abandon ship, the *Electra*'s hull flashed. A web of purple light fractured in every direction, snapping through the air. And then it went out. The hull was dead.

CHAPTER THIRTY-EIGHT

Caledonia raked her gaze across the enemy ship. The flare of energy had pushed every Bullet away from the rail. The air smelled like smoke, and the way was clear.

"Brace!" Redtooth cried.

The final distance between the two ships vanished. The *Mors Navis* drove into the *Electra*'s side with a vicious metallic shriek, her nose puncturing the ship by several feet. The *Electra* began to roll away, dragging the *Mors Navis* with it. With a shock, Caledonia realized the ships were locked together, and they were still rolling. They'd rammed with too much force. Both ships would capsize, and all would be lost.

The ships groaned, listing hard. Water sloshed over the *Electra*'s rail, and the *Mors Navis* shuddered against the strain. Bullets slipped down their deck, gripping at the rail or tumbling into the cold waters just beneath. Caledonia could feel the tension in her own deck as every rivet resisted the pull of the *Electra*.

Then, just when it seemed the *Electra*'s momentum

would doom them all, the ships stopped rolling. The orange numbers of the countdown flickered and went out. They froze for the barest second, then rolled upright once more.

Caledonia stood tall. Alert and ready. They were wedged into the dead centre of the *Electra*, her side crumpled around the sharp nose of the *Mors Navis*. Before her, the deck was littered with Bullets struggling to regain their feet, the railing peppered with the bodies of a few who'd failed to step back while the electro-mag did its work. She tried not to worry that they were dead. That any one of them could be Donnally or Ares.

"Latch on!" Caledonia cried, instructing the crew to deploy the grapples and hooks that would keep them connected to the *Electra*. "Haul over!"

Now the fight began. Her girls leaped across the railings, their mouths open with cries and roars and high-pitched screams, their swords and guns high, their sisters at their sides. Before them, Bullets quickly came to their fighting minds and greeted them violently on the deck.

The air was a constant scream punctuated only by occasional gunfire. With Pisces at her side, Caledonia joined the fight, her pistol in one hand, long knife in the other. Every time she met a Bullet, she sought a sigil on his face, pulling her punches just long enough to do it. Her girls did the same – curtailing their blows until they knew their opponent was neither Donnally nor Ares, leaving themselves vulnerable. It was a terrible way to fight. A long way to fight.

They had no sharpshooters to assist them, no confidence that any kill was a good one, only their quick minds and strong fists to rely on.

And Oran's information.

The fight spread across the *Electra*'s main deck, putting too much distance between her girls. Every battle-honed instinct Caledonia possessed told her this was a mistake. She needed to pull them together, drive forward as a unit, and give the Knots room to fire. But it wasn't enough to win this fight; they had to win it the right way.

With a roar, Caledonia dived forward, knocking a Bullet's shotgun away with her blade. Before he could recover, she drove the flat of her palm up into the underside of his chin. He was pale enough to be Donnally, but in that moment, she registered that his hair was blond. That was enough for her. She pulled back and lunged with her sword, burying her blade in his chest.

As frustration wormed towards desperation, Caledonia reminded herself that they never expected to find Ares in this first volley, and Donnally wouldn't be in the thick of things. The only way to give her girls the ability to fight without caution was to find the boys and get them out of the fray by whatever means necessary.

Pulling in close to Pisces and Hime, she took a single precious moment to study the evolving field. The fight was concentrated here, in the centre of the main deck. The Bullet force was furious and strong, but thin thanks to Amina's electro-mag. The railing was still littered with those too near the blast when it went off, and the remaining force was equally matched by her own. If her girls felt free to fire at will, this battle would be that much closer to being over. As it was, they traded blows for blood, relying on their fists and swords more than guns.

"Any sign?" Pisces shouted.

"None yet!"

The cold air was bright with the scents of blood and smoke. Caledonia felt the tug of guilt in her throat, the desire to tell her girls to use every weapon available to them. But then a single Bullet caught her eye, standing far up the forequarter with his eyes trained on the battle below. It only took a second to realize it was the Ballistic. His dark hair wasn't long enough to curl, but it was black as the night sky, the skin beneath it pale.

Donnally.

He was changed from the small boy she'd known on the *Ghost*. He was tall, with hollow cheeks and broad shoulders like their father's had been, but it was him.

It was *him*.

Caledonia no longer felt the cold of the northern sky. She moved through the fight like a spreading fire, consuming all she touched. Her hand and blade were slicked with blood, and pain sang distantly in her head, but she pressed on, desperate and determined to reach Donnally before anyone else did.

Finally, she was through the throng. There was nothing but open space between her and the ramp leading up to the bridge. The Ballistic's attention wasn't on her. His face was turned away, held in profile so she could just see the tip of his nose and feel a skip in her lungs. She had the element of surprise. She could knock him out before he even knew she was there, secure him before he had a chance to resist. She was ready to run. Then something crashed into her from behind as a gun fired past her ear, and she was on her knees, her gun sliding across the deck.

She rolled, lashing out with the butt of her long knife, only to find that the thing that had crashed into her was Amina, pushing her out of harm's way. The girl never stopped moving. She rolled smoothly to her feet, braids twisting around her body like the lashes of a whip, and drove her own sword into the belly of a charging Bullet. He stopped, eyes wide and angry, then Amina braced her foot on his thigh and shoved him to the ground, blood falling from her blade in a steady stream.

Caledonia allowed herself one small breath of relief before she turned around, again searching for the Ballistic. She found him in an instant, his attention and his gun fixed on Amina.

Dread burned instant and hot in Caledonia's gut as she realized she would be too late to push Amina out of the way.

She flew to her feet.

The gun cracked.

But it wasn't Amina who hit the ground. It was Redtooth. She appeared just in time to make a shield of her body. Her chest jerked as the bullet pierced her back. Her hands brushed Amina's shoulders as though she had something to say. There was a second where all was still but for the stray locks of blonde hair, curling in the air like autumn leaves. Then red bloomed between her shoulder blades and her body hit the deck at Amina's feet.

And that was when Caledonia heard Amina's roar. The girl raised her gun, and without a second thought, without waiting to look for a sigil, she fired at the Ballistic.

Caledonia screamed. Twisted in time to see the Ballistic's hand clutch his chest in surprise. A small trail of blood slid down his chin, and he toppled over the rail of the bridge. Lifeless.

Her ears filled with a cottony buzz. Behind it, the distant sound of her girls holding their ground. She stood trapped between the body of one of her sisters and that of her brother. Numb.

Amina was screaming. She was standing over Redtooth's body. She was fighting anyone who came near. Amina was screaming, and the sound of it was the only thing strong enough to penetrate the fog around Caledonia's mind.

Trusting Amina's sword, she crouched at Redtooth's side. The girl's blue eyes were open, her expression locked in one of love. For Amina. For the crew she'd served so well.

With a shaking hand, Caledonia closed Redtooth's eyes.

"Amina!" she shouted as she pulled Redtooth away from the fray.

Amina moved instinctively. Guarding her captain and her fallen sister as they moved to the wall of the command tower. Tears covered Caledonia's cheeks, and she didn't fight them as she tucked Redtooth against the wall and turned her steps towards her brother.

Now the world narrowed to the gleam of blood on his sky-dark hair. It was all Caledonia could see as she moved to his side.

"Donnally?" she whispered, kneeling in the blood pooling beside him.

Why hadn't she told them? Why hadn't she immediately shared that he was the Ballistic of this vessel? Why had she assumed she could get to him first? Her fault. Once again her foolishness had cost him everything.

"Cala?" Pisces's voice was strong in her ear. "Cala, be steely."

"It's him, Pi." There were tears in her eyes, in her throat, and on her face. "Oh, spirits, it's him."

Gently, Pisces gripped the man's head and lifted it from the deck. His chin was covered in a thin stubble and the lines around his eyes suggested he'd seen more years than Caledonia. Beyond that, his temple bore no tattoo.

"It's not," Pisces confirmed.

Caledonia breathed the battle back into her lungs in one long gulp. Blood. Gunpowder. Salt. The world came back in a rush.

Pisces gave her shoulder a firm squeeze. "On your feet, Captain."

It wasn't him. It should have been, but it wasn't. Any number of things could have happened to remove him from command. Caledonia tried not to dwell on them. She didn't have time to dwell. Only to find him. Answers would come later.

The clip was thin now, and without their Ballistic at the helm, their confidence visibly waned.

And then there was Redtooth. Crumpled against the command tower wall. Her blonde braids staining red all the way to her scalp. There was such a wave of sadness waiting there. One that was sure to pull them all under if they let it. But right now, the sight of her body led to a terrible keening screech. It built slowly, travelling from one girl to the next until no other sound might be heard.

A few of the Bullets continued to fight, their minds dedicated to the task no matter the circumstances, but more faltered in the face of that scream. Their blades hesitated, and the girls took every bit of that advantage.

Caledonia saw Nettle darting between Bullets to slash their calves from behind; she saw Tin and her sisters weaving their blades into deadly webs; she saw Hime wielding her dual swords with furious grace. She saw the battle bending towards them, and before long, the day would be theirs.

Caledonia climbed to the bridge where the Ballistic had stood. She looked over the waning battlefield and shouted,

"Throw down your weapons, and we'll let you live!"

The transition took a few minutes, but soon the remaining Bullets stood ringed by her crew. She spied the site where Redtooth had fallen and clenched her jaw; her blood was a bright flag against the rusted metal deck.

"If they don't have a sigil," Caledonia said, voice girded with steel, "kill them."

"Bind them!" Pisces shouted, breaking the moment in two.

Caledonia climbed down from the bridge, fury fresh on her face. But Pisces met her with an unbending stare.

"Why are you challenging me?" Caledonia gestured to the sea of Bullet faces before them. "These aren't our brothers."

Pisces stepped forward and pressed her shoulder to Caledonia's chest so she could speak in her ear. "If we're going to remind them who they were, we can't forget who *we* are."

Caledonia wanted blood. Revenge for Redtooth's death. Her body trembled with it. She imagined the deck of the *Electra* covered in the bodies of spent Bullets, the surface bright with the blood of all the boys who were not her brother. She imagined it, felt that dark kernel deadening her heart, and she shivered. "Bind them!"

CHAPTER THIRTY-NINE

Not a single Bullet on this deck bore the sigils of Caledonia's family or of Pisces's.

Fear was starting to sing from a knot in Caledonia's throat. They had trusted the word of a Bullet, attacked a mighty ship, and lost several of their own, and all for what?

"Cala." Pisces gave her hand a tug. "Belowdecks. C'mon."

While Amina and her Knots remained topside with their barrels trained on their prisoners, the rest of the crew was taking care of the wounded and ensuring the *Mors Navis* was undamaged and ready to sail.

Caledonia opened her mouth to shout for Redtooth and stopped abruptly. She cleared her throat. "Nettle!"

The small girl appeared at her side. Blood stained her front and she'd taken a blow to the cheek, but she seemed otherwise unscathed.

"Captain?"

"I need you to work with Tin, organize a retrieval party. Anyone who will recognize value in ship parts when they see it. They should come through after Pisces and I do our sweep."

"On it." Nettle flashed a brief smile, and then she was gone.

"Let's go."

Caledonia moved ahead of Pisces as they entered the first level. The hallways were wider than those of the *Mors Navis*, though the piping was just as low. They cleared room after room, moving carefully and quietly through the unfamiliar corridors.

When they were satisfied that the first level was clear, they travelled down the ladder to level two. Immediately, they heard voices. Hushed and tense.

Caledonia met Pisces's eyes, and the two girls moved silently towards the voices. It was a small room in the centre of the ship. If Caledonia had to guess, she'd say they were directly below the bridge.

Pisces held up two fingers. Caledonia nodded in agreement. There were only two of them in there. Caledonia tried not to hope that they would be their brothers. But it was a losing battle. Even as she listened, she searched for some hint of Donnally in those tones. Some promise of Ares.

The girls raised their guns. Pisces was around the corner first, with Caledonia shortly behind.

"Hands up!" Caledonia shouted.

Tools clattered to the ground. The two Bullets were too surprised to do anything other than put their hands up and let Pisces bind them. Caledonia waited with her gun poised and her breath stuck in her chest.

But Pisces shook her head, the hope in her eyes withering. It wasn't them.

They took their new prisoners topside before resuming their search, but the rest of level two was just as empty as level one. Every corridor, every bunk carried only the memory of Bullets.

Caledonia and Pisces moved faster and faster towards level three and the engine room. They didn't say it out loud, but both were chased by a clawing panic that Oran's information was too old and their brothers were no longer here. And if they'd done all of this for nothing, if Redtooth had given her life for *nothing*, then what?

The door to the engine room was pulled shut. Caledonia held her pistol ready while Pisces gave it a shove, entering the room faster than she should have.

A hand reached out. Pisces's wrist was snatched, and before she could resist, she was dragged bodily into the room. Her gun clattered to the floor, but she did not scream.

Caledonia followed, her own gun trained on the boy who now held Pisces against him, her head cinched between his strong arms, his hands poised to snap her neck.

He was tall. His skin a warm, sunny brown. His eyes beaded with gold and shadow. His black hair cropped short. And there, on his temple, tucked close to his hairline, the sigil.

"Ares," Caledonia said, voice destabilized by relief. "Ares, it's us!"

He didn't snap Pisces's neck. But he didn't release her either. His eyes narrowed, and he didn't speak.

Pisces didn't struggle. Her eyes grew wide, and her hands landed softly against Ares's arm.

Caledonia's heart was suddenly wild in her chest. If Ares was here, then surely Donnally was, too. They simply hadn't found him yet. The weight of all her hopes was crushing, but she forced herself to stay grounded in this moment. This was not a time to be careless with her feelings.

She let her gaze travel around the rest of the room, confirming there was no one else here. At least, no one she could see. The centre of the room was occupied by large engine blocks, the ceiling layered with pipes. If there was someone else here, they had plenty of places to hide.

"Ares," Caledonia tried again. "I know you remember us. Look, that's Pisces. Pi. Your sister. You're holding your sister right now."

Ares shook his head. "My sister died a long time ago."

"On the *Ghost*, right?" Caledonia held her gun steady, aimed directly at his forehead. "She wasn't on board when it was attacked. Remember that? She went to shore. With me."

A frown pressed Ares's brow, but he didn't look away. Instead, he studied her more intently, taking in her red hair and the sigil on her cheek. Still, his arms tightened around Pisces's throat.

Pisces gasped. "Ares. Look." With one hand, she lifted the charm she wore to the level of his eyes.

Ares's eyes settled on the little charm. He frowned, and then suddenly his arms snapped open, and he took a startled step backwards. With a gasping breath, Pisces spun to face him.

"Ares," she repeated. She held her hands out, palms up and as non-threatening as she could make them. "It's me. Pisces. See?" She turned her cheek so he could clearly see her sigil.

Caledonia kept her gun trained on his chest. High and to the right. If she did have to shoot him, she'd make it survivable.

Ares stood very still for a moment. His hands hung at his sides like they were filled with lead. On his face was an expression that looked very much like pain.

Finally, he spoke. "You've cut your hair," he said.

"You're taller!" Pisces laughed, rushing forward and into his arms.

At first, he didn't move. He was unbending as a tree even as Pisces wrapped her arms around his neck. Then a small shudder moved through his body and he whispered, "Spirits." He bent and lifted Pisces clear off the deck as though he didn't even notice. "Oh, spirits."

Caledonia's throat was tight. Tears coated her eyes. She bit them back, anxiously scanning the room for a sign of Donnally. She was glad to see Ares. So heart-stoppingly glad, but she needed to see her brother, too. And when she couldn't wait a second longer, she interrupted their reunion.

"Is there anyone else here?" she asked. "Ares, where's Donnally?"

"Donnally?" Ares gently set his sister on the ground again. "He's not here."

"Here, in this room?" Caledonia demanded.

"Here, on this ship." Ares frowned. "Cala, I'm sorry, but he left a month ago."

CHAPTER FORTY

She didn't hear a word more. She turned and just started walking.

She barely saw the corridors of this dreadful ship. She followed the natural progression of stairways until she was back on the main deck, where there was more to fill her ears than the hollow sound of her disappointment. Where the sun was warming the air and everything smelled like blood.

The Bullets had been bound more securely and now sat on the rear deck, far from the centre of activity. Nettle was organizing the retrieval operation with expediency, ensuring that their efforts to strip the *Electra* of her most valuable and portable parts went as quickly as possible. All the wounded had been taken back to the *Mors Navis*, and Tin stood in the midst of the scene, conducting all operations with a firm touch.

Everything was going as it should be.

Spotting Caledonia, Tin moved across the deck. Her expression was one of grim resolve, and instead of a blade she now clutched her notebook in one hand. The news it contained would likely break Caledonia in two. She wished briefly that her heart might be like self-healing glass, repairing itself the instant a fracture was formed.

When the girl was near enough, Caledonia nodded, asking simply, "How many?"

"A dozen wounded," Tin said, voice steady. Evidence of the battle was splattered across her pale face. "Five dead."

"Who?" Caledonia clenched her jaw tight.

It took Tin a moment to answer. She stared down at her notes, perhaps willing them to appear in Caledonia's mind so she might avoid speaking the names aloud. Finally, she cleared her throat. "Alesa, Quinn, Thatcher, Maddy and—" Her breath caught, stealing the final name.

"And Red," Caledonia finished for her. "Where is she?"

Tin pointed to the command tower. In its shadow, Caledonia could make out the shape of a body lying on the ground, blonde braids stained red. They'd left her for the captain. As was right.

"Thank you." Caledonia aimed her steps for Redtooth.

The girl was taller than Caledonia, with more muscle and weight. Though Caledonia's body was weak from the fight, she crouched and pulled Redtooth into her arms.

"Let's go home, my friend," she whispered.

Slowly, she rose to her feet with Redtooth's body gripped firmly to her chest. All work ceased as she moved across the deck towards the gangplank. The eyes of her crew tracked her until she and Redtooth were safely aboard the *Mors*

Navis once again. Caledonia let the tears roll down her cheeks. For the loss of her friend, for the loss of her crew, for the loss of her brother, again.

"I have her, Captain." Amina met her on the main deck, taking Redtooth into her own arms.

"You have her," Caledonia repeated.

Caledonia watched them go belowdecks, then climbed to the command deck, where she could be alone for a minute.

They'd done what they'd set out to do. They'd rescued Ares, and that was no small victory. The *Electra* was in no shape to gather recruits. The colonists would enjoy a temporary reprieve at the very least.

Still, it was hard to find anything but a deep sense of defeat in this moment. Five crew members were lost, Donnally was nowhere to be found, and the brief hope that had lived in Caledonia's heart was gone for good.

"Captain." Tin stood before her, a look of concern on her face. "Captain?"

Caledonia blinked and cleared her throat. "Yes."

"We've got trouble. Our scouts spotted a Bullet fleet on approach. They're ten miles out, coming from the east and moving fast."

So they would have to run. They would leave this ship without her brother and run for their lives. Again. Caledonia's heart felt too heavy and too numb for anything other than this steadying sense of responsibility.

"How many ships?" she asked, voice and spirit tired.

Tin's eyes tracked every movement on the deck even while she answered Caledonia's questions. "Scouts saw at least six. They look like the same ones that chased us out of Lower Cloudbreak."

"How so?"

"They said the nose of the flagship was covered in baleflowers."

Baleflowers.

Lir.

"Set the charges," Caledonia said with renewed urgency. "And bring our girls home. It's time to go."

CHAPTER FORTY-ONE

Caledonia couldn't think. She raced to her cabin, where she threw her weapons to the floor. And for a moment, she felt everything.

Her heart tapping a frantic rhythm against her chest, her tears burning her eyes and washing her cheeks, her breath whistling in and out, struggling against her lungs. There was Redtooth's death, pinning a hole in her gut. There was Ares's return, fluttering between joy and sorrow. There was Donnally's absence, straining in her chest. And there was the fury of Lir's approach, twisting around her ankles, urging her to run, to kick, to *move*.

In the midst of that storm, only Lir felt solid. With Oran's information exhausted and out of date, Donnally was out of reach. There'd be no way of finding him in the whole of the Bullet fleet. That was a hopeless, helpless dream now.

But here again was Lir. And this wasn't like Cloudbreak. There was no need to ask her crew to take on this fight. There was no promise of brothers to be found in her future. There was only Lir and the promise of revenge. If she couldn't have one, at least she could have the other.

A plan began to form, knitting together from the broken plane of hope in her heart. She would take her revenge, and she would do it without asking anyone else to risk their lives. She would do it without losing anyone else. Her body filled with the heady sensation of purpose, her mind suddenly clear and calm.

She spun, and there was Oran. Standing just inside her cabin with his wide dark eyes. He was saying something, asking something. His mouth was moving.

Caledonia didn't hear it. She crushed the distance between them, pressed her body flush against his, pushed her hands along his cheeks and into his hair. And then she took her kiss from his lips.

If he hesitated, she didn't feel it. He met her kiss with a full one of his own, wrapping his arms around her chest, hands pressed flat against her shoulder blades. There was no room for tenderness between them. The moment was burning around them, tricking them into thinking there was only this kiss.

Caledonia kissed him harder, letting the fire of this moment obliterate every other thought in her head. Letting it make her bold and daring.

"Cala!" Pisces shouted, driving the two of them apart.

Caledonia pushed Oran away, spinning to face Pisces. "What?" she demanded.

"We need you topside." Pisces looked between Caledonia

and Oran, muscles tense. Her gaze narrowed on Oran before returning to Caledonia, landing even harder than before. "Now."

She was gone before Caledonia had caught her breath. "Spirits," she muttered, reaching for her coat before remembering she'd ditched it on the bridge just before battle.

Instinctively, Oran stood aside to let her pass. But before she left the room, he caught her wrist. "I didn't know," he said. "I didn't know he wouldn't be there. That's what I came to say."

Even through the fabric of her shirt, his hand was hot. "I believe you."

As she surfaced on deck, she felt the ship drifting slowly away from the *Electra*. The crew had worked hard and fast to disengage from the collision. Any lingering hull damage from the hit would have to be addressed on the move. Their ten-mile lead wouldn't last long.

She found Pisces on the command deck with Amina and Hime. Somewhere on this ship there was Ares. But even that victory was missing from their expressions. They regarded her cautiously and, she realized, with a hint of their own grief over her still-missing brother. And over Redtooth.

Pisces greeted her with a cool glare. Whatever her opinions of the kiss she'd just witnessed, they weren't good, but she wouldn't share them here.

"Options," Caledonia demanded.

Run west, find a cove for cover. Hime looked uncertain even as she said it. *Hide until they're gone.*

"Too risky," Caledonia said. "Others?"

"Run west," Amina began. "Use the coastal topography for cover and keep going."

Caledonia nodded. It was her thought as well.

"Cable mines." Pisces crossed her arms as she thought. "We'll set them adrift as we leave the cove. It won't be much, but it will give us a little edge."

The pause that followed was so natural. They all expected a fourth and even a fifth opinion to fill the space between them. But none came. Redtooth was gone.

"Good. We'll do both." She turned towards the bridge and raised her voice. "Nettle, take us out, slow and steady. We don't want to leave them a trail if we can help it."

Nettle's response was in the quiet churn of her engines. The ship moved through the water with as little chop as possible.

"Amina, time to get those mines ready. Hime, we need you back in the med bay." The two girls nodded and moved off in a hurry. Caledonia waited until they were alone before speaking again. "Pi, I need you to take command."

"Command?" Pisces asked suspiciously. She planted her hands on hips and lowered her voice. "What's going on?"

There was too much to say, and Caledonia had no idea how to say it. The sun above was heartless and cold, everything she needed to be in this moment. Pisces might curse her today and tomorrow and even the next day, but eventually the pain would ease.

"Listen to me, Pi." Caledonia drew her down the command deck, to the very tip of the nose, where no one might overhear them. "You have Ares, and the loyalty of this crew. As soon as I'm gone, take the ship and run. Use Oran and Ares to figure out how to punch the Net and get out of the Bullet Seas for ever."

Pisces studied her through narrowed eyes.

"Why are you talking like this? What do you mean, gone? We have the lead. We're fast and smart, and we've just sailed those waters. This is no worse than anything we've faced before."

If she'd found Donnally, things might be different. She could imagine running with them, fighting for a life beyond the Net. But she hadn't found Donnally. He was as absent as he'd been since the destruction of the *Ghost*. And the person responsible was headed straight for her.

"I'm leaving," Caledonia stated. "There's something I have to do. Just stick to the rules and you'll be fine."

"The rules?!" Pisces couldn't decide between a laugh and a sneer. "The ones you follow so well? We fight together or not at all, remember that one?"

Her stomach twisted and her cheeks burned. "I have to go. This is my best chance."

"For what? Cala, talk to me. Whatever it is, let us help you. You said it yourself, you're here because of *us*. Without us, you fail. Or were you lying up there?" She drove her finger in the direction of the bridge, where just hours before Caledonia had stood to rally her whole crew.

"I wasn't lying. But this time I need you to go, leave me. Let me keep you safe."

"That's not what this looks like. It looks like you're making a reckless decision, and I care about you too much to let you." Pisces reached for her hand, twisting their fingers together. "I love you, Cala. More than anyone else in this world, I love you."

"You shouldn't." Ice and grimy oil slid through Caledonia's heart, leaving a nauseated feeling in the centre of her chest. It was time. "I'm the reason our families were killed. Me. I broke the rules. That night on the island, I met a Bullet. Instead of killing him, I let my guard down. Gave away the ship. If it weren't for me, they'd still be here. All of them."

She waited for the horror to sweep across Pisces's face, even for a blow to follow it. But nothing changed except for the depth of Pisces's frown.

"Why don't you look surprised?"

"Because this isn't surprising. You showed up with a gut wound you never explained, and you've always felt guilty for that night."

"I feel guilty because it was my fault. I met a Bullet on the beach and gave away the *Ghost*. It's *my* fault." The memory filled her like a breath and left her just as quickly. "I can't do anything about that, but I can do something about that Bullet."

"We were fourteen turns. And we were alone." Pisces was so calm, so sure of herself in the face of this confession. She was like a piece of flint; where she'd been broken, her edges had become sharp and beautiful; struck hard enough, she'd start a fire. "You are no more responsible for what happened than I am."

"I don't accept that." Caledonia looked over the steel-grey ocean to where Lir approached.

Pisces grabbed her by the shoulders. "You made a mistake! We've all made mistakes."

"Well, mine get people I love – and people you love – killed!" she shot back.

"Our first family shall not be our last," Pisces stated.

A crack opened in the wall around Caledonia's heart. She'd done an unforgivable thing, and Pisces was comforting her. It didn't make sense. "I got them killed, Pi. Just like Lace and Red. I got them all killed."

"Cala, I forgive you. Is that what you need to hear? I forgive you. But if you do this – if you leave your crew *now* and go off to fight this Bullet on your own – then you're betraying the family you've built. Is that what you want?"

Caledonia shuddered. Lir was out there. He was coming to this very spot. She would never succeed in bringing Donnally home, but at least she could do this. At least she could root out the cause of all their pain and leave her crew in better hands than her own.

The tears burning her eyes were unrelenting. They

slipped down her cheeks in a constant stream, but she stared through them, let them run from her eyes unblinking. She tipped her face up to find Pisces's eyes and gave the only words she could find.

"I'm sorry."

Chapter Forty-Two

Darkness was thick beneath the ocean's surface, an unknowable world she had no choice but to enter. Caledonia hated it. The morning of battle had carried them into a dusky afternoon, and while the cover would only work in her favour, she wished it wasn't so dense. But dusk was nothing to the ocean. Dusk and dawn were for the sky.

As the *Mors Navis* sailed smoothly towards the mouth of the cove, Caledonia dropped into the water after the tow with her crew none the wiser. All except Pisces, who stood on the rear deck watching with her arms pinned across her chest. As terrible as it was to be leaving her, Pisces had her brother back and she was loved by the entire crew. She'd be fine. Even if it took a while for her to find the bright bits again.

Nettle hugged the shoreline as tightly as she dared as they neared the edge of the tumbling hills, bending the ship around the peninsula to avoid being spotted too soon. In their wake, they dropped a dozen mines. Those mines now hung in the water between Caledonia and her ship. Even if she wanted to go after them, she couldn't.

They would run. They would survive. Pisces had been right all along. Caledonia's crew was the finest on the seas. They were smart and brave and skilled, and she was so proud to have been their captain. She hadn't trusted herself to say goodbye in person, so she did it now as she floated in their wake. In her mind, she listed the names of her entire crew one after the other, alive and dead. She imagined the funeral they would hold for Redtooth and the others they'd lost. She imagined how Nettle's skill would grow, how Tin would find her stride, how Amina and Hime might allow themselves to be happy together. She imagined Pisces leading them to a better life and Oran and Ares discovering who they were without Silt in their veins. And as the *Mors Navis* disappeared from view, she imagined her heart a stone, tumbled smooth by the ocean and lost far beneath its surface. The ship had been her home for her entire life. It had been destroyed and repaired and made into a home for so many others. Now it was gone. And she felt certain she would never see it again.

There was no time to waste. She needed to get close to the battered *Electra* before the fleet arrived so she was in the best position possible for boarding the *Bale Blossom*. The tow moved forward at a steady pace, churning the water softly around her. Breathing through the blue lung was odd and it took her several minutes to adjust to seeing water beyond her mask and inhaling safely anyway. Her wetsuit made the biting cold just bearable. Beneath it, she wore a fitted black biosuit that would reflect her body heat back to her skin once she was clear of the water. On her back, she carried a small waterproof pack containing a single remote charge and her gun.

And in her belt, she carried a simple dagger.

Though her compass glowed softly in the dark and the needle was clear to see, she felt as though she moved aimlessly in the dark. Maybe Pisces found the sensation relaxing, but Caledonia was not so friendly with the underside of the sea.

She heard them before she saw them. The roar of their engines carried under the water, bringing her to the surface in a rush. Six ships poured around the eastern peninsula, ghost funnels crooning their discordant tones, with none other than the *Bale Blossom* in the lead.

Lir.

She imagined his face, smiling on the beach. She imagined the stiff sweep of his hair and the crooked tilt of his ear, the star-pale glimmer of his eyes.

Her sadness burned away until all that remained was her fury, black as a solar scale and full of power.

She waited until the *Bale Blossom* slowed its pace. They would take only a few minutes to study the scene before one if not all of these ships turned to track her girls. The mines would slow them down, and by the time they were pursuing in earnest, they'd have lost the trail entirely. In order to pursue at all, they'd have to send ships in three different directions. That was the promise of the open ocean. With enough time and distance, you could lose anything.

But before any of that happened, she would be aboard Lir's ship.

She might have missed her chance to save Donnally. But there was a small dagger tucked into a sheath at her waist. And it was time to return it to its rightful owner.

CHAPTER FORTY-THREE

The hull of the *Bale Blossom* was smooth under Caledonia's cold fingertips. The air snaked around her body as she climbed, attached to the bend of metal at the hands and knees by mag-grips.

She'd stripped out of her wetsuit before leaving the water and abandoned it along with her tow. It would circle at a depth of thirty feet while it had the power to do so, and if by some perfect sequence of events she made it back to the water, all she'd need to do was press the remote tucked safely inside her sack and it would return to her. The biosuit was nothing but a thin layer of black fabric, but with the hood cinched tight beneath her chin and her hair tucked away, it cut through the chill and kept her teeth from chattering.

Her muscles strained with effort and cold, but she kept her movements controlled and precise, ensuring her mag-grips connected with the hull as soundlessly as possible. Finally, she was over the railing and sliding into the protective shadows of the command tower.

A roar of laughter from belowdecks brought her to a full stop, body pressed against the wall, but the top deck of the *Bale Blossom* was mostly free of its crew. Everyone was in their stations, and the few who weren't were moving so quickly they barely gave her a second glance. Still, she proceeded with caution.

It was eerie to be here. The ship was as tidy as her own but ringed with evidence of its terrible trade. The entire railing was lined with steel spits of varying lengths and widths, pointing in all directions. Most were decorated with bones in several stages of decay. Others were bare, ready to receive a fresh kill. High on the tower, a ghost funnel was mounted with its metal mouth stretched wide to catch the wind. It was simple, almost elegant, but managed to look haunting. Like the mouth of a great whale poised to engulf anything in its path. Standing beneath it, Caledonia couldn't help but imagine its thin screams. How terrible would it be to hear them this close?

Based on the very little she knew of Lir, she expected his cabin would be as convenient to the bridge as possible, giving him the quickest access at all times. Caledonia prised her eyes away from the funnel and moved carefully towards one of two hatches directly beneath the bridge. Pausing outside the first, she listened for anything that might suggest the room was occupied. Then, readying her gun, she pushed through the hatch.

Inside, the room was beautiful. Lined with panels of

polished wood and filled with handsome chairs, a low table, a desk. But Lir wasn't here. The room was empty.

Though she would have loved to investigate, to run her hands across the gleaming surface of the walls and search for information about Aric's Bullet fleet, it wasn't her mission. She pulled the door softly shut behind her and moved to the next room, again pausing to listen for any indication that someone was inside. Hearing nothing, she pushed the hatch open to find what was clearly Lir's chamber.

No simple Bullet would enjoy the luxury of a private room. The bed was large and made with sheets that were as smooth as a mirrored surface. One entire wall was painted to match the hull and was covered in a riot of baleflowers. A doorway to her left led to what must surely be a private bathroom, and at the foot of the bed sat a large metal chest decorated with exquisite twists of multicoloured metal she'd only seen in one other place.

She hurried to the bed, slinging her sack around to retrieve the charge she'd taken from Amina. It was a failsafe. She wanted to kill Lir with her own two hands, but if that didn't happen, she'd either need a distraction or a backup plan. It wouldn't do much to damage the ship, but it would be more than sufficient to take out a single person. Flipping the sensor, she crouched and secured it beneath the bed.

She stood, eyes coming to rest once more on the mural.

It had been painted with a skilled hand. The flowers curved in and around one another, bending over the porthole window so gracefully they seemed to be in motion, and brushed into the centre of each one, a faint blush of blue. Had it been Lir? It was strange to ascribe this kind of art to any Bullet, least of all the man who slaughtered her family. Still, there was something about her memories of the boy from the beach that lent themselves to this kind of work.

"They are perfect, don't you think?"

Caledonia tried to spin, but hands closed firmly over her arms, holding her still. She tried again to yank herself free and felt the rock of his chest.

"I think they're perfect." He spoke again, voice curling like a smile. It was a voice she'd recognize anywhere. "Symmetrical and persistent. Rather like you, Caledonia Styx." Her hood was ripped from her head, snapping the clasp beneath her chin and revealing her red hair. Lir leaned even closer, his breath burning along her cheek. She couldn't see it, but she was sure he smiled.

A dark realization snaked through Caledonia's mind: he wasn't surprised to find her here.

"Did you know that in the old world, scientists engineered them to survive?" Lir continued. "The story goes that they were in crisis; crops were failing the world over partly because bees and insects were coming out too soon or too late to pollinate. As a result, all sorts of crops failed to produce their fruits and vegetables. So scientists selected a flower for its grace and endurance and used its genes to create a new flower that could bloom under nearly any circumstance all year round. Of course, this was the old world, and while they wanted to prolong its life, they also wanted to defang its dangerous medicinal properties – to divorce the flower from its spirit! They created a disease to wipe out the original flower so that when they released their improved version, it would flourish. But do you know what happened?"

Caledonia didn't care. She jerked against his hold again.

"One survived."

He was taller than she was but not by much. And overconfident. She brought her heel down in a sharp kick to his shin. There was slack in his grip for only a second, but that was all she needed. She threw her head back into his face, felt the crack of bone against bone, and then she was free, swivelling to face him.

Him. Lir. The boy from the beach.

Time had pulled additional sharpness into his features, making a dangerous edge of his jaw and cheekbones. His hair was still a study in motion, the blond spikes reminding her viscerally of the metal spits along the railing. And his ears, though still seeming to reach for the sun, were less awkward than they'd been four years ago.

He dragged a thumb across his bottom lip, now bloody from colliding with her head. And he smiled. "One survived, and it was her survival that led to the rise of the baleflower.

Her genetic material mixed with that of the engineered blossom, and several generations later..." His eyes floated to the mural behind her. "Perfect symmetry. Like this moment."

"There is nothing perfect about this moment." Caledonia tried to ignore the velvet press of his voice in her ears. Tried not to recognize the way her cheeks so vibrantly recalled the graze of his fingers. "Not until I have your blood on my hands."

"I always wondered what happened to your ship," he said, moving easily past her threat. "I went back, of course. We always go back once the fires have gone out, to collect whatever remains and fold it into our fleet, but your ship was gone."

Caledonia shuddered to think of her family ship in the hands of Lir or Aric. They would have taken their home and used it to enslave and punish, decorated its perimeter with spits covered in death.

"I am always happy to disappoint you," she said.

Lir nodded. "It was a disappointment, Caledonia. At the time, it was the only part that felt like a failure. Aric does not appreciate waste." His eyes took on a distant look, and his hand moved absently to a spot on his arm. It lasted only a breath, then his eyes focused on her and his smile returned. "I imagine you were similarly disappointed today." His eyes skimmed to the sigil on her face, satisfied and knowing.

Caught off guard, Caledonia let panic drive her words as

she aimed her gun at Lir's chest. "My brother," she gasped. "Where is my brother?"

Lir raised his hands. "Aren't you going to demand I fall to my knees?"

"Where is my brother?" she demanded again.

His expression grew serious. "Interested in joining him? I'm not sure you'll like where that takes you."

Forgetting the gun in her hand, Caledonia lunged. She delivered two quick blows, driving him back. He retaliated instantly. His fist crashed into her gut, another into her chin. She staggered back but found her footing again. Before he could close in with another blow, she spun around him, whipping her elbow against the side of his face.

Lir smiled a bloody smile and struck back hard. Soon, blood spilled from her nose, and her breath was sharp in her lungs. Still she fought with every ounce of rage she had to muster. She fought for her mother's gap-toothed smile, for her father's quick wink, and for Donnally's beautiful voice. She fought for Pisces's family and every other family from the *Ghost*. And she fought for Lace and Redtooth and her fierce and loyal crew.

They spilled through the open hatch and onto the deck, where the cold night air revived them. But they weren't alone. They stood in a ring of boys and men, Bullets come to attend their leader.

Caledonia paused at the sight. It was too much of a hesitation. He grabbed her hair and pulled. Her head was wrenched around as Lir turned her to face him, pointing a dagger beneath her chin. He bent close, so close she felt a drop of his blood slide down her cheek towards her ear. His grip tightened.

"Do you know what I find so exciting about your survival?" Lir's voice dripped against the side of her face like blood. His blade pressed beneath her chin kept her still.

"Don't mistake my presence here for interest in your thoughts." She spoke boldly, letting derision coat her words.

"I think you'll find this one interesting." Lir's fist tightened in her hair, his other hand shifted on the knife. "You survived when you shouldn't have, and you've turned yourself into quite the thorn in Aric's side. Your death will bring him more pleasure than the deaths of your parents and everyone else on that boat. You gave me a great gift that night, Caledonia. And you're going to give me another tonight."

The crew surrounding them began to roar. Lir dragged her around in a tight circle, ensuring she felt the full press of their dangerous rage. They wouldn't move unless he said so, and until then, they were like sharks in the water. They had the scent of her blood and it left an unnerving light in their eyes.

Caledonia bared her teeth, the pressure in her scalp growing tighter.

"Bale Blossom." Lir moved closer, pressing the side of his face against her cheek. "You survived. And now I get to kill you again and go after your beautiful crew. Where have they gone, by the way? Tell me and this will go much better for you."

She drove her elbow into Lir's stomach and in the same moment reached up to grip his knife hand. There was a flash of a second where she knew this could be the last move she ever made. She had no good options, so she took the one that came with hope.

His thumb was loose and in her grip. She twisted. Hard. Spinning on the balls of her feet to put distance between herself and the blade. She heard a small pop as Lir's thumb came out of its socket. He growled, and the knife clattered to the deck.

She was free. She was completely surrounded by Bullets, but she was no longer in the hands of one.

"You do like to relieve me of my weapons." Lir's voice had lost its edge of delight. "But do you remember last time, Bale Blossom?"

She caught the familiar look in his eyes just as he charged.

Too late, she realized she had positioned herself very near the railing. He drove into her, lifting her from her feet and carrying her backwards. She was stopped by a sudden pressure. Digging into her back beneath her ribs and so familiar it brought tears to her eyes. On either side of her, metal spits reached in all directions. One of them sliced through her back and into her gut.

She gasped. Unable to move.

"You missed one," Lir said, running a thumb over her bottom lip. "Again."

Her hands shook, but she pushed her fingers into her belt and freed the small remote.

"So did you."

She pressed the button. Behind them, an explosion broke the night sky wide open, spilling fire and screams. The blaze burned upward from Lir's chambers, twisting around the tiers of the command deck.

Lir was thrown aside in the blast, creating just enough space for Caledonia to leverage her body off the spit. She spotted Lir's prone figure on the deck just a few feet away. Unmoving, but not dead.

Blood made a hot trail down her back. She pulled her sack from her shoulder, removed the second remote that would call the tow, then tightened the strap low around her middle to stanch the blood.

It wouldn't be long before someone took notice of her. And she was out of fight. She'd failed, but she'd rather die in the black water below than give Lir the pleasure of killing her a second time.

With weak steps, she hurried towards the quarterdeck where she'd come aboard only an hour earlier. Her vision wavered. She moved, but her feet felt very far away. And suddenly she was in the water.

She pressed the button. Pressed it again. But the tow didn't come and she was too weak to wait. Her head slipped beneath the water.

She sputtered. Breathed in air. Her eyes were so heavy.

The world was so heavy. She was draining away and all she wanted to do was sleep.

"Hoist your eyes." The once familiar words seemed to travel over a great distance, seemed to be in the voice of her father. "Hoist your eyes!"

She blinked. And now it was her mother's voice calling, "Caledonia, hoist your eyes!"

The night was full of screams and fire. Her family was dying. Just as she was dying.

Something bumped into her side. Pain was a lance through her body. She wanted to sink into it, to let it obliterate her senses.

She reached out, felt the smooth handle of the tow beneath her fingertips, found the strap of the blue lung next to it.

The water lapped all around her, hungry, insistent, frenetic. It didn't care if she slipped beneath its surface or if she floated half-gasping above. It would push and pull at her body like it was a toy, helping and hindering in equal measure.

"*Hoist your eyes!*" The call came again as though from some faraway world. "*Nia, hoist your eyes!*"

Donnally this time. The brother she'd loved. The brother she'd lost. The brother who was still out there.

Her thoughts were slow, like the flow of an icy river. But beneath them was something that burned, a flame that wasn't ready to go out. Beneath them was the toss of her mother's red hair, the steady hand of her father, and Donnally's song. Memories banked like the embers of an old fire. She wasn't ready to let any of them go.

Caledonia wrapped cold fingers around the handle of the tow. And then she opened her eyes.

CALEDONIA'S STORY
CONTINUES IN

STEEL TIDE

READ ON FOR A PREVIEW

BEFORE

The stars felt close tonight. Cradled in the nest, far up the mainmast, on a night as dark as this one, Donnally felt they were especially near, almost within reach. He loved that illusive, unsettling feeling of suspension. If he held still, breathed just right, he could convince his mind that it was as possible to sink upwards into the sky as it was to slip into the sea. For a split second, his body was as light as air, and the entire universe was at his fingertips. When he reached up to pluck a single star from the glittering array, the illusion broke. In a flash of disorientating dizziness, he was part of the earth again, with feet firmly planted on the floor of the nest and head tipped up.

"Would you quit picking at the sky?" Ares slumped against one side of the protective bowl that encircled them both, bored and tired. The combination made him irritable. Like his older sister, he was destined to be tall with broad shoulders and long arms. His skin was the same sunny brown as Pisces's, and his hair was long and black.

"Why does it bother you?" Donnally asked, tipping his

head backward over the lip of the nest so that the ocean became the sky.

He heard Ares sigh and crack his knuckles. The truth was it probably didn't bother him. What bothered him was being awake at this hour and the way the nest tipped back and forth like a pendulum. At twelve turns each, the boys had been friends long enough for Donnally to recognize when Ares's irritation was an arrow in need of a target. And he'd been the target frequently enough to know he'd rather avoid it, so when Ares didn't answer, Donnally didn't press.

They'd been posted as lookout for nearly an hour, long enough for Caledonia and Pisces to reach the nearby island called the Gem and start foraging, but not quite long enough to expect them to return anytime soon. Donnally leaned even further over the edge of the nest, letting his arms hook around the railing and the blood rush to his head. The ocean was all gentle black chop. It lapped against the hull of the *Ghost* as the tide swept in, pushing them back and forth.

Suddenly, Donnally felt a foot hook beneath his own and kick upward. The force lifted his whole body, and he began to slip over the edge of the basket. He shrieked, arms flailing. Then hands gripped his knees and tugged him right back into the nest, where Ares was hooting with laughter.

"You know you're strapped in, right? You can't actually fall?" Ares laughed all the harder, bending over to brace his hands against his knees.

Donnally didn't find it funny in the least. He lunged for

Ares, aiming a fist for his face. But Ares was taller and stronger. He deflected Donnally's blow easily, snatching the arm of his grey jacket and whipping it off him in one smooth motion. The jacket flew into the air and fluttered towards the deck below, where it landed in a heap.

Now Donnally was mad. He felt his temper burning in his cheeks and in the curl of his fists. He roared and dived for Ares again.

"Boys!" The voice belonged to Donnally's dad, and it stopped them dead in their tracks. They'd both be in trouble for this. It didn't matter that Ares had started it. There was no rough-housing in the nest. "Sounds like you need something else to keep you occupied."

Donnally peered over the edge, sure to keep a firm grip on the railing this time. He spotted his dad standing near the port rail, chin tipped up to watch the boys, a grey coat pulled over his shoulders.

"Found your coat," he called to Donnally.

Ares laughed again while Donnally fumed. "Thanks."

They were definitely in trouble. Donnally could see it in his father's expression. They were going to be on kitchen duty for weeks, peeling and canning whatever fruits and vegetables the girls brought back, forced to endure Cook Orr's protracted stories about the way things used to be. It was going to be hot and boring and tedious, and it was all Ares's fault.

"Hey," Ares said, voice capped with humour. "Donnally,

I'd never let you fall. I was just playing."

Donnally was preemptively plotting his revenge when three gunshots pierced the night sky.

The entire ship went still as a stone. Donnally met Ares's eyes for one brief second, then the two of them turned to search the waters around the Gem. They looked for anything – light, movement, their sisters – but there was nothing for them to find.

On the deck below, the crew vaulted into silent action. They moved in all directions, readying the ship for sail. The laundry lines came down, the goats were taken below, the box gardens were carted away, and it was all done without a word, every single command given without making a sound. It was a familiar sight. Rhona ran this drill regularly, kept the ship parts seamlessly oiled and cushioned. They would be ready to go in moments.

The stretch of ocean between the *Ghost* and the Gem gave no indication of the little boat that carried Caledonia and Pisces. Donnally watched the choreography unfolding below him in a sort of suspension, stuck between the comfort of routine and the fear of knowing this time it was real. They were preparing to flee.

Ares gripped Donnally's shoulder, alarm making his eyes wide. He whispered, "We won't leave them, will we?"

Donnally wanted to deny it, but there was a coil of dread in his stomach, writhing like a snake. "Never be seen," he said, citing the first rule of the ship.

The strength leached out of Ares's grasp. He looked horrified and then suddenly angry. "No."

Before Donnally could stop him, Ares had unsnapped his harness and climbed out of the nest. Without taking the time to hook on to the safety line, he began to climb down. Donnally followed. He detached his own harness and moved down the mainmast as quickly as his shaking hands would allow.

They reached the deck to find their world unravelling. Their parents stood near the bridge with their shoulders together, engaged in tense conversation.

The boys made straight for them, pushing into the circle just in time to hear Ares's mother say, "And what if it's nothing? What if they fired at an animal and we abandon them?"

"If that's the case, they'll survive two days." Rhona Styx stood with her arms crossed and a rifle slung over her shoulder. "I don't like this any better than you do, Agnes, but our girls know what they're doing. They'll wait for us."

"But we should be the ones waiting for them." Agnes planted her hands on the round curve of her hips.

"Boys!" Donnally's father cried in alarm. "Who's on watch?"

Whatever happened on Donnally's face was answer enough. His father cursed and raced towards the mainmast, but it wasn't soon enough.

"Captain," a young man named Bandi called from the

bridge tower. "We've got trouble. An assault ship. They're close, and they're on course to box us in."

"Damn." Rhona's jaw fixed in place as she swivelled to search the ocean.

Each and every time the *Ghost* had encountered a Bullet ship, they'd taken a single course of action: run. While Donnally was too young to remember any of their more narrow escapes, he'd been raised to believe that running was the only way to ensure they survived.

Right now, running was the furthest thing from his mind.

All he could think about was his sister. Had she fired those shots? Or had those shots been fired at her?

Would he ever see her again?

"Rhona?" Donnally's father asked, coming to stand at her side. "Captain, your orders?"

Rhona's eyes fell on Donnally. Her gaze was as powerful as the sun, and he felt warmed and emboldened at the same time. He feared for his sister almost more than he could stand, but he smiled for his mother, to show her he was afraid and also brave.

Rhona nodded and swallowed hard. "I'm afraid we have no choice," she said. "Weigh the anchor and grab your guns. We're going to fight."

In the wake of those words, the ship seemed to transform. Commands were shouted in all directions, the anchor clanked in its channel, even the sea seemed to slap at the hull with more vigour than just a moment ago. Rhona swept forward, gathering her son into her arms and holding him tightly. She kissed his head and released him, saying, "Do as your father says. I love you, my brave boy."

"I love you, too," Donnally said, and then she was gone, climbing towards the bridge and disappearing inside it.

"Let's move." Donnally's father caught his hand and pulled him towards the quarterdeck, where the rest of the children were being herded by a few tight-mouthed adults. Agnes was there, helping each of them over the side railing and into the remaining bow boat on the water below.

"I don't want to go," Donnally protested, fear spiking through him. "I want to stay with you."

But Donnally's father pulled him along, stopping only when they reached the railing. "You must go. We'll come back for you, but for now, you need to get as far from this ship as you can. Head for the Gem. Find your sister."

In the distance, a deathly crooning pushed through the air, growing closer and louder. The crew of the *Ghost* had lost all pretence of quiet now. They'd become a different kind of machine right before Donnally's eyes, one that sounded like bullets snapping into chambers.

"Tagg!" called Agnes. "We're out of time."

Suddenly, Donnally was pressed against his father's chest.

"Find your sister," he repeated, squeezing the boy more tightly than ever before. "Find your sister and live."

Before he knew it, Donnally was over the side of the ship and tucked into the boat waiting below. There were eight children already aboard. Astra, Derry, Lucero and Jam sat silently, their eyes pinned to the hull of the *Ghost*, while the others searched the darkness for the approaching ship. Ares and Lucero, oldest and strongest of the small group, took up oars, and soon their small boat was cutting a shallow path through the water, heading for the same island as Caledonia and Pisces.

For a few precious moments, there was nothing but that steady wail of the ghost funnel and Astra's sniffles. Time felt like a vice around their little vessel. Donnally kept his eyes on the dark outline of the island just ahead, wishing they could stay locked in this moment indefinitely. Then, a flare of light. The terrible cry turned into a deafening roar.

Donnally couldn't help himself. He turned to watch as the Bullet ship closed in on the *Ghost*.

Red dripped down the nose of the Bullet ship like a bloody gash. Men swung in harnesses, armed with magnetic bombs and roaring with fury. Spikes studded the ship's perimeter like thorns, bodies in many stages of decay impaled on each one.

Every muscle in Donnally's body clenched. The little boat was moving faster now, assisted by the wake of the Bullet ship. Behind him, Donnally could hear Ares calling a rhythm to Lucero, keeping their oars synchronized.

In the next minute, the *Ghost* was in flames, and the children knew speed would not save them.

There was a small but bright part of Donnally's mind that

was as calm and distant as a star. It was the part of him that marvelled at how quickly the Bullet ship subdued the *Ghost*. The seeming chaos of their fury was only an illusion. In reality, they were an expertly conducted choir, striking the deadliest of notes at precisely the right moment. After their magnetic bombs weakened the *Ghost* and forced half the crew belowdecks, the attacking Bullets easily bested those who remained topside. Donnally watched the battle unfurl with sense and strategy, and slowly, his body began to still.

"Stroke!" cried Ares.

But Lucero's oar slowed. One thing Bullets knew how to do was find running children, and a bow boat was already in the water, racing towards them.

"Stroke!" Ares cried again, panic making his voice thin. The approaching Bullets pulled alongside, and still Ares kept rowing. He didn't stop until the Bullets circled them twice, then fired a single shot into the nose of the small boat.

Ares's fingers tightened around his oar as though he were considering whether or not to fight. His rebellious thoughts were clear: if they were going to die, they might as well take a Bullet or two down with them.

"Two choices, recruit." The Bullet who spoke had fresh blood smeared across his cheek.

Choices. Live or die.

"Ares," Lucero whispered from the rear of the boat. In a few short moments, they'd become their own small crew, and every child on this boat now turned to Ares to lead them. Donnally put a hand on Ares's back, and the older boy's grip loosened. He shook his head and lowered the oar.

The Bullet smiled. "Good choice."

The Bullets lashed the children's boat to theirs and sped across the water towards the ship with the red stripe across its nose. The *Ghost* slumped awkwardly in the water, smoke curling away from the deck, a hole ripped into one side. The closer they got, the more Donnally's mind clung to that distant star. He smelled the smoke, heard the screams, and when the gentle thump of a body against the side of the boat made the other children cry, he thought only that whoever it was would probably prefer their watery grave to what awaited the rest of them.

His gaze drifted towards the steel pikes studded around the perimeter of the Bullet ship. One by one, they were plucked from their brackets, like the petals of a flower, and placed on the deck where he could not see. He held his eyes wide as the stakes were lifted once more, this time with the skewered forms of people he loved put on display for them and for any others who might dare evade the Father's arm.

His heart fluttered in his chest, signalling a great swell of something hard and unfamiliar pushing up from the bottom of his lungs. But in his mind, that star cast a cool, soothing light, and he remained still.

It wasn't until he saw a grey coat flapping loosely around a familiar shape that his first tears fell. As the Bullets lifted the boys and girls onto a ladder and told them to climb, he saw them impale his father's body on a pike near the front of the ship. That distant star in his mind crashed to the ground, and in a single disorientating moment, Donnally was on his feet and running towards his father.

"Don't touch him!" He was shouting, he hardly knew what. "I'll hang you! I'll drive your bodies on spits and roast you!"

The Bullets abusing his father's body ceased their work long enough to watch his approach with bemused expressions on their faces.

Donnally stood before them, angry that they touched his father, angrier still that they didn't think him more worthy of respect than amusement. His mind spun until all that was left was perfect anger.

He drew a deep breath, and he roared.

The sound filled him up. It was raw and ugly and loud. It was like a fever racing through every part of him, changing every part of him.

"Now, *that* is a battle cry." An older boy came to stand before Donnally. He had a crown of blond hair and a face like a collection of knives. He met Donnally's glare with piercing blue eyes of his own.

"That kind of rage will serve you well," the boy said. "What's your name?"

Donnally raised his chin and sharpened his eyes.

The boy was suddenly very close. He gripped Donnally's jaw and tilted his head back, exposing the tattoo at his temple.

Recognition lit the boy's eyes, and he released Donnally.

"Your sister was very brave."

At first, the words didn't make sense. Donnally assumed he was speaking to someone else. Then a new, horrible reality ripped through his mind like a wind scouring everything in its path.

"Will you come with me, little brother?" the boy asked, not unkindly. "Come with me, and I will teach you to be just as brave as she."

An image of Caledonia appeared in Donnally's memory. She was laughing and proud and her hair tossed behind her in a friendly wind. How had she died? The boy standing before him wanted him to ask. Wanted to tell him. He was sure of it.

"Don't you want to be brave?" the boy asked. "Tell me your name."

Tears slipped down Donnally's cheeks. He felt them on his skin, but not in his heart when he answered, "Donnally."

The knife-faced boy smiled again. "Hello, Donnally. I'm Lir," he said, extending a hand. "Your new brother."

STEEL TIDE
COMING SUMMER 2020

ACKNOWLEDGEMENTS

I wrote *Seafire* during one of the most challenging years of my life. It was a time of loss and heartbreak, and the crew of the *Mors Navis* was a much needed constellation of hope. Bringing them to life took the combined efforts of an incredible team of friends and colleagues. I am grateful for all of them.

First, the agents who have made my career possible: Molly Cusick, John Cusick and Lara Perkins. The three of you have been the best mentors and colleagues I could have asked for.

My eternal thanks to Team Alloy: Josh Bank, Sara Shandler, Romy Golan, Laura Barbiea and especially Lanie Davis, whose careful eyes have studied every last word of this novel (and frequently suggested a better one). My just as eternal thanks to Team Razorbill: Marissa Grossman, Ben Schrank and Jessica Almon. You are the kind of crew I always want on my side.

Many thanks to the sharp-eyed team of copyeditors and proofreaders who have made sure my messes didn't end up in this final copy: Krista Ahlberg, Samantha Hoback, Janet Pascal, Ashley Yee and Abigail Powers. Of course, any messes still present are entirely my own.

I am incredibly thankful to my publicist at Razorbill, Lindsay Boggs, the entire sales and marketing team at Penguin Young Readers, and everyone at Rights People. To everyone who has worked behind the scenes, thank you!

My friends have supported me in laughter, tears, lattes and beer, and I am more human because of them. A great big THANK YOU to: Lydia Ash, Megan Bannen, Dhonielle Clayton, Becca Coffindaffer, Zoraida Córdova, Laci Gerhart, Bethany Hagen, Sarah Henning, Christie Holland, Tara Hudson, Dot Hutchison, Justina Ireland, Kate Johnston, Chris McKitterick, Julie Murphy, Robin Murphy, Joane Nagel, Kaitlyn Sage Patterson, Amanda Sellet, Miriam Weinberg and the entire crew of FMC.

Thanks and apologies to my father, who I bothered with many technical questions about warships and their combat capabilities. He answered them all with patience and a willingness to speculate. He gets credit for all the things I got right, and none of the blame for the liberties I've taken.

My family is spread out across countries and oceans, but their support has been unwavering in spite of the distance. Special thanks to my mother, who always catches the last round of typos.

And finally, my wife, Tessa Gratton, who has been here every step of the way. I love you and I like you.

ABOUT THE AUTHOR

Natalie C. Parker grew up in a Navy family, finding home in coastal cities from Virginia to Japan. Now she lives surprisingly far from any ocean on the Kansas prairie, where she runs Madcap Retreats, an organization offering workshops for aspiring and established writers, with her wife.

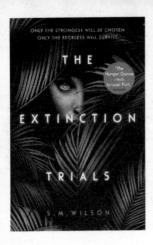

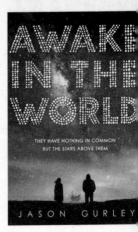

Love this book? Love Usborne YA

Follow us online and sign up to the Usborne YA
newsletter for the latest YA books,
news and competitions:

usborne.com/yanewsletter

 @UsborneYA

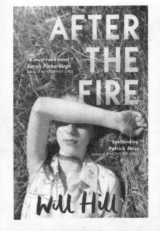